ALEXANDER'S LEGACY
THE THREE PARADISES

ROBERT FABBRI

CORVUS

First published in Great Britain in 2021 by Corvus,
an imprint of Atlantic Books Ltd.

This paperback edition published in 2021.

10 9 8 7 6 5 4 3 2 1

A CIP catalogue record for this book is available from the British Library.

Paperback ISBN: 978 1 78649 803 8
E-book ISBN: 978 1 78649 802 1

Corvus
An imprint of Atlantic Books Ltd
Ormond House
26–27 Boswell Street
London
WC1N 3JZ

www.corvus-books.co.uk

Printed and bound by CPI Group (UK)Ltd, Croydon CR0 4YY

To my daughter, Eliza, and her husband-to-be,
Tom Simpson, wishing you both every happiness in
your lives together.

A list of characters can be found on page 410.

PTOLEMY.
THE BASTARD.

ARMIES ALWAYS COMPLAIN, Ptolemy mused, stepping out of the boat and over a severed arm washed up on the eastern bank of the Nile, *but this one has more cause than most.* With a smile and a nod he acknowledged the Macedonian officer, ten years his junior, in his mid-thirties, awaiting him with two horses; a mounted escort stood a few paces off, the rich glow of the westering sun on their faces. 'They are ready to talk, I take it, Arrhidaeus?'

'They are, sir,' Arrhidaeus replied, offering his hand as Ptolemy slipped on the mud edging the blood-tinged waters of Egypt's sacred river.

Ptolemy waved away the proffered help. 'The question just remains as to who will lead their delegation, Perdikkas or one of his senior officers?'

'I spoke with Seleukos, Peithon and Antigenes; they agree that Perdikkas is the obstacle to peace and, therefore, if his intransigence continues, he needs to be removed.'

Ptolemy grimaced at the idea, rubbing his muscular neck and then clicking it with a swift head movement. 'It would be better for all of us if he can be induced to negotiate sensibly; there's no need for such extreme measures.' He gestured up and down the riverbank, strewn with bodies in various states of dismemberment; the work of the river's many crocodiles. 'Surely having lost so many of his lads trying to cross the Nile he will see sense and withdraw with a face-saving compromise.'

'He'll never forgive you for hijacking Alexander's funeral cortège and taking it to Egypt; his officers don't think he will come to the table unless you give it back to him.'

'Well, he won't get it.' Ptolemy grinned, his dark eyes twinkling with mischief. 'Perhaps I'm the one who is being intransigent, but it's for my own sake; interring Alexander's body in Memphis and then moving it to Alexandria once a suitable mausoleum has been built gives me legitimacy, Arrhidaeus.' He thumped his fist on the boiled-leather cuirass covering his chest. 'It proclaims me as his successor in Egypt and I fully intend to stay here. Perdikkas is welcome to whatever else he can hold but he won't get Alexander back and he won't get Egypt.'

'Then my feeling is that he won't be at the negotiations.'

'Unfortunately, I think you're right. He was a fool, was Perdikkas; he should have kept the body in Babylon and concentrated on securing his position in Asia rather than attempting to get the whole empire by taking Alexander home to Macedon. Everyone knows that Kings of Macedon have traditionally buried their predecessors; he wanted to be king of us all: unacceptable.'

'Which is why you were right to take the body.'

'It wasn't just me, my friend. You were the one in command of the catafalque; you allowed me to steal it from Perdikkas.'

'It was a pleasure just to imagine the expression on the high-handed, arrogant bastard's face when he heard.'

'I wish that I'd actually seen it, but it's too late now.' Ptolemy sucked the air through his teeth, taking his horse's bridle and stroking its muzzle. 'That it should have come to this,' he confided to the beast, 'Alexander's followers killing each other over his body.' The horse snorted, stamping a foot. Ptolemy blew up its nostrils. 'You're wise to keep your own counsel, my friend.' Ptolemy looked over to the Perdikkan camp, a little more than a league distant, hazed by the heat and the smoke from many cooking fires, and then heaved himself into the saddle. 'Shall we go?'

Arrhidaeus nodded and mounted, then eased his horse into a gentle trot. 'Just before I sent the message for you to cross the river, Seleukos guaranteed your safety in the camp and said that you would be allowed to address the troops. He's very keen to come to an accommodation with you.'

'I'm sure he is. He's the most ambitious of Perdikkas' officers; I almost like him.'

'And I'm sure that he almost likes you.'

Ptolemy threw his head back, laughing. 'I'll be needing as many almost-friends as I can get. I imagine he'll be looking for something lucrative: Satrap of Babylonia, for example – should the post become vacant and we get rid of Archon, Perdikkas' nominee, that is.'

'I would say that is exactly what he wants. Like all ambitious men he can see opportunity even in defeat.'

'Perdikkas and his allies may have lost to me here in the south but not in the north; they still haven't heard that Eumenes defeated and killed Krateros and Neoptolemus.'

A conspiratorial smile played on Arrhidaeus' lips. 'If they had then I'd wager that they would not be in the process of assassinating their leader should he not agree to talks.'

Ptolemy shook his head, frowning, unable to suppress the regret he felt at the murder of a fellow member of Alexander's bodyguard, seven in number. 'That it should really come to this and so soon; once we were brothers-in-arms, conquering the known world, and now we slip blades between each other's ribs, and all because Alexander gave Perdikkas his ring but then refused to name a successor. Perdikkas the Half-Chosen now becomes Perdikkas the Fully-Dead.' He leaned over and clapped Arrhidaeus on the shoulder. 'And, I suppose, my friend, that you and I must bear a lot of responsibility for his death.'

Arrhidaeus spat. 'He brought it upon himself by his arrogance.'

Ptolemy could see the truth of that statement. In the two years since Alexander's death in Babylon, Perdikkas had tried to keep the empire together by assuming command in a most high-handed manner purely because Alexander had given him the Great Ring of Macedon on his deathbed saying: "To the strongest", but neglecting to say exactly whom he meant by that.

Ptolemy had realised immediately that the great man had sown the seeds of war with those three words and he suspected that he had done so deliberately so that none would out-shine him. If it had been an intentional ploy it had worked magnificently, for the previously unthinkable had happened: Macedonian blood had been spilt by former comrades-in-arms within eighteen months of his passing. Indeed, war had flared almost immediately as the Greek states in the west had rebelled against Macedonian rule and the Greek mercenaries stationed in the east had deserted their posts and marched back west. More than twenty thousand had joined in one long column and headed home to the sea; they had been massacred to a man, at Seleukos' instigation, at the Caspian Gates as a warning to others seeking to take advantage of Alexander's death.

In the west, the Greek rebellion had been crushed by Antipatros, the aged regent of Macedon, but not without considerable difficulty having been defeated and forced to withdraw to the city of Lamia and there endure a winter siege. It had been the vain and foppish Leonnatus who had come to his aid, breaking the siege, but he had lost his life in the process thus becoming the first of Alexander's seven bodyguards to die. Antipatros had regrouped back in Macedon and, with the help of Krateros – Macedon's greatest living general, the darling of the army – had defeated the rebellion and imposed a garrison and a pro-Macedonian oligarchy upon Athens, the city at its head.

With the west secured, Antipatros had then declared war on Perdikkas for marrying and then repudiating his daughter, Nicaea, at the same time as conspiring to marry Kleopatra, the full sister of Alexander. And thus the first war between Alexander's successors had commenced with the diminutive Eumenes, Alexander's former Greek secretary, and now Satrap of Kappadokia, supporting Perdikkas. But Eumenes had been unable to prevent Antipatros and Krateros crossing the Hellespont into Asia due to the defection of Kleitos, Perdikkas' admiral. Underestimating Eumenes' martial abilities, Antipatros and Krateros had made the fatal mistake of dividing their forces: Krateros had been despatched to deal with the Greek whilst Antipatros had headed south to confront Perdikkas. But the wily little Eumenes had shown a degree of generalship that had not been expected of a man who had held no significant military command and, despite his former ally, Neoptolemus, switching sides, he had defeated Krateros, killing the great general and the treacherous Neoptolemus in the process.

This fact was, as yet, only known to Ptolemy as it was his navy that controlled the Nile and he had prevented the news getting quickly through to Perdikkas' camp: had they known of their victory in the north and that Antipatros' army was now between them and Eumenes, their willingness to make peace might have been severely dampened.

And thus was Ptolemy a man in a hurry.

SELEUKOS.
THE BULL-ELEPHANT.

SELEUKOS GLANCED AT the blood coating the naked blade clasped in his fist as he stepped out into the crowd surrounding Perdikkas' tent; broad-shouldered, bull-necked and a head taller than most men, he looked down at the, mainly, full-bearded faces around him, most in their forties or older – at least ten years his senior. All were veterans of Alexander's campaigns and all now found themselves fighting for Perdikkas against fellow Macedonians who, by force of circumstance, were in Ptolemy's army. It had been the promise of a share in Egypt's riches that had motivated these men to turn on their former comrades; but those former comrades had defeated them, denying them passage across the Nile. Many had been swept away when the silt on the river's bed had been dislodged by the army's elephants that Perdikkas had ordered into the river upstream of the crossing in an attempt to slow the current; the disaster had attracted crocodiles who had relished the feast that had resulted from this blunder. And so it was in anger that the crowd jostled around their commander's tent, anger for the grisly death meted out to many of their fellows; to die in the maw of a reptile having conquered so much of the world was a fate unacceptable to Alexander's proud veterans – and it was clear to them who had been responsible.

'What have you done?' a voice to his right growled.

Seleukos turned to see Docimus, ever faithful to Perdikkas, walking towards him with his hand on the hilt of his sword. 'I'd turn around if I were you and go to find your little friend, Polemon, and get out of here before you get lynched, Docimus; your protector is dead.' He held up the bloodied knife. Behind him, Peithon and Antigenes, they too with blood on their hands, smiled, thin and threatening. Docimus paused, looking again at the blood before walking away at pace.

Seleukos turned, dismissing Docimus from his mind as an irrelevance; he had a far more important task to accomplish. Feeling no fear, he stepped up onto a cart and held his bloodied dagger above his head; behind him, Peithon and Antigenes, his two fellow conspirators, joined him on the makeshift dais. *They will either lynch us or laud us; yesterday it would have been the former but after today's debacle I rather suspect it will be the latter.* At the sight of Perdikkas' three most senior officers openly acknowledging their guilt in the assassination of the bearer of Alexander's ring, received from his own hand upon his death bed, the veterans growled their approval – an act unthinkable just two years previously, soon after the great man's untimely demise. But then two years previously it would have been unthinkable that a Macedonian should spill a fellow-countryman's blood.

So much had changed.

'Perdikkas is dead,' Seleukos announced, his voice high and resounding so that it carried over the few thousands in the large crowd. 'We three took it upon ourselves to remove the one obstacle to peace; the man whose arrogance has caused the deaths of so many of our comrades. The man who recklessly married and then repudiated Nicaea, the daughter of Antipatros, the regent of Macedon, thus setting Asia against Europe; the man who then intrigued to marry Kleopatra, Alexander's full sister, in order to make himself king. King! King, when he was sworn to be the regent for his two wards, the rightful kings, Alexander and Philip.' Out of the corner of his eye he caught sight of two women turning away, with their retinues, and each making their separate ways back to their tents: Roxanna, the mother of three-year-old Alexander, the fourth of that name, and Adea, now known as Queen Eurydike since her marriage to Alexander's imbecilic half-brother Philip, the third king of Macedon to be thus called. *Now that you know just what your erstwhile protector really had in mind, you might both find it politic to be a little more grateful and a little less vocal, bitches.* 'I suggest that in the spirit of reconciliation and in acknowledgement of Perdikkas' folly – a folly that we all shared in – we should ask Ptolemy to act as the regent of the two kings.' He studied his audience but could find no trace of dissent. *I think that I may have timed this just right. If they'll not object to my suggestion that Ptolemy become regent then I'm sure that he'll show his gratitude by giving me Babylonia in return. It's down to Ptolemy to continue in a spirit of reconciliation.* 'Ptolemy, our brother whom, through a collective madness stoked by Perdikkas, we were forced to fight, is coming across the river to talk peace; we shall ask him then.' Mutterings of agreement greeted this statement. 'Kassandros is also here.' He pointed to where he had last spoken to Antipatros' eldest son just before he had entered Perdikkas' tent, and failed to spot his pinched, pock-marked face in the crowd. 'He comes with an invitation from his father, Antipatros, for us all to meet at The Three Paradises in the cedar hills above Tripolis in Syria and there we shall make a final settlement.' He paused for the expected cheer, only to be disappointed by its volume.

'A settlement to include all,' Kassandros shouted, springing onto the cart behind Seleukos, taking him by surprise. He smiled at the crowd with all the charm of a rabid dog, his pale, sunken eyes, either side of his beak of a nose, dead to emotion; with lanky, spindly legs, narrow shoulders and a weak chest, he looked out of place in the richly decorated cuirass and pteruges of a Macedonian general, an avian error in uniform, and yet he had a presence that could command attention; the crowd stilled. 'My father has called for all the satraps from all over the empire to be present, even Eumenes, despite – or perhaps because of – his support for Perdikkas. My father and I are determined that never again shall Macedonian fight Macedonian! My father and

I will ensure that you, brave soldiers of Macedon, will never again suffer at the hands of your comrades.'

The cheer thundered into the darkening sky as Kassandros held both arms aloft, hands clasped, as if he had just won a wrestling bout at the games.

Seleukos shared a brief, but significant, look with Antigenes and then smiled at Kassandros, placing a well-muscled, hirsute arm around his tall but wiry frame. *I can see that I'm going to have to watch you, my ugly worm; no one gets a louder cheer than me from my own men and expects to go un-humiliated.* 'That was well said, Kassandros,' he shouted for all to hear. 'I can see we have a common purpose.' Although his response was positive, one look from Kassandros' pinched face was enough to disabuse Seleukos of the notion; a fact that did not surprise him. *And what would I possibly want to achieve with you?* He turned back to the crowd and gestured for silence. 'For now, though, we will mourn our dead and at dawn tomorrow we will convene an army assembly and there we will hear what Ptolemy has to say.'

'Is it right to allow Ptolemy to address the men?' Antigenes asked, as he, Seleukos, Peithon and Kassandros waited for the Satrap of Egypt to arrive; night was falling and, with it, the temperature. A dozen lamps and a couple of braziers heated the command tent and lit the dark blood stain on an eastern-made carpet, testimony to the crime committed not three hours previously; the hard evidence, the body itself, had been removed in secret to prevent it becoming a focus for dissent of the new regime.

'What choice do we have?' Seleukos countered, downing a cup of wine in one.

'You say "we" but it was actually only you who gave your word to Arrhidaeus; and you did so without consulting Peithon or me.'

'I gave you both the chance to object but neither of you did.' Seleukos waved away the criticism. 'Anyway, Ptolemy has to be allowed to speak. He has Alexander's body; he must defend his taking it. When he justifies his actions then he makes Perdikkas' decision to go to war with him even more dubious.'

'And if Ptolemy can't explain himself to the men's satisfaction?' Kassandros asked.

Seleukos grunted and gave a half-smile. 'Have you ever known Ptolemy to be unable to talk his way out of a situation?' He stopped abruptly, as if he had just remembered something of vital importance. 'Oh, of course, silly me; you were left behind in Macedon weren't you, Kassandros? So you probably hardly remember him at all anymore; although you did briefly know him during the few months after Alexander's death before he went to Egypt.' Seleukos feigned a look of concentrated recollecting. 'You *were* in Babylon at that time, weren't you?'

'You know perfectly well that I was.'

'Of course, I remember now; you arrived the day before Alexander fell ill. You'd come all the way from Pella because Alexander had sent Krateros to replace your father as regent of Macedon and you were bearing a letter from him asking for confirmation of the order. Strange, we all thought, Antipatros sending his son as a post boy when anyone would have done; especially as the mere sight of your face would have been enough to send Alexander into a fury, such was his aversion for you.' He smiled pleasantly at the scowling Kassandros. 'Still, it didn't matter in the end, did it? Alexander was dead within three days of your arrival.' He gave Peithon and Antigenes a knowing look. 'Conveniently.'

Kassandros sprang to his feet. 'What are you insinuating?'

Seleukos motioned for him to sit back down. 'Nothing, Kassandros, nothing at all. Your younger brother, Iollas, was Alexander's cup-bearer; allowing him to mix his wine and water shows just how much trust Alexander placed in your family, despite his hatred for you personally.'

Kassandros shot Seleukos a look of pure loathing, but slowly backed down as the bigger man casually cracked his knuckles.

'I mean nothing by it, my friend,' Seleukos said, refilling his cup with un-watered wine and shrugging his shoulders. 'Nothing at all. But there could be more than a few who might make some unwarranted connections should rumour run unchecked. Wouldn't you agree, Antigenes?'

18

The veteran general scratched at his bald pate, sucking on his lip, as if he were considering a matter of great import. 'Yes, I'd agree. A few of my lads have already wondered at the coincidence but I've told them not to be so suspicious and I still have to keep on doing so from time to time.'

Seleukos gave him a look of sympathy. 'It would be a shame if you stopped.'

'Oh, I don't think that I would do that.'

Seleukos nodded in agreement. 'No, I don't think that you would, not unless someone tried to make himself too popular with our lads, giving rousing speeches and getting hearty cheers.' He looked directly at Kassandros. 'Then we might have to, how should I put it? Poke the embers of rumour?'

'You wouldn't. Especially when you know that I had nothing to do with Alexander's death.'

'Do I, though? Do I really know that you had nothing to do with it?' Seleukos looked at Peithon. 'Do you, Peithon?'

Peithon frowned, his slow mind turning at full speed. 'I don't know.' He frowned again. 'Do I?'

'Never mind. Antigenes, what about you?'

'At the moment I know that he had nothing to do with it,' Antigenes asserted, but then raised a warning finger. 'But if he were to come between us and our lads again, as he did just now, then new evidence might well come to light.'

'You bastards,' Kassandros spat. 'People from country families like you, bumpkins with sheep shit on your cocks, threatening me, the son of the regent of Macedon; how dare you?'

'How dare we?' Seleukos looked incredulous. 'My father, Antiochus, was one of Philip's generals, as was Peithon's father, Creteuas. Antigenes may have worked his way up from the ranks but is now highly respected throughout the army; don't forget that until recently he was one of Krateros' senior officers and you don't climb much higher than that in this army. We dare threaten you, Kassandros, because for all your father's fine words about peace and cooperation, we don't like you wheedling your way into favour with our men; we don't want you gaining their loyalty and we don't want you becoming a contender. Another contender is not what the empire needs at this time.' He held out his hand. 'The ring, please.'

Kassandros looked shocked. 'What?'

'Alexander's ring, please. Don't play dumb; I know you've got it. We three came out of Perdikkas' tent leaving him dying with his ring still on his finger, but when we had the body removed it was gone. I looked for you outside as I was addressing my men and you were absent, only to suddenly appear behind me on the cart, coming from the direction of the tent. The ring, please.'

Kassandros did not move.

'You're a dead man if you try to leave this tent with it; we killed Perdikkas today, Kassandros. For all his faults he was a great man in many ways. I don't think any of us would notice the passing of a turd like you. The ring!'

Slowly Kassandros opened a pouch on his belt, his eyes blazing his fury at Seleukos. He pulled out the Great Ring of Macedon, indented with the sixteen-point star-blazon, weighed it in his hand and then tossed it at Seleukos as if it were of little consequence.

Seleukos grabbed the ring out of the air.

'Good evening, gentlemen,' Ptolemy said as the guard let him and Arrhidaeus through the entrance. He cast his eyes around the company. 'Nothing troubling you all, I hope? What was that that Kassandros just gave you? A ring, if I wasn't mistaken? Rather a big one at that.' He looked with exaggerated disapproval at Kassandros. 'What was such a weak man doing with so big a ring?'

Kassandros jumped to his feet. 'Don't you talk to me like that, Ptolemy!'

'Like what?' Ptolemy asked, surprised. 'I was merely stating the facts: it is a big ring and you are a weak man. Not small like Eumenes, I grant you, but weak nonetheless. Why, you haven't even killed your first wild boar.'

Kassandros sneered. 'You think that you're all so clever and that you can bait me because I didn't share in the greatest adventure of the age, because I stayed behind. Look at Kassandros, he's a weakling. He hasn't even killed a wild boar on a hunt let alone faced a Persian army in battle; he's nothing but someone to jeer at. Well, I'll tell you what, brave heroes: I may not have the right to recline at the dinner table because I've never taken my boar, and you might think that I feel the shame every meal, sitting upright on the couch like a youth with the first growth of hair on his lip. And you may suppose that I regret, every day, being left behind by Alexander because he could never tolerate me for the weakness that he – wrongly – perceived in me. But you would be mistaken because, you see, I don't think the same way as you.' He smiled, baring caninesque teeth. 'I take no pleasure, nor hold any worth, in hunting or feats of valour on the field of battle, why should I? I'm not built for it as you all endlessly observe. My priorities are different and, gentlemen, soon you will find out that they are superior.' He turned and walked from the tent without looking back.

'That seemed to hit a nerve,' Ptolemy remarked with a bemused look. He turned to Seleukos. 'I assume that's Alexander's ring.'

'It is,' Seleukos said, holding it out to Ptolemy.

'So I assume that Perdikkas is dead, seeing as he's not here and yet the ring is.'

'We had no choice.'

Ptolemy took the ring and slipped it on the end of his forefinger. 'What was Kassandros doing with it?'

'He'd stolen it from Perdikkas' corpse and thought that I wouldn't notice.'

'Had he now? I wonder what he meant to do with it; give it to his father or keep it for himself?'

'Give it to his father, surely,' Antigenes asserted.

Ptolemy looked at the veteran, unconvinced, as he sat in Kassandros' vacated chair. 'After that little exhibition, I'm not so sure; I would speculate that the little weasel has high ambitions.'

'Delusions of grandeur,' Arrhidaeus said, also sitting.

'Weakling!' Peithon snapped.

'Never underestimate a man who feels that he is alone against the rest of the world; Kassandros is one such like, if ever I saw one. Unfortunately, he can't be got rid of without seriously upsetting his father and I'd say that is best avoided at the moment, wouldn't you?' He took the ring from his finger and leaned over to hand it back to Seleukos. 'What are you going to do with it?'

Seleukos glanced at his two companions, who both indicated acquiescence. 'At the moment I hold it, but we had thought of offering the regency of the two kings to you.'

'To me?' Ptolemy laughed in genuine amusement. 'And what would I do with the regency? Why would I want to bother myself with that burden when I already have Egypt and Cyrenaica? What possible pleasure could I get from having a toddler along with its vicious, poisoning mother, as well as an idiot and his ambitious queen under my protection?'

Seleukos' face betrayed genuine surprise. 'But we thought you would be grateful.'

'Grateful? Grateful enough to offer you Babylonia? Is that what you hoped?' Ptolemy grinned at the sight of Seleukos' discomfiture. 'Come, Seleukos, you don't really imagine that I want to set myself up as a second Perdikkas, do you? No one can hold the empire together as he proved so convincingly. No, Seleukos, I'll be happy for you to have Babylonia, and I know that is what you want as I've watched – and been impressed by – your manoeuvring to becoming the obvious choice to take it when Perdikkas inevitably fell; but you won't get it from my hands. You keep the ring and give yourself Babylonia.'

Seleukos looked at the ring and then back to Ptolemy. 'I don't want it.'

'Of course you don't; for the same reason as I don't. So let us come to an elegant solution, you and I: let us appoint deputies, one each who will share the regency; if I were you I would nominate Peithon as I believe he owes you a big favour for the way you massacred those twenty thousand Greeks before he was tempted to incorporate them into his army and go into open rebellion. As he owes you his life it is the least he can do.'

Peithon scowled.

Seleukos contemplated the notion for a moment, smiling. 'Of course, Peithon would be perfect because he is so unsuited to the position.'

'But he'll do until a full council can convene. I believe Antipatros has summoned you all to The Three Paradises, you can all decide then who should be regent together.'

'"You"? Surely you mean "we"?'

'No, Seleukos, I mean you. I won't be going. In fact, I don't think I'll ever leave Egypt again unless to travel to one of her domains. I have all I need. And Peithon can give you what you want.'

Seleukos nodded. 'All he has to do is to confer Babylon on me and then Antipatros will find it impossible to take it away unless he wants to go against the spirit of cooperation that he is hoping to achieve at The Three Paradises.'

'Exactly. And your position will be made so much the stronger by an endorsement from my nomination: Arrhidaeus.'

'What!' Arrhidaeus turned to Ptolemy in alarm. 'Why do you choose me?'

'By way of thanking you, of course; you surrender your part of the regency to Antipatros and he will reward you with a satrapy, something I can't do. I'm sure there'll be a vacancy soon; in fact, we both know that one has already become free.'

Arrhidaeus' eyes widened. 'Ah.'

Seleukos frowned. 'What? What do you know that you aren't telling us?'

Ptolemy shrugged. 'Well, I suppose you would have found out sooner or later, but eight days ago Eumenes defeated and killed Krateros.'

Seleukos, Antigenes and Peithon stared, incredulous, at Ptolemy.

Seleukos was the first to recover. 'That's impossible.'

'Evidently not. To make it all the more impressive, Neoptolemus changed sides; Eumenes captured his army's baggage and then killed Neoptolemus in single combat before taking the combined army on to face Krateros. Apparently he didn't let his Macedonian troops know who they were facing; Krateros fell to his Asian cavalry. Now he's dead, the satrapy of Hellespontine Phrygia is vacant.'

'But if Perdikkas and we had known that his cause had won in the north...'

'He probably wouldn't be dead now. I know; that's why I kept it from you.'

Seleukos' huge frame tensed with anger. 'You scheming bastard!'

'Am I? Perhaps I am. I'm certainly a bastard and I suppose I could be accused of scheming. But I had to make sure that we could all talk sensibly: had Perdikkas known of Eumenes' victory it wouldn't have made much difference to his position, other than to have strengthened his unwillingness to negotiate; but you three would certainly have been much more averse to assassinating him. In fact, I don't think that you would have.'

'You forced us to kill him.'

'I wouldn't say forced but, yes, I did do my best to ensure that you would if he proved to be intransigent. And I think that we'll all find that it was for the best. Now, shall we eat? I'm tired as I fought and won a battle today and in the morning I have to address your men.'

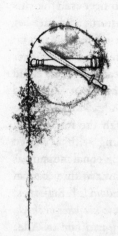

ADEA.
THE WARRIOR.

IT WAS MORE imperative than ever that she should conceive now; her life depended on it. Adea cursed the necessity that was so repugnant to her. In the six months that she had been married to King Philip and become Queen Eurydike, she had only allowed him to cover her at the height of her cycle every month and each time the experience brought her to the point of vomiting: the masculine stench, the bestial grunting, the drool flowing from his slack lips dripping onto her buttocks and the humiliation of kneeling before him as he grunted his way to his pleasure, with no thought of her own; none of the tenderness that she found in the female lovers that she took to her bed throughout the rest of the month. Still, it was better than lying on her back and having to endure his breath as well.

But now she knew that she would have to resign herself to the experience more than just once a month, for if what Seleukos had said was the truth – and she had no reason to disbelieve it – then she really did need the weapon of a child, a son. A son who could claim to be the grandson of Philip, the second of that name, on the father's side and his great grandson on her side; a pure-blooded, royal prince of the Argead royal house of Macedon. Never again would it be possible for someone such as Perdikkas – a man of distant royal blood – to seek to marry Kleopatra and make himself king through her weak, female inheritance. Her son with her idiot of a husband would have the strongest claim to being Alexander's heir; stronger even than his own son and namesake through that eastern wild-cat, her deadly rival, Roxanna, for she was from far-off Bactria and no Macedonian blood flowed through her veins. The younger Alexander would have to wait at least ten years before he could sire a child, and a lot could happen to a person in ten years. *And Roxanna will be only too aware of that fact.* Adea looked over to her husband, thirty-eight years old but with the mind of an eight-year-old, sitting in the corner playing with a carved wooden elephant, trumpeting and drooling in equal measure as his personal physician, Tychon, watched over with a look of indulgence on his lined face. *Roxanna will redouble her efforts to poison Philip now that Perdikkas is not around to keep her in check, if only I knew what he had on her that she feared him so.* Adea swiped the whetstone along the blade she honed, enjoying the metallic rasp of sharpening iron. *I wish Mother was still with me, she would know how to keep that man-child safe as her mother had kept her safe from Olympias in her turn.* Her idiot husband had been made imbecilic as a child by Alexander's mother, Olympias, attempting to remove another rival wife; the dose she had given her pregnant victim had been insufficient to kill the child she bore, but it had done a decent-enough job.

But Cynnane, her mother, was dead and Adea, at seventeen, had to fend for herself in a man's world. Her mother, however, had brought Adea up in the ancient way of Illyrian princesses for Cynnane had been sired by Philip of Macedon on Audata, a princess of Illyrian Dardania, given in marriage to seal a treaty. Audata had taught Cynnane the art of the blade, in all its forms, and, in turn, Cynnane had passed this knowledge on to Adea. It was with her skill at weapons and her size – as tall and broad as a man and with muscles to match – that Cynnane had hoped Adea would survive when she had sought to marry her to Philip and make a bid for empire. But Cynnane had been killed by Perdikkas' younger brother, Alketas, as he attempted to turn the two women back before they reached Babylon.

Such was the outcry from Alexander's veterans that a half-sister of his should be murdered in cold blood that Perdikkas had been forced to allow the marriage to go ahead against his wishes. Thus Adea became a queen and thus she had earnt the everlasting enmity of the deadly Roxanna, so free with her potions.

But what good was a blade against the poisoner's draught? Roxanna had already managed to poison Philip once but had been coerced into administering the antidote by Perdikkas; who would have that power over the eastern bitch now?

It was with heavy heart and dragging legs that Adea set down her blade, walked over to her husband, took his hand and led him to her bed, screened off from the rest of the tent. Tychon followed and together they undressed Philip who panted with excitement for he knew what treat was in store for him and being the possessor of a prodigious penis took great pleasure in wielding it. Removing Philip's loincloth, Adea massaged the organ to ensure its readiness as Tychon held his charge, restraining him in the way that he and Adea had evolved over the months to make the act safe for her, as Philip knew not his strength, nor had he empathy with his partner. Indeed, two unfortunate slaves had bled to death in his early years.

Once satisfied that all was ready, Adea turned around and knelt upon the bed, buttocks raised; she pulled up her tunic and, nodding to Tychon, grabbed the pillow and closed her eyes. As Philip thrust into her without preamble, she turned her mind to the man she assumed would be the new regent, Ptolemy, and whether he would be able to protect her. Egypt, she considered, as her husband pounded away under the watchful eye of Tychon, could suit her well.

'Although I am deeply flattered,' Ptolemy declaimed with the risen sun glowing golden in the east before him, 'deeply flattered, my brothers, I am not the right man to assume the regency and take on the guardianship of the two kings. We propose that Peithon and Arrhidaeus should jointly take up the role until the meeting at The Three Paradises can decide a long-term solution.'

Adea's hands involuntarily gripped the arms of her chair and she cast a fleeting, sidelong look at Ptolemy; he was standing at the front of the dais with the senior officers around him, before the whole army, parading in rigid units, throwing long shadows. Her husband sat next to her, a fixed and vacant grin on his face as Ptolemy invited the two temporary regents to step forward and commended the choice to the army. Beyond Philip sat Roxanna with the infant king on her lap; heavily kohled, cold eyes flashing from the narrow slit in her veil, chilling Adea with the depth of their loathing as she glanced at her and then Philip. *She thinks that now is her chance, Peithon and Arrhidaeus mean nothing to her.* Instinctively, she reached over and took Philip's hand and heard Roxanna hiss at the sight; she felt her Illyrian bodyguard, Barzid, move closer to her in reaction to Roxanna's naked hatred. *Antipatros will be our best hope now.*

'...and to help heal the wounds caused by Perdikkas' foolish declaration of war against me,' Ptolemy continued as the infant king burst into a wail; his mother's long fingernails had dug into his arms, so consumed was she with loathing for his co-monarch next to her, 'I have had the bodies of your dead comrades retrieved from the river and individually cremated with honour; as soon as the bones are cooled they will be collected and sent to you, their messmates, for you to deal with as you wish.'

The cheers this announcement brought briefly drowned the child's cries; buoyed by the good feeling emanating from his audience, Ptolemy let them laud him with his arms open, embracing them all.

Adea almost felt pity for the infant as Roxanna thrust the mewling brute into the arms of the waiting nurse who acted far more maternally towards him than did his mother; indeed, she knew from a spy in the household that Roxanna only ever held Alexander when she appeared with him before the army assembly. But Adea was not the only person to observe the scene: from within the crowd of officers surrounding Ptolemy,

Kassandros' pale eyes hardened as he watched the exchange before his gaze caught hers; he inclined his head, his expression chill, and she knew that in him she had yet another who, if he did not actively wish her harm, was not her friend. *With his eldest son against me, how can I appeal to Antipatros for protection? Still, judging by the way Kassandros looked at them, he is no friend of Roxanna and her whelp either; evidently of the same mind as Perdikkas. A man to watch and to avoid.*

Signalling for silence, Ptolemy began to wind up his oration. 'Finally, Brothers, I have to be the bearer of bad tidings; news of the worst degree.' He paused as if he were trying to find the words to express the depth of the tragedy. 'It's no use, Brothers; I cannot sweeten the blow so I shall just say it how it is: Krateros is dead.'

A few moments' stunned silence and then a howl of grief erupted from the army; it rose and rose as the enormity of what had occurred sunk in. Krateros, the greatest general after Alexander himself, was dead; the darling of the army, never defeated, beloved for his prowess and his willingness to share in the hardships of his men, always eating whatever fare they had to make do with, and respected for his conservative views on the diluting of the Macedonian army with easterners: a soldiers' soldier; one whom they had known for most of their military lives.

It was with genuine surprise that Adea saw tears flooding down grizzled faces; men hardened by years of campaigning seemed to be brought low to snuffling wrecks as if they had just discovered their entire families raped with their throats cut and the loot of many years of campaigning gone.

Two veterans, well into their sixties, climbed onto the dais, tears drenching their beards. 'Tell us how this happened,' one shouted at Ptolemy over the grief.

'It will give me no pleasure, Karanos.' Raising his hands into the air, Ptolemy sought to quieten the assembly and soon the mourning was limited to stifled sobs. 'Eumenes, Perdikkas' supporter, refused to see sense and surrender to Antipatros and Krateros; in the ensuing battle he treacherously withheld the fact from his own Macedonians that it was Krateros whom they faced. Our great friend died at the hands of Eumenes' barbarian cavalry.'

This was too much for men who had spent the last years crushing every barbarian standing in their path; they howled for Eumenes' death and then for the deaths of Alketas, Perdikkas' brother, and Attalus, his brother-in-law, as well as Polemon and Docimus, his two leading supporters, recently fled from the camp. Again, Ptolemy begged for silence. 'It is the right of the full army assembly to pass judgement upon individuals deemed to be guilty of crimes against army. Is it your wish to pass sentence on Eumenes for his part in the death of Krateros and on Alketas, Attalus, Docimus and Polemon for their support of Perdikkas?'

The answer was unambiguous.

'Death to all his supporters and family,' the second veteran demanded.

'Is this what you wish too, Karanos?'

'It is.'

The cry was soon taken up by the entire army and its will was immovable.

Ptolemy turned to the officers standing behind him on the dais and none made to object. 'So be it,' he shouted, 'a sentence of death is hereby passed upon Eumenes, Alketas, Attalus, Docimus, Polemon and all Perdikkas' supporters and family; anyone who has the opportunity to execute any one of them may do so. Failure to carry out that duty—'

But a woman's screams cut him short; Adea searched the crowd for their source. With clothes torn and hair awry, a woman was being dragged towards the dais. The men parted for her, hurling abuse as they did but offering her no physical violence. Closer she was hauled, and Adea could detect a look of regret passing over Ptolemy's face for he too had recognised who she was and what the men would demand of him for she was Perdikkas' sister, Attalus' wife, Atalante.

'Ptolemy! Ptolemy!' Atalante shrieked, writhing in the grip of many hands. 'Ptolemy, demand that they release me.' In her mid-thirties, she possessed, still, beauty and confidence, but neither of these were now on display; nor was the hauteur which she had always shown Adea during the few dinners that they had shared around Perdikkas' table; Adea felt the change suited her. She still resented Atalante for defying her by saving her brother, Alketas, from the justice of the mob for the killing of Cynnane, her mother. *The gods laugh at me one moment and smile upon me the next.*

Screaming another appeal to Ptolemy, Atalante fell to her knees, panic in her eyes as the realisation of who she was spread through the men closest to her and they crowded towards her. 'Ptolemy, save me!'

But Ptolemy could do naught but shake his head in regret.

Adea could understand Ptolemy's predicament. *The sentence has been passed on Perdikkas' family, men and women alike; he's caught. He can do nothing for fear it will seem like weakness in him.*

But it was as Atalante's garments were ripped, exposing her breasts that Ptolemy could no longer be a by-stander. 'Hold!' he roared as Seleukos pushed through the officers on the dais to stand next to him. 'You will not dishonour her.' He jumped down into the crowd, with Seleukos close behind, and pulled her dress together to cover her modesty. 'No matter that she is Perdikkas' sister, you will not dishonour her.'

Atalante embraced Ptolemy's legs. 'Thank you, thank you.'

Ptolemy reached down and eased away her grip. 'Don't thank me, Atalante, I can't save you, the sentence is passed; but I can ensure that it is carried out cleanly and that your honour remains intact.'

Dark eyes, clouded with misery, stared up at him and a thin wail grew and then died in her throat.

I would take no pleasure in her suffering at the hands of the men, but her death is something that I'll not regret; not after she affected to look down on me, a queen, and she being nothing but the sister of the regent – the late regent. But it serves as a warning as to just how quickly our fortunes can change in such volatile times and just where the real power lies: it's the army that has its way now, not the generals. That is my way forward.

Between them, Seleukos and Ptolemy cleared an area around the condemned woman as the entire army cried for her blood. Adea saw Ptolemy share a questioning look with Seleukos and then shrug his shoulders as a thought occurred to him as if he suddenly saw a positive side to the situation.

Atalante caught the meaning of the gesture and it seemed to steady her for she rose to her feet and held her head high and her shoulders back. 'Very well, if I am to be executed for the deeds of my brother then let it be done with dignity so that you can all witness how a high-born Macedonian woman can die.' She turned to Ptolemy and pulled open her dress. 'If you say you cannot save me then it shall be you who should carry out the sentence.' She lifted her left breast and pointed to her heart. 'Strike here and strike hard.'

Ptolemy's normally relaxed demeanour slipped for a few moments as he contemplated her exposed chest. He drew his sword. 'Hold her shoulders firm, Seleukos, so that she doesn't flinch and I miss the mark.'

Atalante pushed Seleukos away. 'I'll not flinch, Ptolemy, but you're more than welcome to have him steady your arm should your nerves at killing a woman in cold blood cause it to shake.'

Ptolemy smiled, his composure returning. 'I'll not miss.'

It was with a flash of burnished iron in the growing sun, the dull thud of a blade striking flesh and bone and the shocked exhalation of Atalante's breath that Ptolemy drove his sword, up, under her ribcage, deep, through her heart to jag to a halt on the inside of her shoulder blade. Blood oozed from quivering lips and her eyes widened; she looked down at the wound as if to fully comprehend the reality of it. Putting a hand on Ptolemy's shoulder, she let her legs give and, in stages, down she went. Seleukos placed a hand under her arm and eased her descent so that there should be no final slump. She came to her knees, rested a hand on the ground and then, with Seleukos' and

Ptolemy's help, lay down on her side, drawing her legs up, blood now flowing free from the wound as well as her mouth and nose. In the foetal position she looked up to Ptolemy, the light now dimming within her. 'I did nothing wrong.' Her mouth slackened; her body went limp.

If I ever share her misfortune I hope that I will face it in such a manner. But one look at her husband showed that he had not taken the same lesson from Atalante's execution, far from it judging by his obvious excitement. Disgusted with the man and yet feeling a strange urge to protect him at the same time, Adea took his hand and led him from the dais as Ptolemy pulled the sword from Atalante's breast.

'The sentence has been passed at the army assembly,' she heard Ptolemy shout as she descended the wooden steps, 'and once it is passed only the army can rescind it. It gave me no pleasure to execute a woman, but it is done now and through this act we have passed the point of no return; there can be no understanding now between us and Perdikkas' followers. They will not be coming to The Three Paradises to make a final settlement with Antipatros; it is now to the death. All of them, especially Eumenes.'

Adea smiled to herself as she led her husband away, holding his wrist firmly to prevent him playing with himself, her confidence growing for she had seen her way forward. *I may not have many friends at the moment but I would hazard that, soon, after talking to Karanos, I'll have a few more than Eumenes. And then, despite Kassandros, Antipatros will have to deal favourably with me.*

ANTIPATROS.
THE REGENT.

'AND WHERE'S NICAEA?' Antipatros asked his eldest son, having been apprised of the news from the south; the information had made him far more well-disposed towards Kassandros than would normally be the case and he smiled at him in a manner that could almost be construed as natural and easy. They sat, along with Nicanor, Kassandros' younger full brother, and his half-brother, Iollas, under an awning looking out over the sea, on the beach at Issos, the site of Alexander's stunning victory in which Darius, the King of Kings of the Persian empire, had been utterly defeated and forced to flee deep inland. The sun hung low in the west and around them the army of Macedon prepared the evening meal, filling the atmosphere with the smell of grilled seafood and thousands of voices.

'Still in Babylon, Father, where I left her,' Kassandros replied, tearing at the loaf of bread before the slave had even placed it on the table.

'Then at least she is safe for the time being.'

'Safe enough, yes; but technically she was condemned to death along with the rest of Perdikkas' friends and family.'

'I don't think they'll worry about her until they find Alketas, Attalus, Docimus and Polemon,' Nicanor observed. Younger than his sibling by three years, he lacked the same wiry, lanky frame, the pinched features and surly manner and was far more pleasing to both the eye and the ear.

'As soon as they heard what had happened to Perdikkas they knew they would be condemned; Alketas, Docimus and Polemon slipped away, but no one knows where to, and Attalus withdrew his fleet from the Nile delta and sailed to Tyros.'

'Tyros?' Antipatros groaned. 'Of course he would, there are eight thousand talents in the royal treasury there; that will buy a lot of men for his ships and equip Alketas with an army if they join together. Alexander took two years to take Tyros. I don't suppose anyone will be able to do it quicker without the help of treachery; the Perdikkans are a long way from being totally defeated even though they've lost their leader.'

'And then there's Eumenes,' Nicanor said, equally downcast, looking nervously at his father as he brought up what he knew to be a very painful subject. 'He may have been condemned by the army assembly but he's still controlling Kappadokia and Phrygia since he defeated Krateros.'

'And he makes me look a fool! But I'll have him, the sly little Greek, and regain my honour. Whatever happens, I'll see him dead. I'll try sending Archias the Exile-Hunter after him, but it's one thing assassinating unprotected exiles, it's quite another trying to kill a general in the midst of his army. Still, he's the best there is at his trade.' Antipatros contemplated the humiliation inflicted on him by Eumenes for a few moments and then shook his head in disbelief. 'Just how did a secretary defeat and kill a general as experienced as Krateros?'

'You shouldn't have divided your forces, Father,' Kassandros said, almost flinching in anticipation of a sharp rebuke.

Antipatros glared at his son but said nothing. *Unfortunately he's right, with the benefit of hindsight. But now is the time for looking forward, not back.* 'How long did it take you to get here?'

'Three days; Ptolemy lent me a ship. I was just behind Attalus' fleet as it sailed into Tyros.'

Antipatros beamed, feeling more optimistic at the news. 'Ptolemy helped you? The good lad; he's proving to be a compliant son-in-law. He'll ingratiate himself even more with me by returning Alexander's body; what he wants with it in Egypt I just don't understand.'

Kassandros shook his head. 'It would be a useless demand, Father; best not to make it and avoid looking weak when he refuses you. Alexander stays in Egypt whether Ptolemy's your son-in-law or not; he sees the possession of it as a way of establishing his legitimacy. He has no need to ingratiate himself with anyone; he was just being civil in lending me that ship as a brother-in-law should be.'

Antipatros felt his warmth towards his son-in-law diminish. 'Then we had better send it back to him with a strong letter reminding him that we are family and need to work together for our common good, hadn't we?'

'The ship's already gone; but not back, on.'

'On? Where to?'

'I didn't ask the triarchos,' Kassandros replied through another mouthful of bread. 'It came as a surprise to me; he literally dropped me off and then, as soon as I was on dry land, left.'

'On, eh?' Antipatros' good feeling towards Ptolemy evaporated entirely. *This is so tiresome; I'm getting far too old for these games.* 'The conniving bastard must be sending a message to Kleopatra in Sardis. He knows that she will write at once to warn Eumenes. Ptolemy is, as usual, playing both sides and I'll wager that the ship will carry on to Macedon and deposit a messenger heading for that witch, Olympias, in Epirus. I'll have a quiet but firm word with him at The Three Paradises.'

'I'm afraid you won't, Father, he's not coming.'

This was too much for Antipatros. 'Not coming! Not coming to the most important conference since Alexander died? Why ever not?'

'He doesn't see the need to talk about the rest of the empire when he is perfectly happy in Egypt and has no wish to leave. He told me he would be content with whatever settlement we came up with so long as it left him alone; he added that he wouldn't want things to become unpleasant.'

'Unpleasant! I'll give the ungrateful bastard unpleasant! How am I meant to organise a lasting peace if we don't have everyone who matters around the table; even Lysimachus is coming, for Aries' sake, and he's got no interests outside Europe at all, being quite content to spend his time subduing the northern Thracian tribes. Ptolemy has to come!' Antipatros rubbed his forehead with a wrinkled and blotchy-skinned hand, feeling every one of his eighty years. *That's just it: he doesn't have to come. To all intents and purposes, Egypt is an island and if Ptolemy wants to stay there then there is nothing that I can do about it. Gods, how I wish Hyperia were here; I'm in dire need of the comforts of a wife.* Controlling himself, he looked back to Kassandros and Nicanor and then to Iollas, his third eldest son, leaning against one of the awning's poles. 'So, Perdikkas is dead, boys, and Eumenes and his other supporters have a price on their head which I'm very sure that the Exile-Hunter will be only too pleased to claim. Where does that leave us?'

'On top, Father,' Kassandros replied without pause for thought.

'Think before you answer,' Antipatros snapped, his mood towards his eldest now fragile. 'If the two temporary regents decide that they would rather be permanent, then who are we to force them to stand down without the threat of violence; the very thing that I've called The Three Paradises conference to put an end to? But persuade them we must, for if I want to bring stability to the empire, and avoid further conflict, then it's imperative that I have the two kings back in Macedon where they belong. To do that I must be not only the regent of Macedon but of them as well, in order to prevent Olympias using the young Alexander as her route back to power.' He looked down at the skin on the backs of his hands. 'There are few enough years remaining to me and I want them to be as peaceful as possible. I've had my share of struggle and now I wish to enjoy some rest; that will not be possible if I have to contend with Olympias scheming to get hold of her grandson and trying to murder the fool.'

Antipatros stood and stretched his legs, rubbing his thighs and grimacing as the aged limbs creaked with sitting too long. Always an active man, a contemporary of Philip, he had been appointed regent of Macedon by Alexander as he left for his glorious conquest of Asia; he had ruled almost as a king there ever since. This, however, had brought him into regular conflict with Olympias, Alexander's mother, whose lust for power was almost as great as her ability to abuse it. Antipatros had spent much of his energy in keeping the former queen from meddling in the affairs of the kingdom. Whilst Alexander had lived he had an ally; but now, with him gone, there was no one with enough influence over the woman to help him in his endeavours against her. He was well aware that once she knew of Perdikkas' death – which would be sooner now, rather than later, thanks to Ptolemy – she would work to bring Roxanna and her child under her care and use them to wield power in Macedon and wreak bloody vengeance for all the slights and insults her crazed mind perceived she had received since Alexander left – and they were, no doubt, innumerable.

Antipatros sighed, slumped back down on his chair and looked at Kassandros, trying to keep the dislike he felt for his oldest son out of his eyes now that his good mood had died. 'So, Peithon I know of old: ruthless but not very bright and hardly likely to want to stay as regent to the kings.'

'He did try to incorporate the Greek mercenaries he had been sent to prevent leaving the east into his army rather than fight them,' Kassandros said, looking at his father out of the corner of his eyes now that he sensed the old enmity returning. 'Had he been successful, and if Seleukos hadn't have had them massacred before he could do so, only the gods and he know what he had planned to do with the army. So I would say that is evidence of some ambition, even if he set about it unsubtly.'

Antipatros considered the thought. 'I don't think he's up to doing anything too threatening now. I'm told that Seleukos keeps a wary eye on him. But it's Seleukos who interests me. I vaguely remember him in Pella but he was an unformed youth at the time; I'm curious to know what sort of a man he's grown into.'

'You would like him more than you like me, Father.'

Antipatros started at this remark. 'What do you mean by that?'

'I mean that he is everything that I'm not in your eyes. He's a bull-elephant of a man, taller than me and twice as broad across the shoulders as I am. He is liked by people immediately upon their meeting him as opposed to the distrust and distaste that I engender. He's clever; he's able to reason clearly. For example, he knew that—' Kassandros stopped, a guilty look in his eyes. 'What I mean to say is that he has the ability to make a decision and draw people along with him without having to cajole or bribe them and he can more than hold his own in a fight – indeed, people would go out of their way not to fight him one on one.' Kassandros creaked his pinch-faced smile with no joy in his eyes. 'You see, Father: everything that I'm not.'

Antipatros remained silent, his eyes cast down upon the sand around his feet.

Iollas shifted uncomfortably from one leg to the other and back again as he waited for his father's reaction. Nicanor muttered something in a positive tone, but could not bring himself to look at his elder sibling.

'I have tried,' Antipatros growled, 'but you were never a pleasant child, always howling to get your own way and acting in a spiteful manner with other boys in the court. I watched you cheat and lie because you felt that you could not compete with them and the shame burned in me.' He levelled his gaze at Kassandros. 'But there is no reason why our past relationship should impinge upon the present; do as I ask and make me proud, Kassandros, and perhaps we may learn to like one another a little more.'

'It is always under your terms.'

'Well, under whose terms should it be, eh?' Antipatros jumped to his feet and pointed at his chest. 'I'm the father and you are my son, it's your duty to obey me and please me. If you cannot get that into your head, as Nicanor and Iollas have managed to, then I don't know how I can help you by becoming more amenable.'

Kassandros held his father's look and then lowered his own in a token of submission.

That's the first time I've seen him do that.

'I'm sorry, Father,' Kassandros said, his voice small, 'you are right.'

Antipatros waited but Kassandros left it at that; he sat back down. 'Very well, son. You can start by telling me what you think Seleukos wants.'

'That's simple: Babylon.'

'Does he now?'

'Yes, and I believe that he's already got it.'

Antipatros waved the suggestion away. 'Impossible, only the regent can dispense satrapies; besides, Archon is still in place.'

'Yes, but he was Perdikkas' appointment and one of the first things that Peithon and Arrhidaeus did when they were appointed joint-regents was remove Archon and confer Babylon on Seleukos.'

Antipatros stared at his son and then pinched the bridge of his nose, screwing shut his eyes. *Of course; that's clever and there is nothing I can do to reverse it without causing serious offence. I can see Ptolemy and Seleukos working together for this. Arrhidaeus was Ptolemy's man; bringing the catafalque over to him ties his fortune to Ptolemy completely and so he would do anything he was asked. Peithon is in Seleukos' debt for preventing him from making a serious error of judgement by incorporating the rebel mercenaries into his army, thereby making himself an outcast.* 'Do Ptolemy and Seleukos seem to be friendly?'

Kassandros shrugged. 'Well, they certainly like one another more than they like me.'

In the spirit of improving relations with his son, Antipatros resisted the temptation to express a lack of surprise at this observation. 'Babylonia allied with Egypt would be a tough proposition; it would effectively make a north–south divide in the empire. I need to counter this possibility before it becomes an established fact.' He paused for reflection and then continued: 'Kassandros, go to Babylon at once and bring Nicaea to me at The Three Paradises, I'll be there in a month. I don't want her becoming a pawn to be used by men who may well turn out to be my enemies.'

'Yes, Father,' Kassandros said, suddenly looking concerned. 'Do you think that they will really threaten you?'

'Me personally, no; but what I stand for, yes. I see what they are up to. They have no wish for power over the kings otherwise they would have had themselves made joint regents, instead they use proxies. The kings are irrelevant to them and so they are quite willing to give them up to me, thinking that the vast distances from Macedon to their satrapies will keep them safe because if I have the kings I won't feel the need of going to all that effort to trouble them.'

'It's a fair assessment.'

Nicanor and Iollas both murmured their agreement.

'It is, except they have forgotten one thing: that little bastard, Eumenes.'

'What about him?'

'If the army assembly has outlawed him then we ought to bring him to justice; and the gods know just how much I would love to do that after being so humiliated by him. But always put yourself in your enemy's position: if I were him, I would fall back east looking for allies and that will force Seleukos to declare either for Eumenes or me, thus prising him away from Ptolemy, whomever of the two he chose.'

Kassandros considered this. 'It could work, but are you really considering making such a long campaign following Eumenes east at your age – with all due respect?'

Antipatros laughed. 'No, my boy, no I'm not. I prefer to remain at home whilst others do my dirty work; in this case either Archias or Antigonos.' He turned to Nicanor. 'Sail immediately to Cyprus and tell Antigonos to return to the mainland as soon as he can; I want him and his army to be at The Three

Paradises in under a month, so he had better hurry up and finish dealing with Aristonous. Tell the Resinated Cyclops that I plan to have him made commander-in-chief in Asia and his first job will be to root out Eumenes, if the Exile-Hunter doesn't manage to get the sly little Greek first.'

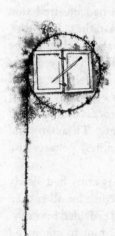

EUMENES.
THE SLY.

EUMENES HAD WATCHED them go the previous evening, almost twelve thousand of them; there had been nothing he could do to stop them. Twelve thousand veteran Macedonian infantry, Krateros' former men, old in the ways of war and wise in the ways of living off the land; perfect troops for him, Eumenes reflected. *Had it not been for the fact that I'm responsible for their general's death and that I have the temerity to be a Greek, and not a very tall one at that.* He shook his head as, from the vantage of a knoll, he surveyed what was left of his army camped on the western side of the bridge that took the Royal Road across the River Halys from Phrygia into Kappadokia. It had never been a great army in numbers but it proved to be remarkably loyal to him. *Despite me being a former Greek secretary.*

It had been the five hundred Kappadokian cavalry, who had come over to him during the siege of Mazaca, the capital of Kappadokia, that had formed the nucleus of his army: tall, proud, bearded men, dressed in brightly coloured embroidered trousers and long tunics, very close to the Persian style, and protected by scale armour and high helms and riding partially armoured horses. These men he had come to love for their horsemanship and their fearlessness; they, in turn, had come to respect him for he had brought them nothing but victory.

In persuading them and their commander, Parmida, to change sides during the siege, Eumenes had ensured that Perdikkas had defeated the rebel satrap Ariarathes. After that, Eumenes and his new cavalry had then set about subduing the rest of Kappadokia, the satrapy he had been given by Perdikkas as a form of joke, it having never been completely conquered by the Macedonians. Together they had swept away the last resistance to Macedonian rule and in the process he had added to his army many mercenaries, mainly Thracian and Paphlagonian as well as some Greek hoplites, peltasts and sundry light troops.

As the empire slipped into civil war, his army had slowly grown but Macedonians had been hard to come by, other than the few companion cavalry who had always provided his body-guard ever since Alexander had promoted him to command rank; this had changed when he defeated Neoptolemus and Eumenes had taken the oath of his ten thousand-strong phalanx. It was, therefore, with a respectably sized field army that he had faced Krateros and beaten him. He had taken the surrender and oath of Krateros' cavalry but his infantry numbered too many to control after they had laid down their arms; and so he had been powerless to stop them once they had decided to return to Antipatros. Two victories he had won, two victories for Perdikkas and still he had been unable to do what he had been tasked with: to prevent Antipatros' forces from coming south whilst Perdikkas dealt with Ptolemy. Two victories and still Antipatros' army had gone by and Perdikkas would be trapped; his cause, the cause of the Argead Royal House, would be crushed.

Despite Eumenes' shabby treatment by Perdikkas, he had remained loyal to him for Perdikkas was the regent to the inher-itors of the Argead royal house; it was to Alexander's sire Philip, and therefore his family, that Eumenes owed everything. After the murder of his father and much of his family by Hecataeus, the tyrant of his native Kardia, Eumenes had taken refuge in Pella; Philip had seen his intelligent and ordered mind and, despite his young age and foreign blood, made him his secretary.

And so, here he was, fighting on the losing side because of his unshakeable loyalty to the heirs of Philip and Alexander and he was painfully aware that he only had himself to blame. 'I should never have let Perdikkas out of my sight,' he said to his companions, Parmida the Kappadokian cavalry commander, Xennias, the commander of Krateros' defeated cavalry and Hieronymus, a compatriot and friend since youth newly arrived from Kardia. 'He's too unsubtle and arrogant for sound politics.' Again he shook his head as the horns sounded within the camp and tents began to come down. 'I told him to marry Kleopatra and politely refuse Antipatros' offer of his daughter, Nicaea, on the grounds that Ptolemy and Krateros were married to the old man's other two daughters and therefore the club was not exclusive; but no, the idiot decides to try to marry both Nicaea and Kleopatra as if no one will notice.'

This was news to Xennias. 'You wanted Perdikkas to marry Kleopatra?'

Eumenes looked up at Xennias, ten years his junior, in his thirties, and a head taller than him, and frowned. 'Of course; it was the logical thing to do.'

'But you said that you remained loyal to Perdikkas because he was the regent to the two kings and you will always support the Argead royal house; had he married her, he could—'

'Have claimed the throne. Exactly.'

'But then what would have happened to the two kings, the real—'

'Heirs to the Argead house?' Eumenes shrugged as he watched a distant rider canter along the Royal Road towards them, from the west. 'Secluded somewhere quiet until it was certain that they had no further use. It's the house that is important, not the individuals: who would you rather serve, a babe and a fool or Kleopatra, the full sister of Alexander, married to Perdikkas, who has plenty of royal blood in his own right?'

'I see your point.'

'Do you, Xennias?' Hieronymus, a martial man running to fat, a soldier turned historian, asked. 'I struggle to, but then I suppose that's why I've come to witness this struggle at first hand to gain a better understanding of it all.'

Eumenes smiled. 'You've been too long locked away with your books at home, old friend. My reasoning was sound.'

Xennias contemplated the notion as the rider neared. 'Antipatros would have been—'

'Unable to oppose that claim. I know. That was the whole object of the exercise.' Eumenes sighed with regret. 'There would have been a peaceful settlement; no civil war. Krateros would have been still alive – as would Neoptolemus, come to think about it, but I suppose things must always have their negative aspects – and we could have concentrated on governing the empire and becoming fantastically wealthy. And it nearly happened; it really did. I was on the verge of undoing the damage that the idiot had caused in marrying Nicaea by getting Kleopatra to agree to wed Perdikkas despite his being already married. Antipatros had already declared war on Perdikkas for his treatment of Nicaea but, even at that late stage, hostilities could have been avoided. Antipatros couldn't have stood against Perdikkas, married to Kleopatra, coming to Macedon with Alexander's catafalque to inter him in the homeland; no, he would have had to back down and swallow the insult to Nicaea. It would have been over before it started. But then I made the most terrible mistake: Kleopatra refused once she heard he had lost Alexander's catafalque to Ptolemy; and it was me that told her. Me! I could cry for the shame of it. Me! After all those years of court intrigues and diplomatic missions I, who really should know better, let out a piece of information that the person I was negotiating with did not know. That's what I did! Can you believe it? Can you believe how stupid I was?'

Hieronymus, aware it was a rhetorical question, said nothing and Xennias, being first and foremost a soldier, did not know whether to say he believed it or not and so shrugged in a non-committal way but Parmida, used to the machinations of the Kappadokian clan-leaders, tutted in disapproval. 'No, lord, I can't; it was stupid to the point of madness.'

'I was being rhetorical,' Eumenes said, frowning at the overt criticism.

Parmida spread his hands. 'I'm sorry, lord. I am still not used to not saying what I think when talking with Greeks.'

Eumenes stared at the Kappadokian commander but could see no guile. *Of course, all this fighting The Lie with The Truth in their religion; I keep forgetting that you have to be literal with easterners.* 'Yes, well, never mind. Anyway, Kleopatra didn't know that the catafalque had been hijacked; I could have easily made up some sort of cover story, obfuscated, glossed over the issue, until I'd got Perdikkas to Sardis and the ceremony was done.' Eumenes rubbed his head and tried to ignore that his hair seemed to be thinner every time he touched it. 'But there you have it: my elementary mistake has led now to war and I've just had to allow twelve thousand men who really should be my prisoners, or actually in my army, to go south to join the enemy. I've failed on all fronts, militarily and diplomatically and now I'll never be forgiven by any Macedonian because I'll always be seen as the man who killed Krateros, even though it was I who did more than anyone to try to prevent this war and his death.'

Xennias looked down at his new commander. 'So, what do we do now?'

We? He said we; that's the first time for a long while that a Macedonian has asked me 'what do we do now'. If only Perdikkas could have done the same then we wouldn't be in this mess. 'We go on fighting for the Argead royal house; so we go south to help Perdikkas and hope that we are not too late.' Eumenes took the helmet from under his arm and set it upon his head as the rider trotted through the gates of the camp. 'Come, gentlemen, by the looks of him, that horseman is an imperial courier, perhaps he brings counsel. The question is: is he from Perdikkas or Antipatros?'

But he was from neither as Eumenes realised when he looked at the seal on the scroll-case. 'Kleopatra? Intriguing.' He broke it, pulled out the letter and unrolled it.

My dear Eumenes, this is written in haste as it must outrun the assassins who will inevitably wish to claim the price that is now on your head; I know for a fact that Antipatros greatly prizes the skill of Archias the Exile-Hunter. I have just received a despatch from Ptolemy sent by the fastest of his ships. Assuming Antipatros receives the news by overland courier then he would have heard it a day or so before you; however, if the news travels by sea his assassins could already be closing in on you. Perdikkas is dead, murdered by Seleukos, Peithon and Antigenes; the new regents are Peithon and Arrhidaeus until a settlement is agreed at a conference at The Three Paradises as soon as all can assemble there. You will not be receiving an invitation to attend as when news of Krateros' death was given to the army assembly it immediately passed a sentence of death upon you. You are now outlawed; as I see it, you have but two choices: flee the empire or tell your men before they find out from another source and pray that they stay loyal to you.

'"There will be no chance of removing the sentence."' Eumenes paused and looked up from the scroll across the faces of men in the front ranks of the units closest to him in the army assembly he had called immediately after reading the letter; none were hostile now that they too knew of its contents. '"And so you will find no allies anymore. I wish you luck. Your friend, Kleopatra."' Eumenes rolled up the scroll; silence enveloped his entire army. He opened his arms. 'Here I stand, condemned to death. Is there any man here who wishes to carry out that sentence?' Still there was silence. 'Shall I flee the empire?'

The response to the negative surprised Eumenes by its vehemence. *Being popular is a new sensation; I find it rather disconcerting.* 'Then I stay.' With a roar his men saluted him, helmets raised in the air and feet stamping the dust-dry ground. Such was his surprise at the warmth in which his men held him that Eumenes let the ovation run on for longer than good manners dictated. 'If I stay,' he shouted as at last he begged for silence, 'then there is no alternative but to fight. As soon as I stop I am a dead man.

Now I understand that in supporting me you are also sharing in my sentence and therefore I release any man who is unwilling to be condemned to death on my behalf.' Again he paused but none made to move away. 'Very well; we'll cross the river back into Kappadokia and winter there around the fortress at Nora. In the spring we will take to the field back in the west and choose our ground against the army that I am certain Antipatros will send against us.'

ANTIGONOS.
THE ONE-EYED.

NOW I'LL FINALLY *get to see what Aristonous is made of.* With his one eye, Antigonos surveyed his enemy's ranks of pike-armed Macedonian phalangites, screened by light archers and slingers, facing his own troops armed in exactly the same fashion and formed up in a similar manner as if a giant mirror had been placed before them. They were two opposing armies both fighting for control of Cyprus, the key, along with Rhodos and Tyros, to naval power along the Asian coast. But it was not just two armies, one fighting for Perdikkas and one for Antipatros, that contested the day, just to the south of the city of Salamis, on the east coast of the island. Antigonos felt a surge of delight as his gaze roved along the opposing phalanx, past the local Cypriot light infantry and cavalry, covering its right flank on the beach, and then out to sea to the two fleets lined against each other. With over a hundred vessels in each, drawn up, in deep water, ready to do battle, they were a formidable sight. *Today it will all be decided,* Antigonos mused, lifting a wineskin to his lips and taking a long swig of resinated wine, as he watched the distant figure of Kleitos the White, the captain of his fleet, walk to the bow of the leading ship, naked but for a cloak that fluttered in the breeze, and shake his trident at the enemy. *And with Poseidon on my side, how can I fail?* Dismissing the eccentricity of his admiral, he turned to look at his inland flank and the massed, lance-armed cavalry led by his seventeen-year-old son, Demetrios, resplendent in a purple cloak. *The cocky little bugger dressing as if he were royalty; where did he get that cloak? I'll have it off his back once we've dealt with Aristonous. And I'll have his skin along with it if he fails to obey my orders again.*

Satisfied that all was ready, Antigonos handed the wineskin down to a groom, wiped a tear from the seeping ruin of his left eye, and then dismounted, giving his horse to the groom to be led back through the sixteen ranks of his four-thousand-strong phalanx. Rubbing his hands together in excited anticipation of the looming battle, he took his place at the very centre of the front line.

A grey-bearded man, with eyes to match, grinned as he handed Antigonos his sixteen-foot-long sarissa, the pike used by the heavy, close-formation Macedonia infantry, whomever they were fighting for.

'Thank you, Philotas,' Antigonos said, testing the weight of the weapon in both hands. 'How many does this make it today?'

'It's the sixty-fourth time we've stood together shoulder to shoulder, old friend.'

'And yet I still feel the same excitement as I did the first time. Gods, this will be good. We may not have big armies, but they're big enough for an excellent scrap and the fleets will have a good go at each other. I've a mind to be generous with Aristonous; I've always rather liked him and he's been a worthy opponent here in Cyprus.'

And it had been an enjoyable three-month campaign that had seen Antigonos cover most of the island as he and his adversary had played cat and mouse with one another, trying to get the advantage of ground because, numerically, their armies were about equal. With the civil war escalating on the mainland there had been no question of reinforcements for either side, so Antigonos and Aristonous contented themselves with fighting on a smaller scale in a smaller theatre; the one variable had been the fluctuation in loyalties of the petty kings who infested the island, but their troops were so poor that they were often more hazardous to their own side than to the enemy. And so the engagements that they had fought had been inconclusive and, as both armies were supported and supplied by fleets of equal size, neither could corner the other to try to starve them into surrender.

But now, as the campaigning season was drawing to a close, both Antigonos and Aristonous seemed to have, as if by mutual consent, decided upon a battle on even ground, advantageous to neither side as both their armies were so similar. It was as if the two generals had tired of the niceties of campaign strategy and tactics and decided, rather, just to settle the issue much as two boxers at the Olympic games, toe to toe, blow for blow.

Looking back at his trumpeter, six ranks behind him, Antigonos gave a nod. 'Sound the advance.'

At almost the identical moment, the same signal resounded from the other side of the field and both armies began to close on each other whilst, out at sea, glistering in warm afternoon sun, the shrill pipes of the stroke-masters wailed over the cries of gulls flocking around the ships, scavenging their waste.

Gods, this will be good. We just need to hold them as Demetrios outflanks their cavalry and sweeps around to the rear of the phalanx; and if Kleitos can break through and land his marines behind them as well, then Aristonous' lads are bound to surrender. Not too much Macedonian blood should be spilt; although I wouldn't want my pike-blade to come through completely unsullied. He glanced up at his weapon, still held in one hand upright, resting upon his shoulder, so that he could keep his round shield – slightly smaller than that of a hoplite – firm with the left, protecting him fully as the phalanx trudged across the sparsely grassed sandy ground.

On they went, with the light troops screening them and releasing volley after volley of arrows or slingshot, mostly at their opposite numbers as to shoot at the enemy phalanx at this distance was a wasted effort, their shields also being still held before them.

The distance between the two sides closed; at a hundred paces Antigonos turned and nodded to his trumpeter. A call rang out to be repeated to either side along the formation; down the sarissas came in a gentle wave spreading along the frontage, like a roller hitting the beach. Each man now needed two hands to wield his weapon and could not, therefore, hold a shield rigid before him; they were, instead, slung over the left shoulders to provide limited protection. And this is what the light troops had been waiting for: no longer focusing their attentions on their opposite numbers, they raised their aim and sent their volleys over the skirmishers' heads to land in the mass of barely shielded close-formation infantry. But only the first five ranks had their pikes at the horizontal, the next eleven held the weapons at progressively steeper angles so that they broke the flight of many an arrow or stone; but some got through, thumping into helm, leather cuirass, shield or flesh. The first cries rent the air as the wounded and dying clattered to the ground, disorganising their comrades around them as they strove to keep their feet and formation.

And then the skirmishers fell back for fear of coming between two great weights of infantry; through special, thin gaps left in the formations they filtered to spill out the other side, reform and then send high looping volleys over the heads of their phalanx to rain down upon the enemy.

As the last of the light infantry slipped past, Antigonos felt his comrades to either side close on him; the phalanx tightened its ranks, ready for impact. *Not far to go now; finally I'll get to see exactly what it is like to face a phalanx.* He glanced down and saw that the fifth ranker's pike blade was just past his belly, exactly where it should be, with the fourth ranker's a pace and a half further forward and then the third, second and finally his own: five blades coming to bear on the enemy for every man in the front rank; he felt the familiar pride of leading an exceptionally fine body of men into battle but knew that they faced an equally skilled and disciplined army; for this was civil war and many of the men opposite would have been trained by him or his officers.

Closer they came, both sides with the sixteen-point star of Macedon emblazoned on their shields, the whites of eyes clearly visible; the pike-blades of the two front ranks passed each other with a mass of metallic rings and wooden rasping as haft scraped haft. On came the wicked blades, coming closer and closer, bringers of death glinting in the sun. *Gods, this is going to be good; phalanx against phalanx, who'd have thought it would ever come to this.* 'Now!' he cried as he thrust his pike forward to the extent of his reach, ramming it into the throat of the man directly opposite. Forward the first, second and third ranks thrust, blades flashing in both directions, jamming into flesh, armour or just waving in thin air. Heaving forward, Antigonos ducked under a vicious jab and drove his skewered adversary back into the man behind, halting his progress and preventing any further advance by that file. All along the line, on either side, similar incidents were occurring as the far-reaching sarissas pushed forward and stopped dead the advance. Rear rank troops heaved on the backs of those in front of them, attempting to push them forward but none was willing to venture further into the razor-sharp hedge of points. Five paces apart, the two phalanxes came to a halt and a stabbing match ensued. Blades dripped red; men fell, crying to the gods, wounds gaping, to be replaced by the man behind.

On and on Antigonos thrust his pike, back and forth, stabbing, stabbing, stabbing, all the while dodging the honed iron hissing around him intent upon taking his life, and trying to ignore the missiles clattering down through the forest of pike-hafts above him. Philotas, next to him, as ever bawling every obscenity he could think of as he too worked his blade, attempted to push forward, past the second rankers' weapons, to fall to a thrust to the thigh from the next line of glistening pike-tips. Down he went, ignored by all as the battle continued, both sides knowing that it was futile and that they were at stalemate but also sensing that to lessen their endeavours would mean the other side gaining the upper hand. *It's all down to whatever is happening on the flanks and out at sea; we must hold them until that is resolved.* But marooned as he was in his own small realm of violence, he could see no further than ten paces; the flanks might as well have been on another island.

Blood and viscera tanged the air, slopping to the ground and the footing grew treacherous, but still the pikes punched and still they found their mark. But it was with equal success on both sides; neither, therefore, could advance, and to withdraw would be certain death. *With the phalanxes cancelling one another out, I can see that I'm going to have to develop a different way of going about things if this civil war continues.* But this thought was a brief flash across his mind as from the rear ranks of the enemy a great scream arose and the stones and arrows that had tormented them from above ceased. As quickly as the scream had started, it stopped; Aristonous' phalanx began to sit down.

Pikes dropped to the ground and the enemy sat or squatted, a mass of men in surrender. 'Enough!' Antigonos called; behind him his trumpeter sounded "disengage". Over the surrendering phalanx Antigonos saw horses and within that formation was a distinctive purple cloak. *Good lad, Demetrios; you managed to do exactly as you were told for once.* He dropped his weapon and stepped forward to Philotas, lying face down on the ground. 'How are you, old friend?'

Philotas turned over and took his hand from his wounded thigh. He smiled in relief. 'It's not spurting blood, just oozing. I'll be alright after it's been strapped up. Hurts like rough buggery, though.'

Antigonos clapped him on the shoulder. 'I want you ready for our sixty-fifth battle, brother.' He turned to the men in Philotas' file. 'Get him to my doctor. Gentle as you can with him; he's getting on a bit, you know.'

'Goat turd,' Philotas said through clenched teeth as he tried to stand. 'I'm six months younger than you.'

'Antigonos!'

The shout prevented his response to Philotas' insult as Antigonos looked around for its source.

It was obvious: an officer, ten or so years Antigonos' junior, in a high-plumed, gleaming bronze helm and a fine silver-inlayed breastplate rode a magnificent white stallion through the surrendered phalanx. Antigonos gave a grim smile. 'Aristonous, it's been a while.'

'Thirteen years, my friend, since we said goodbye when Alexander left you to conquer the rest of Anatolia.'

'That long, eh? And now we find ourselves fighting each other.' He indicated to the tidemarks of dead and wounded that showed the extremes of each side's advance. 'Good lads too; well, most of them.'

'I would that it could have been avoided but our masters both sent us to hold this island and now, I think it's fair to say, I have done all that honour dictates and you have possession of it.' He drew up his horse in front of Antigonos and looked across to the beach, past where Kleitos' marines had landed behind his army's flank and on out to sea where his fleet lay scattered. 'And you also have possession of the sea. I surrender. What will you do with my men?'

'Bring them into my army; I imagine they don't much care whom they're fighting for as long as they *are* fighting and are getting paid well and regularly.'

Aristonous smiled at the one-eyed general and dismounted. 'You know the men so well, Antigonos, and you make it sound so simple. So, what about me? What will you do with me?'

'Give you a cup of wine, I should think; you must have worked up quite a thirst.'

'That is much better,' Aristonous said, holding his freshly drained cup out for the slave to refill. He looked over to Antigonos and Demetrios, reclining on the other side of the low table, loaded with many varieties of seafood. 'Do we know how many died yet?'

'Enough for honour's sake,' Demetrios replied, adjusting his folded-up cloak so as to cushion his elbow better. 'The phalanx surrendered once we had seen off your cavalry and got behind it at the same time as our marines landed to its rear on the beach.' He looked to his father. 'Although I don't understand just why you felt the need to take away from my glory by having the marines share the victory; I was managing perfectly alright by myself.'

Antigonos gave his son a one-eyed glare as the puckered scar of his other wept a clear pink fluid. 'My arse! You think you were on your own, boy? My damp, hairy arse, you weren't! You had close on a thousand men with you, each one at least your equal in arms; you can't fight without your men and never forget that. Share your glory with them or you might one day feel a knife slip into your back during a fight; unpopular officers are often dealt with that way.' Demetrios began to protest, but Antigonos cut across him. 'And I had the marines land because in your first battle you got carried away and chased the enemy all around Kappadokia for a couple of days. I can't trust you not to just disappear off the battlefield chasing a routed foe.' He leaned across and grabbed the cloak, swiping it from under Demetrios' elbow. 'And only kings wear purple, Demetrios, you have a long way to go.'

Demetrios jumped to his feet, outraged. 'Don't you humiliate me, Father! Especially in front of a defeated enemy.'

Antigonos pointed to Aristonous. 'In this man's forty years in the field he has seen more battles on a greater scale than you are ever likely to see. He may have been defeated today but he is not an enemy; he was one of the King of Macedon's seven bodyguards. And I am not humiliating you, I'm teaching you; if you can't tell the difference then I suggest you go back to your mother and learn how to sew because you are of no use to me.'

Demetrios looked between the two older men, his mouth opening and closing.

'I dare you,' Antigonos snarled.

But it was a laugh that burst forth from the younger man, not a tirade of teenage invective. He sat back down. 'You're right, of course, Father. And my apologies to you, Aristonous, I spoke out of turn.'

Antigonos reached over and cuffed his son around the ear. 'You didn't speak out of turn, you spoke without thinking; there's a big difference. But you did well today; exactly what I told you to without getting carried away.' He grinned. 'Next time, perhaps, we won't need the marines.'

'You have a guest, Antigonos,' Philotas said, limping through the entrance on a crutch.

Antigonos turned round. 'Who is it?'

Philotas signalled the waiting man in. 'A messenger from Antipatros.'

'Nicanor,' Antigonos said as Antipatros' son came into the tent. 'This must be serious.'

'So I'm to be executed by vote of the army assembly,' Aristonous said once Nicanor had briefed them on the developments since Perdikkas' ill-fated attempt at crossing the Nile; he drained his cup and looked at Antigonos. 'You had better do your duty by the army and get on with it.'

'I've never heard such rubbish in my life!' Antigonos thundered. 'Execute one of our own? My arse, I will!'

'I can see that Alketas must die,' Philotas said, cracking a crab leg with a hammer, 'if only because he was responsible for Cynnane's death. Attalus condemned himself the moment he took those eight hundred talents from the Tyros treasury, but what happened to Atalante was shameful.'

Antigonos shook his head, anger burning in his eye. 'But you, Aristonous? You are a man of honour; I'll not see you executed because of some misguided, emotional decree. The men should have been better handled. It was Eumenes who killed Krateros, let him be the one to pay for that, just as Attalus and Alketas should pay for their crimes.'

Aristonous inclined his head. 'You are a comfort, old friend.'

'As for Atalante, Ptolemy should have ensured that women

were exempt from this vindictive decree. Has it come to this that we execute our women? What sort of men are we? When I find the ringleaders who called for her death I'll make them into women before I execute them.'

'It was a foolish move,' Aristonous agreed. 'With that one death we've ensured that there can be no peace, no reconciliation until Attalus and Alketas are dead for they are honour-bound to avenge a wife and a sister. Such a blunder; so much so that it makes one wonder whether it wasn't deliberate.'

Antigonos frowned and looked at Nicanor. 'Could Ptolemy have prevented her death?'

Nicanor shrugged. 'I wasn't there.'

'Ptolemy never does anything without a reason,' Aristonous pointed out. 'And it's normally a self-serving reason. Who benefits most from war in the north?'

Philotas wiped his fingers on a napkin and helped himself to another crab leg. 'Ptolemy's certainly ensured that we'll be busy even after Eumenes has been defeated.'

'He was ever the clever one, and always had ambition added to his love of the finer things in life.'

Antigonos grunted in disapproval. 'There's nothing to be done about him now. I must garrison the island and then take the rest of the army over to The Three Paradises; we'll be busy for the next few days if we're to be there on time.'

'And me?' Aristonous asked.

'I'll give you a ship, two ships; take your companions back to Macedon, retire to your estates and don't draw attention to yourself.'

'That is all I've wanted to do since Alexander died.'

'Then you have it; I'll settle the matter with Antipatros.'

'Thank you. I'm in your debt, Antigonos.'

'I know, and you are in the position to repay it.'

'I am?'

'Yes, your estates are to the west near the border with Epirus, are they not?'

'Ahh, I see what you want.'

'Yes. Antipatros will become regent to the two kings so I want to hear any rumours coming out of Epirus; I want to know what *she* is up to. I want to know, before Antipatros or anyone else, what Olympias' plans are.'

OLYMPIAS.
THE MOTHER.

T HE SNAKE FELT cool on her body; it slithered across her belly and then onto her thighs, working its way down her legs, its skin glistening in the red light of many flaming sconces. The low chanting soothed Olympias and, as the first serpent cleared her feet, she felt a second slide up onto her shoulder; a soft hiss in her ear, and then it began to traverse her breasts. For the first time in months she felt a modicum of peace; finally she could push the hatred that burned constantly inside her to the back of her mind as she focused on the purity of the snakes and on the question she had asked them.

Behind her, she heard the priestess remove the lid from another basket and felt the rush of pleasure that she had experienced all her life at the thought of contact with another of those magnificent creatures. The raw power in their sleek bodies and the death in their fangs thrilled her to the point of worship; other than the rites of Dionysus, this ritual satisfied her the most, both spiritually and sexually. Again she squeezed her legs together and felt the head of the de-fanged serpent writhe within her and she let out another long moan of pleasure.

The chanting increased as the second serpent completed the journey down her body and the priestess placed the third snake next to Olympias' head; once again the creature hissed and climbed onto her shoulder and then travelled down all the way to her feet. That was three in a row; there could be no better omen – one that she had witnessed, but on a couple of occasions – three snakes in succession all making the same journey from her shoulder down to her feet.

Three times they had replied in the affirmative; that was enough to give her the answer she had looked for.

She squeezed her thighs together again repeatedly and, with chest heaving and throat contracting, let the rapture of the snake moving within build and take her to places that could not be found in the physical world, until she lay, sweat-covered and panting, limbs awry, trying to focus on the room around her and finding it a sad disappointment after the inner road upon which she had just travelled. Olympias felt the priestess remove the snake from between her legs and heard the soft shuffle of her and her chanting acolytes withdrawing to leave her alone with her thoughts.

And what thoughts they were: dark and grim; full of hate, spite and malice.

For a while she allowed herself to wallow in them but, from much previous experience, she knew that she could only indulge for the shortest of time as she exhausted herself in the depths of her malevolence.

The sweat on her body began to cool with the early autumnal mountain air gusting, despite the shutters, through the room, fluttering the sconce flames so that the vivid murals of women – and a few men – copulating with snakes seemed to come alive, moving in the flickering light and shadow. She shivered and sat up, rubbing her upper arms and pulling her thoughts away from the vengeance that was rightfully hers for being excluded from the heart of power for so long; for the thirteen years since her son, Alexander, had gone east.

But now the snakes had spoken and soon all would change, for soon Perdikkas would defeat Ptolemy and regain Alexander's catafalque; of this she was certain for the news had come that morning of Eumenes' defeat of Krateros and the death of that great general. With Antipatros now caught between Eumenes and Perdikkas he would be obliged to turn and face the Greek, leaving Perdikkas free to concentrate all his strength on defeating Ptolemy; and defeat him he would, for he possessed the larger army in terms of veterans – Ptolemy's force being mainly local conscripts armed in the Macedonian manner.

No, it was certain that Perdikkas would triumph and, between them, he and Eumenes would defeat Antipatros. With the body reclaimed, Kleopatra would then agree to marry Perdikkas and, in interring Alexander's remains in the royal tomb at Argeas, he would claim the throne, adopt the child, Alexander, as his heir, and then, through her daughter and her grandson, Olympias would finally wield power. The snakes had spoken: her wait was over.

And then what a reckoning there would be. The first who would suffer would be that toad Antipatros and his loathsome sons; they would make a fine beginning. It was all for certain for the snakes never lie and three in a row had slithered the length of her body, something that had happened only twice before and on each occasion they had answered the question true.

Pulling on a robe and a pair of fleece-lined slippers, Olympias clapped her hands, summoning her body-slave. 'Prepare my bath,' she ordered the middle-aged woman who had served her all her adult life but had never once been addressed by her name. 'And lay out my finest dress, the saffron one with the golden thread embroidery, and have the slaves ready for my hair and make-up; I'll decide what jewellery to wear once I've seen the final effect. Warn the girls that I must look my best for my inter-view with the king or the skin will be coming off their backs and yours. And send Thessalonike to me.'

With a bow, the slave retired to do her mistress's bidding, well aware that this was no idle threat, having been subjected to many a whipping throughout her life of misery.

Savouring the look of fear in the woman's eyes, Olympias went to the window, threw open the shutters and breathed deep of the air coming down from the Pindus mountains away to the east. Feeling the mists of religious and sexual ecstasy blowing clear by the cleansing breeze, she composed, in her head, what she would say to her cousin, Aeacides, the young King of Epirus, to persuade him of the necessity of lending her the Epirot army. She intended to threaten Polyperchon, Antipatros' deputy and ruler of Macedon during his absence in Asia, should he decide to oppose Kleopatra's and Perdikkas' arrival in Macedon. If necessary, she would invade from the west as Perdikkas came from the east; she would not stand one moment of delay to his and, therefore, her return; especially after she had received such a clear answer to her question.

For too long she had been confined to Passaron, the capital of this mountainous realm of Epirus, but, despite her status, she was excluded from Epirus' royal counsel by her insect of a nephew. Powerless, isolated, with no one of her standing, other than her adoptive daughter, Thessalonike, to keep her company, now that Kleopatra resided in Sardis awaiting Perdikkas, Olympias yearned for her return to the centre of politics and attention – and then what a reckoning there would be.

Olympias savoured the thought of revenge as she awaited Thessalonike. Thessalonike was the daughter of her husband, Philip, and his third wife, Nicesipolis, born ten years after Alexander, a long time after Philip had deserted Olympias' bed for younger flesh. But Olympias was nothing if not resourceful and just because the child had been sired upon another did not mean that it could not be hers – if it were a girl, that was; had it been a boy it would not have survived its first night. Fortunately for the babe it had been a girl, but that fact spelt death for her mother, slowly poisoned over twenty days so as to look like a natural decline after giving birth. Selflessly, Olympias had offered to bring up the child as her own, thus gaining herself another daughter with whom she could make advantageous political marriages that would help secure her position in the future. Although not nearly as pure-blooded as her natural daughter, Kleopatra, Thessalonike was still of Argead blood and Olympias now had a use for her stolen child, for that future she had foreseen had arrived.

'You sent for me, Mother,' Thessalonike said, gliding into the room, her movement elegant and her deportment graceful; together they provided a powerful shield that masked her true nature, a nature that had been imbued by her adoptive mother. *I was far more successful with this one than I was with Kleopatra; this one is all mine.*

'I did, child,' Olympias replied, indicating that they should both sit. 'We are coming to interesting times and we need to take advantage of every opportunity to confound our enemies and strengthen our position.'

'The snakes spoke?'

'They did. I asked them as soon as I heard of Eumenes' victory; it was the best of omens.'

'What was the question?'

'Is my time of waiting for power in Macedon over?'

Thessalonike looked surprised. 'Surely that was a little vague? Why did you not ask whether Perdikkas would defeat Ptolemy and then Antipatros?'

'The priestess of the snakes will only allow questions about oneself, not the fortunes of others; it was ever thus.'

'If you would allow me to be initiated then I would know such things.'

'A virgin cannot serve, for obvious reasons.'

Thessalonike snorted. 'Mother, you know perfectly well that I am not.'

'Whatever you get up to with your slaves or bodyguards is between you and them. To the world you must be a virgin and therefore you cannot serve; and you do well to remember that on your wedding night and refrain from doing tricks that one meant to be unschooled in the art of love would find difficult to explain away.'

Thessalonike held Olympias' gaze. 'I am twenty-four; I should have been married eight or nine years ago. You can't expect me to do without the pleasure of men just because you haven't found the appropriate husband for me – or rather, for *your* purposes.'

That's it, girl; stir up a bit of resentment, you will feel so much better for it. 'Don't talk to me like that. I've sacrificed much to give you a life; who knows what would have happened to you had I not intervened and took you for my own.'

'You would have poisoned me most likely, as you did—' Thessalonike clamped her mouth shut.

Olympias waited a moment for the sentence to be completed but it was left hanging. 'As I did what – or who?' *Of course she has guessed by now; I've brought her up to think the way I do. How can she have not seen the truth? So much the better.* 'But come, my dear, it is about your marriage that I wish to talk to you.'

'You want me to marry Eumenes?'

My, she is quick, this one. 'It would seem the logical thing to do.'

'Because my real mother was a Thessalian of little consequence but of great beauty, whom Philip took out of lust rather than for dynastic reasons?'

'One could put it that way.'

'And so as a half-blooded Argead I can be given to a Greek from Kardia without causing offence to Macedonians but still binding Eumenes even closer with Perdikkas and his new bride, Kleopatra, because she is my half-sister.'

'Exactly; you've read the situation perfectly, my dear. It will secure our position. No matter who Antipatros marries Phila to, now that Krateros has left her a widow, he won't be able to drive a wedge between Eumenes and Perdikkas because of you and Kleopatra; he will be forced to come to terms with them or face the utter destruction of his house. I would wager that he will choose to spend what little time is left to him in retirement on his estates.'

Thessalonike studied her adoptive mother, weighing her words. 'Mother, I understand your position but I'll make no commitment until we know for certain the outcome of the struggle.'

'We already do, the snakes have spoken.'

'They may have spoken, but you asked the wrong question.' Thessalonike rose to her feet. 'Having never witnessed the ceremony, I can place little faith in its validity.' She turned and walked away as the slave-woman appeared in the doorway. 'After all, Mother, you're fifty-four, that's quite an age; your time of waiting for power in Macedon could well be over any moment when you drop down dead.' She paused at the door and gave a sweet smile, much exaggerated, over her shoulder. 'It's just an observation.'

'Your bath is prepared, mistress,' the slave said as Thessalonike left the chamber.

'Get out!' Olympias screamed, flinging a miniature statue of Dionysus at the woman.

Doubts now plagued Olympias, normally so firm in her convictions. *The trouble is, she's right; it was the most unsatisfactory form of question. I'll redo the ceremony after I've spoken with Aeacides.*

'And who will pay for all this?' Aeacides asked.

It had been the first question that Olympias had expected of her weak and avaricious nephew and she was prepared. 'Perdikkas will, as a debt of gratitude for you supporting his claim to the crown.'

Small bloodshot eyes peered at her from a face already falling prey, despite the king's age, to the ravages of excessive drinking. 'And what if I muster the army and we lead it over the mountains and into Macedon, or at least to the border and wait only to find that Perdikkas is not installed as king? Who will pay then? Antipatros? I think not; no, it'll come out of my treasury.'

The relaxing effects of her bath, the pleasure of having her slaves whipped and the sweet anticipation of another snake-ceremony, once she had got her own way with the little fool, were rapidly wearing off; Olympias struggled to keep her temper as she always did when having an audience with her kinsman. 'Perdikkas will be installed as king and Kleopatra will be his queen.'

Aeacides affected to look puzzled. 'I don't think that even a daughter of yours would care to share a bed with a dead man; and I certainly don't think the Macedonians would take kindly to a corpse sitting on their throne.' He smiled at Olympias in triumph. 'Because that's what Perdikkas is, cousin, a corpse.'

Olympias felt her belly sink and instinctively she knew the truth of the statement. 'How do you know?'

Aeacides produced a scroll. 'Ptolemy sent this to you; unfortunately you were otherwise engaged, shall we say, when the messenger arrived a couple of hours ago, so I thought I'd better check its contents to see if it were important enough to disturb your devotions, as I know – from the noise – how seriously you take them.' He flicked the scroll to Olympias; she read with increasing despair as her plans and schemes were exploded by misfortune. *The fool, Perdikkas, the fool. And this part here where Ptolemy says that the news of Eumenes' victory came just too late to save him; don't think me a fool, Ptolemy, I can see what you have done.* She screwed up the letter, threw it to the ground and stormed from the throne-room. *Calm, I must have calm to think this through. Antipatros now has Phila and Nicaea widowed; two daughters to dispose of. Who will he give them to? To whom can I offer my two now? Who would be the most likely king?* She halted and a smile of comprehension crept over her face. Forgetting dignity, she turned, broke into a run and only slowed as she entered her suite. Sitting at the desk she arranged her writing implements. After a moment's pause for reflection she dipped her nib into the inkpot. *Olympias, Queen of Macedon, greets her sister and fellow queen, Roxanna.*

ROXANNA.
THE WILD-CAT.

*S*HE IS THE *first to recognise my right to be addressed as queen,* Roxanna noted with approval as her secretary finished reading the letter – a queen has no need of reading or writing when there are plenty who will do it for her – *but is that just to get my attention?*

Roxanna waved the secretary away and pondered the problem, ensconced within the pile of cushions that formed the day-bed in her living-wagon as it swayed and bumped its way north. The living-wagon was but a tiny component of the huge column that made up the army of Babylon, now within sight of the manicured hunting parks of The Three Paradises, spread over many a rolling hill and punctuated with grand pavilions and prodigious cedars. Cool breezes now made the journey more bearable; a gentle rain fell intermittently.

It had surprised her to receive a letter from Olympias; she had never had any contact with the woman who was the grandmother of her child and she was intrigued. It was obvious, however, what she wanted when she requested that Roxanna should bring young Alexander to Epirus – wherever that was – so that they could both come under her protection now that Perdikkas was dead. It was also obvious that they both had the same objectives: the death of the fool, Philip, his unnaturally masculine wife and the eventual sole rule of Alexander as the fourth of that name to be King of Macedon and its empire. In the meantime, Roxanna wondered, *what plans does she have for the regency?* And that was just the problem for Roxanna: whoever had her child controlled the regency and, as an outsider, a barbarian in Macedonian eyes, it could never be her. She needed an ally, one with power; one whom she could control now that the bitch, Adea, had gathered so many followers. It had made Roxanna want to weep and tear at her garments and hair to see the ease with which the man-woman married to the man-child had gathered so much support from the soldiery during the slow trudge north, over twenty days, from Egypt; now it seemed that the whole army listened to her.

The fact that Adea could bring herself to talk to people so far beneath her showed, to Roxanna's mind, just how unfit she was to hold power; yet the army now recognised her right to speak for the fool of a king. The two new regents, the idiot Peithon and the non-entity, Arrhidaeus, could do nothing because Adea had united the men behind her by championing a cause about which they cared more than anything else; more than Macedon, more than glory or family or the gods: money. Money had proven to be the issue that roused them, for they had none. Nor was it likely that they would get any until Antipatros arrived at The Three Paradises. Adea had exploited this grievance to the extent that it had made Roxanna feel physically sick. And it was not only their back pay that the men of the army of Babylon were aggrieved about; it went far deeper than that: all the veterans whom Alexander had discharged had been given a talent of silver each, but many of them had re-enlisted with Antipatros once they had returned to Macedon and had been allowed to keep the payoff. Here, in the army's very midst, were Antigenes' three thousand Silver Shields, living proof of the one talent bounty that had been paid; none could deny it for each man's share was travelling in their baggage. Alexander had promised the bounty to all, discharged or not, it was claimed – although none could remember exactly when this pledge had been made – and since they had failed to share in the riches of Egypt, the men were unanimous that the alleged verbal contract should be kept.

Every evening, as the slow-moving column had made camp, Adea would wander around the men promising them that her husband would ensure that they had everything that they were due paid to them, back pay and bounty. If they supported him, with her as his mouthpiece, they would never find themselves in the position where they were so behind on their pay again. *As if she could keep such a promise. Pah!* Roxanna threw a cushion at one of the two girls who cowered by the door awaiting her pleasure. 'Bring me a sherbet!'

But the cool, refreshing drink did not calm her and, halfway through it, that too was hurled at the unfortunate slaves. *If I cannot find a way of poisoning the fool and his wife then I need to either undermine them or make myself obviously superior to them. Perhaps Olympias may be of use.*

More than ever she felt isolated; her son, travelling in the wagon behind so that she did not have to endure his petulance, was not a talisman for the soldiery as she had refused to let the men near the child; such was her aversion to the low-life scum that made up the army of Macedon in Asia. Or any army for that matter; they were there to fight and die for their king without question, such was the nature of things, surely? And now, in a small recess in the part of her mind that had become less eastern in outlook over the years she had been travelling with the Macedonian army, she began to question that premise. *If the man-woman gains safety and support by currying favour with the common men perhaps I could do the same by cultivating the lesser officers? Are they so beneath my dignity that they cannot be of use to me?* 'Summon Peithon and Arrhidaeus,' she ordered her slaves, 'tell them I wish to see them as soon as we make camp at The Three Paradises.

'You have kept me waiting,' Roxanna said, trying not to sound too snappish without losing what she considered to be her innate authority; she glanced up and struggled to hide her surprise at seeing Seleukos standing before her. 'Where are Peithon and Arrhidaeus?'

Seleukos looked down at her, lounging on her many cushions

under an awning protecting her completely covered body from the last of the sun; two dark eyes looked back from within a narrow slit in her veil. 'Firstly, I am not late; I come and go as I please. And secondly, Peithon and Arrhidaeus are not coming as whatever it is you have to say can be said just as easily to me as it can to them; and, besides, they're busy.'

'Too busy to come when their queen demands?'

Seleukos sighed and sat on the camp-chair that his slave had brought for him, being perfectly aware that no such courtesy would be provided by Roxanna. 'One is dealing with the army's demands and the other is with another trying woman who likes to call herself queen; although being married to a king makes her more so than you who is just the mother of a king.'

Roxanna, with great restraint, held her temper even as it threatened to thunder from her. *I need him on my side, however insolent he may be.* She composed herself. 'I shall ignore that remark – although I won't forget it.'

'I am terrified. Now say what you have to so that I can get on to more pressing affairs.'

Despising more than ever the arrogance of these Macedonian upstarts who believed themselves to be the equal of Alexander, Roxanna sipped her sherbet beneath her veil to moisten her angry, dry and tight throat. 'I wish you to procure me a ship.'

Seleukos looked as if he had misheard her. 'A ship?'

'I wish to take my son, the king, to visit his grandmother in Epirus; she herself has written requesting this and, as she is the mother of Alexander, I expect her will to be obeyed. As a favour, I shall allow either you, Peithon or Arrhidaeus to accompany me – you may draw lots – as I assume that the man who reunites that great woman with her grandchild, the rightful king, will receive magnificent gifts and preference.' Roxanna watched as Seleukos sat before her, his mouth agape, his brow furrowed, his eyes incredulous. The laugh that then exploded from him was as loud as it was insulting: never before had she been laughed at to her face. She launched a cushion at him. 'How dare you amuse yourself at my expense!'

Seleukos rubbed his eyes with the cushion as he brought his mirth under control. 'You honestly think that anyone in their right mind would allow Olympias – someone who, incidentally, makes you seem like an undemanding, kind and considerate person – access to one of the kings so that she can use him as a pawn in her never-ending quest for power?' Again Seleukos hooted with laughter. 'And you really believe that if one of us were foolish enough to allow this and accompany you and your child then Olympias would shower us with gifts?' Another peal of mirth followed as he contemplated the mental image. 'No, Roxanna, this time you really do ask too much and you display a complete lack of understanding of Macedonian dynastic politics. Olympias is toxic and she will never be allowed to meddle in our affairs again. In fact, I would say that a hatred of her would unite every Macedonian; me, Ptolemy, Antipatros, Attalus, Kassandros, Alketas, anyone you care to name, all of us.' He got up to leave. 'There will be no ship. Your fate, and the fate of the kings, will be decided soon now that we've arrived at The Three Paradises. Antipatros and the others will be here in the next few days. Good evening to you.'

SELEUKOS.
THE BULL-ELEPHANT.

THAT OLYMPIAS IS *scheming means that she must have heard of Perdikkas'* death. Seleukos considered the implications of the letter to Roxanna as he left her part of the encampment, still smiling at the depth of the wild-cat's delusion. *That she is trying to get influence over her grandson means that she is uncertain how to use Kleopatra now that she isn't going to marry Perdikkas. Antipatros will be very interested to hear about that letter, especially as he has two newly widowed daughters. That will help soothe him if he finds confirming my appointment as Satrap of Babylon unpalatable.*

Making up his mind to seek a meeting with the old regent as soon as he arrived at The Three Paradises, Seleukos walked back towards his tent; around him the army of Babylon made their way, with purpose in their steps and anger in their voices, towards the western perimeter of the camp. 'Where're you all going?' he asked a group of Hypaspists, the elite infantrymen known as the Silver Shields, commanded by Antigenes.

'Ain't you heard, mate?' an old hand replied. 'The king and queen have called an army assembly; they want to—' He stopped as he recognised who he was speaking to.

'Yes?' Seleukos said with a dangerous smile. 'They want to what?'

The veteran swallowed and his comrades suddenly found the need to disassociate themselves from him. 'They, er, they want to… Well, they want to consult us.'

'Consult you about what?'

The veteran's face grew very uneasy as he realised that his mates had completely abandoned him in the face of the largest man in the army and so very far above him in rank. 'They didn't say.'

Seleukos glared at the man. 'All you Silver Shields were paid the talent bounty when you were discharged with Krateros; why are you getting involved in this argument over money?'

'It's the back pay; we've received nothing since we left Babylon more than two years ago. Perdikkas promised to pay us from the treasury in Tyros but now Attalus controls that; so where is our money coming from?'

Seleukos held the man's eye for a few moments, nodded, and then turned to go, to the veteran's obvious relief. *Discipline is going and the army's disintegrating; it's time for a harsh lesson to be administered. I'd better listen to what Adea's filling their heads with. The trouble is that since that idiot, Alketas, killed Cynnane, Adea is invulnerable; to kill her would mean a mutiny.* And Adea was taking advantage of exactly that; a harsh lesson was the last thing that Adea suggested to the army assembly as she harangued them from an uncovered wagon with her fool of a husband sitting drooling to one side – his four Macedonian bodyguards around him – and Barzid, her own bodyguard, standing on the other. 'I accept the need for a regent,' she shrilled, her normally deep voice raised high in excitement. 'And I accept the reasons why we now find ourselves with two regents. But what I don't accept is that these co-regents make decisions without reference to me, the only person able to speak for my husband, the king.'

There was much sympathy for this contention, surprising Seleukos with the extent of support the seventeen-year-old had amongst the grizzled veterans as well as the younger men. *We've let this get too far without knowing it.* 'Support me in my claim for the sake of my husband, Alexander's brother, in whose veins flows true Argead blood; support me so that I can make his voice heard. Support me and I promise my husband will ensure that the talent of silver bounty is paid to all who have yet to receive it.'

A massive cheer arose and Adea held her arms wide to accept their accolade.

How does she think she will be able to pay such a vast amount?

But the answer to that question came sooner than Seleukos expected as a Macedonian officer got up onto the wagon beside her.

'And here is the man who can set a wrong right.'

Silence fell over the crowd as those closest to the new arrival recognised him and his name filtered back.

Attalus! What's he doing here? And then Seleukos understood and his respect for the young queen doubled. *Ohh, that* is *clever.*

'Yes, I know that the army assembly has condemned this man to death,' Adea continued, 'and yes he was a close supporter of Perdikkas, but, consider this, soldiers of Macedon: he was only keeping faith with family, as any one of you would have. He was married to Perdikkas' sister whose death you demanded and he has this offer to make to you. Hear him.' She indicated that Attalus should address the assembly.

'Comrades,' he declaimed, 'and I am proud to say "comrades" even though you have laid a sentence of death upon my head. Comrades, I have suffered at your hands; I have had my wife taken from me and for what? What had I ever done to you to deserve that? I commanded the fleet, I had nothing to do with Krateros' death; nor could I influence my brother-in-law and dissuade him from invading Egypt where we lost so many, such was his arrogance towards the end.' He paused to let his words have an effect. 'I have this offer to make to you: remove the sentence of death hanging over me and I will seek no revenge for the killing of my wife. And what is more; I have taken Tyros with my fleet and in Tyros I found a treasury with more than eight thousand talents in silver and gold. Gold! Not just silver. Do this for me and you will not find me ungenerous.'

Nor did the army think he would be, judging by the acclaim with which they acquitted him.

Seleukos hurried away as Adea called through the cheers, imploring the men to escort her and her husband to confront the two regents. *I think it's advisable to bring forward that meeting with Antipatros.*

'And so I rode to meet you as fast as I could,' Seleukos said, having told Antipatros of the developments in the army of Babylon's camp. 'Antigonos is keeping an eye on the situation. He arrived just as I was leaving yesterday; he camped on the other side of the river to them so as not to let his troops be infected by the mutinous atmosphere.'

'Both Peithon *and* Arrhidaeus have resigned the regency?' Antipatros asked as they began another climb through wooded, resin-scented hills; the army of Macedon from Europe snaked out behind along the winding track until it disappeared in the depths of the valley below.

Seleukos nodded, stroking his stallion's neck. 'They didn't want to stand up to Adea with the army in mutinous mood behind her; they've declared that the regency of the kings should pass to you seeing as you're also the regent of Macedon. To be honest, Ptolemy and I didn't expect them to last long.'

Antipatros turned a knowing look to his companion. 'Just long enough for them to appoint you Satrap of Babylonia which I suppose I will have to confirm for the sake of keeping the peace and as a thank-you for the information about that witch's letter to Roxanna.'

Seleukos shrugged but made no comment; they rode on in silence.

'Attalus came to the camp,' Seleukos said after a while. 'Adea invited him to speak to the men.'

Antipatros looked at him in surprise. 'And is he dead now?'

'Far from it: the Assembly rescinded his sentence and he returned to Tyros with four thousand deserters bribed by the promise of the silver talent bounty.'

'Why didn't the rest of the army go with him?'

'He said that he would only take the first four thousand who volunteered; there was quite a scrum.'

'I can imagine.'

'Our intelligence tells us that Attalus has only got troop transports for two thousand men.'

'So he plans to make two journeys to Pisidia before the sea-lanes close for the winter.'

'Pisidia?'

'It's where Alketas is hiding; he's raising an army and doing quite well by all accounts. Attalus' four thousand will be a real bonus to him. What sort of troops were they?'

'Phalangites; mostly veterans.'

'What about Antigenes' Hypaspists?'

'They've had their bounty, they just want their back pay; they were tempted to go but Antigenes put their baggage under guard. I think you'll have most trouble from them if you can't come up with any money.'

Antipatros sighed. 'How can I come up with any money for them when the treasury in Macedon is barely enough to keep this army going, Attalus has commandeered Tyros and the chances of getting anything out of Ptolemy is nil? All the money is out east; they'll have to wait.'

'They won't like it.'

'They'll have to. I'll talk to them as soon as we arrive.'

ANTIPATROS.
THE REGENT.

I'M TOO OLD to be shouting like this. Antipatros tried to make himself heard over the baying of the furious mob of soldiery pressing close around him so that the shields of his dozen bodyguards were compressed back into their wielders' chests. 'Will you let me speak?' he roared with as much volume as his octogenarian form would allow.

'Where's our money? Where's our money?' the crowd chanted, raising fists in the air in time to the beat; the veteran Hypaspists, grizzled and grey, to the fore, leading the insubordination.

Seleukos didn't exaggerate; I've never seen the lads so het up. He looked over to Adea, seated on a raised chair next to her husband, smiling at him with a calculating look. *Adea has a lot to answer for and, by Aries, answer she will; what does she expect to gain from a mutiny?* He dodged a half-eaten onion but a well-aimed apple found its mark. 'How can I address your grievances if you won't let me speak?'

But it was no use. On and on they went with the same chant, never allowing Antipatros to respond, and all the time Adea sat there doing nothing to control the beast she had birthed.

It had been thus since Antipatros had arrived at The Three Paradises in advance of his main army, such was his determination to stifle the nascent revolt. Antigonos and Seleukos had both offered to come with him but he had refused their suggestion, vastly underestimating the depth of feeling in the camp across the river.

Impotent, Antipatros stood in the midst of the Assembly, to be verbally abused and the target of many a shied fruit or vegetable. Never had he felt so humiliated; never had he seen the soldiery of Macedon so mutinous. *But then I wasn't in India when the infantry forced Alexander to turn back; I imagine it was something like this, with the Hypaspists leading the revolt, but without a teenage harpy stirring them up.*

Once more he tried to make himself heard and once more the chant drowned him out; so it was with a great degree of surprise that he witnessed Adea silencing the crowd solely by getting to her feet.

'Soldiers of Macedon,' she cried. 'Loyal subjects of my husband.' She pointed at Antipatros. 'This is the man to whom Peithon and Arrhidaeus wish to bequeath their regency. Here he stands before you and his king. I will put my husband's question to him; a question that is very dear to his heart because it concerns the welfare of his soldiers. Antipatros, where is the back pay of the army of Babylon and where is their promised bounty?'

Antipatros drew himself up and cleared his throat. 'You will all have your money but it will take a bit of time as it has to be transferred from the treasuries out in the east. It is in the east that Alexander left his wealth and it is from the east it must be carried.'

'Ha!' Adea exclaimed over the discontented murmuring that met this answer. 'Ha! What use is this old man as regent for my husband if he cannot even pay his troops when they ask for their dues? What use, I ask? Three days ago, Attalus came and addressed you; he gave out money; he paid debts that were not even his to pay. Would he not be more suitable as regent to my husband? He would consult with me, I who have the ear of the king; I who alone can speak for him. King Philip would finally have a voice; the brother of Alexander would finally be heard. Soldiers of Macedon, I put before your army assembly the notion that Antipatros should be deposed and Attalus made regent with King Philip, the third of that name, having an equal status with him. What say you, soldiers of Macedon?'

And what they said was demonstrated by the way they broke through the thin cordon protecting Antipatros, seized him and held him bodily aloft. 'Let me down, comrades,' Antipatros said in as dignified a manner as possible for a man being carried against his will, 'and we will talk further.'

'There ain't nothing to be said, old man,' a disembodied voice in the crowd shouted, 'except by you deciding whether you want to throw a lot of money at us or would rather we throw a lot of stones at you.'

Harsh laughter greeted this statement; Antipatros was tossed up into the air and then caught by ungentle hands, fingernails grazing his skin and tearing his tunic.

'We've already killed one commander, old man, what difference would a second make?'

Seleukos, Antigenes and Peithon also have a lot to answer for, the bastards. 'Put me down!'

Up again he went, limbs flapping and back arching, to the accompaniment of growing laughter, raucous and overflowing with disrespect. And then down he came, but this time the hands were not nearly so quick in grappling him and his back jarred against stony ground. Grimacing and straining with every fibre of his being not to cry out, undignified, in pain, Antipatros ceased to struggle, realising that his fate was, literally, in the hands of his men and there was little he could do to influence them.

'Put him down, you mutinous maggots! How dare you manhandle the regent of Macedon, appointed by Alexander himself?'

At the mention of that sacred name the laughter died and the grip on his person grew slack; Antipatros found himself sitting on the ground looking up at bearded faces who could barely meet his eye. *To be treated like this at my age! I'll have some heads for this.* He pushed himself to his feet, trying not to wince as his aged knees and hips clicked, slapping the dust from his tunic as he rose. Twenty paces from him, sitting upon a horse was Antigonos, in full armour as if he were going into battle; which, indeed, he could well be, Antipatros reflected, feeling the anger all around him.

'Hand him over!' Antigonos ordered; behind him came Seleukos with a substantial cavalry escort, ploughing their way through the mass of disgruntled soldiery.

'We keep him until he's paid,' a veteran replied, placing an iron-hard grip on Antipatros' shoulder; others crowded around him, preventing flight.

'The longer you keep him, the longer and more severe the punishment will be,' Antigonos barked.

'Don't listen to him,' Adea shrieked. 'He has no authority over my husband and my husband orders Antipatros to be detained until he has paid what is owed.'

'Quiet, bitch!' Antigonos' one eye roved over the crowd. 'Is this what it has come to? Is it? Grown men of pure Macedonian blood listening to the uninformed words of some pubescent amazon?' He pointed to Adea and Philip, sitting drooling next to her, his face creased with confusion. Barzid put his hand on his sword's hilt, tensing. 'Look at her! Guarded by an Illyrian and yet claiming to be a Macedonian queen. What is she really? Yes, she's Philip's granddaughter and, yes, she's married to Philip's son. And yes, she is of the Argead royal house and should she bear her husband's child and it be a boy then it would have the strongest claim to the throne of Macedon than anyone else alive – even over Alexander's son sired upon the eastern wild-cat – because we men of Macedon choose our kings, we don't have them foisted upon us, we choose them from the Argead house.' He looked at Antipatros and gave him the briefest of nods as he carried on. 'But that is where our choices end, soldiers of Macedon, choosing the king. After that it is by his choices that we are ruled and Antipatros was chosen by Alexander to be regent; it is not down to us, or that harpy over there, to question those decisions.' Again he gave Antipatros a surreptitious nod as

Seleukos and his men pushed their way to the heart of the crowd, mere paces from Antipatros.

He means to provide a diversion so that Seleukos can get to me.

'And yet you let yourselves be influenced by her, a woman, a very young woman at that. Would you take the advice or act upon the whims of your daughters? Of course you wouldn't; only fools are swayed by women's opinions. The only influential part of a woman is her cunt and the last time I looked at one it was free of opinion.' This produced the ribald laughter that it was meant to and grabbed the men's interest.

With a wife like mine I wouldn't necessarily agree with that assertion, but I'm not going to argue the point here. As Antigonos expanded on his theme, at great length, Antipatros felt his captors' concentration slipping away from him. He glanced up at Seleukos who winked back and nodded at a riderless horse amongst the troopers next to him.

Antigonos spoke on, developing his premises of loyalty, obedience and patience, arguing that although money was important, indeed, of prime importance, there was just as great a consideration to be taken into account and that was unity. 'And she,' he bellowed, levelling an accusatory finger at Adea, 'she is not conducive to unity. All she has done on the march north from Egypt, if I understand matters correctly, is try to divide and thereby rule. Is that the way that Alexander ruled? Or his father before him? No, brothers, it is not, for had it been then we would still be confined to the limited boundaries of Macedon and not rulers of the world. She is a corrosive influence who must put up and learn her position.'

'He lies!' Adea screamed, causing all to turn their heads towards her.

It was the moment Antipatros needed: barging through the cordon surrounding him, he scrambled towards the horse as Seleukos drove it in his direction. With a strength that he had not felt in years, such was his awareness of the desperation of his situation, he grabbed the saddle as his legs launched him onto the beast's back and, in a fluid continuation of the motion, he pulled the bridle, turning the animal and driving it into the relative safety of Seleukos' cavalrymen.

Outrage erupted, drowning out Antigonos as he raged against Adea and her perceived undermining of Macedonian unity and he, too, became a target for the men's fury; as Antipatros was hustled away by Seleukos and his cavalry troopers, beating the mob back with the flats of their swords, he glimpsed an isolated Antigonos being pulled from his horse.

ANTIGONOS.
THE ONE-EYED.

B LOOD SPRAYED FROM the flattened nose, soaking Antigonos' knuckles as he sprang to his feet, hitting out and roaring defiance at the attackers surrounding him. His horse reared, forelegs beating the air and cracking open the heads of a couple of the Silver Shields who had recently dragged its rider from its back.

'Don't be bigger fools than you've been already,' Antigonos shouted at the men squaring up to him. 'Pulling me from my horse is the same as striking a superior officer; that's death in any army. Death!' This last word was growled with the same ferocity with which the fire of anger burned in his single eye. 'Death!' he repeated, looking around at the soldiers encircling him. 'And leave my horse alone,' he shouted at the men trying to calm the beast before it killed anyone else.

His evident fury and absence of fear caused his assailants to pause and glance at one another, seeking reassurance; they found none, for the collective madness which had overcome them had dispersed with the sight of two of their number lying dead on the ground, skulls shattered and brains oozing.

'That's better,' Antigonos snarled. 'You seem to be thinking for the first time today.' He pointed at each of the veterans surrounding him. 'I know your faces; all of you! Your lives are now in my hands. Sure, you could try to protect yourselves by killing me but I promise you that if I don't return to my army, alive, the Silver Shields will cease to exist due to the demise of every one of its members.' Again he stared at each man, none of whom could look him in his eye. 'Now, if you want me to forget your faces, start telling your mates to stop listening to that silly little girl and to wait until we've all sat around the table with Antipatros and decided upon how things will be organised in the future.' He turned and pushed through the crowd of veterans, who gave way, muttering, and, taking his horse's bridle, swung himself up into the saddle. 'Lysimachus is due here the day after tomorrow, lads, then the talks will begin and your back pay will be high on the agenda.'

'Make them go and get it themselves,' Lysimachus said, leaning on the polished cedar wood table around which the successors of Alexander had gathered. 'I believe the contents of the Susa treasury should easily cover the back pay for the entire army; a one and a half thousand league round trip on foot to bring it here should keep the Silver Shields quiet. As the saying goes: there have been more tears shed by wishes granted than by those still unfulfilled.'

Antigonos smiled to himself. *Lysimachus was always a ruthless bastard with a poetic sense of justice. Robbing the east of a great bulk of its wealth when the satraps aren't there to defend themselves and at the same time punishing the Silver Shields is a master-stroke; Peucestas will be furious.* He looked around the table at the ten other men present: all but Antigenes and Peithon seemed to be appreciating the idea.

'That will take us months,' Antigenes complained.

'They should feel themselves lucky that they have months,' Lysimachus retorted. 'Had they been in my army the whole lot of them would have been given the choice of losing their hands or their head and then having the one that they didn't choose removed.'

Antigenes folded his arms and looked, hard, at Antipatros. 'And if I refuse to go, what then?'

Antipatros gave a weary sigh. 'Then you won't get to your satrapy.'

'My satrapy?'

'Yes. I think that everyone here recognises that you should be rewarded for your part in removing the problem of Perdikkas; Seleukos seems to have been awarded Babylonia and Peithon, well… Anyway, Susiana seems to me to be an appropriate gesture of our thanks.'

'But Peucestas—'

'Has Persis as well as Susiana. Once I've emptied the treasury at Susa he won't argue for fear of me taking the treasury at Persepolis; now do you accept?'

Antigenes' face brightened. 'I do.'

'Good. I will tell your mutinous command that when, and only when, they have brought the Susa treasury to the fortress of Cyinda in Cilicia will they get their back pay.' Antipatros looked around the table. 'Now that deals with the Silver Shields. I will speak to them when we've finished here for the day. Any questions?'

Lysimachus leaned forward again. 'Yes, why have we been wasting time talking about the Silver Shields' back pay?'

'It's the whole army's back pay and also it's the issue of whether to give the one talent of silver bounty to every man and not just those who are being decommissioned.'

Lysimachus' face, now covered in a black, fertile beard, grown since Alexander's death, crumpled into a frown of shocked disbelief. 'Pay them before they're decommissioned? Who in Hades came up with that ridiculous notion? You'll be telling them next that just because they're in the army it doesn't mean that they have to risk their lives by fighting and, oh, by the way, here's a free boy each to enjoy instead of going on parade and route marches.'

Antipatros sighed again. 'It's because the Silver Shields and some other lads took the bounty and either didn't go home, like the Shields, or did but then re-enlisted with me and still kept the money.'

'Well, that was their choice, wasn't it?' Lysimachus waved his hand dismissively. 'I'm certainly not going to pay my army a talent of silver each. What about you, Antigonos?'

'My growling arse, I will.'

'Nobly put. For a start, can we afford it, Antipatros?'

Antipatros rubbed his temples with his middle fingers, looking down at the desk. 'Perhaps, but it would come close to bankrupting the empire.'

Lysimachus slammed his fist down. 'Then why in Aries' name are we even contemplating it, let alone actually discussing it?'

'Agreed,' Seleukos said. 'The contents of the Susa treasury will sort out the back pay issue and then that is as far as we should go. A bounty is only payable on demobilisation and, once paid, if they decide to re-enlist then that's up to them but they won't receive a second bounty the next time they are decommissioned.'

Good man, Seleukos, now perhaps we can get on with discussing things much more important. 'And anyone who doesn't like the terms will just be drummed out of the army without any bounty and they can moan about it in poverty. Now, let's get on. Peithon and Arrhidaeus have both resigned their positions as joint regents.' He looked at the two men who confirmed this statement with a nod, Arrhidaeus placing the Great Ring of Macedon on the table. 'I move that we offer Antipatros the regency of the kings and that he takes both of them back to Macedon where they and their troublesome female appendages can far easier be managed and silenced; a repeat of the near mutiny we witnessed here, three days ago, would be intolerable.'

'I agree.' Kleitos the White, commander of the fleet, boomed with nautical force. As he was not aboard ship, he was dressed in military uniform and not as Poseidon – naked apart from bits of seaweed – much to all's relief – although he had brought his trident, which was leaning in a corner by the main door. 'We need one central leadership with which we all agree and whom we trust not to try and lord it over us as did Perdikkas.'

'Yes,' Asander, the Satrap of Caria, said. 'And if I may say so...'

This is going to be a long and dull few days if everyone is going to have their say on every topic. And as Asander said so, to great length, Antigonos sat back in his chair and looked out of the large window, dominating the western wall of the commodious, high-ceilinged audience chamber of the main palace in the sprawling hunting groves and fields. It was a refreshing sight: huge cedars speckled the parkland that stretched as far as he could see towards the sun, dipping into the west, back-lighting the monster trees so that each was defined with an exactness that made them seem as if they had been painted on the wall and were not actual living things in the distance.

With everyone in the room taking their turn to praise Antipatros and add their support for him becoming regent to the two kings as well as of Macedon, Antigonos let his mind wander, keeping half an ear out for mention of his name during the discussions as he pondered his position. Antipatros, as all could see, was not going to last much longer; indeed, the recent exertion of the wars against the Greeks and then Perdikkas had left the old man looking every one of his eighty years. *And what then? Who will take his place? Kassandros? I think not; no one will stand having that pimpled prick lording it over them. He may well get to hold Macedon and he'd be welcome to it; but the east, where the wealth really lies, will be up for plucking by the strongest. And just who will that be?*

Antigonos cast his eye around the table, dismissing most of the men seated as either lacking in ambition, like Kleitos or Asander or the non-entity Philoxenus, Satrap of Cilicia, or too unpopular like Lysimachus of Thrace or Peithon of Media or the absent Kassandros himself or just plain too old like Antigenes. It was Seleukos who caught his eye. *There's the coming man; young, ambitious and popular and a good soldier into the bargain. He'll get to keep Babylonia, Antipatros won't dare take it from him; and with Antigenes now his neighbour in Susiana I imagine he'll double his territory in the very near future. Peucestas will also see it is far more in his interest to support Seleukos rather than looking a thousand leagues west and north to whosoever has control of Macedon.* He smiled inwardly and considered the absent Ptolemy, concluding that other than Cyprus and the Palestine portion of the Syrian coast to act as a buffer state, he was unlikely to concern himself with the East. *He's far more likely to look west to Carthage. No, Seleukos is the coming man but he won't be able to hold it all, and nor, if he's sensible, would he want to. Let him have Babylonia, Susiana, Persis, Media and Assyria even; and then let him see if he can hold the Satrapies further east whilst, meanwhile, if I leave Lysimachus alone in Thrace, protecting my northern frontier, from Phrygia I could take the rest and then we shall see.*

With this pleasing, and not unrealistic, view of the future Antigonos emerged from his reverie as Antipatros thanked all present for their unqualified support and placed the Great Ring of Macedon on his forefinger. 'But, gentlemen, although I accept the nominal post of regent to the kings, I do not think it right to take them back to Macedon whilst there is still a war to fight here. To give the Royal Army legitimacy they must stay with it. I will not be leading that army.' He looked to Antigonos. 'As a reward for his bravery the other day I appoint Antigonos guardian of the kings and to be the royal general in Asia responsible for concluding the war against Eumenes and the remaining supporters of Perdikkas.'

Now that's a welcome surprise. Antigonos bowed his head in acknowledgement. *He's just made me the most powerful man in Asia once he returns to Macedon.*

'And now, gentlemen,' Antipatros said with a look of benevolence, 'I will give some thought to the dispersion of the satrapies overnight so I suggest we adjourn for the remainder of the day and resume tomorrow at noon. Take advantage of the magnificent hunting if you will; I have to see the Silver Shields and then have my final interviews to explain the new situation to the two young bitches who consider themselves to be queens.' Antipatros smiled knowingly at Antigonos.

The inner glow of well-being within him was suddenly doused as Antigonos realised that the gift was a double-edged sword. *The crafty old sod has just managed to lumber me with the two most vicious harpies ever created.*

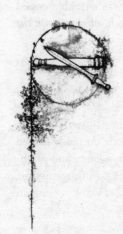

ADEA.
THE WARRIOR.

IT WAS NOT yet over, not yet. Surely she could still exert influence over the men who had so easily followed her on the march north from Egypt? Surely they still wished for their bounty even if their back pay was to be settled? Surely they would still come to her call in the name of her husband, the true king? Adea looked around her sumptuous apartment in the main hunting lodge of The Three Paradises, decked with more luxury than she had ever seen displayed in one place, and tried to fight the notion that this was no more than a magnificent prison cell. She and Philip had been escorted there soon after Antipatros' escape from her men; for their own safety, they had been assured, but the two guards outside the door made a mockery of that claim. She knew that they were there far more to prevent her from getting out, or her friends from getting in, than they were for her safety. Although Barzid still remained in name her body-guard, he was not allowed within the apartment, and she had no friend with whom she could share her fears. She looked over to her husband, gazing at her from a seat by the window; as their eyes met he smiled, set down his toy elephant and, whimpering, began openly masturbating.

'Stop that!' she yelled, bile rising in her gorge.

But Philip just grinned and slobbered and addressed himself to his task with increased vigour.

She resisted the urge to strike him; she had never struck him and, notwithstanding his overwhelming superiority in strength, he had never attacked her, despite his urgent sexual compulsions. She well understood that if she were to be the first to offer violence then that delicate balance between them would shift and she would find herself in constant danger of assault and brutal rape and her only recourse would be to slit the man-child's throat – a self-defeating act.

She felt a fresh surge of revulsion for her husband as the realisation grew within her that she had been outmanoeuvred by Antipatros now that he had assumed the regency and promised the contents of the Susa treasury as back pay, thus quelling the burgeoning mutiny. This man-child of hers was king only in name; in reality he was but a slobbering imbecile to whom her fortunes were inextricably linked. And yet, deep within her lurked pity for the ruined man and an urge to protect the child that he would always remain. *But what can I do? Mother would have known; she wouldn't have let Antipatros or Antigonos into the camp for a start. That was my big mistake: as soon as my men touched either of them in violence they committed capital treason that could only be forgiven by abject surrender.* And abject surrender was what they had offered, giving up Adea and Philip as a sign of good faith; Barzid had been compelled to surrender his weapons. A tear welled in both eyes but she fought them back; she had never been one for crying and had sworn to herself to endure her confinement dry-eyed.

With a series of gross grunts, Philip ejaculated, his gaze firmly fixed on her breasts, indistinct beneath her tunic. *Let him spill his seed wherever he likes; it's of no use to me.* And, indeed, it was not. Despite the many couplings she had endured on the march north, no child grew within her and she had begun to despair of ever conceiving with this brutish man; and without a child her life was in constant danger. *Still, I must persevere; there may still be a chance.* She looked with distaste at Philip's penis, glistening in his hand, oozing as much drool as his mouth, and again fought the urge to cry. *Whatever he is, however disgusting I find him, it is beyond his control and I must keep him safe. Without him I am nothing and without me he is a voiceless imbecile despite his royal blood. And yet, does it have to be by him that I'm impregnated? Who would ever know? I just need to get someone past the guards…or maybe the guards themselves would suffice; two would double my chances.*

Adea called for one of the two slave-girls she had been allowed to bring with her – a pretty little pale-skinned thing who gave her much delight – and ordered her to clean up her husband's spillage and then to bring her a cold sherbet.

And it was thus, sitting by the open window, reflecting upon her new problem but drawing consolation from the fact that at least her deadly rival, Roxanna, was enduring a similar confinement, that Antipatros found her not long after.

'I trust I find you and your husband well, Adea,' Antipatros said as the slave girl showed him into her chamber.

'You find us deprived of our loyal bodyguard and confined against our will, Antipatros,' Adea replied, deliberately not using his title as he had not used hers. 'But then you are well aware of that seeing as you ordered it.' *Diana, he's looking weary; there'll soon be nothing to fear from this old man.*

'Don't get up.'

'I wasn't.'

'Even so.' Antipatros smiled and sat down, uninvited, laying a couple of scrolls out on the table next to him. He winced and then rubbed the small of his back before gesturing to Philip, now fully absorbed, once more, by his toy elephant which he was charging up and down a pillow whilst making screeching trumpeting calls. 'And how is the king?'

'No different from how you see him; happy in his world.'

'So he has lost all the concern that you professed he had for the men's back pay?'

Adea's smile came nowhere near her eyes as they bored into those of Antipatros. *I'll not play his game and just end up incriminating myself.*

Antipatros contemplated her for a few moments. 'I see: to answer that question you realise that you would have to admit that it was you that stirred this mutiny up; you alone for your own personal gain and it was nothing to do with the noble feelings of an imbecilic king for the welfare of his men. No, Philip has more concern for his elephant than for the financial well-being of his army.'

Adea did not lower her eyes, but sat there, mute. *We both know the truth but I'll not admit it to him.*

'Very well,' Antipatros continued once her silence had spoken for itself. 'Let us get down to business because, as it will not surprise you to learn, we both need each other for the time being.'

I'll be interested to hear why.

'I shall be returning to Macedon soon and, although I've been appointed regent, the kings will remain with the Royal Army under Antigonos' guardianship. There will be no repeat of your recent behaviour.'

I'll make him no promises.

'I see that you're going to need some persuading to good behaviour.' Antipatros picked up a scroll, unrolled it, and perused it with a thoughtful countenance, shaking his head. 'Fascinating, absolutely fascinating.'

He'll tell me what's written without me having to stoop to asking.

Antipatros put the scroll down and fired a question: 'Are you pregnant?'

Adea was startled by the suddenness of the enquiry. *I'll call his bluff and worry about the guards later.* 'Yes.'

Antipatros showed exaggerated concern. 'How far gone?'

'No more than a moon; too early to be safe and sure.'

'Then perhaps you should take things a little easier and refrain from enticing men to rise against their commanders.'

Again she made no reply. *He seemed to take that far too sanguinely; perhaps he already suspected that I was.*

'Do you know what this is?' Antipatros asked, proffering the scroll.

You're just about to tell me.

'It's an account by Perdikkas of how Roxanna was prepared to substitute her baby, had it been a girl, with the brat of a slave.'

Now that is interesting.

'And how Perdikkas kept the slave so that he could have control over the eastern wild-cat by threatening to tell the army that she was willing to kill Alexander's offspring and replace it with a substitute for her own ends. Roxanna, quite rightly, realised her peril.'

'And that's how Perdikkas persuaded her to give my husband the antidote after she had poisoned him.'

'Exactly.'

'And where is this woman?'

'Ahh, that is something that you would dearly love to know, I suspect.'

The old bastard's got me to show him a weakness. Oh, Mother, that you were here to guide me.

Antipatros rolled up the scroll. 'Suffice it to say that she is safe and Roxanna knows that she is alive.' He rubbed a red welt on his left forearm. 'I have just come from an interview with her; she didn't take too kindly to the news and hurled ornaments at anyone within range but the knowledge has persuaded her not to make another attempt upon yours or your husband's life – for the present, that is, as I can dispose of the slave any time you decide to make trouble.'

'I see.'

'Good. That brings us onto the contents of this second scroll.' He unfurled it, humming quietly.

He is looking remarkably pleased with himself; no doubt he is in the possession of a vile piece of information that I shall just have to deny.

'It makes for fascinating if repetitive reading.' Antipatros mused as his eyes shifted down the scroll. He handed it to Adea. 'I think you'll agree.'

Adea stifled a cry with a hand over her mouth as she realised exactly what she was looking at. *How did he get this? How dare he? And it is so complete.*

'As you can see, it's a complete record of all your moons since marrying Philip. At every one of them you have bled as it waxed from half to full.' He leaned over and pointed to the last entry. 'I'd like you to take especial notice of that one and then answer my earlier question truthfully: are you pregnant?'

He knew perfectly well I wasn't when he asked me before; it was a trick question to see how far he could trust me and I totally failed. Oh, Mother, I'm struggling. Adea swallowed the fury rising fast within; she felt naked, her most intimate functions exposed to be the subject of discussion. *Who is the traitor in my bed chamber?*

'I know what you're asking yourself: how is it that I have all this information? The answer is because I need it. You can kill every member of your household and live in a cave by yourself but I will still find out whether or not you bled this month.' Antipatros patted her knee. 'It could have been any one of the girls with whom you share your bed; perhaps even one of the women who does your washing or mends your clothes.' He paused to think. 'Could it even be Barzid – is he as loyal as you think? Or perhaps it was Philip's physician, Tychon, or Philip himself – no, that's too far-fetched – perhaps it was that delightful little thing that let me in. Such a shame if it was and you punished her; such a waste of perfectly good cunt, wouldn't you say? So, do everybody a favour and punish no one; carry on as normal and know that if you try to fool me by foisting a cuckoo upon the empire, just as Roxanna contemplated, then I will know; and it won't be just a friendly little chat like this that we'll be having, believe me.'

Adea looked up at the old regent as he stood; the hold that he now had over her transformed him from the world-weary man who had entered the room into a powerful figure demanding of respect. Believe him she did, and now she understood that, because it was so, she would have to fight even harder to free herself from his grip if she were ever to be a contender for power again in the struggle for Macedon.

'So, as I said at the beginning of this interview: we both need each other. You need me to keep Roxanna in check and in return I need you to stay out of Macedonian politics.' Antipatros looked down at her. 'And if you don't, well, quite frankly, it makes little difference to me if there is one king or two. I think we understand one another. Now if you will excuse me, I have the fate of the empire for the next few years to decide.'

Again the tears welled but again she battled to suppress them. Everywhere she looked now there was danger. Never had she felt so alone and unprotected. *I wish I were a man. May the gods curse that bastard, Antipatros.*

ANTIPATROS.
THE REGENT.

IT HAD BEEN pleasant work, dealing
with Adea and Roxanna. Antipatros
had always been exceptionally fond of
women and relied heavily upon the advice
of his wife, Hyperia, but he found it hard
to countenance the more outspoken members of the sex. It was,
therefore, with a feeling of contentment at a job well done that,
in the cool dawn the following morning, he embarked upon the
next phase of his effort to manufacture a settlement that would
hold for at least the rest of his lifetime. *I've managed to dodge the
issue of whether Macedon rules the empire or the empire rules
Macedon by keeping the kings in Asia and me returning as regent to
Europe; now I need to ensure that an army's route from one to the
other remains guarded by a trustworthy man – although I don't
think I've ever heard anyone accuse Lysimachus of being such.*

It was, therefore, with a deal of confidence that Antipatros
picked up his bow and stepped into the waiting chariot and,
greeting Lysimachus in the vehicle next to his, ordered the
driver to head out to the deer park for a morning hunt before the
conference began again at noon. Behind them trundled a train
of carts filled with hunting tools and weapons, refreshments,
awnings and slaves to see to their needs.

'That was a fine shot,' Lysimachus shouted as the roebuck's
limbs collapsed in tangle and its head dived into the lush grass,
eyes wide in death, 'for a man of your advanced years.'

Antipatros gave as good natured a chuckle as was possible upon the fourth time of hearing the same joke during the course of the hunt. 'If you can still shoot as well in forty-five years' time, be sure to tell me when you cross the Styx.' He signalled to his driver to halt and, stepping down, walked towards the kill; Lysimachus sent another arrow, juddering, into the corpse annoying Antipatros still further.

'So let's stop pretending that this is just a social hunting session, shall we,' Lysimachus said as they knelt over the buck, admiring its physique and drawing his hunting knife. 'We're in the middle of the most important conference of our age; what do you want?'

What do I want? I want to be free to live out my last few years in peace, begetting as many sons on my wife as my frail libido will allow. 'Kassandros arrived here last night.' He could tell by the unveiled look on Lysimachus' face that it was not news which filled him with joy – Kassandros had that sort of effect on people. 'He's brought his sister from Babylon.'

'Nicaea?'

'Indeed. Have you ever seen her?'

'A few times before we left for Asia, she was just a little girl then.'

'Well, she's a widow now.'

Lysimachus worked his knife, slitting the belly open. 'And?'

'And I need to bind you close to me if we, in Europe, are to keep ourselves safe from what will be the inevitable series of wars in Asia.'

'I already have a wife.'

'She's a Persian whom Alexander forced you to marry at Susa; take another, Lysimachus, a proper one this time; we need to stand together and the only way that we can both trust each other is if we're family.'

Lysimachus ceased eviscerating the kill and looked at Antipatros, his eyes searching. 'What do you want from me?'

'I want you to guard the Hellespont; I need you to ensure that no army ever crosses it from south to north. I want to guarantee

100

that the upheavals that Asia will undergo after my death won't affect what relative peace we might achieve in Europe.'

Lysimachus carried on his bloody work, slicing through fur and muscle. 'And you think that we can avoid war on our side of the Hellespont? With that witch Olympias always looking for a way back to power?'

Antipatros shrugged and held the belly open as Lysimachus pushed his hands in. 'Perhaps there'll be war in Europe but it'll be a small-scale affair; it won't completely ravage the country as it would if one of the huge Asian armies became involved. Let them stay here and fight it out amongst themselves. Antigonos, Ptolemy, Seleukos and whoever else; they can do what they want as long as they don't do it in Europe.'

Lysimachus looked down at the pile of steaming innards spread on the grass. 'I take your point. And, for my part, in being married to your daughter I can guarantee that you won't try to march into Thrace from the west so technically, in your eyes, I would just have the south to defend. But then there is my northern border: the Danubus. Do you ever consider what's in the north?'

'Barbarian tribes?'

'Lots of them, stretching beyond imagination. I fight against, or deal with, the closest of them, but the rumours I hear of what is beyond those could make our plans of defending Europe from the south irrelevant.'

Antipatros frowned. 'What rumours?'

'The tribes to the north are being pushed by a movement that is bigger than ever before, and that's according to prisoners I took the last time I fought the Getae, as well as a Scythian king with whom I was negotiating a treaty; have you ever heard of the Galatai and the Gallaeci, two tribes of a people known as the Keltoi; huge people, all at least half a head taller than us?'

Antipatros thought for a few moments and then slowly nodded. 'A few years ago, Alexander of Epirus crossed to Italia to come to the aid of Terrentum – he managed to get himself killed for his troubles. Anyway, obviously I had spies in his army and they told me of an invasion of Italia seventy or eighty years previously by a people call the Galli, huge men who tower over us; would they be the same?'

'More than likely if they're also giants.'

'Apparently they sacked many towns in the north of the peninsula as well as Roma, which is the city that seems to be the coming power in the region; they were eventually beaten back and settled vast tracts of land in the north. I've also heard from agents in Massalia, a Greek colony on the coast beyond Italia, that another migration of them has crossed the mountain range that borders the Iberian peninsula. And Pytheas the explorer told me, on his return from his voyage in the northern seas, four years ago, that others went north and some even crossed into Hyperborea, if you can believe it exists; although Pytheas assures me that it does and that it's an island. He claims to have sailed around it.'

Lysimachus' expression conveyed a complete lack of geographical knowledge of lands so far removed. 'Well, it seems that another migration, who have yet to find land to settle, are slowly moving south and east; towards us.'

'How long?'

'Oh, a few years yet, decades even; they're not a horse-people, they move slowly and only if threatened by other tribes equally as barbarous. But they will come; and from what I hear there are tens of thousands of them. You won't live to see it and I'll be a lot older.'

Antipatros wiped his hands on the flanks of the buck and then held them out for a slave to pour water over them. 'I'm pleased to be spared the worry, but I fear for my children.'

'You are right to. Anyway, it seems to me that we need to be prepared so I've instigated a fortress-building programme. The Danubus is no barrier to all of them as those that invaded Italia are to the south of it; however, there are more to the north of the river in the great forests of the interior. So I'm going to build a series of forts along the river to try to prevent the two arms of the migration from joining up and then I shall build a fortress overlooking the Succi pass which is the only viable way over the

Haemus Mountains into southern Thrace. If they cross that then Macedon and Asia will be at their mercy.' Lysimachus stood and wiped his hands on a towel held by a slave. 'But this will all cost a lot of money.'

'I see; you're asking for a considerable dowry to come with Nicaea.'

'It's not for me; it's for Macedon and her empire. If they come and we can't stop them, we're finished. We'll be slaves in our own lands.'

Antipatros looked thoughtful. 'As has already happened to the people of the north of Italia and, no doubt, Hyperborea too.' He shook his head at the thought of such an outlandish-sounding place being a physical reality. 'Very well, Nicaea will come with a dowry that will help you to build your forts.'

Lysimachus shook his head. 'Not help to build but build entirely.'

'I have to finance the whole project?'

'Not you personally but the empire; it's for all of us. And I suggest that you start by stopping giving away so much of its wealth in bounty.'

Antipatros considered his prospective son-in-law's remark and then held out his hand. 'You make a persuasive case, Lysimachus, we will look to the north and hope that between them, the Danubus and the Haemus Mountain range can keep us safe. You will get your money.'

'Then I will marry your daughter.'

'It gives me great joy.'

'Out of interest: who do you plan to marry Phila to now that Krateros has seen fit to make her a widow?'

'Antigonos' son, Demetrios.'

'But she's more than ten years older than me,' Demetrios protested as he stood before his father and Antipatros.

'Then she might just have the stamina to keep up with your sexual excesses,' Antigonos said, enjoying the way his son was, for the first time in his memory, showing signs of fear.

103

'She's not a virgin.'

'Oh, stop being silly. Neither are you and I don't suppose she'll be complaining. Far from it as she'll know that she might have a puppy for a bed-mate, but at least the whelp has some idea what to do with her.'

'It's of vital importance that we tie our families together,' Antipatros insisted in the face of Demetrios' defiant look. 'And you will do what your father and I tell you to otherwise there is a strong chance of us becoming enemies and that would help no one's cause.'

'It's for all our good,' Antigonos reminded his son, trying to keep a straight face at the now-naked terror in his eyes. 'To paraphrase Euripides: One must become a spouse, despite oneself, for the sake of gain.'

'Yes, but the original quote is slave, Father. Slave not spouse; I'll be an older woman's slave. She will never bow to my will.'

'Ah, so that's what the problem is, is it? You're afraid that you're not man enough to take on this formidable woman?'

'I didn't say that.'

'Then what are we arguing about! I don't want to hear another word about it; you marry the woman and that's that. Now get out before I take my belt to you as I used to.'

As the door slammed, both Antipatros and Antigonos waited a few moments and then burst into laughter; belly-bursting, throat-constricting, tear-spurting mirth.

'I wouldn't like to be Phila on the wedding night,' Antipatros managed to get out, eventually.

Antigonos wiped his eye. 'No, the little brat is going to have a few points to prove, that is for sure.'

'Yes, in the morning it'll take her slaves twice as long as normal to make her look presentable, the poor girl. But as she is my daughter you can bet she'll consider it worthwhile. Now if you'll excuse me, Antigonos, before we sit down again, I need to speak in private to Seleukos.'

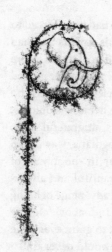

SELEUKOS.
THE BULL-ELEPHANT.

S ELEUKOS SAT BACK in his chair,
only half listening to Antipatros as
the regent confirmed those who
had remained loyal to his cause in their
satrapies and replaced those whose alle-
giance could not be counted upon with those whose could. He
vaguely noticed Eumenes' removal from Kappadokia and his
replacement by Antipatros' son, Nicanor; and as he sank
deeper into thought he barely registered surprise as Kleitos
the White replaced Menander in Lydia and Arrhidaeus was
rewarded with Hellespontine Phrygia, a far greater plum than,
surely, he deserved.

The expression on both Antigonos' and Kassandros' faces
when they heard that Antipatros had appointed his eldest son as
second-in-command of the Royal Army passed completely
unnoticed, which was a shame as Seleukos would have particularly enjoyed the sight of Kassandros being forced to do something
against his will and that of Antigonos registering outrage at the
fact that, despite the forthcoming marriage of their offspring, his
own ally had so blatantly put a spy in his camp.

But Seleukos had more pressing concerns and he barely
managed a nod of gratitude as his satrapy of Babylonia was
reconfirmed, such was his puzzlement at his meeting with
Antipatros just before the conference resumed. *The old man
must either be going senile or there is something that I am just not*

seeing. And why would he ever think that I would be happy to divorce my wife?

Unlike the rest of his contemporaries who had been forced to take Persian wives at Susa, Seleukos loved his Apama and had no intention of renouncing her for a Macedonian of status. More to the point, she had borne him two children, a daughter named after her and a son, Antiochus, named after Seleukos' father who was now dead and much missed; to repudiate her now would be, to his way of thinking, the act of a callous, ungrateful man. Although she came from the wildlands of Sogdiana, way out in the east, Apama was not an untamed harpy in the mould of Roxanna. Far from it: she was, naturally, beautiful and always elegantly attired but she also had the distinct advantage of being moderate and reasonable in her behaviour and, above all, she was not grasping, which made Seleukos want to grant every one of her few wishes. In short, he knew that he would never find a woman so suited to his needs in combination of her beauty, character and family, for she was of eastern royal blood and that would be of great service to him should he think of expanding his influence over the eastern satrapies in the future; being a man of great ambition this was an object of prime importance to him as the troops those satrapies could provide would help him secure his portion of the west.

But that was the future, the near future to be sure, and a great factor in the long-term plan that had been formulating in Seleukos' mind ever since Alexander had looked unlikely to survive his illness. Now, however, he was trying to fathom the present and Antipatros' news: his receiving of Babylonia would not to be as straightforward as he had hoped. According to Kassandros, who had just returned from the city, Docimus had fled back east, to Babylon after Perdikkas' death and, killing Archon, had proclaimed himself satrap. As Seleukos had no army of his own other than what was now in Docimus' hands in the satrapy he had stolen, that left him, Antipatros had rightly pointed out, somewhat disadvantaged. Antipatros had offered to provide him with a modest army, indeed, he would be only too pleased to, but on one condition: that he divorce Apama and marry Kleopatra, Alexander's full-sister. This would by no means give him a claim to the throne of Macedon, Antipatros had explained, as it would have done Leonnatus and Perdikkas for they were possessed of some Royal blood; it would, however, do Antipatros the big favour of getting Kleopatra out of the way as well as giving Seleukos some legitimacy for whatever he planned to do, the regent had added with a knowing look. *What good would Kleopatra do me? Apama is a far more useful consort when dealing with the east. Yet why did he make me that offer?* He had, of course, refused it out of hand for he had no wish to divest himself of the woman whom he loved for a woman who would see herself as his superior, if, indeed, she could be persuaded to marry him at all. No, it just did not make sense and the fact that it evidently had made sense to Antipatros and he, Seleukos, could not see why, worried him immensely, even more than the prospect of having to oust Docimus without the benefit of an army.

Sighing inwardly, he resolved to just let the problem percolate in the back of his mind and hope that an answer would come to him.

'On your way back to Caria, Asander,' Antipatros was saying as Seleukos brought his attention back to the proceedings, 'I want you to remove Alketas from Pisidia and send me his head and his men.'

Asander looked less than thrilled at the prospect. 'But I don't have enough men.'

'You'll get men; just do it. March hard and fast and take the bugger by surprise.'

I can't say I think much of your judge of character; Alketas is more than a match for that pleasure lover.

Antipatros stared Asander into submission and then returned his attention to the meeting. 'And that, finally, brings me to the issue of Ptolemy, who has seen fit not to join us in our deliberations.'

Our deliberations, old man, there has hardly been any "our" about it.

'He has asked me to speak on his behalf,' Arrhidaeus said from down the end of the table.

Antipatros looked as if that was not news to him. 'Did he? Well, go on then, speak.'

'He asked me just to say this: he sends his greetings to his brothers-in-arms and wishes nothing but the best for you all. He would hope that in the new spirit of cooperation we would all leave him alone and recognise his right to Cyrenaica as a spear-won land, something that Perdikkas refused to do. He asked me to particularly stress that this would be very important to him and, along with one other condition, would encourage him to keep his eyes looking west and not east.'

Antipatros almost choked. 'The insolent young puppy making conditions: is he threatening me with his bringing an army east if I don't let him have Cyrenaica?'

'Not at all; Cyrenaica is non-negotiable, he's keeping it whatever happens; he just wants you to recognise it. He says that he won't bring an army east to take southern Syria if you give him Cyprus, as he only needs one or the other.'

Seleukos choked back a laugh into a fit of coughing – he was not alone in this. *You have to admire him.* He risked a look at Antipatros and was unsurprised to see the old man puce with indignation.

The explosion came. 'I've given him one of my daughters and this is how he treats me? At my age? How dare he make demands? I'll strip him of Egypt. I'll…'

Seleukos watched, amused, as Arrhidaeus sat with his eyes lowered until the storm passed and he could once again make himself heard. 'He said to point out, in the event that you should react as you just have, that he has the largest fleet in the sea and all it would take him to do is make an alliance with Attalus in Tyros, combine their two fleets under his command and Cyprus would be his within a month. But he doesn't want to do that as he knows that it would upset you and that's the last thing he would wish to do to his dear father-in-law.'

This was too much for Antipatros; he slammed the table with both fists, inchoate with fury as those who had been Ptolemy's companions during the conquest of Asia, and knew him well, tried but failed to hide their amusement.

'This is no laughing matter!' Antipatros roared as soon as he was able to formulate words. 'If Ptolemy dares to—' But what Ptolemy should not dare was lost as Antipatros' eyes opened in pain and, clutching at his heart with one hand whilst leaning on the table with the other, he sat down.

All laughter ceased as the old man struggled to draw breath, gasping and choking. It was Kassandros who reacted first, taking his father and laying him on the ground as the others in the room gathered around, anxious as they looked down at the man who could keep them united. 'Someone, fetch his doctor,' Kassandros ordered as he placed a cloak beneath his father's head.

And yet, despite of his outward concern, Seleukos noticed a predatory look in Kassandros' eyes. *Don't die now, you old bastard, not before I'm safely in Babylon.*

But Antipatros, in spite of his years, was strong and not long after the obviously nervous doctor had slipped a draught down his throat, his breathing became more regular and his eyes focused. 'What are you all looking at?' he growled at the concerned faces looking down at him. 'Stop gawping and help me up.'

Many hands lifted the old regent to his chair, where he fought off the doctor's entreaties to retire to his bed, pushed Kassandros away, insisting that the conference should continue and once all were again seated he carried on as if nothing were amiss. 'If Ptolemy dares to bully me into giving him Cyprus, then he is sadly mistaken with his choice of tactics.'

'We have no choice in the matter,' Antigonos said from across the table. 'What he says is quite true. His ships, combined with Attalus', will be more than a match for Kleitos' fleet. If we were to resist Ptolemy's claim then he would carry out his threat and annex Cyprus nonetheless; we would be unable to resist him thus making us look weak and putting ideas into the head of anyone who fancied building on their power.'

The Resinated Cyclops just turned his eye on me as he said that; he either wants my support in this or he thinks that I am one of those who might wish to imitate Ptolemy. I'll play safe and, besides, Antipatros isn't the only one with troops to dispense; if Ptolemy hears I supported him...' I agree with Antigonos. Ptolemy could easily take both Cyprus and southern Syria, so it's best to give him just the one he asks for and keep at least a semblance of peace between us all; which is what we need as we fight Eumenes.'

Antipatros looked around the table to see many of the heads nodding in agreement. 'You can't seriously think that we should give Cyprus to Ptolemy?'

PTOLEMY.
THE BASTARD.

'HA! IT'S TAKEN three months but I knew the old man would be forced to agree, eventually.' Ptolemy slapped the letter between his palms, directing his exuberance to the cat that dozed in the shaded corner of the terrace where he sat, breakfasting. 'Although I feel that Seleukos is rather exaggerating the parts he played.' He returned to the letter as the cat was clearly not going to venture an opinion either one way or the other, content as it was to snooze in the cool January breeze wafting in from the great harbour of Alexandria.

With another exclamation of triumph, Seleukos clapped his hands. 'Wine, Sextus! This calls for celebration.'

'Yes, master,' his body-slave replied in his thickly accented Greek, scuttling off.

'You seem to be having an enjoyable breakfast,' Thais, his mistress of twenty years, said, joining him on the terrace wearing an almost sheer gown; to her certain knowledge it was Ptolemy's favourite breakfast attire.

'Seleukos,' Ptolemy said, not looking up.

'What about him?'

'It would seem that I find myself in his debt.'

Thais sat down and helped herself to a couple of dates. 'What for?'

'Cyprus.'

'But you demanded it from Antipatros.'

'Yes, but he wasn't at all keen to agree.' He looked at Thais for the first time and smiled with appreciation at her choice of dress; absent-mindedly he reached up and stroked the back of his hand down the side of one breast. 'Seleukos has spent the last three months at The Three Paradises persuading Antipatros that he had no choice but to agree.'

'That seems an inordinate amount of time.'

Ptolemy put the letter down. 'Well, obviously he wasn't at it all day every day. Antipatros was busy reorganising the army, taking units of his, Antigonos' and the army of Babylon and mixing them together so that the more mutinous elements are dispersed. And then, of course, he was writing to all the satraps and to the rulers of kingdoms outside the empire and waiting for their replies; he wants to go back to Europe leaving Asia reasonably stable. And I don't blame him.'

'Which is how Seleukos managed to persuade him to give you Cyprus, I assume.'

'Indeed. Seleukos knows me far better than the old man does; he knows I would carry out my threat to invade southern Syria.'

'But why was it in his interest to fight on your behalf?'

Ptolemy looked out over the great harbour to the construction site that was in the process of dividing it in two as a mole was sunk to join the Pharos Island to the mainland. *Progress on every front.* 'The fact that Antipatros is forming the three armies into just two, by incorporating the army of Babylon into the army of Macedon and into Antigonos' army, has not gone down well with Seleukos who needs men to push Docimus out of Babylon; an objective that I thoroughly applaud. However, Antipatros sees things differently and has made demands – what, I don't know – that are unacceptable to Seleukos.'

'Thus he's turning to you.'

'Exactly.'

'And will you give him the troops?'

'Most certainly; once I've occupied Cyprus by the end of spring. Seleukos can expect to have them by beginning of summer, I should think; that should give him plenty of time to get rid of Docimus. He can meet me in Damascus and we'll sign the agreement there.'

'But I thought you said that you would never leave Egypt again unless it was to visit one of her possessions.' She looked at him, her mouth and eyes wide with surprise before her face transformed into a disbelieving smile. 'You cunning old wolf. You were always going to invade Syria whether Antipatros agreed to you having Cyprus or not.'

Ptolemy leaned across and kissed her on the lips, lingering at their sweet taste, dismissing Sextus with a wave as he heard him return, his need for wine now secondary. 'Why fight two battles if the objective of one of them can be achieved by other means? To get Cyprus I would have had to make a deal with Attalus, something that many people, myself included, would have found repugnant; indeed, I might never have been forgiven for it, which would have made negotiations on other matters more difficult in the future. Much better just to use the threat of a deal with him rather than actually conclude one; and then if I did do a deal with him, what would I have done with the odious man afterwards? Logically, I should kill him as he would just have been a nuisance, but after I did who would ever trust me enough to form an alliance again? No, this has worked out very well: by the middle of next year I shall have Cyprus and southern Syria, up to Damascus and perhaps beyond, safely in my hands and then I can work on getting Attalus out of Tyros and who will be able to level any criticism of my actions against me if I do that?'

'You'll have Cyprus, Tyros, Damascus and the other ports of southern Syria in six months, and, added to that, a friendly and grateful Seleukos as your neighbour in Babylonia, all with very little loss of life.'

'None at all, I would hope.'

Thais giggled, but not in a young girl's manner. 'Antipatros will hate you for it.'

'He might, but how much longer is he going to be around to hate me for? Besides, I'm married to Eurydike and, as you know and he will soon, she's pregnant; would he attack his own son-in-law, the father of his grandchild?'

'He'll still hate you.'

Ptolemy shrugged as he stood and offered Thais his hand. 'Let him. Come, my dear, I have an interesting man waiting to see me but, first, it would be a shame to see all that effort you've put into your appearance go to waste.'

But fortunately it was not wasted and it was a very refreshed Ptolemy who walked into the audience chamber, which still smelled of new plaster and paint, no more than an hour and a half late for his meeting with the wiry little sea captain bowing with deference before him.

'Onesecritus, sire,' Lycortas, Ptolemy's chamberlain announced once Ptolemy had made himself comfortable on his chair. 'Former triarchos under Nearchos the Cretan, admiral to Alexander.'

Ptolemy nodded in a good-natured fashion and then picked up the scroll on the table next to him. 'This is your memoir, I believe: *Voyages with Alexander.*'

'It is, sire.' Despite his small frame, the man's voice was surprising low and vibrant. 'I wrote it soon after his death.'

'So I believe. It has been circulating amongst my troops here in Egypt. How many copies did you have made?'

'Ten, sire.'

'There are three here; where are the others?'

'I gave one to a friend with Kleitos' fleet, one to another old shipmate who is with Attalus in Tyros at the moment. One went to my cousin who sails in Antipatros' navy and the rest are either with the army of Babylon or the Euphrates river fleet.'

'I see. That's a wide circulation, especially if all the owners lend out their copies; I assume you asked them to.'

'Of course. Yes, sire, I want it to be as widely read as possible.'

'For your own personal glory or to circulate the accusations that you make at the end that certain people conspired to murder Alexander?'

Onesecritus swallowed. 'I just wanted to write a book.'

'Yes, don't we all? It satisfies the vanity. I'm writing one about Alexander's conquest but I name names. What is the point in writing a book if you make allegations against unnamed people accusing them of doing unspecific things but, nonetheless, murdering Alexander.'

'I was afraid to name them for fear of reprisals.'

'Well, my friend, there will be reprisals if you don't name them now; rather nasty ones, I can assure you. How do you know these things that you're too afraid to speak of?'

Again Onesecritus swallowed; he wrung his hands and looked around; there was no escape. 'My cousin, who sails with Antipatros' navy.'

'What about him?'

'He was the triarchos of the trireme that brought Kassandros to Asia when Antipatros sent him to have his orders confirmed: Alexander had summoned him to Babylon and sent Krateros to Macedon to take over as regent.'

'Yes, yes, I know.' Ptolemy was immediately interested. 'Any messenger would have done and yet Antipatros sent his own son to confirm orders that seemed to all to be quite clear enough; and then Alexander falls sick soon after the pimply little shit's arrival.' Ptolemy thought for a few moments. 'Nothing was ever conclusively proven, of course, but I still find it amusing to goad Kassandros with the possibility whenever I can. What do you know about it?'

'Only what my cousin told me.'

'I'm listening.'

Again Onesecritus swallowed, then grimaced, squeezing his eyes tight shut before letting out a sigh of resignation. 'Kassandros came aboard in Pella, at night and in great secrecy; then, the following morning, Archais the Exile-Hunter and his seven Thracian killers came aboard making a great show of their presence.'

'So spies in the port would not suspect Kassandros of being aboard, just Archias off on another mission of murder for Antipatros.'

'You understand all too well, sire. Once they were on, my cousin was ordered to sail. When they got to Tarsus, Archias disembarked first and disappeared for a couple of hours. When he came back he had a bag that he gave to Kassandros; he looked inside, smiled and brought out a mule's hoof that had been formed into a little box. He opened the lid, sniffed its contents, nodded to Archias and paid him, what seemed to be, a great deal of money. Kassandros then left with a cavalry unit that had been waiting for him at the port and Archias ordered my cousin to take him to Ephesus where he had business for Antipatros to do.' Onesecritus spread his hands and shrugged. 'And there you have it, sire.'

'But do I, though? All you have given me is that a well-known assassin gave a box to Kassandros when he arrived in Tarsus, which, presumably, he took with him to Babylon. If it was poison then his brother Iollas could have quite easily administered it to Alexander; but there is no firm proof that Kassandros did bring poison or that Antipatros was behind the assassination, if, indeed, it was such and not swamp fever.'

'Ah, but it's what Archias said as he handed over the hoof; it was a quote from Aeschylus: "no convulsions, the pulses ebbing out in gentle death."'

'One of Cassandra's lines in *Agamemnon* as she enters death's realm; well, that certainly sounds like something Archias would say, having been a tragic actor before deciding that murder was more lucrative. But it is by no means conclusive.' Ptolemy considered the problem. 'However, I've never let lack of proof get in the way of a good story.' He looked back at the triarchos. 'You will be well rewarded, Onescritus, but for the time being you will stay here in Alexandria.'

Onescritus was about to ask why, but bit the question back.

'You said you have an old shipmate who is with Attalus in Tyros?'

'Yes, sire.'

'He may be of use to me; later in the year I might need you to contact him. Until then you will live very well.' Dismissing him,

Ptolemy turned to his chamberlain, plump and refined in long, loose-fitting robes, with a shaven head and an inscrutable expression on his pudgy-lipped visage. 'Lycortas, find me the best literary mind in the city.'

'As you wish, sire.'

'I want a book written in an exemplary style that will put names to all those people that Onescritus refused to mention and quite a few more besides. I'm going to make it official that Alexander was murdered and that it was Antipatros who instigated it, supported by a few other people whom I consider to be nuisances – Peithon for one.' He paused for a look of extreme pleasure. 'And then, just to make matters really interesting, the book will also exonerate – apart from myself, obviously – Perdikkas and Eumenes, thus making the little Greek seem like a man of honour standing up to the assassins of Alexander; that will divide some loyalties and put a strain on Antipatros' settlement. In those circumstances I might even take southern Syria unnoticed.'

'A bold scheme, sire, but may I suggest just one refinement?'

'I'm always intrigued to hear your refinements, Lycortas.'

'Would it not be better if it were actually the proven truth?'

'It certainly wouldn't hurt. Are you going to tell me you know where the Exile-Hunter is?'

'Antipatros sent him to assassinate Eumenes, four months ago now; and, as far as we know, Eumenes is still alive.'

'Of course; the Exile-Hunter never leaves a job unfinished. He'll still be hunting Eumenes.'

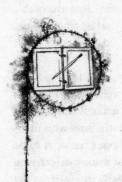

EUMENES.
THE SLY.

T HE WINTER HAD been a long, lonely time for reflection for the little Greek. Yes, he was surrounded by his army and, yes, he had some amiable companions amongst his officers, however, they were but social comfort, tied to him by a mixture of personal and financial loyalty. What Eumenes had missed was an ally who saw the future of the empire in the same way as he did: Europe, Asia and Africa united under the royal house of Macedon with Macedonians and Greeks ruling the satrapies and getting fabulously wealthy. He missed someone who really cared that Ptolemy was virtually autonomous in Africa, that Antipatros showed no signs of ruling much more than Macedon, thus leaving Lysimachus independent in all but name in Thrace. He wanted someone who cared that, if nothing was done, Asia would split into rival kingdoms that would, necessarily, be constantly changing allegiance and fighting one another. He needed to share his thoughts with someone who understood these things, unlike Hieronymus, Parmida and Xennias, his main dinner companions. Parmida was Kappadokian and therefore could not be expected to understand and Xennias did not see far further than his own purse and those of his men. Of the three, Hieronymus displayed the most understanding but it was much more from an objective point of view, studying the history in the making, rather than caring about one particular viewpoint.

It was with interest, therefore, that, as the snows were melting, he sat listening to Babrak, a Paktha merchant whose constant perambulations around Asia in the service of trade made him an excellent source of news and gossip. Babrak himself enjoyed being the conveyer of tidings to all who would seek him out as he was as loquacious as he was appreciative of the fine food and wines that always accompanied these sessions; neither was he averse to coinage being as forthcoming as his tongue.

'So Peucestas has taken it unsurprisingly badly that control of the treasury at Susa was removed from him?'

Babrak's dark eyes twinkled in the lamplight and his weathered, high-cheekboned face broke into a grin revealing red-stained teeth. 'Master, when one sees the object of one's desire being violated by another and one can do nothing but stand and watch, it greatly affects the view one has of one's own manhood; of course one would still desire the boy but would one have the courage to force one's attentions on him knowing that he had already enjoyed the ardour of one more powerful?'

'I see,' Eumenes said, not seeing at all but pleased at the plain fact that Peucestas' source of finance had been greatly limited. *A man who lacks money is ever keen to make friends.* 'And Antigenes has set out west again, from Susiana?'

'He was still there when I left four months ago in January. Indeed, I had a very pleasant evening with him; he was more than generous as you—'

'Can imagine being in control of such a haul. I'm sure I can; it's always easy to be generous with other people's money.'

'Master, it is the only money one should be generous with; to be generous with one's own is an act of folly and the sign of a weak man.'

'Alexander was always generous with his and I wouldn't call him weak.'

'With respect, master, Alexander was generous with the wealth of Asia; it was not his it just fell into his hands. But I digress; Peucestas has vowed to have vengeance on Antipatros for the shabby way, as he sees it, that he has treated the East. As you know, Peucestas is much taken with the East and its people and customs – the wearing of trousers being an outward manifestation of such – to the extent that he speaks three or four languages now with admirable fluency. He does not see the East as being—'

'An inferior appendage of the West.' *He would happily split the empire East from West which is against what I believe in and yet he and I could make common cause against Antipatros.* 'Thank you, Babrak, old friend; as always you have been most informative and I shall be only too pleased to take your shipment of linen off your hands for the price that you mentioned.'

Babrak rose and bowed with the middle finger of his right hand touching his forehead. 'The master is too kind, but if I may, I would also—'

'Ask a favour of him?'

'The master has a talent for—'

'Finishing other people's sentences? Yes, most people find it annoying. Name your favour.'

'I believe your destination is Sardis?'

Eumenes looked at the Paktha in surprise. He had not divulged the army's destination to anyone; he had just set out west along the Royal Road from Kappadokia the moment it was clear of snow. 'What makes you think that?'

'To ravish the boy one must first catch him out in his field.'

That did nothing to enlighten Eumenes. 'Meaning?'

'I mean, master, that if you are to defeat Antipatros you must take the fight to him; if you stay in Kappadokia you will become increasingly irrelevant, especially seeing as Nicanor is now the satrap and you are an outlaw. So it makes sense that you go west and it makes sense that you go and seek the help of the only person who you might consider a possible ally, seeing as both Alketas and Attalus have made it perfectly clear—'

'What they think about Greeks.' *He is well informed; Alketas refused his brother's direct order to help me subdue Kappadokia and there is absolutely no reason that he would join with me now, even though we have a common cause.*

'So therefore Kleopatra is your only option and I would like to accompany you there for safety; I have some valuable merchandise that is destined for that fair city.'

Eumenes smiled. 'You would be most welcome, Babrak.'

'The master is too kind.' Again a bow. 'However, I feel obliged to inform you that we will not be the only ones upon that road. Archais the Exile-Hunter has been waiting for you to leave Kappadokia in the hopes of acquainting you with the sharpness of his blade before you reach Sardis.'

But it was not the sharpness of Archias' blade that Eumenes became acquainted with on the road to Sardis but, rather, the sharpness of Kleopatra's tongue upon his arrival. 'You should not have come here!' He voice was imperious and quite unlike her manner the last time he had had an audience with her; when he was still pressing Perdikkas' suit as the doomed man chased Alexander's funeral cortège south. She had refused to marry him once she had learned that Ptolemy had taken the cortège to Egypt whence it would never return, thus lessening considerably Perdikkas' claim to the crown – Macedonian kings traditionally claimed legitimacy by burying their predecessor.

'At least listen to what I have to say, Kleopatra,' Eumenes pleaded. 'You saw my army parading before the walls of Sardis this morning; you saw the professionalism of my Kappadokian cavalry as they went through their evolutions; you heard the spirit of my Macedonian phalanx as they cheered you, and hailed you as the sister of Alexander; you saw what power I have behind me, did you not?'

Kleopatra, now in her mid-thirties but still retaining the bloom of beauty that both she and her brother had shared, flashed angry blue eyes at him as she looked down from a dais; she dismissed the speech with a wave of her hand. 'I saw a force that numbered less than fifteen thousand; Antipatros is marching north with almost twice that number and Antigonos is heading east to circle around you, trapping you with almost the same total. Nicanor has taken your old satrapy of Kappadokia; you have nowhere to go now. You don't stand a chance, Eumenes. I'll not ally myself with you, an outlaw, and go down with you; not even for old friendship's sake.'

Antigonos is heading east to get around my flank; that is unwelcome news but the last thing I should do is appear desperate to her. 'Kleopatra, you are coming to the end of your child-bearing years, the two children you had with Alexander of Epirus can have no claim to the Macedonian throne so if you wish for Alexander's line to continue through you it must be with a suitable Macedonian husband. But there is no one left, Antipatros has seen to that by marrying one of his daughters to Ptolemy, the most eligible. Who else is there now? The only remotely feasible candidate after Ptolemy was Lysimachus and Antipatros took him out of the running by marrying Nicaea to him. Phila went to Demetrios should you consider the younger generation; the old man has covered all your options. Admit it, Kleopatra, you will sit here fading until it is time to make the last journey.'

'That journey will come sooner than you think if I were to ally myself to you; I can't marry you, you're a Greek.'

'I'm not asking you to marry me!' Eumenes' voice had risen considerably; he paused, took a sip of the chilled wine at his elbow and gave a deep breath. 'You and I are both second-class people in the Macedonian world, Kleopatra: me because I'm a Greek and you because you're a woman. We stand no chance to influence matters on our own, but together? Together we can have power. Antipatros has been named regent of the two kings although Antigonos has custody of them to keep them with the Royal Army in Asia. But by what right? Answer me that? If you were to stand up and claim the regency as Alexander's sister then your blood would outdo your sex. It would be impossible for Antipatros to resist the claim especially because it would be backed by force, my force and the size of it won't matter for who would go against an army that stood for Alexander's sister and the kings?'

Eumenes could see that the force of his argument was working on Kleopatra; her expression mellowed as she considered the proposition. *Now I'll give her the harsh reality of her situation.* 'Your mother is constantly plotting against Antipatros; what's to stop him coming here on the way back to Macedon, forcibly removing you and taking you with him as another prop to his legitimacy and to make it seem that Olympias is so desperate for power that she would even plot against her own daughter? Who knows, he might even manage to force you to marry that pimply son of his.'

'I'll never marry Kassandros.'

'Never is a very long time but you don't have much of it left; at least the offspring of a union between the sister of Alexander and the son of his regent would have credibility and who knows how desperate you might become as your body draws nearer to the change?'

'Never that desperate.'

'Can you be certain? At least you would know that your son would take the throne; he would be chosen over the half-breed. You and I both know how conservative your people are.'

'I would never have anything to do with any of Antipatros' family, especially not one who is rumoured to have killed my brother.'

'Then do it, Kleopatra, claim the regency. Claim it and in one blow we defeat Antipatros and bring the empire back into the hands of the Argead dynasty for real and put an end to this sham whereby Antipatros holds all the power by proxy; he has not long to live and then what then? Will the regency become hereditary and Kassandros assume full power? Is that what you want?'

Kleopatra considered Eumenes for some time; he shifted under her gaze but never took his eyes from hers. *I've done all I can; it's down to her to make the right decision.*

'No, Eumenes, it's not what I want but, nevertheless, I won't claim the regency.'

Eumenes could not stop his face from falling. 'But why not?'

'Because what you said will come true, my mother would see to it that it does, constantly dripping poison into my ear: I would be tempted to act as regent not for the two kings but for my child, whoever I chose to conceive it with. I would necessarily become the murderer of my half-brother and nephew. I dare not put myself into that sort of temptation. No, Eumenes, I shall stay here and grow old; I shall send for my two children from Epirus and they shall bring me consolation and I shall resign myself to the fact that I shall never marry again.'

Eumenes was finding it hard to believe what he was hearing. *How can she just throw away the chance of real power and the opportunity to ensure that the true Argead line survives?*

'No, Eumenes,' Kleopatra said, holding her palm towards him. 'I know what you're thinking and I won't be persuaded. Go now and do what you will, but don't involve me in your plans; you have made me see the futility of my situation. Now I must acknowledge the fact that Antipatros has beaten me.'

It's pointless to argue further. 'In that case I'll keep my army out on the plain outside the town and wait for Antipatros; they'll fight better knowing that the sister of Alexander is within.'

'No, Eumenes, just go. Take your army far away from here; I want none of it.'

'But—'

'Go!'

'She would not let herself be persuaded,' Eumenes said to Xennias as they walked down the steps of the palace; their companion cavalry escort waited with the horses in the bustling agora below. 'She seems to have given up hope, resigning herself to fading into obscurity.'

'Did you try to induce her with money?'

'Thank you, Apollonides,' Eumenes said as he took the bridle of his horse from the young commander of the cavalry escort and mounted. 'Kleopatra doesn't do anything for money, Xennias, that's something that everyone knows. Her honour is in inverse proportion to her mother's. In fact you could almost say that she was fashioned to cancel out Olympias' deeds.' Eumenes smiled at the thought. 'And I like both of the ladies very much, but for very different reasons.' He kicked his horse and led his men through the busy agora, market day being in full progress; the crowds parted for them, well used to the behaviour of soldiers when impeded. 'But this time I'm afraid to say that the shadow of Olympias has ruined my plans; the daughter knows the mother only too well.'

'Do we stay here or move on?' Xennias asked as they left the agora and clattered down the Sacred Way, lined with the elegant two-storeyed buildings of the rich merchant class, towards the east gate at its end.

Its hiss was just audible but the impact of the arrow in a wooden shutter just to Eumenes' left was violent and reverberating, as were the cries of two of the troopers punched from the saddles by better-aimed projectiles.

'On!' Eumenes cried, kicking his horse, leaning forward his head on the left side of the beast's neck.

Three more shafts thumped in from above, taking down two horses and a trooper.

Eumenes felt his mount accelerate, aware in its equine mind of danger closing in. Behind him, the pounding of the surviving escort's hooves on stone echoed off the buildings, magnified out of all proportion in such a confined space. His horse shuddered, mid pace, and gave a bestial shriek but pressed on at great speed despite the arrow now buried in its rump. But speed suddenly ceased to be the issue as, up ahead, four men spanned the street; fox fur hats adorned their heads, blending with their long beards of the same hue, almost obscuring their faces. Knee-length leather boots they wore as they stood, foursquare, on the road, brandishing the long-handled, curved-blade weapons that, Eumenes knew, could slice a man in two: the rhomphaia.

A quick look over his shoulder showed Eumenes the four archers jumping down from their vantage places, drawing their sleek weapons from sheaths down their backs; with no alleys to either side in this stretch of the street there was no way out. The Exile-Hunter had chosen his ambush site well. There was nothing for it but to press on and chance that barrier of honed iron knowing that a rhomphaia would hardly notice a horse's leg.

"'And in full charge he ran at Diomede, and he at him,'" Archias declaimed from the *Iliad*, spinning his rhomphia in the air, catching it with two hands over his right shoulder and then springing into a reckless sprint, his hair flowing out beneath his cap and a wild grin of pure pleasure on his round, almost boyish, face. His three companions, roaring in their own guttural language, followed with equal enthusiasm.

He'll jump to his left as his rhomphaia is to his right. It was now strength against agility. Eumenes urged his horse, his equine battering ram, directly at the charging Archias. But a horse, even at full speed, is of little threat to a small, dispersed force of infantry; such is their agility. At the last moment, as Eumenes swerved right in anticipation of Archias' move, Archias jumped to his right, reversing his weapon in a flash and skimming it down into the path of the beast that thundered on despite leaving its left foreleg behind. Down it crashed, screeching, blood spurting from the fresh-hewn stump that worked on as if it were still a whole limb.

Eumenes jumped clear, hitting the ground, rolling into a ball, his momentum taking him a dozen paces down the road, as his men crashed through the three Thracians in a swirl of hissing blades; two more horses came down, the rider of one sharing in his mount's sudden amputation, both man and beast flung wailing to the floor.

Speed now was paramount; Eumenes leaped to his feet as soon as his motion slowed, drawing his blade in one fleet action. But Archias was already bearing down on him, striding with purpose, calm in his savage intention.

"'Caught in a tide of death from which there is no escaping,'" Archias quoted again, this time from *King Oedipus*, Eumenes recognised, as he held his rhomphaia, two-handed, towards Eumenes.

Eumenes backed away from the fearsome blade, keeping his sword pointing towards it. *I'll be lucky to come out of this with a single limb unless I think of something.* And then he tripped; onto his arse he fell, the stone that his right heel had hit rolled back with him and it was by an unconscious instinct that he grabbed it. It was just a flick of the wrist but done so fast it was as if the stone had left a sling. Straight it went, blurred by speed; the crack of bone and the sharp exclamation of pain seemed to be detached from the chaos around; Archias' backwards, arched-spined fall, arms flying up, launching his blade skyward, all happened in very slow time.

The Exile-Hunter crumpled to the ground as Xennias raced up to Eumenes, his mount still possessing all the limbs it had come into the world with. 'Up,' the Macedonian shouted, reaching down.

'But he's still alive!'

Xennias was not interested and grabbed his general under the arms, lifting him bodily as he sped away with Apollonides and the few remaining survivors racing after him.

'He's still alive,' Eumenes shouted again.

'And just be thankful that you are too; and in one piece.'

At the gate Xennias put Eumenes down so that he could mount up behind him. He looked along the Sacred Way and saw Archias staggering to his feet, all seven of his Thracians gathering round him to help him up. He pushed them away and stood firm. Looking to Eumenes, he raised his hand in greeting. 'And fate? No man alive has ever escaped it – I tell you, Eumenes, it is born with us the day we are born.'

With that, he turned away and Eumenes knew that he had not seen the last of Antipatros' assassin.

ANTIPATROS.
THE REGENT.

ANTIPATROS THUMPED THE tent pole in frustration. 'Seven months! It's been seven months that you've been chasing him, Archias, and the sly little Greek is still in one piece and still leading a rebel army. I thought you were meant to be the best.'

'"But the gods give to mortals not everything at the same time,"' Archias said, totally unconcerned by the anger in his patron's voice.

'Fuck Homer and fuck all tragic playwrights whilst we're about it. You're meant to be an assassin, not an actor anymore; if you want to go back to the theatre then give me the money I paid you upfront and get going and I'll get someone else to do the job.'

'That won't be necessary, Antipatros,' Archias said, his face hardening. 'I'll get him. But what you have to understand is that he wintered in Kappadokia; I don't know if you've ever been there but in winter nothing happens because of the snow. He didn't move around in the open and we couldn't get to him, so I waited until he came out and took him on the first occasion that he wasn't surrounded by fifteen thousand men.'

'Well, you missed.'

Archias' smile was cloyingly sweet. 'And I won't next time. I'll fling a spear myself and leave the rest to Zeus.'

'Forget about divine help and aim the spear yourself properly. And make the next time soon because, according to my spies, he's now two days away from Sardis heading back east again. Why you are even here now and not following him is beyond me. Really, Archias, I think you're losing your touch.'

'There's nothing alive more agonised than man, of all that breathe and crawl across the earth.'

'Oh, stop it! Get out of my sight and go to work!' Antipatros watched the Exile-Hunter stalk from the room as he tried to calm his breathing. *Why does that little Greek plague me so? He should have been dead last year and Krateros should still be alive.* He closed his eyes and shook his head. *Would that he were still, then I wouldn't have the problem as to whom I leave the regency. I don't have much longer left to me; any fool can see that. Oh, Krateros, you would have been the perfect successor; Alexander even named you himself. Kassandros could never have argued with my choice if you were it.* But wishing for what could not be was a thing of the distant past for Antipatros and he quickly dismissed the thought from his mind as futile. It was with a weary sigh that he went to address the real reason he had come to Sardis.

'I had no choice but to see him,' Kleopatra asserted. 'Whatever he's done, he's an old friend. I told him that he shouldn't have come and then I listened to what he had to say.'

'And what was that?' Antipatros asked, wrinkling his nose at the sharpness of the ice-cool sherbet.

'I will not betray a confidence.'

'He's an outlaw, he can't have confidences.'

'That may be your opinion but it isn't mine.'

Antipatros examined the drink in its glass tumbler of various shades of green. 'Do you really like this Asian muck?'

'I do; I find it very cooling.'

Antipatros grunted and placed his glass back down onto the table. 'Kleopatra, as you know, I had tremendous respect for your father and brother, as I do for you. But I have to question your motives when you grant the empire's most-wanted man an interview, refuse to tell me what was discussed and, more to the point, did not detain Eumenes when it was within your power to do so. Whose side are you on?'

Kleopatra's smile widened and she laughed through her nose. 'Sides, Antipatros? I wasn't aware that there were sides. As far as I'm concerned we are all on the side of the Argead dynasty; it's just that there are different thoughts on how that is best supported.'

'Don't try to be clever with me, Kleopatra.'

'Why, because a woman should just sit demurely and do what she's told?'

'You know perfectly well that I have more respect for women than to think that. Eumenes has been outlawed by the army assembly for his responsibility for the death of Krateros. You should have detained him.'

'I should have done no such thing. But I did tell him to leave and take his army with him; he was going to wait for you here on the plain.'

'Again! Why did you do that? I would have welcomed the chance to settle it once and for all. He's the reason why this war drags on.'

'He's not! It's you, Antipatros,' she snapped, pointing a finger at the old man, 'it's you who could stop all this by granting him a pardon for something that only happened because he was defending himself. This could all stop now if *you* wanted it to. But, no, you don't want it to, do you? And would you like me to tell you why?'

Antipatros ran a hand over his bald pate. 'Not really, but I suppose I have no option but to hear it.'

'Because you can't bear it that you and Krateros made the classic mistake of dividing your forces, thereby letting a Greek get the better of two great Macedonian generals, killing one into the bargain. Eumenes' very existence is a reminder of your incompetence; you think that his death will bring back your self-respect.'

Antipatros waved her theory away. 'Eumenes is an outlaw.'

'Because he killed a Macedonian in open battle; whereas you, Antipatros, you do similar things but in a different way and yet you are not an outlaw.'

Antipatros frowned. 'What are you talking about?'

Kleopatra clapped her hands; a buxom woman bustled in with a scroll case. 'Thank you, Thetima,' Kleopatra said, taking the case, opening it and pulling out a tightly wound scroll. 'Are you a literary man, Antipatros? Did you ever read *Voyages with Alexander* by a Greek named Onescritus?'

Antipatros' attitude was dismissive. 'If you're talking about the unsubstantiated allegations he makes at the end then it's a pack of lies made up to sensationalise the book to gain wider circulation.'

'I was actually and, frankly, I would agree with you. Would have agreed with you, I should say, until this arrived.' She handed him the scroll.

'What is it?'

'It's a book called *The Last Days and Testament of Alexander*. It makes for some quite interesting reading as it puts names to all the faceless people who appeared in Onesecritus' book. One of them is Antipatros and another is Kassandros and a third is Iollas. You can have that; I had it copied from my original.'

'Where did you get this?'

'Oh, it arrived a few days ago.'

'Where from?'

'The ship that brought it was one of Ptolemy's fleet which he sent to occupy Cyprus as a part of your agreement. So I suppose the book originally came from Egypt.'

'Ptolemy! The lying bastard!'

'Is he though? Is he really, Antipatros, because it all fits? Kassandros always hated my brother and you always loved the power and independence you have as regent of Macedon. The motive is established and with Iollas acting as Alexander's cup-bearer and Archias the Exile-Hunter always doing your dirty work, the method is also established. Interestingly it also mentions Peithon, Antigonos and Roxanna as being a part of

131

the conspiracy as well as completely exonerating Ptolemy, Seleukos, Eumenes and, most interestingly, Perdikkas, Alketas and Attalus.'

'It's lies, all lies; propaganda to suit Ptolemy's agenda.'

'You might think so, Antipatros, but the people who will read it may well take another view. And if I choose to believe what I've read, I could make life very difficult for you. In fact, I might even do what Eumenes suggested I do and claim the regency for myself and have you and your pimply son executed for regicide.'

'You wouldn't dare!'

'Of course I would; and there would be nothing that you could do to stop me. You're a dead man if you kill the sister of Alexander; and you'd also be a dead man if I happened to meet with an unfortunate accident or succumbed to a strange disease as I've left letters accusing you of plotting my surreptitious death.'

'You little bitch.'

'Don't you call me names, old man! You used to take orders from my father and brother so I'll not have you lording it over me. Now you listen to me, Antipatros, I will make no pronouncement supporting the accusations in this book, but you can wager everything you own that my mother will jump on it. She will see this as another chance of ousting you; but my remaining silent will still keep an element of doubt in your favour.'

'If you think that I am going to be grateful to you—'

'Be quiet and listen to me. In return I want you to get out of Asia and take your army with you. Stop prosecuting this useless and vindictive war against a man who only has the best interests of my house in mind. It is in all our interests to get the army assembly to reverse its verdict.'

'And what about Alketas and Attalus?'

'Them too; although the murder of Atalante was a serious error and probably means that although Attalus has professed himself willing to forgo revenge, I doubt Alketas will surrender his arms, even if they are pardoned.'

'I rather think that Ptolemy had just that in mind when he executed her.'

'I'm sure you're right but that doesn't mean there is no reason to try and make peace with them both.'

Antipatros looked at the imperious woman, now standing on her dais and looking down with iron eyes at him. 'Why are you doing this, Kleopatra?'

'Why am I trying to establish a peace?'

'No, why are you trying to humiliate me?'

'Why did you marry your daughters to the men who could have been fit husbands for me?'

'Ah!'

'Yes, ah. You may have defeated me in that respect but I now hold your life in my hands; that book will get a wide circulation and with it I can protect myself against what I now see is your ultimate ambition: to force me to marry your pimply son and combine your family and mine in a new dynasty.'

'This is Eumenes' work, isn't it?'

'So you don't deny it?'

'Of course I deny it; I know the true nature of my son and I wouldn't wish him on anyone and especially not you, Kleopatra. More than that, he would be intolerably cruel and vengeful if he came to the throne. Eumenes has misled you there to a certain extent, because although it is not my ambition I'm sure that within the dark recesses of his mind Kassandros has nurtured the idea and has set it as a goal.'

'Then this book is as much my protection against him as it is against you.'

'Do you think so?' Antipatros gave a rueful smile and shook his head. 'I care how I am seen in this world; Kassandros does not.' He got to his feet a wearier man than when he had sat down. 'But maybe you're right; perhaps it is me who is dragging out this war against Eumenes, but he has to be defeated as he is fighting against this.' He held up the Great Ring of Macedon. 'So I'll only do part of what you say, Kleopatra: I'll not try to have the convictions overturned in the assembly because I know the men won't do it, they loved Krateros too much, and I'll just end up looking weak. However, I will go back to Europe and leave Antigonos to prosecute the war.'

'Why? Ultimately, Eumenes is fighting for the same thing: my house.'

'No, he's fighting for Eumenes; but I'm tired of it. I can see that nothing will stop the war entirely, not even Eumenes' death; nothing, until there is only one man left standing. Surely you know your people well enough by now? It is inevitable.'

But if Antigonos can defeat the little Greek there may be peace for the short span I have to go, Antipatros reflected as he rode back to his camp, the same field that Eumenes had vacated just two days earlier. It was a pleasing thought and he smiled to himself as he trotted along the wagon-rutted track enjoying a breeze sweeping down from the rugged hills to the north, hills he would soon be traversing as he left Asia for the last time.

He nodded to the sentries at the camp gate and greeted the officer of the watch by name, dismounted and gave his horse to a waiting groom to be taken to the horse-lines. With his mind completely settled on his course of action, he walked to his tent at the centre of the camp.

'Father,' Iollas said, getting up from the camp chair in which he had been waiting, as Antipatros came in.

'What is it, my boy?' Antipatros slapped his son on the shoulder, feeling his benevolent mood increase at the sight of him.

Iollas looked at his feet and then met his father's eyes. 'We've just had a message from down south.'

Antipatros' good humour expired outright. 'Ptolemy?'

'Yes, Father. I'm afraid so.'

'What's he done now?'

Iollas paused. 'He's invaded Palestine.'

'But the deal was that he got Cyprus and then kept to his borders.'

'With forty thousand men.'

'Forty thousand? But that's a massive force. What does he intend to do with it?'

'He's taken the city of Hierosolyma without a siege.'

'Without a siege? Did the city just open its gates to him?'

'No, Father, it seems that the population are a strange race of monotheists that call themselves Jews; no one has ever really taken any notice of them before. They have the rather odd habit of taking every seventh day off in praise of their god. During this day they are not allowed to do any work which also includes fighting. Ptolemy got wind of this so managed to capture the city by the simple expediency of entering it on what they call their Sabbath. No one lifted a finger to defend themselves and it fell without loss of blood.'

The crafty bastard; I can almost admire him for that.

'He then defeated a Jewish army sent against him on a day that they did allow themselves to fight and defeated it totally; sending thousands of prisoners back to Egypt to help in the construction of Alexandria.'

'He's done all this so quickly without us knowing? How?'

'He cut all the roads heading north so that no word could come through. And, of course—'

'And, of course, he now has Cyprus and so, therefore, control of the sea between it and the mainland seeing as Tyros is still in Attalus' hands.' Antipatros slammed a fist into his palm. 'What a fool I've been! He always planned to do this whether I gave him Cyprus or not; he played me so easily and saved himself a protracted blockade of the island. The bastard waited until Antigonos and I were too far away chasing Eumenes to be able to do anything about it. Where is he now?'

'He's coming up the Jordan river; we believe he's heading for Damascus.'

Antipatros slumped into a chair and put his head in his hands. 'What an idiot I was not to give Seleukos some men; he could have at least done a delaying action giving us some time to get there and stop the bastard in his tracks and then kick him all the way back to Egypt.'

'Are we sure he's heading for Damascus?'

'Yes, Father. It seems that he's meeting someone there.'

'Who?'

'Seleukos.'

SELEUKOS.
THE BULL-ELEPHANT.

T HE GREAT SHADOW trailing back across the land had been coming steadily closer for the past three hours; now flashes of sun reflecting off polished metal could be discerned, and the types of troops in the van of the army were recognisable. But Seleukos, surveying the scene from the topmost tower of Damascus' citadel, held no fear of that army for he knew that soon a part of it would be under his command; Ptolemy had brought forty thousand men with him, far too many for his current purposes, but enough to lend him ten thousand which would be sufficient for his plan to take Babylon. He turned to the commander of the city's Macedonian garrison. 'Are your lads all settled, Dreros?'

Dreros, an old veteran, running to fat, having been eight years in this cushy billet, scratched at his grey-flecked beard. 'The few that weren't have been locked up; the rest of the boys are overjoyed at the prospect of being in Ptolemy's pay as it's rumoured that there's a lot of it.'

'There is indeed, my friend. Ptolemy likes to make sure that his men have all that they need to have a good time – when they're not fighting for him, that is. And, unlike some people, he does actually pay it.'

'Which is more than we've had for the past couple of years; we hardly ever see a pay-chest anymore. The whores now have

137

more money than our lads which makes them very fussy about who they do business with; I've never known a place where prostitutes have all the airs and graces of an eastern queen.'

'Well, Dreros, go and open the city's gates to him and Ptolemy will put an end to your whore issues for all time; in a few days they'll be feeling mighty stupid that they weren't more generous with their favours when the lads were suffering from a paucity of coinage.'

Dreros saluted, grinned and then clattered down the stone steps towards his men, awaiting him in the courtyard below.

Seleukos rolled his shoulders, glanced once again at the approaching army and then followed Dreros down. *Ten thousand men; in twelve days we'll meet the transport fleet on the Euphrates and then south to Babylon. Now comes my time.*

It had not been difficult negotiating with Ptolemy for the troops, indeed, Ptolemy's gratitude for Seleukos' persuasion in the matter of Cyprus had rendered him so amenable to Seleukos' requests that he regretted considerably not asking for more.

'But ten thousand will be ample,' Ptolemy said as they relaxed later on a high, shaded terrace overlooking the bazaar that was now packed with soldiers spending freely and bringing a welcome boost to the local economy. 'If you felt as though you would need more then you should have asked before I set out; I need the balance to besiege Tyros.'

'You plan to lay siege to Tyros?'

'Of course; if I kick Attalus out then Antipatros can have nothing to say to me about my invasion of southern Syria as I can legitimately claim that it wasn't an invasion at all, I just happened to pass through it on the way to Tyros. I was forced to leave garrisons in all the major cities to protect my supply lines.' Ptolemy made a good effort at making a contrite face. 'I'm sooo sorry I didn't ask you, Antipatros, but as you were busy dealing with little Eumenes, I thought it best just to get on with ridding ourselves of the dreadful Attalus. And, no, I won't remove my garrison from Tyros and, no, Kleitos may not sail his fleet into the harbour and, yes, from now on all of the city's taxes will be collected by Egyptian officials and sent back to Memphis.'

Seleukos almost choked on his wine, a dribble of which oozed out of his nose. 'He'll hate you for that.'

'He already hates me, my friend, for being here in the first place so a little more won't do any harm. I have to say that Eurydike is taking my defiance of her father in very good heart, she's only reprimanded me once and that was none too seriously. I think her being pregnant takes her mind off my misdemeanours.'

'Congratulations,' Seleukos said, with a degree of warmth that genuinely surprised him.

'Thank you. A legitimate heir will make me feel far more secure; what's more, the little brute will be Antipatros' grandson and, therefore, would have a claim to the regency of Macedon if the old man decides to make it a hereditary office and that little shit, Kassandros, becomes regent. Not that I'm thinking of invading the homeland, but if I did I would have a very good pretext and I don't think in those circumstances that anyone would lift a finger to help the pockmarked little coward. The shit hasn't even killed his boar yet and thinks nothing of sitting up to eat.'

'That's assuming that Antipatros does leave it to him instead of, perhaps, to Nicanor.'

'I doubt it, Kassandros would murder his brother and Antipatros knows that; but he could, of course, nominate one of us.'

'Or leave it to Polyperchon who's filling in as his deputy whilst he's over here in Asia.'

Ptolemy shook his head. 'No, he's too much of a pedantic nonentity; he wouldn't be able to command enough respect and Olympias would tear him apart. Anyway, we shouldn't have long to wait to see; when he gets the news that I've lent you ten thousand men it could well be the thing that finishes him off, finally. And, even if that doesn't, you taking Babylon most certainly will; he was quite happy with the present arrangement. Docimus posed absolutely no threat to him seeing as the army of Babylon has now been dispersed between his army of Macedon and Antigonos' army of Asia. No, a new power to the south will not please him at all, which, of course, is why he didn't give you the troops himself. I'll bet he's regretting that stupid error greatly; one should never force a talented man such as yourself into the hands of someone as unscrupulous as me; such a foolish mistake.'

'But one I think we are both very grateful that he made; an alliance between Babylon and Egypt is a thing of great strength.'

'And beauty, my friend; strength and beauty.' Ptolemy raised his cup to the toast and downed the contents. 'Standing together, we will both be able to assert our independence from Macedon and begin new dynasties.'

Seleukos studied his ally for a few moments before deciding that the time was right for what he had to say. 'You do realise, Ptolemy, that should I be successful, and I don't doubt that I will be, and Babylonia falls into my hands then there is one other thing that I must have?'

'Access to the sea?'

Seleukos tried but failed to conceal his surprise. 'Yes. How did you know?'

'Well, it stands to reason, doesn't it? To be secure you will have to control both the Tigris and the Euphrates as far north as Armenia so therefore you annex Assyria. That is a huge area and the trade that you would oversee will be worth fortunes, but it would be worth even more if you also had access to our sea and could therefore levy a customs duty on all goods embarked or disembarked.'

'That's the way I see it too.'

'And if that's what you want then just make sure that you don't do anything to upset me. We will split Syria between us; Tyros is mine, Damascus is mine, Berytus is mine, so that confines you to the northern coast of Syria, up by where we defeated Darius at Issos.'

'But there is no big port up there, only Rhosus, and that isn't large enough for my purposes; nor is there a city of any reasonable size.'

'Oh, Seleukos, how are you ever going to make a tolerable ruler if you worry about things which aren't? If something's not there then build it. There's a navigable river up there, the Orontes, build your port at the mouth of that and build your city next to it. I am.'

'That will bring me into conflict with Antigonos.'

'We're always going to be in conflict with Antigonos: me because he'll want to take Cyprus off me and you because he'll always want to push south out of Anatolia and into your piece of Syria and Assyria. But together we will be able to beat him.'

Seleukos pondered this as he sipped his wine. *I can now understand why Ptolemy is being so helpful: all the favours he's doing me now will have to be repaid in the form of alliance with him against Antigonos and whoever takes the regency from Antipatros. He's making a north–south divide and completely doing away with the idea of a united empire once and for all. Our two realms in the south will balance Macedon and whatever is carved out in Anatolia. Once we have some sort of stability I will be able to look to the east. And then we shall see.* He raised his cup. 'To our friendship, Ptolemy. Long may it last.'

Ptolemy smiled and raised his wine. 'Let's not go too far, Seleukos. To our mutual assistance and may it be passed down at least one generation.'

They drank to that.

As Ptolemy placed his cup down, he looked thoughtfully at Seleukos. 'Although I think it's inevitable that somewhere along the line our descendants may not be as amenable to one another as we are.'

And as he watched rank upon rank of his seven thousand infantry embark upon the transport fleet, twelve days later, to be ferried down the Euphrates, keeping pace with the cavalry upon the shore, Seleukos reflected upon the wisdom of that toast and Ptolemy's observation afterward. It was now clear to him that Eurydike's pregnancy had made Ptolemy consider his position in a dynastic way; indeed, he had even used the word. Up until now Seleukos had been thinking only in terms of his coming to power in Babylon and then expanding that base both to the east and the west; his ambition had been solely focused upon area with no consideration for time, other than the natural wish for his own longevity. Ptolemy, however, had grasped the full implication of taking power: dynasty. That being the case, Seleukos realised that, having but one son, Antiochus, and one daughter, he should now think about getting Apama pregnant again; sons and daughters, especially daughters, could be very useful diplomatic currency; if a dynasty was to survive then its seeds needed to be spread far.

It was with the growing and sobering realisation that what he was embarking upon was not just a power grab by a single man for his own lifetime but, rather, the beginning of a journey that would propel his descendants into history when the record of the time was written, that Seleukos gave orders for the fleet to sail the following morning. As he did, he knew that, whatever came to pass, it was to Ptolemy that he would always be grateful. Whether or not they eventually came to face each other with arms, Seleukos would always know that his portion of Alexander's empire and that of his heirs had come to him through Ptolemy's good services.

PTOLEMY.
THE BASTARD.

'**O**F COURSE IT was the right thing to do,' Ptolemy said, standing at the starboard rail of the quinquereme, gliding slowly through the blockading fleet outside Tyros.

Thais looked at him, far from convinced. 'But if you give Seleukos access to the sea then he immediately becomes a rival.'

'That might be so but, at the same time, he is also a buffer.' Ptolemy paused to admire the forty warships patrolling up and down in squadrons of eight beyond the great harbour mouth, barred by a chain of prodigious-sized links. They were far enough out to sea for it to be a clear blue rather than the sludgy greyish-green of the port water; with no wind, the surface was so still as to reflect the towering sea-walls of the city that had taken Alexander two years to subdue. It was an impressive sight, the fleet before Tyros, and it had the gratifying effect of keeping Attalus' navy bottled up for the past half-moon as well as preventing any shipping from entering the town with fresh supplies – the landward access having been cut off by Ptolemy's besieging army. Attalus, however, was cooped up inside entirely of his own volition: upon his arrival at the blockade, the previous day, Ptolemy had offered Attalus free passage north with his fleet provided that he leave his army behind and the treasury full; he had declined the offer, a move that had neither surprised nor concerned Ptolemy.

Ptolemy brought his mind back to Seleukos and his long-term strategy. 'Think about it, my dear, if Seleukos holds all the land from Babylon, up the Tigris and Euphrates and then across to the north Syrian coast, then I have only one neighbour to deal with. He has the problems of Antigonos to the north and whoever else manages to carve himself a slice of empire to his east; for any of them to get to me they first have to go through him. Cyprus protects me by sea and Seleukos by land; you could say I've wrapped myself in Seleukos and Cyprus. Of course, he didn't see what I was doing and I believe he is charmingly grateful even though it is I who should be thanking him for all of my battles that he'll be fighting whilst I lie back in your arms and watch.'

Thais smiled up at Ptolemy, linking her arm with his. 'And I wrap myself in you, which must make me the safest person alive.' She nuzzled her cheek against his shoulder.

Ptolemy felt a surge of well-being within; he placed his arm around the woman whose love he cherished above all others. *Life seems to be treating me far too well.* He held his thumb between his fingers to ward off the evil eye. *Don't think such things; that's when it can often start going so very wrong.*

And so it did: with a speed that surprised even the most experienced of the triarchoi in Ptolemy's fleet, the great chain across the harbour mouth loosened with a series of sharp metallic reports, splashing into fetid harbour waters. No sooner than there was adequate draught above it as it sank, the first of the triremes appeared, timed to perfection, already at attack speed, the shrill pipe of its stroke-master piercing the clanking of the chain's descent. Two more ships followed in short order and then four more surged through the opening, now free of its constricting chain; another four followed, and then four more and more.

Taken completely by surprise, the Ptolemaic fleet scrambled to form into line of battle from the loose patrolling in squadrons of eight. Accelerating now to ramming speed, on came Attalus' lightning attack, spear-headed and long-shafted as yet four more triremes, line abreast, sped from the emptying harbour, fire arrows bursting from each in arcing streaks of flame-trailing smoke.

Ptolemy closed his eyes rather than watch the chaos of his fleet caught mid-manoeuvre as ship fouled ship, entangling oars and cracking on hulls. But it was the hollow boom and screeching of wood torn through by metal that forced him to open his eyes to behold the lead attacking ship rip into the broadside-on hull of a quinquereme half again its size. Smashing oars aside as if they were naught but dry twigs, the stout copper-headed ram thrust into the ship's hull with the urgency and ease of a voyage-weary sailor taking a dockside whore already greased and slack from many couplings.

The screams of the stricken crew rose above the wrecking of their vessel as the counter motion of the two ships tore at the wound, splintering it open still further so that the sea surged in with the force of a mountain waterfall in the thaw. Down came the fire arrows, like a burning, staccato hail spewed by a raging volcano, slamming into the decks of the closest squadron or splashing, hissing and steaming, into the sea. And thick and fast they fell, for Attalus was leaving Tyros with his whole army as well as his fleet; the decks of each of the ships in the haft of the formation were crammed with men, now all bow-armed, with fire pots scattered throughout their ranks to ignite their massed volleys and it was with haste that they released them as they knew, to be sure of escape, overwhelming force was required.

And overwhelming it was as the next two ships, with thunderous impacts, struck triremes with decks already ablaze to either side of the first casualty, now listing as its tormentor withdrew, oars backing, from the ghastly rent in its side. Rowers slithered out of oar-ports, chancing the open sea rather than being taking down by their ruined vessel; deck crew and marines leaped overboard to fight their crewmates for flotsam or jetsam to keep afloat as others grasped one another in a mutually destructive attempt to embrace life, sending them both, thrashing, below.

With awe and respect did Ptolemy watch the breakout as the ranks of four ships following the initial assault triremes split, two to either side, and raced through the Ptolemaic formations now backing off to avoid the burning deluge; none of the surviving five ships from the first squadron of eight had escaped the flames and their crews rushed with buckets to extinguish fires before they could take hold of the bone-dry decking caulked with pitch and horse hair; such was their concern with their task that none made any attempt to block the fleet as it fled north; indeed, the remaining four Ptolemaic squadrons moved out of its way as none could withstand such condensed and constant volleys of blazing missiles.

And thus Ptolemy watched as his quarry escaped, taking his full force with him.

'Shall we give chase, lord?' the triarchos shouted above the din of battle.

Ptolemy did not hear him at first but eventually responded to the repeated question: 'No, let them go.' His voice had a weary lilt to it, he looked down at Thais with a rueful smile. 'One must always see the positive of a situation, my dear. I offered to let Attalus go north to join with Alketas, should he wish, with just his fleet on the basis that the two of them would make more trouble for Antipatros to be kept busy with and I would gain Tyros, another few thousand men and a considerable amount of money. However, now he's gone taking the men and money I had hoped to gain, the positive side to it is that he will be an even bigger nuisance to Antipatros who will now be far too busy to argue with me about Tyros, which,' he indicated to the empty harbour mouth hazed in smoke from many burning vessels, 'as you can just about see, I still have gained. Let's go and see what Attalus has left me.'

'Nothing's in there, lord,' the keeper of the treasury said, bowing and wringing his hands and keeping his eyes averted. 'He forced me to remove everything overnight and load it onto his ships.' He gestured to the open door of the vault, deep within the heart of the citadel.

Ptolemy pushed past the man, annoyed by his obsequiousness. He walked into the vault, twenty paces square, lit by a dozen flaming torches whose smoke blackened the ceiling; he paused and looked around the empty shelves and then bellowed with laughter.

'What is it?' Thais asked, running to join him.

Ptolemy's laughter continued as he pointed down to the floor. 'Such generosity!' There, in the exact centre of the room, lay a single gold coin. 'Attalus can now argue that he did not take the entire contents of the treasury with him and he split it with me.' He bent to pick up the coin and held it up to Thais' face. 'It's one of the pieces that I had minted with Alexander's face on it a couple of years ago.'

She took it from his fingers. 'The first time that a mortal had ever appeared on a coin; it made you look as if you were his rightful heir, a masterful stroke.'

'I thought so too. Seeing this now, I wonder whether I should go one step further.'

Thais frowned and then nodded with slow comprehension. 'Of course: put your own head on a coin; that would really advertise you to the world as being the master of Egypt.'

'It would indeed.' He mused for a few moments. 'The question is: would it be seen as an act of provocation that would finally goad Antipatros into turning his attentions away from Eumenes, Attalus and Alketas or would it just be a clear signal that Egypt and I are now independent.'

'I think, my love, that it would be best to let it lie for the time being; leave Antipatros alone to deal with his problems in the north and then return to Macedon to die.'

'Yes, you're right, there's plenty of time for coinage after the old man has gone and I consider assuming the title of Pharaoh. Besides, we've yet to see what his next move will be in the propaganda war now that he will have definitely read *The Last Days and Testament of Alexander*.'

ANTIPATROS.
THE REGENT.

'I T WILL BE added to the end of *The Royal Journals*, which I intend to have published once they have been collated,' Antipatros said, handing a scroll to Kassandros, 'completing the story of Alexander's conquest with an eye-witness account of his death.'

Kassandros perused the document, his lips mouthing the words as his eyes scanned the letters. 'I don't see how that helps.'

Suppressing an urge to sigh in frustration, Antipatros took the scroll and pointed to the relevant lines. 'Here it says that Alexander did not have a sudden, stabbing pain but rather made a gradual descent into the fever and finally into unconsciousness before he died.'

Kassandros scratched the back of his head. 'But how does that imply he wasn't poisoned?'

'Because it didn't just suddenly happen.'

'But he still died and people will still blame us for it because of the lies in *The Last Days and Testament of Alexander*.'

Antipatros stared at his son. 'Are they lies, Kassandros? I don't know. What I do know is that I didn't order you to poison him but that doesn't mean that you didn't.'

Kassandros looked away. 'Of course I didn't.'

He can't meet my eye as he lies to me. Still, it's best that I don't force the issue; what do I gain if I make him admit it? 'Perhaps, therefore, to make that abundantly clear we should add that you arrived after Alexander first fell ill; that way there can be no dispute that you were responsible. I'll have the clerk redraft it and then we can have the whole thing published and circulated as widely as possible and put a stop to those filthy rumours once and for all.' Antipatros waited for a reaction from his son but was disappointed. *He doesn't care what people think; well, I suppose that's a strength rather than a weakness.* He rolled up the scroll and laid it down on the table between them before getting on to the real reason for Kassandros' visit to his camp at Sardis before he, Antipatros, began his journey home to Macedon. 'How's the war against Eumenes going and how is Antigonos behaving himself?'

'It's bad news and bad news, Father.'

Antipatros heaved a sigh. *Why is it always bad news?* 'Give me the least bad first.'

'Eumenes moves so quickly through the hills and mountains of the interior of Phrygia, and because he has been made an outlaw he feels that he can behave as one: plundering towns, selling their populations into slavery—'

'What! That is outrageous; you can only do that on enemy territory, not here, within the empire.'

It was Kassandros' turn to suppress a sigh. 'Don't you understand, Father? Because he's been made outlaw, everywhere for him is enemy territory; he doesn't care. All that matters to him is to keep his army together and if that means taking what he wants when he wants it to pay his men, then so be it. He doesn't have access to the treasuries as do you and Antigonos, so what do you expect?'

'I expect him to be caught and executed. We've put a price of a hundred talents on his head, for the love of the gods, we've publicised the fact heavily; why have none of his men betrayed him?'

'Because he's a sly little Greek. When he heard that his troops had been reading your leaflets he convened an army assembly and told them that it had been him who had circulated them as a test for the army; he told them that they had passed admirably and thanked them for their loyalty.'

'The sly little bastard. And they believed him?'

'Yes. He said that it could not possibly have been you and Antigonos who offered the bounty as you were far too intelligent to do that, knowing that any general who offered bounties would be creating a weapon that could be turned back against himself.'

Antipatros lifted his hands to the air in exasperation. 'The gullible fools.'

'The gullible fools voted immediately that he should have one thousand extra bodyguards in case someone takes the *test* seriously.'

'I suppose that's why the Exile-Hunter hasn't finished him yet, he's guarded too well. Have we heard from him?'

'Archias hasn't been seen since you last spoke to him and he left Sardis; there is a rumour that he and his men were seized and taken off, but by whom and to where is unknown. What is for sure is that he is not chasing Eumenes anymore.'

Antipatros drummed his fingers on the table. 'Gods above and below, I want Eumenes dead.'

'Yes, especially as he has just taken Celaenae.'

'The capital of Phrygia!'

'Yes, Antigonos left his capital undefended.'

'What's Antigonos doing? Why isn't he hunting him down?'

'This is the point, Father. In answer to your second question, Antigonos is hunting Eumenes, but he's doing it badly and I believe he is doing it badly on purpose. He's one of the most experienced generals in the army and yet he makes the basic error of leaving his capital wide open to the enemy.' Kassandros hunched his shoulders in disbelief. 'Of course he knew what he was doing and of course he feigned surprise when he heard that Eumenes had walked in; but really? No, he knew what he was about.'

Antipatros frowned. 'What was he about?'

'He was about making you look stupid and impotent.'

'But he's the one who has had his capital seized.' *Wait a moment; oh, I see.* Antipatros groaned and put a hand to his forehead. 'Of course, the cunning old dog. He makes a great show of running around the country trying to corner Eumenes, but never quite managing it – on purpose, no doubt; he's so stretched that he can't even spare troops to garrison his own capital such is his keenness to stop Eumenes stealing estates and looting towns and, meanwhile, what am I doing? I'm still here in Sardis preparing to go home, looking to the common man as if I'm doing nothing even though I'm trying to keep an empire together and running, if not smoothly, then at least with some semblance of efficiency.'

Kassandros nodded. 'Whereas Antigonos is seen to be darting around the countryside at least trying to do something about the Greek and, meanwhile, Eumenes ravages the land, causing untold suffering to the population.'

'Who see me as nothing more than a spectator to their suffering, when, by rights, as regent I should be out there doing something.'

'Precisely, Father. And what with that idiot Asander's complete failure to remove Alketas from Pisidia and Attalus reportedly on his way to Rhodos with his fleet, which would give him a formidable base, people are starting to wonder what would happen if Eumenes could persuade those two to join forces with him. And that's not the worst of it.'

Oh, not more bad news. 'Go on.'

'Over three thousand men under Antigonos' command have deserted; it may be that they are imitating Eumenes and have decided that banditry is profitable during times like these.'

'But?'

'But their commander, Holcias, has been suspected of having sympathy for the Perdikkan cause.'

'What's Antigonos doing about it?'

Kassandros shrugged. 'He sent Leonidas, one of his officers, to join them as if he too has a grievance; the plan is that he will gain the deserters' confidence and then betray them. In the meantime, Antigonos is keeping between them in Kappadokia and Eumenes in Phrygia so that they can't go over to him.'

'Well, at least he's doing something right.'

'Yes, but a desertion of that magnitude has added to the sense of Eumenes being on the rise and our cause being in serious difficulties. People are starting to wonder if they've backed the right chariot.'

Antipatros knew that his son was in the right of it; he wrinkled his nose, disliking Kassandros, irrationally, more than usual because he had been the one to point out his mistake.

'Then I had better cancel my plans of going home and leaving the war to the Resinated Cyclops and take my army north to deal with the little Greek myself to make sure that eventuality doesn't arise. If I can coordinate with Nicanor coming in behind him from Kappadokia it might be a success. Who knows but between us we might even shame Antigonos into doing a little better.'

'You can try, but, frankly, I don't trust him.'

'I don't trust anyone but that doesn't mean I won't try to bend people to my will.'

'I get the feeling that Antigonos now has an agenda of his own and it doesn't involve you.'

I'm too old to be dragging my weary body out on campaign, but I can see no choice if I want to keep respect and be able to choose my successor from a point of strength. Antipatros got to his feet, decisive and ready for action. 'Well, we shall see about that after I've caught Eumenes. You get back to Antigonos and keep me informed of anything that smacks of growing ambition. I'll take Iollas with me, he could do with the experience; together we'll take back Celaenae.'

'He's gone, Father,' Iollas reported as he led a unit of cavalry scouts, fresh from a reconnaissance of Celaenae, back into Antipatros' slow-moving column. 'According to the Elders, he left with his whole army two days ago.'

Antipatros shifted his stiff buttocks in the saddle and looked around the jagged hills of the valley through which the column trailed. 'Two days? Which way did he go?'

'That's just it, Father. He went in all directions.'

'All?'

'Yes; he's split his force into four or five units, the reports vary, and has taken to the hills.'

'Hiding?'

Iollas shrugged.

Antipatros looked again at the hills to either side. 'We'd better send patrols up to either flank, Iollas; I've just had the feeling that I'm being watched. Take whatever other light cavalry you need; I want you to spring any ambushes.'

But it was not Antipatros himself who was the target for malevolent eyes, as he realised less than an hour later when screams rose from towards the rear of the column, half a league away. Antipatros turned in his saddle to see wisps of smoke rising from the baggage; eastern horsemen swarmed around it. 'With me!' he shouted to the commander of his bodyguard as he swung his horse around and kicked it towards the column's rear.

On he raced with a hundred companion cavalry following; down the ranks and ranks of infantry, many looking nervously over their shoulders as the screaming and the din of battle grew from the baggage train. To either side of the valley he could see swift light cavalry racing down the hillside as others sped back up, loaded with booty. A unit of Thracian mercenary cavalry, stationed at the rear of the column, was being held off from relieving the baggage train by enemy heavy cavalry whose handling of their mounts was far superior to anything that Antipatros had seen thus far in Asia. *They must be Eumenes' Kappadokians of whom I've heard so much; this could be our chance to finish them if we can take them from behind.* As he watched, horse-archers began to strafe the Thracian cavalry from the flank, bringing more than a few down.

Urging his mount on, Antipatros glanced behind; his unshielded, lance-armed companions had their sleek weapons ready for the charge and had formed a wedge of which he was the tip. *I shouldn't be doing this; fighting in the front rank at my age.* But there was no choice for Antipatros; to slink back to the rear ranks so close to impact would bring only shame, despite his record as a fighting general. 'At them, lads!' he cried, kicking his horse into full stride. Lacking a lance, he drew his sword as the wind of the charge ripped at his cloak and massed hoof-beats thundered in his ears.

But the Kappadokians were not commanded by a fool with eyes only for what was in front of him; as Antipatros' men came to within hundred paces of their rear, a horn blared from their ranks and, as one, they pulled their horses around, turning to face the new threat; their erstwhile opponents withdrew in the face of mounting casualties from the horse archers to their flank.

It had been an age since Antipatros had been involved in a cavalry charge and the joy of it now surged through him and a sense of youth returned, firming up his thigh muscles as they gripped the flanks of his speeding mount; he found himself screaming at the top of his voice and laughed inwardly, feeling the pent-up tension from the pressure of trying to hold the empire together since the death of Perdikkas flow from him.

But his opposing commander was wily and wise in the ways of horse-war: not for him the head-on clash of scores of beasts but, rather, a subtler approach. And it was with a shock that Antipatros registered one man in Greek tunic, bare legs and cavalry boots amidst the betrousered Kappadokians. *Eumenes himself! This is far too good to be true.*

With twenty paces separating them, the Kappadokian horn blared once more; down the middle they divided, veering away right and left, skimming down the widening flanks of the wedge, just out of range of the lance tips bristling from it. One javelin apiece they hurled as they passed and many found their mark, punching riders from mounts, slamming into the great chests or rumps of the beasts or skewering their skulls. Such was their skill, their complete oneness with their animals, that not one of the Kappadokians was unhorsed as the last of them cleared the rear of their enemy leaving dead and wounded – both man and beast – strewn in their wake.

The shock at being so outmanoeuvred slapped Antipatros in the face as he pulled his mount up, looking over his shoulder at the Kappadokians streaming away up the hill, screened by their retreating light cavalry, many of whom had sacks of booty from the baggage-train slung across their horses' rumps. Smoke now drifted on the breeze as wagons burnt and the cries of women filled the air as the camp-followers mourned the dead or bewailed stolen goods. On the far side of the column, enemy cavalry could be seen retreating back up the slope towards the safety of the hills.

The column behind the baggage had ground to a halt, blocked by the chaos, whilst the rest had marched on, splitting the army into two uneven parts.

Antipatros slammed a clenched fist on his thigh, regretting it the moment it struck. *I've been made to look a fool by a Greek leading a pack of barbarians.* 'Get the wreckage out of the way!' he shouted at the commander of the baggage train, running towards him to report. 'And get moving as quickly as possible, Andros; I can slow the column so that you can catch up, but I don't want to halt it completely, not after that.'

'Yes, sir,' Andros replied, giving a cursory salute and turning to run back to his ravaged command.

Antipatros looked around at the Macedonian dead and dying and finally understood the scale of the problem he faced. *With cavalry like that and using hit and run tactics, Eumenes can hold out for as long as he likes, running rings around us, wearing us down, chipping away at our morale and always being one move ahead. Perhaps I've been too hard on Antigonos; Eumenes is a trickier foe than I've given credit for. I need to get him to face me in open battle but the trouble is: why would he want to do that?*

But further thoughts on the subject were interrupted by the skidding arrival of a mounted messenger. 'Sir! Sir!'

'What is it?'

'The van is under attack!'

Antipatros looked back to the head of the column to see cavalry again flowing down the hills to either side, releasing javelins or arrows and then speeding away as others took their place; to his left, almost directly above him, the Kappadokian heavy cavalry had rallied and were now making their way, at speed, towards the head of the column. 'Back!' he yelled. 'Back before they have the opportunity to bring a charge home.' Without waiting for his companions to form up, Antipatros pushed his tired horse into a gallop, a sickening feeling brewing in his belly; he was being toyed with and there was little he could do until he got his army to the relative safety of Celaenae. As he rode past the ranks of infantry he reflected on the unsuitability of heavy infantry in this rugged terrain and wished that he had not given so much of his mounted force to Antigonos.

And then it hit him: he had sent Iollas to spring any ambushes, and yet here they were charging down the hill at him.

Iollas!

With desperation clawing at his heart, Antipatros spared not his mount as he flogged it on with the flat of his sword. Although slower than before, the column still moved forward, the units under attack sheltering behind their shields as they kept going. Cavalry from the vanguard at the very head of the army had doubled back and was now forming up for an organised charge rather than piecemeal action. But still the enemy swarmed down the hills in a fluid motion, releasing an arrow or hurling a javelin before streaming away to let others inflict more damage. Hundreds of them had now joined the attack, they ebbed and flowed like the sea breaking on the strand and then rolling away, wave after wave in an incoming tidal surge.

With no thought for his own well-being, Antipatros crashed into the nearest group, javelin-armed Paphlagonian light cavalry, just as they veered away, back uphill, having launched their weapons. Sword swirling above his head, iron grip belying his octogenarian status, he brought it down to take the arm of a surprised sparse-bearded youth, before crashing his mount past him and cutting the blade back up into the face of an older man in elaborately embroidered long tunic and trousers. Blood exploded from the shattered visage as the victim arched back, Phrygian cap flying through the air, with a bestial scream dying in his gorge as it filled with gore. On Antipatros went, through the loose formation, slashing left and right thinking nothing but death, uncaring of the growing precariousness of his position the deeper he delved. And then a shudder ran through the enemy before him and, with great urgency, they retired, many looking over their shoulders: the cavalry of the vanguard had charged home, scattering those they could hit and inducing flight in the rest, relieving the pressure on the hard-pressed van who cheered their saviours as they continued their march. Away sped Eumenes' cavalry, heeding not the solitary Macedonian in their midst such was their desire to avoid the needle-sharp lance tips that had already reaped many of their lives.

As the enemy cleared, Antipatros found himself alone in front of the vanguard cavalry as his companions finally caught up with him. He nodded to the commander and then turned to look up the hill at the fleeing mass. His breath caught in his throat: for there, high above and to the right of him came Iollas' troop, slanting away from the retreating foe, taking advantage of their disorder to make a run for the front of the column and relative safety.

But the sight of an isolated, weak enemy proved far too alluring for Eumenes' cavalry whose skirmishing had been curtailed by a far stronger force; three or four score veered towards Iollas' men with impetuous haste and ululating cries celebrating the excitement of the chase not more than three hundred paces from them but further up the hill.

That Iollas would be intercepted was likely but not inevitable. 'After them!' Antipatros screamed at the commander of his companion cavalry, beating his exhausted horse once again with the flat of his sword; the beast whinnied in protest, rising on its hind legs and flattening its ears, but consented to move forward with a leap upon receiving a second stroke. Struggling to maintain his seat as his horse careered away, Antipatros sent up a prayer to Aries, the god of war, to hold his hands over his son until he could come to his aid. The column's cheers for the vanguard cavalry turned into shouts of warning for Iollas' men, urging them on to more speed.

Having seen the danger, Iollas changed his path dead away from his pursuers, now a mere hundred paces from them, and for a few moments held his distance as Antipatros and his companions raced after. But, with a jangling of harnesses, snorting and a stamping of hoofs, Eumenes' Kappadokians appeared over a crest, high on the hill, ahead of the chase. Without hesitation, the little Greek urged his men forward, straight down the steep slope at breakneck pace. Shouts from the column grew more desperate as it became increasingly apparent that Iollas' men were destined to lose the race.

Desperation grew in Antipatros' breast as he felt his mount flagging, oppressed by the distance already galloped and the incline of the current slope; no amount of beating could make the beast move faster and he turned to see that his companions' horses were also on the verge of exhaustion, sweat-foamed and frothing at the mouth.

But even had they had the speed of Pegasus, they would not have prevented Eumenes from smashing his Kappadokians into the flank of Iollas' troop. In they thrust, sending beasts crashing onto their sides, shooting men into the air; equine limbs thrashed as they tumbled down the steep incline over and over, crushing their erstwhile riders and snapping bones in a chorus of bestial shrieks and human anguish.

'Iollas!' Antipatros cried as he saw his son fending off the sword thrusts of two men as he strove to pull himself out of the chaos. Again and again he parried with increasing desperation as men all around him fell to overwhelming odds. And it was with an inevitability that broke Antipatros' heart that Iollas' frame jerked and then became rigid.

'My son!' Antipatros cried to the sky as the sword dropped from Iollas' hand and he slithered from the saddle.

'Hold!' shouted a disembodied voice from within the Kappadokian formation. A horn sounded thrice and disengagement was immediate, allowing those of Iollas' men still mounted to beat it back down the hill without pursuit.

The Kappadokians pulled back, all except one man; Eumenes dismounted and knelt beside the motionless Iollas, cupping his head in a hand, as Antipatros pulled up his horse and leaped from the saddle.

'My men will stay back if yours will,' Eumenes said.

Antipatros nodded and turned to his companions. 'Stay where you are.' He came to his son's side, looked down at the vacant, staring eyes and collapsed in violent, chest-heaving sobs.

'I didn't realise that it was him until it was too late,' Eumenes said, his voice quiet. 'I'm sorry.'

Antipatros let his grief run for many racing heartbeats, tears streaming onto Iollas' face and chest as he hugged the lifeless body. After some while he sucked in a few huge lungfuls of air and brought himself back under control. 'It's the madness of it all, Eumenes, we're killing each other but for what?' He gestured down at his dead son. 'Why did he have to die?'

'Why did any of them have to die, for that matter?' Eumenes replied, looking around at the dead scattered about.

Antipatros raised his bloodshot eyes and looked at his enemy. 'All because that arrogant young pup refused to name an heir. "To the strongest": with those three words he condemned Iollas to an early death and here we are, you and I, fighting each other for control of his legacy. And for what?'

Eumenes was certain of his answer. 'I'm fighting to ensure that the Argead royal dynasty remains supreme in the empire. And you?'

Antipatros thought for a few moments, looking at the ring on his finger. 'So am I; at least I thought I was. Which was why I opposed Perdikkas, who seemed to want to take the kings' power for himself.'

'And I supported Perdikkas because he represented the kings.'

'But then, when you defeated Krateros and made me look stupid for dividing my forces, I made it personal. It was my mistake, my pride; had it just been kept to a business level we could have come to an accommodation, I'm sure of it. There was only a very fine line between us; but that doesn't matter now.' Antipatros shook his head and spat. 'But what do I care anymore? I'm done with it.' He gestured at Iollas. 'No cause is worth the death of a son and certainly not this one. Keep your war or settle your differences; it's all the same to me now. I'm going back to Macedon to die a grieving man.'

'And the kings?'

'I'll take them with me; I'll not let them be used as pawns in the power game anymore.'

'Will Antigonos let you have them?'

'Of course he will; he's not interested in them, they serve no purpose for him. He doesn't care about legitimacy, like you and me. He's just biding his time with a view to making his own bid for power once I'm gone. Face it, Eumenes, the empire is lost; the Argead royal house consists of a fool, a child and Alexander's bastard, for I'll take Heracles with me as well.'

'What about Kleopatra?'

'What about her? I ensured that all her potential husbands are taken; I didn't want the situation complicated any further by her marrying and becoming pregnant. She can stay in Sardis or return to Macedon; her time is over.'

'And me? Will you secure me a pardon from the army assembly? If you do I could come to an accommodation with you and Antigonos.'

'Frankly, I don't care one way or the other. I'm leaving Asia; you can fight for it or not, it's none of my business anymore. I tried my best to make a settlement at The Three Paradises, but it has failed. I don't believe that you will be able to come to an accommodation with Antigonos unless you agree to serve him as he attempts to sweep all before him.'

'In that case I would certainly have to oppose him; I'll only serve the blood of the Argead house.'

Antipatros got to his feet and looked at the little Greek with a mixture of incredulity and pity. 'And so the war will just continue. Dream on like that, Eumenes, and the inevitable result will—'

'Be more sons dying.' Eumenes also stood. 'If I were to cease fighting for the Argead house then all the lives already lost in that struggle would have died for nothing. Get me that pardon and I'll still champion the kings' cause again rather than just fighting to survive.'

Rueful was Antipatros' smile as he looked to Eumenes and then down at his son. 'Do your worst, the lot of you: you, Antigonos, Ptolemy, Alketas, Attalus, Seleukos, all of you. You deserve one another.'

SELEUKOS.
THE BULL-ELEPHANT.

THE MOON HAD set and darkness enshrouded the fleet; darkness made to feel more absolute by comparison with the glow in the distant sky to the south: Babylon.

Seleukos, standing next to the steering oar of the leading ship – the only trireme in the fleet of troop transports – looked to the heavens to estimate the time and judged that it was right; he turned to the triarchos. 'Remember, as quickly and quietly as possible, no pipes for the stroke, just hand signals.'

The man nodded and stamped his foot three times on the deck. Below, the stroke-master raised a fist and brought it down; with a repressed groan, the hundred and twenty rowers pulled on their sweeps and the ship moved forward. Behind came the armada of transport vessels, each filled to capacity with men who longed to feel dry land beneath their feet once again; they hoisted sails that filled with the breeze to carry them out into the current. They were underway.

Now all that mattered was for the fire to be set on time.

Fire and surprise were the two ingredients upon which Seleukos now relied to oust Docimus from Babylon and install himself as satrap.

Surprise he felt he had achieved. In the days and nights of sailing down the Euphrates, the fleet had stopped any ship from going ahead of them; that contingency, along with travelling as fast as possible without pause, so as to outrun messengers on land, would, he felt, prevent the news of their coming from reaching Babylon before them. His cavalry, split into two, travelling down either bank of the river added insurance to this hope.

And so they glided down the Euphrates, sped by the current and the breeze; on either bank, unseen but just audible, the cavalry moved in tandem with the fleet advancing at a speed that would quickly take them to their destination, now just three leagues away.

But all would be for naught if the fire was not ablaze by the time the fleet sailed down the river to where it bisected the two halves of Babylon. The western side of the city was mainly residential and commercial, and although it was protected by a sturdy wall to the landward side, the river bank itself was embanked with a series of quays and markets, easy to land an army on but useless as there was nothing of strategic value in that half. The palace and the fortresses and the heart of Babylon lay on the eastern bank and this had a formidable wall along it – two, in fact, the second wall thirty paces behind the first; and this was the arrangement for the entire length of the eastern wall, the height of ten men and tiled in deep-blue glazed tiles interspersed with animal and astrological motifs. There was no way to cross that wall without a lengthy siege involving tens of thousands of men, most of whom would, in all likelihood, die of disease before the city fell. And even to get an army there from the landward side, a further outer wall, enclosing the summer palace to the north of the city and its gardens surrounding the entire eastern half – the gardens for which Babylon was famous – would also need to be taken. No, there was only one way in, as far as Seleukos could see, and he had studied the problem in depth when first the idea of him taking the city had entered his mind as Perdikkas grew more and more arrogant: the two halves of the city were joined by one bridge across the Euphrates, two hundred and fifty paces wide. One bridge that led to a towering gate on the eastern side, a gate that was closed each dusk and opened again at dawn. Beyond this gate was a further gate in the second wall and beyond that was the city. Open those two gates at night and the city would fall if enough men swarmed through them. Seleukos had the men, but the gates were locked. And that was why he needed fire.

Seleukos walked along the deck, through his seated companions, fifty-strong, who would be fighting on foot alongside him this night, muttering a few encouraging words as he did, and went to lean against the rail in the bow of the ship. His thoughts turned to Apama, his Persian wife, who had, along with their two children, remained in Babylon when he had left with Perdikkas' army, acting as the second-in-command, over half a year ago; if all went well he would be with her by midday. *And then there will be time to start working on creating the raw material for dynastic marriages.* He chuckled to himself at the way he had expressed the sentiment. But however flippant the thought might have been, it was a serious consideration for once he had Babylon he did not intend ever to lose it.

He had no concern for the safety of his wife and children in Babylon; no Macedonian would sully his honour by using a woman or a child as a means of attacking a rival – the case of Atalante had been an aberration, a thing never to be repeated – at least, not by honourable men, no matter how hated their enemy was. And this was just the point: he did not like Docimus but nor did he hate him either and neither, as far as he knew, did Docimus hate him, so there was absolutely no need to be excessive in his dealings with him. He would be allowed to depart the city with his family to go wherever he wished, just as Seleukos had given him the chance to leave the camp after Perdikkas' assassination. This sort of attitude would be impossible if they all started executing each other's families. No, Seleukos that night wished for nothing more than a simple transfer of power, with as little blood spilt as possible as, with their former master treated with respect and few of their number killed, he might reasonably expect to swear the garrison into his service as he would be desperately short of troops once he sent those Ptolemy had lent him back to Egypt.

If I do send them back, that is.

He contemplated the rights and wrongs of keeping the men and decided that it would be impossible to do so against their will; and given the choice between Egypt and Babylonia he guessed that most of them would plump for the first, especially as most of them would have women there by now. No, if he was going to expand his army, and that was essential, then he would have to look for troops elsewhere. But that was a problem for tomorrow, for now, huge against the light rising from it, the silhouetted shape of Babylon was clear ahead of them; it was now time to concentrate on his plan. And as his vessel passed the summer palace, to the north of the city, Seleukos strained his eyes looking for any signs of a fire on the eastern bank, just past the bridge, now only half a league away.

Nothing unusual could he see as the outer wall, the height of five men, enclosing the palace gardens that surrounded the eastern city, glided by, dimly backlit by the light emanating from the palace itself until that faded and merged into the murk of night. No shouts came from the shore as the fleet drifted on with the current, sails having been furled some time ago to make the ships less conspicuous.

Soon, the northern fortress loomed ahead, standing outside the city's main walls and guarding the Ishtar Gate where the Processional Street from the palace entered the city. Now the outer wall was replaced by the blue-glazed city wall with the southern fortress, twinkling with many lights, just beyond it. On the west bank lay the watchtower that marked the beginning of the wall protecting the landward side of the western half of the city; there were now buildings to either side of them and it was with little surprise that Seleukos heard the first cries of alarm coming from both the southern fortress and the western watchtower, having known that detection would be most probable now that there were wakeful eyes on either bank. The bridge was clearly in sight, a little over one thousand paces away, illumined with torches along its length, a strip of fire across two hundred and fifty paces of dark river. Seleukos' heart leaped for, as he watched, figures streamed onto the bridge from the eastern side; this could only be possible if the gate had opened. And then, sure enough, the flicker of flames could be seen beyond the wall: the outhouses around the Esagila, the Temple of Marduk, were burning; thus threatening the very temple itself. This, and only this threat, Seleukos had judged was the sole thing likely to get the gates opened so that the hydraulic pumps that were used to supply water to the gardens via leather hoses could now be brought to the bridge and used to save the temple just next to it. And save the temple they would, Seleukos would make sure of that. Indeed, it was a crucial part of his plan that he should.

'On!' Seleukos cried now that stealth was less of an issue than speed. Out went the trireme's oars and up went the transport vessels' sails, harnessing the warm breeze and driving the fleet forward at renewed pace. Arrows flicked in from either side but did little harm as the fleet stayed mid-stream, towards the limit of their range.

'Faster!' Seleukos ordered, just five hundred paces out, as he saw that the men on the bridge were so busy with the pumps and the hoses that they were yet to notice the hostile threat. On the trireme surged, pulling away from the transports and veering towards the east bank. Arrows thudded into the deck with juddering reports as they came more within range. Seleukos and his companions knelt beside their shields taking little notice of the incoming missiles, their concentration focused on the still-open gates.

Two hundred paces out and the men manning the pumps began to shout and point at the fleet, but they were cuffed back to their duty by officers and priests to whom the lives of the insignificant were nothing compared to the beauty of the Temple of Marduk.

Seleukos smiled to himself: it was what he had expected. Now he knew that the gates would remain open for the hoses to pass through on their sacred mission. 'Ladders ready!'

Ten short ladders, no more than the height of two men, were brought to the front of Seleukos' companions; five men lining up behind each.

At fifty paces the ship slewed, the larboard oars backing; round it came. On a bellowed command the starboard oars were withdrawn just before the hull cracked against the eastern-most pillar of the bridge. Up the ladders went and up them streamed Seleukos with his men. Over the bridge's parapet he leaped to clatter down on the paved surface, his men just moments behind him. Now the bravery of the pump handlers was stretched to breaking point; most ran in the face of armed men charging towards them. But they need not have worried, for they were not the target of the attack, no man was unless he got between Seleukos and his objective: the second gates.

Through the first gate Seleukos ran, jumping over the leather hoses, knocking a protesting priest out of the way. Chest heaving, he sprinted the thirty or so paces between the walls, his men, beating their shields with swords and howling their war-cries, pounding behind him as, ahead, the second gates began swinging shut, on goose-fatted hinges, at a surprising rate. With a final spurt, Seleukos crashed through the closing gates when they were no more than three paces apart, a dozen or so of his men making it through just before they slammed together, crushing the hoses.

But a dozen would do; Seleukos punched his sword into a bearded veteran, evidently the commander of the guard, as he charged towards him, blade raised. Down the man went in a spray of blood, as his companions set about those of the guard with the heart to fight. But there were few of them who were willing to risk their lives fighting their fellow Macedonians for a reason that they did not understand; when those few lay dead or dying, the remainder knelt in submission.

'Open them!' Seleukos ordered.

In the matter of moments the two gates swung open, aided by a counterweighted system of great antiquity. And there, on the bridge, the first units of his men had formed up while behind them more disembarked as empty transports swung away to be replaced by full ones.

Seleukos waited for the lead units to come through the second gate and spoke to the general at their head, a Greek mercenary in Ptolemy's employ. 'Take a hundred men and deal with the fire, Callias; I want the people to know that it was my men who prevented it from burning down the Temple of Marduk.'

Callias frowned. 'But won't they also know that it was started at your instigation to get the gates to open?'

Seleukos smiled and clapped Callias on the shoulder. 'They might think that at first but I shall, of course, deny it and claim that it was divine intervention, proving that the gods are with me in my venture; or some similar twaddle which, if I have it repeated often enough, will soon become the truth. Alternative facts can be very useful. Now, get on with it; I've got two forts and a palace to open.'

The garrison of the southern fortress, set within the city's walls, saw no reason for continuing in their support for Docimus and opened their gates at the sight of five thousand men – half Seleukos' infantry – marching towards them along the Processional Way. The commander of the garrison formally offered Seleukos his sword, which was refused. 'You and your men swear loyalty to me, Temenos, and I will increase what Docimus was paying you and keep you in your posts.'

'You are generous, sir,' Temenos replied, visibly relieved. 'Most of the lads have no wish to leave as they have women here now.'

'As do I; do you have news of her?'

'I would have thought she is still in her suite in the Palace of Nebuchadnezzar, along with the other officers' wives left behind. Docimus didn't touch them.'

'So much the better for him. Send a party of your men to warn her of my arrival, Temenos. They are to stay with her until I get there.'

Pleased to be of service so soon to his new commander, Temenos saluted and snapped to his business.

Seleukos' generous terms were also gratefully accepted by the guards of the Ishtar gate who opened their charge with happy smiles and clear consciences, but the commander of the northern fortress, just beyond the Ishtar Gate, had a different idea of loyalty. 'Why should I surrender? We've got supplies in here that will last us at least six months, by which time relief would have arrived.'

'And who do you think is going to come and relieve you?' Seleukos asked, genuinely interested.

'Alketas.'

Seleukos laughed, throwing his head back. 'Alketas is dug in in Pisidia; he's going nowhere.'

'Eumenes, then?'

'Even less likely; his satrapy is Kappadokia. Why would he want to leave the easily defended mountain fortresses there and expose himself by coming to your aid? No, face it, my friend: you're on your own and likely to be for a very long time. I have half my infantry here with me whilst the other half has gone through the city taking strategic crossings, buildings and gates and garrisoning them. If you would care to wait until the sun rises then you will also see that my cavalry are patrolling in front of all the gates and, as I'm sure you've already noticed, I control the river so that no one can leave or enter the city except with my knowledge so it might be quite a while before you manage to get a message out calling for help.'

Shortly after sunrise, the body of the commander was dropped from the walls and the northern fortress' gates opened; out walked the garrison under an olive branch of truce, with their hands extended to show that they were unarmed. 'It's good to know that I shall be inheriting troops with a decent amount of common sense,' Seleukos commented to Callias as he arrived, blackened by smoke. 'How's the fire going?'

'It's out, sir. All the buildings around the temple were destroyed, the priests' quarters, their kitchens and refectory, the storerooms, but the temple itself was unharmed, just a bit of smoke damage that a new coat of paint and gilt will cover up.'

Seleukos beamed. 'Good, I don't suppose anyone will feel sorry for the priests except for the priests themselves. I'm sure they will be very happy to spread the rumour that the fire was divine intervention in my favour in return for me building them an even more sumptuous residence.'

Callias grinned. 'Comfort is generally uppermost in their minds, sir.'

'Invariably. Now take some men and garrison the northern fortress along with these prisoners after they've sworn loyalty to me and then we shall deal with Docimus before I send for my wife.'

But Docimus did not want to be dealt with by someone he considered to be socially below him; in fact Docimus refused even to come to the palace walls, resplendent with motifs of Babylonian kings hunting lion and other game on a background of emerald-green glazed tiles. Instead, he sent his second-in-command, Polemon. 'And, obviously,' Polemon said in conclusion to a long list of demands, 'he will take the entire treasury with him.'

'Have you finished?' Seleukos asked, his tone exasperated.

Polemon looked down his nose at Seleukos, a task made easy by his relative height on the wall and the size of the proboscis in question. 'I believe so.'

'And he expects me to grant him all that?' Seleukos counted off the demands on his fingers. 'An escort of a thousand men and the ships to carry them, provisions for a month and spare clothing and weapons for all of them. Plus, his pick of the furniture and artwork in the palace, a retinue of personal slaves for him and his household as well as transport for his entire stables and then, on top of that, he announces that of course he will be taking the treasury. Did I miss anything?'

'No.'

Seleukos shook his head, incredulous. 'As supporters of Perdikkas, you are both under a sentence of death which, until a few moments ago, I had no intention of carrying out. If I were you, I would leave that stuck-up prig who believes that people whose family do not come from Pella are nothing better than bumpkins and come down here to throw yourself at the mercy of this rather insulted bumpkin.'

Polemon, whose views on aristocratic blood were much the same as his superior's, looked down his nose again at Seleukos, displaying evident distaste. 'You haven't got the power to order our executions.'

'Now you're just being stupid. I am Satrap of Babylonia, despite what Docimus thinks, and can therefore order the execution of anyone I like or, rather, don't like. And you can tell Docimus that he is climbing higher and higher on that list the longer I am kept standing here – as are you, for that matter. Now go!'

The force of Seleukos' voice visibly surprised Polemon and he stepped back before turning away.

'Just kill them,' Callias said as Polemon disappeared. 'Macedonians are arrogant enough and look down on Greeks, even on Spartans like myself, but when you get ones who looks down on fellow Macedonians, that's intolerable; at least take their eyes so they aren't afflicted by having to look at you.'

'That's a tempting thought, my friend, but what would happen if Alketas and Eumenes did finally manage to make an alliance and managed to take control of Anatolia? Where would I be then if I had executed their allies?'

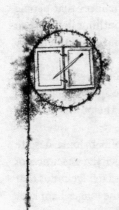

EUMENES.
THE SLY.

'THE TIMING HAS never been better,' Eumenes stated, looking over at Alketas, Attalus, Docimus and Polemon in turn, standing opposite him, the stiff breeze pulling at their cloaks and hair; they were on a hilltop in snow-capped, mountainous terrain just south of Iconium on the border between Phrygia and Pisidia – a branch of truce lay between them and their mounted escorts waited behind them, further down the hill, just out of earshot; Hieronymus sat behind Eumenes taking notes of the negotiations. 'Antipatros is taking the kings and a good part of his army back to Europe. It just leaves Antigonos here in Anatolia; we all know that three thousand of Antigonos' men, commanded by one Holcias, deserted a few months back. His lads aren't happy. If we combine our forces, we will have enough troops to make a fool of him by leading him around western Asia, living off the land, taking what we want as I have been doing but on a much greater scale. Eventually, Antigonos will be such a laughing stock more desertions will deplete his army and the locals will despise him for allowing us to inflict such misery on them without hindrance. He will be forced to negotiate; all we will ask for is a pardon and for everything to be as it was. Thus the civil war will be over.'

'So do I get Babylonia back?' Docimus asked, looking at the little Greek with distaste.

Gods, these high-born Macedonian have as much brain as they have manners. 'Seleukos is satrap there now, on Antipatros' orders; I think it would be hard to remove him, especially as you seized the satrapy without any official sanction in the first place.'

'I'll make the bastard pay for what he did, some day.'

'What? Make him pay for sparing yours and Polemon's lives and giving you safe conduct to Pisidia?'

'Humiliating us; allowing us no escort, no baggage, no slaves, just our wives and children and a few spare tunics each.'

'And your weapons,' Eumenes reminded him. 'You came as free men not prisoners.'

'We didn't have a denarius between us,' Polemon complained. 'Nothing.'

'Yet all your expenses were paid. I think, gentlemen, that you have cause to be grateful to Seleukos. He would have been well within his rights to have had you both executed. Indeed, it could be argued that he broke the law in not doing so.' Eumenes waved these concerns away and concentrated his attention back on Alketas and Attalus. 'Think of it: if we can get them to the table then the war will be over and our positions safe.'

The two men looked at one another and then back to Eumenes.

I think I might be winning the argument; somewhere deep in the dark military mind of a Macedonian is an appreciation of strategy and it may well have just been awakened in these two fine specimens. I'd better tread carefully with the next part. 'Now that we no longer have a navy, the interior is our only option.'

Attalus stiffened and searched Eumenes' face for any implied criticism.

Eumenes held up a hand. 'I don't mean to apportion any blame, Attalus, I just state the facts as they stand: since the Rhodian navy destroyed your fleet in defence of their island, we have no means to counter Kleitos' fleet and must, therefore, stay away from the coast. So bring your men inland to me and together we'll confound Antigonos. What do you say, gentlemen?'

'I will naturally have overall command with Attalus as my second, of course,' Alketas said.

Eumenes gazed in surprise at the younger man, fifteen years his junior. 'Of course you won't; I will command and you can be my second.'

'I'll not take—'

'Orders from a Greek.' *Gods save us from the arrogance of these people; they would rather lose the war and their lives than have their dignity, as they see it, diminished.* 'No, you'll take orders from a proven commander; one who wins. One who beat Neoptolemus and Krateros; one who forced Antipatros to despair and go home; as well as out-thinking Antigonos. A winner, in other words; men follow a winner.' He stared at them, defying them to contradict him.

'We're winners too,' Alketas asserted in a voice that came out less forceful than intended.

That was too much for Eumenes. 'Winners? Attalus has just had almost his entire fleet sunk beneath him in his ill-judged and badly reconnoitred assault on Rhodos; in saying badly reconnoitred I'm doing him the service of implying that there was a degree of reconnaissance, normally considered a prerequisite for a military undertaking, but actually he just blundered in thinking that Macedonian will always outdo Greek. Well, forty ships and almost five thousand men say that isn't true.' Eumenes stood, pushing his chair backwards onto the floor and, fuming, pointed at Attalus. 'Don't even try to defend yourself because that's how it happened. And as for you, Alketas, what have you done but skulk around Pisidia? Oh, yes, you managed to kill Alexander's half-sister, Cynnane; that was a winning move, wasn't it? The army almost mutinied, you had to be saved by your late sister and your late brother was forced to allow the bitch's whelp to marry Philip, thus adding to poor Perdikkas' problems. Well, go back to Pisidia and carry on your winning ways there. Or see sense, and come back with

174

me to Phrygia; join me and together we really do have a chance of winning.'

'Only if I am in command,' Alketas stated.

Eumenes cocked his head as if he had not heard correctly and then gave a weak smile when he realised that he had. 'Gentlemen, I'm wasting my time with you; our business here is done. Good day to you all. Come, Hieronymus, I trust you have sufficient evidence of the bone-headed stubbornness of the Macedonian warrior class.' With that he turned and walked at pace back to his Kappadokian cavalry escort waiting down the hill.

'You're a Macedonian, Apollonides,' Eumenes said to the commander of his escort, having contemplated the stubbornness of Alketas as they descended from the meeting place. A thin snow had started to drift; flakes settling on his horse's neck melted almost instantaneously. 'Why would Alketas rather risk death than take orders from a Greek?'

Apollonides had no hesitation in answering. 'Hundreds of years of being looked down upon as barely literate yokels with a dialect of Greek that would make even an Epirot blush is not easily forgotten by the noble houses. Since King Philip subdued the greater part of Greece twenty years ago, they feel that their superiority has been asserted and are therefore incapable of taking orders from—'

'Inferiors who have been beaten. Yes, I understand all that; what I'm asking is why do they take it to such an extreme so that they would rather die than take orders from a Greek? You take orders from me, after all.'

'Yes, sir, but I'm a soldier who has worked his way up through the ranks; I wasn't born with a sense of entitlement like Alketas. I was born in a hovel and my father cared more for his sheep than he did for me. And rightly so as the sheep could keep the family alive whereas I was a liability until I was six or so and could be of some use looking after the flock. As I was a younger brother I had little choice but to join the army and it has treated me very well; why would I put that at risk just because you are a

Greek? I know that it is my lot to take orders, so who gives them is all one to me. Alketas, however… well, it would be more than his pride and dignity are worth to be seen bowing to a Greek; he could never go home again.'

'Well, he's not going to be going home anyway if he stays in Pisidia without a fleet to protect him,' Eumenes mused, 'so it doesn't make much odds either way, I suppose.'

It was as they approached his camp that evening, three leagues north of Iconium – a town that had already suffered badly from Eumenes' army foraging – that Eumenes realised that something was amiss: one whole section, at the far end, judging by the lack of smoke from cooking fires, looked remarkably empty.

'They left in the middle of the night,' Xennias explained, 'very quietly; by the time I knew they were going it was too late. They were right at the other end of the camp and just crossed the picket lines and headed north; they were half a league away before I caught up with them. Diocles, their leader, refused to stop and, short of attacking them, there was nothing that I could do.'

'How can three thousand men just walk out of the camp "*very quietly*"? Three thousand men in full equipment with all their baggage and everything quiet? No, I think not, Xennias.'

Xennias' face displayed displeasure at being disbelieved. 'Think what you like, sir, but that is how it happened.'

Careful, don't alienate him. 'I'm sorry, my friend, I'm sure you're right. The question is; what to do about it? We can't just allow a fifth of the army to disappear. Do you know where they are going? Antigonos, I suppose.'

'No, sir, it seems that your tactics have shown that banditry pays: those men who deserted Antigonos last month have set themselves up in Kappadokia. Now that Nicanor has been recalled to Macedon, our lads—'

'Have decided to join them. We'll soon see about that; get all the cavalry, all of it, light, heavy, Macedonian, Kappadokian, Thracian, Paphlagonian and any other sorts of "ians" we have, ready to ride as soon as possible. Those bastards will not reach Kappadokia.'

'They're in the valley up ahead, half a league away,' Apollonides said, pulling his horse up with a scattering of gravel; his breath steamed in the cold mountain air.

'Good. We'll just track them for a while to give our horses a rest before we tackle them. How are they formed up?'

'In a standard column; very disciplined, no lagging and the ranks and files are in perfect order.'

Eumenes reflected on that for a few moments. 'So their discipline hasn't gone; that's a good sign. I may be able to bring them back to their duty. Who's at the head of the column?'

'Diocles, still, with a few of his junior officers.'

Eumenes smiled, grim and determined. 'Then he'll be easy to find.'

A moan rose from the column as two files of cavalry raced from its rear, up either side of it, as it travelled through a valley whose dun-coloured slopes were made up of jagged rocks, scree and the occasional patch of snow. As Eumenes neared the van, orders were bellowed and the great snake of men came to a creditable halt; anxious faces looked at him.

What did you all think? That I'd just let you walk out on me, leaving me barely strong enough to survive, whilst you plunder my province? Eumenes drew his mount up at the head of the column, facing it a couple of paces from Diocles, a grey-bearded, brown-leather-skinned veteran of strong build and great age, who noticeably failed to salute him. 'Men, my men, where are you going?' Eumenes voice was high and clear in the crisp air.

'We're heading out on our own,' Diocles said. 'Seeing as we've been nothing but outlaws ravaging the country for this past year and more, we reckoned that we might as well just set up on our own and leave you to it, so as to speak; more for everyone that way, see?' His smile was gapped-toothed and rotten; it came nowhere near his eyes.

'So you all thought that you would go and plunder Kappadokia, my satrapy, did you?'

'Well, you ain't there at the moment, is you?'

'As soon as you started raiding then you would have found me there.'

'And besides, we heard that Antipatros had appointed his son, Nicanor, satrap, in your place.'

'He's not the legitimate satrap. I was appointed by Perdikkas, but I'm not here to bandy words with you.'

'What are you here for, then, Greek?'

'This!' In one fluid motion he pushed his mount forward, swept his sword out and, leaning out, sliced the tip across the veteran's throat.

It was with a look of complete surprise, and then bewilderment, that Diocles clasped his throat but that did nothing to stem the spillage of blood; shock registered on the faces of his junior officers, just behind him, and on the men in the forward ranks of the column. He started to sway, as if inebriated, a gurgle rose in his gorge as blood flowed freely down his leather cuirass. Knees buckled and down he went, legs twitching at a disconcerting pace.

'Seize them,' Eumenes shouted, pointing at the junior officers.

They made no attempt to resist arrest, as there was nowhere to hide from cavalry; nor did they struggle as, one by one, they had their heads struck off.

'They died well,' Eumenes declaimed, sitting on his horse over the headless bodies, 'but they died unnecessarily as a result of stupidity. Did you really think that I or Antigonos would allow you and Holcias' men to join up and ravage a part of the empire? It might even have brought us together for a temporary truce whilst we dealt with you and then it wouldn't have been these few lying here missing their heads, no, it would have been all of you to serve as a lesson to anyone else who thinks that they can take advantage of the civil war. Whatever happens, we will keep order in the empire because without order there is nothing to fight for; not for me, nor Antipatros or

Alketas or Antigonos; do you understand? Now, return to your duty and we'll say no more about it. But mark my words: Antigonos will deal with Holcias far more brutally than I have dealt with you.'

Antigonos.
The One-Eyed.

'T HE REPORTS WERE correct, Father. Leonidas is bringing them down from their camp now,' Demetrios reported, urging his mount to the top of the hill where Antigonos stood with his old friend, Philotas, looking east. 'The ruse has worked.'

Antigonos chuckled to himself, rubbing his hands together, as he looked up to the low cloud shrouding the uplands from where Holcias and his deserters had terrorised western Kappadokia. 'He's a good man, that Leonidas, he must have been very convincingly against me for them to trust him so quickly. Just four months and they elect him as their general. I wonder how he did it.'

Demetrios shrugged. 'Tempted them with a large prize, no doubt. What will you do to them?'

'I'll use them to out-sly that sly little Greek, that's what I'll do with them; now get your cavalry ready.'

Looking puzzled, Demetrios turned his mount and cantered off down to where a force of four thousand cavalry was formed up on the smooth plain of a river-valley – two thousand on either bank of the shallow, fast-flowing stream just ten paces wide.

Antigonos again chuckled to himself and then blew into his cupped palms, warming them against the mountain cold. 'The coming of winter affects me more with each passing year; it gets right into my joints.'

Philotas grunted. 'And that's not all it affects; at our age we're lucky if we can get an erection any time between the autumn and spring equinoxes.'

'Speak for yourself, old friend, I find a pair of warm and willing hands answer very well.' He looked at his pale fingers. 'I just wish I could keep mine warm.' But the temperature could not lower his spirits; things were finally coming together as he had hoped they would. He had, of course, protested in the strongest possible terms – as he would have been expected to – when Antipatros had ordered him to hand over the kings: loss of status for himself, bad for the morale of the men, takes away from the legitimacy of the Royal Army and a whole lot more besides, all convincingly argued and all, thankfully, rejected and he had submitted with gruff grace, a sour expression and joy coupled with relief in his heart. Antipatros was leaving Asia for good and the kings were to go with him – and with them the two harpies who clung to their flesh like things deranged. And, what was more, he was taking that sneaking brute, Kassandros, with him.

It had been the best day's work for a long time, ridding himself of all that baggage and being left in sole charge of the army of Asia; and now that Antipatros was on his way home, Antigonos was determined to deal with Eumenes and, preferably, bring him and his army onto his side for he could never have enough men and enough competent generals to lead them for what he had in mind; and there was no doubting that Eumenes had proved himself to be a very competent general indeed.

From down on the plain a horn sounded.

'The deserters must be in sight,' Philotas observed as the mounted force began to move forward; ranks and ranks of shieldless, lance-armed Macedonian heavy cavalry, whose combined smell, both human and equine, rose to their vantage point imbuing Antigonos with an even greater sense of well-being as it reminded him, vividly, of the pleasures of war.

He inhaled deep for a few moments and turned his face to the sky, revelling in life. 'We had better get going then, old friend.'

The two of them stalked down the hillside in the stiff-jointed manner of older men negotiating an uneven, treacherous surface. Down they struggled as the cavalry moved east along the valley at whose far, eastern, end a column of infantry, supported by a few cavalry, a very few cavalry, flowed down from the mist-wreathed hills.

As the column reached the valley floor, Demetrios' command moved from trot to canter and then to full gallop, covering the half league to the infantry quickly enough to prevent them forming into line; they were caught in the open by cavalry and, with very little horse of their own, their fate was obvious: surrender or be destroyed.

'Well done, Leonidas,' Antigonos said, a short while later, when he reached the captive troops, now all sitting on the ground, whispering amongst themselves and looking nervously around at the cavalry surrounding them. 'That was a fine performance.'

'Thank you, general,' Leonidas said as he rose and grasped his general's proffered forearm. 'Like most of these sorts of creatures, their greed was their downfall.'

'You treacherous bastard!' a voice shouted as Antigonos and Leonidas embraced.

'He may be a treacherous bastard to you, Holcias,' Antigonos agreed, 'but he's a loyal bastard to me. You are the treacherous bastard. Now shut your mouth before I lose my sense of benevolence.'

Holcias, a young officer who favoured Alexander's beardless look, glared at Leonidas and then Antigonos, but kept his mouth shut as advised.

Antigonos leaned closer to Leonidas' ear. 'I have another job for you over the winter, this time in Eumenes' camp at Nora; just find me one officer, preferably cavalry, who will turn for a reasonable amount of gold.'

'It will be my pleasure.'

'Discreet.'

'As always.'

'Good man.' Antigonos clapped him on the shoulder and then turned to address his prisoners. 'You are all treacherous bastards, every one of you. You all deserve summary execution, all of you, here and now.' He pointed to his cavalry all around them. 'They would tear you to pieces; it would only take my word.' To Antigonos' satisfaction none cried out to beg for their lives. *They know I'm right and they expect no less; well, this will surprise them.* 'But I'm not going to give that order. Not today and not any day, provided you take an oath each to your guardian gods: an oath that you will return directly to Macedon and never again set foot in Asia.'

This pronouncement drew looks of surprise from not only the prisoners but also from Antipatros' own men, especially Demetrios, who stared at his father aghast.

'That's right, you heard me correctly. You are free to go if you swear never to come back; do you accept?'

It did not take long for them to make up their minds and the cheering echoed around the bleak valley that, a few moments earlier, none of the deserters had thought they would leave alive.

'Why are you doing this, Father?' Demetrios asked as the oath was being administered.

Antigonos looked at his son, his one eye twinkling with amusement. 'Eumenes executed the ringleaders of the men who deserted him and then took the rest back into his service, splitting them up and distributing them around more reliable units. I've just shown myself to be more lenient than the sly little Greek in dealing with outlaws. Don't forget, Eumenes' men are all outlaws and can normally expect no mercy, but in allowing my outlaws to live it might make more than a few of his men think seriously about coming over to me; and when I get him to stand and face me, his men will be more inclined to surrender knowing that they will get fair treatment.' He gestured at the deserters as they repeated the oaths in front of makeshift altars made of shields set on upright javelins. 'And besides, what good are they to me? I can never trust them again and why would I want to dilute my crack troops as Eumenes had done? No, let these lads go back to Macedon where they can become yet another problem for Antipatros.' He rubbed his hands and chuckled again. 'Not a bad day's work, all in all. Now, Son, let's get out of these mountains and winter on the coast at Tarsus rather than freezing our balls off in Celaenae, assuming we can even get into it; I'm going to spend the winter practising the dark art of subversion with Leonidas whilst you can spend it nicely tucked up in bed with Phila.' He paused and frowned. 'I've been so preoccupied recently I haven't had time to ask you how married life is treating you.'

Demetrios shot his father a glance to see if he was making game of him. 'Very well, thank you,' he replied once he judged the question to be genuine. 'She's as compliant as I could wish although she does read too many books for my liking.'

'Does she now? You should put a stop to that. It doesn't do to allow a woman to be too highly educated; they start having opinions, you know.'

Demetrios nodded. 'Phila's already expressed a few of hers, mostly on literature; I have to say that they're way beyond me, although she does seem to take an interest when I talk to her about Alexander's campaigns and warfare in general.'

'Well, hopefully you'll have a lot to talk to her about in the spring once we've found that little Greek.'

'Eumenes' army is just over two leagues away, over that range of hills to the south-east,' the scout reported to Antigonos as he led his men north at the start of the campaigning season four months later.

'We mustn't let him pass,' Antigonos said after due consideration. 'Tell the scouts to pull back; I don't want Eumenes to know that we have found him and he makes a detour around us.' He looked down at a rough map of Anatolia, so basic as to be of little use, yet it was all he had; Philotas, Leonidas and Demetrios gathered around him. 'He's heading back to Phrygia to carry on raiding this season.' He turned to Leonidas. 'What's the nearest town to here?'

'Orcynia, about ten leagues to the north-west.'

'That'll be where he's aiming for then; we'll stop him there before he does any damage. We'll force-march before him; Demetrios, take your cavalry around his southern flank and get behind the little Greek, cutting him off from his base in Kappadokia. Philotas and I will bring the rest of the army to the gates of Orcynia as fast as we possibly can and offer battle in front of the town. No doubt Eumenes will try to deal with you and your cavalry first with his Kappadokians as he forms up the rest of his force to deal with us. He's going to be in for a nasty surprise.' He looked at Leonidas. 'Can you get a message to our man to tell him the timing of the plan?'

Leonidas smiled. 'I'll sneak into their camp tonight. Don't you worry, he'll be ready.'

Antigonos rubbed his hands together and chuckled softly. It was just as he had hoped it would be as, over the winter months, he had anxiously monitored Leonidas' progress; the price had been high but, if it worked out as it should, it would be worth it. Once Leonidas had reported the success of his mission, just as the snows of the interior had begun to melt so that the Taurus Mountain passes opened – and Demetrios had roused himself from Phila's bed – Antigonos had taken his army back north from Tarsus with a view to meeting Eumenes as he left his winter quarters in Kappadokia. In this he had been successful after just two days waiting close to the border, and now all he had to do was to form up his army before the gates of Orcynia and await his enemy's arrival. *With Demetrios cutting off his retreat, Eumenes will have to fight. Gods, it will be good; nothing better than starting off the season with a set-piece battle rather than dancing around each other for months on end. Still, I hope it's not too bloody as I need as many of his Macedonians to come over to me as possible; and, besides, I rather like the sly little Greek. He never did anything to offend me and I don't think he bears any animosity towards me. He could be a very useful ally.*

*

Antigonos looked east, through soft rain to see the vanguard of Eumenes' army approaching, two days after his scouts had first spotted it; it had been an exhausting time, force-marching his army to Orcynia, a forbidding-looking town of slab-like, grey-stone architecture of great antiquity that had nothing to recommend it other than he was able to choose his ground, at the top of a gentle slope, and stand in readiness for Eumenes' arrival. And here Eumenes now was with an army, according to his scouts and spies in the enemy camp, of twenty thousand infantry and almost five thousand horse. *We're very evenly matched in terms of numbers – for the moment, that is.*

As he watched, a group of horsemen split from the advancing army and kicked their mounts into a gallop; the lead man had a branch of truce tied to his lance. *So he sends to parley, does he? I wonder what he wants.*

'My lord Eumenes sends his greetings, sir,' the herald said, standing before Antigonos seated in a chair under a panoply rigged against the rain.

'Please return mine in turn.'

'Indeed I shall, sir. My lord Eumenes also wishes you and your kin health and long life.'

'Does he now? Does that mean he is surrendering to me without a battle?'

'Indeed not, sir, he just hopes that you and your kin will survive the battle that he very much regrets; but he sees it as a necessity unless you, sir, can see your way to surrendering.'

'He always did have a sense of humour, Eumenes,' Antigonos said with genuine affection. 'Go, return to him and tell him that I am more than willing to take his army under my command, convene an army assembly that would overturn his death sentence and then take him on as my second-in-command in Asia, restoring him officially to the satrapy of Kappadokia.' Antigonos waved the herald away. 'Return as soon as you have his answer.'

'Do you think he'll agree?' Philotas asked once the herald was heading back to Eumenes' camp, being erected half a league away.

'Of course not: he would lose all face. No, he has to fight but, seeing as that herald is going to come back, I plan a ruse that should, along with the defection, make his army quite willing to surrender after a few score casualties; and you, my friend, have a part to play.'

And as Antigonos explained to Philotas his part in the deception, the rain cleared and the sun broke through, warming the cold grey-stone walls of Orcynia with a late afternoon light, making the city seem somewhat less forbidding. All around the camp, cooking fires were set and the scent of wood smoke and grilled mutton wafted through the air as the men's voices grew louder with their evening wine ration lubricating their throats.

It was as Antigonos, now in his tent, drained his second cup of unwatered wine that the herald was announced again. Ushering Philotas out of the back of the tent, Antigonos received the herald alone.

The herald saluted, holding his branch of truce tied to his lance in the other hand. 'My lord very much regrets that he is unable to take advantage of your generous offer – for which he thanks you – for reasons he is sure that you will understand.'

Antigonos made no reply, just nodding.

'He asks you to consider,' the herald went on when he realised that Antigonos was only there to listen, 'that a great loss of blood could be averted if you could see your way to joining forces with him, as an equal partner, sharing command, in order to at least keep the empire in Asia from disintegrating. He would—'

'Antigonos,' Philotas said, striding into the tent in a state of excitement. 'They're in sight; they were spotted just now. They'll be with us before the moon rises.'

Antigonos stood and downed his wine. 'Excellent, old friend, is it the number we were expecting?'

'If anything it is more but only infantry.'

'More? Even better.' He looked back to the herald. 'You were saying?'

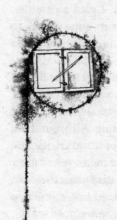

EUMENES.
THE SLY.

'I DON'T BELIEVE IT,' Eumenes asserted.

'I assure you, my lord, that's what he said, the reinforcements were in sight and there were more of them than they expected – all infantry. They will be in their camp by moonrise.'

Eumenes waved his hand in irritation. 'No, no, I'm sure you're right, I believe that's what was said; I just don't believe it was the truth. One of his officers, probably Philotas judging by your description, comes in whilst an enemy herald is being interviewed and gives away a piece of sensitive information just like that? No, I don't believe that at all; it's a ruse to make me think I'm grossly outnumbered and to get me to surrender without a fight. Well, I'll not fall for it.' He turned to his dinner companions, Hieronymus, Xennias, Parmida and Apollonides, all seated around the camp fire with him. 'What say you?'

'I agree,' Xennias said, with complete conviction. 'It was too much of a set-up; no one would let a piece of information like that slip in front of an enemy herald.'

'No one but a fool,' Parmida cautioned, 'but we know Antigonos not to be a fool so if it were genuine he would have reprimanded the officer rather than question him further.'

'Unless he wants us to know that he really has got reinforcements in order to avoid a battle,' Apollonides put in. 'After all, you yourself said you don't really understand why you and

Antigonos are fighting now that Antipatros has gone back to Europe with the kings.'

'Yes, that's true.'

'Whether it is true or not,' Hieronymus said, 'it has caused confusion and doubt and I would hazard a guess that that is what it was meant to do; therefore, I would say it is misinformation planted for that very purpose.'

Eumenes stared into the fire for a while, enjoying the patterns in the glowing logs. 'Ultimately,' he said eventually, 'it doesn't matter whether it's the truth or not; I still have to face him in the morning and with my cavalry superiority I don't have to worry too much about his infantry numbers. No, gentlemen, we can choose to believe it or not, for the present; however, tomorrow shall show us the truth of the matter.'

'The phalanx's frontage must be at least two thousand paces,' Xennias observed as they sat on their horses, watching Antigonos' army form up, soon after dawn the following morning.

'That can't be,' Eumenes said, refusing to believe what his eyes were witnessing fifteen hundred paces further up the gentle slope at its summit. 'That would mean he has something in the region of thirty-two thousand men.'

'They must have been telling the truth about the reinforcements then.'

Eumenes stared, incredulous, at the phalanx as Antigonos' peltasts and cavalry deployed to cover the huge formation's flanks; light troops came swarming from between the files and fanned out, left and right, ready to skirmish when the two armies rumbled towards one another. 'I still can't believe it.' He glanced over his shoulder at his own phalanx at little less than half the size of what it faced: the concern was obvious on the faces of the men closest to him. *They won't stand in the face of that; especially as they know that Antigonos didn't execute his deserters last year.* He looked to each flank, formed of Thracian, Paphlagonian, Bithynian and other mercenary infantry, almost five thousand on either, and then to Xennias' and Apollonides' Macedonian

Companion cavalry on the left flank and his own Kappadokians on the right, both supported by light cavalry of various sorts. *It'll have to be the cavalry and mercenary infantry who win it, if I am to win at all; I'll refuse with my centre, retreating the phalanx facing the enemy and then send the cavalry and infantry mercenaries around the flanks of this monster. If I can seize his baggage, as I did with Neoptolemus, then there is a good chance...* But Eumenes' train of thought was cut short by movement on his left wing: his Companion cavalry were advancing towards the enemy. 'Why are they attacking, Xennias? Who gave the order?'

Xennias looked bemused as he watched Apollonides lead his own and Xennias' men, almost four thousand in total, up the hill, changing from a trot to a canter as they reached the halfway point between the two armies.

And then the ghastly reality of the situation hit Eumenes as Antigonos' men let rip a mighty roar that was acknowledged by the horsemen waving their lances in the air. 'They're deserting, the bastards. Xennias, what do you know about this?'

Xennias shook his head, his eyes betraying his total surprise. 'Nothing, sir, I've had no hint of it from any of my lads and I very rarely talk to Apollonides' men.'

Apollonides and his deserters reached the Antigonoid line and turned; horns rang out and the great army lumbered forward, down the hill.

Without that cavalry, I'm lost. 'Sound the retreat facing the enemy!' Eumenes shouted to his signaller waiting behind him, sharing the terrified look that was now on most of his men's faces.

The call was long and clear and repeated throughout the army and was received with the greatest relief; back they went, pace by pace in the face of the force now coming down the slope at a good pace. Eumenes did not move; he was transfixed: something felt very wrong. And then, as the opposing phalanx came down the slope and it could be viewed at an angle, seeing over the heads of the first ranks, he saw it. 'It's only eight deep!' he shouted at Xennias and Parmida. 'The bastard's tricked us: he's formed up his phalanx at half the depth so it looks twice the size. We can still win this.' He turned to his signaller. 'Sound halt!'

The signal rang out, repeated all along the line, but it was too late: confusion ruled as many of the units did not believe – or want to believe – the order and carried on the retreat whilst other, steadier, units stood to face the enemy; thus the army disintegrated.

And Antigonos unleashed his cavalry.

Down they came, furies from the mouth of Hades, shrieking their triumph at the sight of a disordered and confused army; the three thousand that had originally been with Antigonos plus the four thousand deserters descended upon the flanks of Eumenes' army with the relish of killers seizing upon a defence-less target.

Eumenes took one look and knew that all was lost. *I must save what I can.* 'Parmida, Xennias, with me; we must at least get the Kappadokians out of this!' Turning his horse, he galloped to where his elite cavalry unit waited in silence despite the wave of death surging down the hill towards them. But the sight of that incoming horde was too much for the mercenaries and they turned their backs and fled; as Eumenes sped away with his Kappadokians, Antigonos' cavalry crashed into the fleeing infantry and a great slaughter commenced whilst in the centre, the phalanx sat down in surrender.

Betrayed and bamboozled all in one morning, Eumenes mused as he led his favoured cavalry away from the carnage, *I must be losing my touch; and there was me thinking that I was an intelligent person with a degree of intuition. It's put me right in the mood for administering a deliciously slow death to Apollonides. But all in good time; first I need to get out of this mess.*

It was as the sun reached its zenith that Eumenes judged it safe to call a halt to the headlong flight and assess the situation on a hilltop not far from the Kappadokian border.

'Most of our horse-archers,' Xennias reported after a head-count, 'about half of the Paphlagonian light cavalry and the same proportion of the Thracians have followed us out as well as dribs and drabs of other mercenary light cavalry; about two thousand in all, plus the six hundred Kappadokians.'

'Two thousand six hundred out of twenty thousand,' Eumenes said. Although the number did not surprise him, hearing it stated was sobering indeed. 'The phalanx surrendered entirely so that leaves about eight thousand dead; once he had the phalanx in his hands he would have slaughtered any mercenaries so that he wouldn't have to pay them and they couldn't go and fight for someone else. I know how the Macedonian military mind works and it's far from being a thing of beauty; present company excluded, Xennias, naturally.'

'Naturally, sir.'

Eumenes looked around at the groups of bedraggled cavalrymen rubbing down their sweat-foamed mounts, or trying to light fires with damp wood with the view to a midday meal. 'And, no doubt, he captured all of our baggage?'

'I'm afraid so, sir. He's even captured Hieronymus. He's got everything we own.'

'Well, that will buy the phalanx's loyalty for him.' Eumenes checked himself. 'No, I mustn't be bitter, however much I might enjoy it. Who can blame them, after all?' He looked at Xennias and then Parmida. 'So, gentlemen, we need a course of action. Antigonos will, no doubt, follow up his victory by chasing us all the way back to Kappadokia in an attempt to capture me, thus ending the war in the north. Well, let us help him in his endeavours. Xennias, you lead the rest of the men back to Kappadokia, we'll meet up back at the fortress at Nora.'

'Nora it is, sir.'

'As soon as you get there collect firewood and anything edible in the surrounding area; the fort has been re-provisioned since we left, but who knows how long we might be forced to stay there if Antigonos decides it's worth his while to besiege it.'

'It'll be done by the time you arrive from wherever you're going; which is where?'

'I'm going to take Parmida and his Kappadokians, along with the horse-archers and circle back around Antigonos. He'll have left my mercenary dead where they fell in his hurry to chase me; if I don't see to it that they receive a decent funeral and send them over the Styx in good order I'll never be able to hire another soldier again. And then,' he paused for a vicious smile, 'I'm going to kill Apollonides just to make me feel a little better about myself.'

And it was with the feeling of pent-up excitement at vengeance being nigh that Eumenes, cloaked and deep-hooded, walked through Antigonos' camp the following night. It had been as he had suspected: the dead had lain thick on the plain before Orcynia, a feast for carrion birds and flies. With no ceremony, he sent his men into the town and conscripted its inhabitants – after the summary execution of the half dozen or so, refusing in overloud voices – to help build sixteen great pyres, each containing five hundred corpses, all with a coin under their tongue for the Ferryman; the coinage had been forced from the citizens on the basis that the corpses had been robbed and it was in all likelihood their own money being returned. The smoke they had raised still tinged his clothes as Eumenes made his way towards the heart of the camp with the victorious army sitting around a myriad of blazing fires, drinking to their own health and toasting their luck at capturing the entire baggage train of the defeated foe. Loud was their boasting and singing; intense was their rutting with the new batch of camp followers freshly fallen into their hands who, for the most part, cared not who swived them so long as they were paid, fed and sheltered – and not beaten with undue frequency.

It was through this chaos that Eumenes passed unremarked, a small figure in the midst of thousands, stepping with care over drunken bodies, fornicating couples or groups, waving cheerfully at wineskins extended towards him and declining them in a gruff, disguised voice, making his way ever closer to the heart of the camp where his quarry would have his temporary dwelling. He stroked the knife in its scabbard beneath his cloak. Long and slender it was and double-edged, so that it could slip between ribs with barely a falter: an assassin's weapon; one that gave Eumenes much pleasure.

So it was that he came to the huge pavilion dominating the centre of the camp: Antigonos' headquarters; the place where all his officers would be feasting, congratulating their commander on his stunning victory through treachery and a cunning ruse. *Let them celebrate; they deserve it, all of them except one.* Finding a corner of deep shadow between two tents, Eumenes sat down to keep watch on the pavilion entrance guarded by two bulky phalangites silhouetted by the light that poured from within.

It would be a long wait, of that Eumenes was sure, but better to be early than to miss Apollonides and to risk having to repeat the process the following evening. No, the following evening Eumenes fully intended to be back, safe, in Nora; for it was within the safety of that impregnable redoubt that he would be able to wait out events and, perhaps, receive aid from his unwilling would-be-allies, Alketas and Attalus – although this was an unlikely eventuality. No, it was not aid that he was waiting for but, rather, death: a specific death, that of Antipatros. Eumenes had seen the will to live drain from the face of the old regent as he had grieved for his son, Iollas. He was certain that the event would not be long postponed and when it came...well, who knew what ructions and shifts of allegiance it would cause. From his bolthole in Nora, Eumenes would be able to watch the turn of the tide below him and, who knew, even end up emerging onto firm, dry land.

But that was in the future and there, in the present, Eumenes tensed and forgot his schemes as the object of his immediate attention came within view, laughing with an officer, someone he felt he vaguely recognised, as they both left the pavilion. Right they turned and walked along the torch-lit main thoroughfare of the camp – if such a disordered, haphazard affair could be said to have a main thoroughfare – all the while joking as if they were old friends. Eumenes pulled his hood deeper over his face and followed, trying to keep as much in the shadow as was possible without conspicuously weaving out of the light.

After a while they paused. 'I bid you good night, my friend,' the dimly remembered officer said, as they clasped forearms. 'You will find Antigonos a very generous man as what is waiting for you in your tent will prove.'

'I have no doubt of it, Leonidas,' Apollonides said, 'far more generous than the sly little Greek.'

That's just where you're wrong, you traitorous piece of shit; I've got a very special gift for you, one that will last forever.

The men parted, Leonidas walking further along the thoroughfare and Apollonides entering a leather tent, round with a central pole, the type reserved for officers. With a smile, Eumenes crossed to the neighbouring tent, snuck around it and settled down in the shadows behind Apollonides' to wait. He did not wait long for soon the light seeping out from under the sides faded and the low moans of a woman being pleasured began to rise within, growing steadily, climbing slowly to a rousing crescendo of ecstasy that was interspersed with a series of deep, masculine grunts. The sound of deep breathing was not long in following.

After waiting in the shadows for as long as he could bear, Eumenes lifted the leather enough to be able to see the interior, lit by a small nightlight; dimly he could make out the camp bed: judging by the shape, the woman was still there. *That makes matters a little more complicated; it's a shame for her, of course, but these things can't be helped.* He drew his blade, crept around to where he judged the bed to be closest to the edge of the tent and, lifting the leather, rolled under it. He was in; lying still he held his breath, listening to the sound of sleep. Satisfied that both were undisturbed by his entrance, he got to his feet and, with utmost stealth, went to the head of the bed.

It was quick, so quick her body hardly tensed: one hand over her mouth as the blade slid into her eye and pierced her brain; with a couple of twists of the wrist he made mush of the organ. As soon as it was done he knelt by Apollonides' side, and, clamping a hand over his mouth, pricked the side of his neck with the needle-like tip of his blade. His eyes sprang open.

'Good evening, Apollonides,' Eumenes whispered, the muscles in his arm tensing as he struggled to keep his hand compressed tight on the man's face. 'Now hold very still, we wouldn't want this blade to slip; look what it did to your lovely girlfriend.' He pushed Apollonides' head to one side so that he could see the woman lying on her back with blood slowly oozing from the savaged eye socket. 'Now, much as I'm tempted to ask you why you betrayed me, I think that I'll just have to curb my curiosity as I imagine that the only answer you'll give me if I take my hand away is a loud scream for help.' Eumenes took pleasure in seeing Apollonides' eyes stare at him, wide with panic. 'So instead, I'm going to tell you my theory and you can answer or not with your eyes: I think that you were offered a lot of money, probably by that man who you said goodnight to this evening. Thinking about it he does seem familiar from this winter in Nora. But I suppose it doesn't matter who was the go-between because the end result was the same: you accepted because, despite all you were saying last year about remaining loyal to me because I was your general and you didn't care that I wasn't a Macedonian, you felt that loyalty to a Greek could be discarded for money whereas loyalty to a Macedonian was much more about personal honour. Am I right?'

Apollonides' eyes showed neither admission of guilt or denial; he just lay there, his body stiff.

Eumenes shrugged and punched his blade up under the jaw. 'Well, ultimately, what do I care?' He looked down into a pain-filled face as the back arched and the legs juddered. 'But at least you got to see me before you met the Ferryman.' He twisted the blade, again shredding the brain. 'Although, not for very long, that's for sure, which is a shame for you but a pleasure for me as the sight of you, even dead, makes me feel sick.'

Pulling the blade from Apollonides' skull he wiped it on the blanket, stood and then took a scroll from a pouch hanging from his belt and laid it on the dead man's chest.

*

'"See you at Nora, with a man short,"' Antigonos shouted up at the fortress walls waving the scroll. 'Very witty.'

'Yes, I thought so too,' Eumenes replied, looking down at the small party on the bare rocks below under a branch of truce. 'Although, if I were you I don't think I could have trusted someone who could be bought for mere money so consider his death a favour from me to you.'

'Why, thank you, Eumenes. You've always been known for your unselfish conduct. But it wasn't mere money that bought Apollonides; it was a lot of money.'

'It was still money. But that's all in the past now; I had my revenge as you saw and thoroughly enjoyed it. It was a shame about the girl but, at least, judging from the noise she had been making, she died well fucked.'

Antigonos grinned. 'She was one of my favourites.' He waved her memory away. 'So, Eumenes, are you going to come out of there and talk to me face to face?'

'What guarantee do I have for my safety?'

Antigonos beckoned a middle-aged man forward. 'This is Polemaeus, my nephew. You know him. He stays in the fortress for as long as you sit with me; fair enough.'

'Your nephew's life wouldn't concern the Exile-Hunter; not that I've seen him since he tried to kill me at Sardis.'

'That's because he's disappeared; no one's seen him or his fox-fuckers.'

Eumenes thought for a moment. 'Very well, Antigonos, I'll come and parley.'

'But there is one condition: that you don't—'

'Keep on finishing your sentences for you. Agreed.'

It was with surprising warmth that they embraced; indeed, Eumenes was genuinely pleased to see an old friend after twelve years, despite the fact that he had refused Perdikkas' orders to help him to take Kappadokia, not to mention the recent defeat in battle.

'So, my friend,' Antigonos said after they had been made comfortable beneath an awning, with wine and stuffed vine-leaves, 'are you really going to live in there for ever?'

'Eventually I'll have to come out, but it will be a long time yet.' Eumenes looked around at the crowd, gathering now that word had got around Antigonos' men that the sly little Greek, the killer of Krateros, was talking with their general. 'I seem to be an object of some curiosity; have they never seen a Greek of less than average height before?'

'Many, but not one still in possession of both his legs.'

Eumenes raised his cup and drank to the humour.

'So if you won't come out—'

'And be subject to an execution order from the army assembly.'

'What if I could get that removed?'

'Then we could talk again; you know where to find me. I've supplies for over a year and the world may well be a different place by then. I've dismissed most of the surviving elements of my army with grateful thanks for the loyalty they had shown me – I'd be obliged if when you come across them you would employ them rather than murder them.'

'It depends whether they're any use to me.'

'Oh, they're all good lads, as were the eight thousand you managed to slaughter at Orcynia, had you bothered to have a word with them first.'

'Giving them a funeral was a nice touch; you earnt the respect of a lot of my men.'

'It wasn't their respect I was after, but I thank them anyway.' He raised his cup to the growing audience and was rewarded with a stone whistling just past his right ear; another followed, far better aimed, taking him in the shoulder.

'Murderer!' came the cry. 'You killed Krateros!'

More stones fizzed towards him as the crowd began to close in.

'Get back!' Antigonos shouted, 'Get back, you idiots. Another step and every one of you I can recognise is a dead man!'

The advance halted, but the stones did not; Eumenes was forced into the undignified position of having to hold his chair before him as a shield.

Antigonos went to stand in front of him, arms outstretched. When the first stone hit his back and he turned to face the men, glaring in his full fury, the fight went out of them and they slunk back. 'I didn't realise just how much animosity the lads still bear you,' Antigonos said as he led Eumenes, a protective arm around his shoulders, back up the steep path to Nora. 'You had better get back into the fortress, if only for your own safety.'

Eumenes gave a wry smile. 'You were saying something earlier about having the death sentence removed?'

Antigonos grunted. 'So you're not going to come out and I'm going to be forced to lay siege to this lump of rock.'

'No one's forcing you.'

'You know perfectly well what I mean. Well now, I'll leave Leonidas here, in charge of the siege; I'm going back west to deal with your friends Alketas and Attalus.'

'They're not my friends although, I admit, I did want them to be.'

'Yes, you seem to be rather short of friends at the moment; I've even got Hieronymus in my camp.'

'You keep him for the time being, he'll enjoy witnessing events from your perspective.'

'He does; I've told him all about your sneaking little ways and a lot more besides about all the others.'

Eumenes laughed as the fortress gates opened and Polemaeus walked out. He gripped Antigonos' proffered forearm. 'You hurry back west, Antigonos, and don't you worry about me as you go after Alketas and Attalus. I'll be fine all tucked up nice and warm in this fortress. Come back when you've dealt with those arrogant, ignorant bastards – perhaps you could do me the favour of giving them a slow and painful death seeing as it's partially because of them that I'm here. Come back later on in the year as you may find that we have more things in common than we do now once Antipatros is having a nice little chat with the Ferryman.'

ANTIPATROS.
THE REGENT.

IT WAS A bleak place, high on the cliff. It was bleak despite the warm sunshine and the sea glistering below, far below, stretching away into a deep blue distance. However, it was not bleak because of any device of nature: it was bleak because Antipatros had made it so in his mind, for here, just separate from those of the rest of his family, he had raised the tomb of his son, Iollas. Here, before the sombre edifice, the height of two men and with depictions of its young occupier in battle, at hunt and relaxing in the symposium, cup in one hand, a poetic text in the other, did Antipatros come to weep most days. Here he felt the years press heavy upon him; here he knew, before long, his bones too would rest for he was tired of life and desired nothing but peace. Peace: that was a word that echoed constantly around his head. Peace, how he longed for it, for nothing seemed to give him joy in the world anymore, not even in the arms of Hyperia, his wife, could he find the comfort that would banish the grief he felt for Iollas. But it was not only grief that tormented him; far from it: it was also guilt. The guilt he felt, in every waking hour, and no doubt also in the subconsciousness of sleep; guilt for having made the war against Eumenes a personal affair about his honour and thus not ending it when, from a business sense, it had become pointless. And as he grieved for Iollas, he also wished, with all his heart, that it had been Kassandros who had died and not his younger brother, for he could but feel that Iollas was worth ten of his older sibling. For Kassandros' death would open the way for Nicanor and then…well, then his burden would lessen.

But it was not so: Iollas had passed beyond the Styx and Kassandros still inhabited the realm of the living, watching over Antipatros with barely concealed impatience; for he, too, knew that his father was soon to die and thought only of the benefits it would bring to himself. So now Antipatros knew he would have to make the hardest decision of his life; and, as he sat on a rock gazing, with eyes weighed with sorrow, at the tomb, he struggled to see how the result of what he knew he had to do could be anything other than to bring the civil war into Macedon itself. For he realized that Kassandros would not take being passed over with a mild shrug of the shoulders and heart-felt congratulations to the man who had usurped – as Kassandros would see it – his rightful inheritance.

That the regency was not a hereditary title would not be understood by Kassandros; he would see it as his right, as the elder son, to have whatever his father possessed at the time of his death, his unsuitability to the position never occurring to him. Antipatros gave a rueful smile as he reflected that should Kassandros actually realise his unsuitability to the task that might, ironically, make him far more suitable.

With a sigh he got to his feet, pushing down with his hands down on swollen knees to ease the action, walked across to the tomb and laid a hand upon it. 'I should never have sent you up into those hills, Iollas; I can never forgive myself for doing so.' Another surge of grief passed through him followed by the inevitable guilt as the irresistible wish that Kassandros had been there to lead the scouts came unbidden to his mind and, kissing the cold stone, he turned and walked away to where his horse and groom awaited him.

'You must eat, my dear,' Hyperia said in her gentlest, most wifely voice. 'Just looking at the lamb won't bring you any sustenance.'

Antipatros roused himself out of his reverie. 'Sorry, Hyperia, what did you say?'

Hyperia stretched a hand across the couch they shared and stroked his forearm. 'I said that you must eat.'

'I know I must, but everything tastes the same; there's no joy in food anymore for me.'

'Come, Father,' Kassandros said from the other side of the table where he sat on the couch with Polyperchon reclining next to him. 'Eat, whether the food tastes or not, or you will certainly waste away.'

And how you would love that. Antipatros picked up a chop and ripped the flesh from it if only to help him stay alive a little longer and, therefore, postpone the inevitable. As he chewed he looked over to Polyperchon, bald and in his sixties, with a non-descript, round face, uneventful eyes and a mild manner. He was a thorough second-in-command: reliable and with a good, if pedantic, attention to detail – Krateros himself had chosen him to be his own number two, and that was praise indeed – but a great follower does not always make for a charismatic leader, and it was a leader with charisma that Macedon would need to prevent Kassandros from stealing first the regency and then, the gods forbid, the throne. The throne that belonged to his child-hood friend, Philip, the second of that name, and then to his son, Alexander; the throne that he, Antipatros, had been charged with preserving for the heirs of the Argead line; the throne that he suspected Kassandros coveted – he had, after all, stolen the Great Ring of Macedon from Perdikkas' dead hand. Shame would be brought upon their house for ever should Kassandros achieve that ambition and steal the throne that he, Antipatros, was honour-bound to preserve.

No, it would be Polyperchon to whom he would pass the regency; it would probably be a death sentence for him, but what alternative was there? Should he give it to Nicanor, then he would be dooming one of his sons to murder the other; all the other possibilities were far less suitable and the kings themselves were unfit to rule. Adea or Roxanna would rule for their own

202

ends each, trying to assassinate the other and, besides, the Macedonian aristocracy and army would not accept them. Adea had made another attempt to seize power as the army had journeyed back to Europe, protesting in the name of her husband, Philip, about the men's conditions. Again the troops had mutinied over their pay, or lack of it; but this time Antipatros had just walked away, crossing the Hellespont in secret and returning to Macedon. Once the army had realised that they were stranded and Adea had no answers to the problems they faced, they slunk back across to Europe and begged forgiveness from Antipatros, leaving the young agitator as a spent and broken force; no, she could never rule now. And nor could her bitter rival, Roxanna, excluded because of her outlandish foreignness.

So that just left Olympias, who would bring nothing but vengeance and death. Antipatros put down his cleaned bone and took another chop, shaking his head with regret. *It has to be Polyperchon. I will write to Antigonos, Lysimachus and even Ptolemy and Eumenes begging them to support him against Kassandros. Perhaps with their help Polyperchon can survive long enough for the young Alexander to come of age. But what then? He would be in the power of Roxanna, his mother, and his grandmother, Olympias; what chance would Macedon have then? But at least my line will be spared the dishonour of stealing what I have been charged to preserve.*

'I'm told that Athens is sending an embassy, Father,' Kassandros said, his tone casual as he flicked a morsel of lamb fat off his finger, hitting a slave on the chest.

'You hear correctly,' Antipatros replied with little enthusiasm.

'Concerning our garrison in the Munychia fortress at Piraeus, no doubt?'

'It's all they ever think about. There is a faction, an unrealistic faction, who believe that they can persuade me to remove our troops from the city, knowing that if I did so then many of the democratic exiles would return and the oligarchy would fall, to be replaced by the irresponsible lunacy of democracy.'

Polyperchon nodded, chewing thoughtfully. 'It's democracy that got them into the position they're in now: allowing the vote to people with nothing to their names, who therefore have nothing to lose, breeds suicidal foreign policies.'

Antipatros put down his half-eaten chop, took a green olive and examined it before nibbling on it. 'My old friend Phocion appreciates that, which is why he refused to head the delegation; he wrote to me apologising for the naivety of the anti-Macedon faction in thinking that I would remove the garrison as a mark of respect for him and our late friend Aristotle, thus opening the way for a return to democracy.' He surprised everyone around the table by chortling, the first sign of any mirth since Iollas' death. 'Phocion was schooled by Plato and so understands intimately the follies of that bizarre system.'

Kassandros led the conversation in the manner of one who has a particular destination in mind. 'So if Phocion's not coming, who will head the delegation?'

He knows the answer to that already; what's he planning? 'Phocion said in his letter that Demades has volunteered for the task, along with his son, Demeas. Demades thinks that because he's such a loyal supporter of mine and actively works to get pro-Macedon legislation through the assembly and prosecutes many of his fellow citizens who are making life difficult for me, then I might favour his embassy.'

'Did you say loyal, Father?'

Antipatros looked at his son, frowning. *Ah, so this is it, is it?* 'What do you know?'

Kassandros gave a vicious smile – it was one of the many characteristics that Antipatros found distasteful about his son. 'Just after he was murdered, I slipped into Perdikkas' tent.'

'And stole his ring, I know.'

Kassandros was astounded. 'Who told you?'

Antipatros looked at the item in question on his forefinger. 'Just about everyone; but go on.'

'Well, I had time to look around the place and open a few chests and rummage through some private letters.'

Antipatros found it impossible to criticise Kassandros for this breach of privacy. 'I don't blame you.'

Hyperia added her approval. 'After all, knowledge is power.'

'Indeed. And I gleaned some knowledge which will give us power over Demades.'

'What?'

'A letter, well, three to be precise; they were all bundled together. The first was from Demades to Perdikkas; the second was a copy of Perdikkas' reply and the third was Demades' response to that.'

Antipatros was interested, very. 'And?'

'And in the first one Demades describes you as "a piece of old and rotting rope" that ties down the once glorious city of Athens in spiteful servitude. He then proposes an alliance to overthrow your regency, the armies of the Greek city states and Perdikkas' working in tandem.'

'The treacherous bastard; after all the money I've passed his way. What did Perdikkas say?'

'Well, he was interested, naturally, considering how things were between you at the time, but he wrote saying that if they thought that he would withdraw the garrisons they were sadly deluded.'

'Well, at least he got one thing right,' Polyperchon said, licking his fingers.

'Yes. And then, in the third letter, Demades suggests that if Perdikkas was to declare the freedom of the Greeks, taking away the yoke of Macedon, he would have very willing allies.'

Both Antipatros and Polyperchon choked at the sheer scale of the lie.

'Who would slip a knife into your back as soon as it was turned,' Antipatros said, once he had managed to control himself.

'Even if you have a Greek by the balls and ask him what his favourite colour is,' Polyperchon pointed out, 'you can't be sure that his answer is the truth.'

'Why haven't you told me about these letters before?'

Kassandros shrugged. 'Because they weren't relevant before as we were dealing with the problems in Asia; Europe was relatively quiet. But now we're back I think we would do well to make people realise that we're still in control. What would you like me to do about this, Father?'

'I would like you to make what little is left of Demades' life as unpleasant as possible, but, unfortunately, we can't do that.'

'Why not?'

'Because if we're to have any moral authority over the Greek states then we have to act within the law; so seize him and his son as soon as they arrive and we shall put them on trial so that all can see the impartiality of justice in Macedon. Have Deinarchos, the Corinthian, prosecute them as he is presently in the city; he has always been a loyal friend to me and can be relied upon for a just verdict.'

'And these three letters,' Deinarchos declaimed, holding up the offending items one by one. 'These three letters are all that are needed to prove beyond any doubt, the treachery of Demades and his son, Demeas.' Deinarchos looked around the fifty jurors sat on benches in the court in the agora. 'These are evidence of a deliberate approach to Perdikkas, offering an alliance against Antipatros, the regent of Macedon.' With a dramatic flourish he extended an arm towards Antipatros. 'Palpable treason as Athens is subject to Macedon and Antipatros was at the time and still is the regent of Macedon.'

Antipatros felt a shortness of breath as Deinarchos read through each of the letters in turn and then submitted them to Kassandros, the president of the court, for him to pass around the jurors for perusal. He rubbed his chest and looked across to Demades and Demeas, both of whom had been apprehended the moment they had arrived in Pella. Demades, still a richly dressed, portly dandy despite being close to seventy and bald, was a veteran of many a show trial and he sat with an amused expression, occasionally taking notes. Antipatros enjoyed the symmetry of him now being the accused as it had been Demades who had secured the death sentence for his compatriots, Demosthenes and Hyperides, at

Antipatros' behest and for a very handsome fee, just four years previously. Having taken his money, Demades was getting nothing less than he deserved for throwing it back in Antipatros' face.

Demeas, an elegant and perfumed playboy in his late twenties, the product of a liaison between his father and a notorious flute girl, was looking far less relaxed than Demades; sweat stained his fine linen tunic, a pastel blue with rich embroidery around the hem and sleeves and he continually ran his hand through his oiled curls that fell to his shoulders. *You thought you were coming here on a mission of glory, taking me for granted, young pup, instead you are going to be beginning your final journey.* Antipatros winced as another sharp pain struck his chest; his breathing grew shorter and faster for a few moments before settling down again.

'You are nothing but a Macedonian shrill,' Demades shouted over Deinarchos' long list of other outrages, some true but mostly false, committed by him over the course of his long career of bribe-taking as he worked his way up in life from a mere rower in the Athenian navy. 'A shrill, do you hear? A shrill wielding a thunderbolt borrowed from Zeus because you have no weapon of your own to throw at me. Why are we all wasting our time with this trial when you could have got any tavern-keeper on the road up here to slip a knife between my ribs?' He turned to address Antipatros. 'Or what about your Exile-Hunter, Archias, Antipatros?' He slapped his forehead, theatrically. 'But of course, I forgot: Archias was persuaded to go to Ptolemy's court in Tyros to chat about his role in procuring the poison that Kassandros took to Babylon with him; you know, the poison that Iollas murdered Alexander with.'

As the court erupted in outrage, Antipatros felt his chest tighten again; he drew some quick, shallow breaths. *So that's where he disappeared to; Ptolemy's getting him to corroborate the lies in* The Last Days and Testament of Alexander.

'This seems to me to be a grievous error, Antipatros,' Demades went on through the din. 'It seems to me that it shouldn't be me and my son on trial here but, rather, you and your son on trial for murder; for the murder of Alexander himself.'

This was too much for the jurors, who stood and pointed at the accused pair. 'Guilty! Guilty!' they chanted. Demeas turned to his father in terror but Demades just sat there with the contented look of a man who, on the verge of death, has just sown his last and greatest piece of mischief, for he knew that the reports of this trial would travel throughout the Hellenistic world.

Antipatros gasped and held his chest again as Kassandros pronounced a sentence of death and immediately took matters into his own hands, walking forward with a drawn sword.

With rough handling, Demeas was pushed to his knees by the guards; with no ceremony and a force fuelled by rage, belying his puny frame, Kassandros struck off his head before the horrified eyes of his father that were soon blinded by a powerful spray of warm blood as Demeas' oiled locks wafted to the ground.

To see a son die before your eyes! He did not deserve that, Kassandros; that was cruel for cruelty's sake. If I had a shred of doubt before, it has gone now: you cannot rule. Again another streak of pain shot through Antipatros' chest; he gasped and cried out loud, his cry going unnoticed as Demades' head fell from his shoulders. He struggled to stand and cried aloud once more before the paved stone ground rose to punch him in the face.

'Give him room to breathe, my lady,' a voice said coming out of the darkness. 'He's coming round. If he has enough air he will be fine.'

But Antipatros knew that was not to be the case for he was coming back but not for long; he had one last job to do before his appointment with the Ferryman. He opened his eyes.

'Husband,' Hyperia said, as the doctor peered into Antipatros' eyes. 'I was so worried.'

With a feeble wave, Antipatros dismissed the doctor. 'Don't be, Hyperia, I'm quite fine in my mind. Call Kassandros, Polyperchon and all the heads of the senior families.'

'They're already here, waiting below.' She turned to the doctor. 'Call them in; all of them.'

'But my lady—'

'Just do as I say!'

The sharpness of her tone overcame any medical objections and soon the room was full of people.

Antipatros took the Great Ring of Macedon from his finger and viewed it through dim eyes, then surveyed the faces of those around his bed: Hyperia, Kassandros and Polyperchon; the heads of the high families were arranged behind them; he felt his strength seeping away and his breath fade and then made one last effort. 'Kassandros, you must bear this well.'

'Yes, Father, I will.'

'You are to be the second-in-command to Polyperchon.' He passed the ring to his deputy. 'Polyperchon, in front of witnesses, I name you Regent of Macedon and of the two kings.' He wheezed a couple of shallow breaths, gathering his little remaining strength for a last word. 'Do not ever let Macedon be ruled by a woman.'

KASSANDROS.
THE JEALOUS.

I T WAS FURY, raw, blind fury that raged through Kassandros as his father's hand slumped back down, leaving an astounded Polyperchon holding the Great Ring of Macedon. Fury as Antipatros' eyes glazed over, the light of life fading from them beyond the point of recall. But recalled he must be to redress this terrible injustice.

'Father!' Kassandros shrieked into the immobile face of the man who had just robbed him of his inheritance. 'Father! Father!' He slapped Antipatros across the right cheek and then backhanded the left, back and forth until rough hands hauled him, screaming, from the body. 'Put me down! Father! Father!' He wrenched himself free and turned to the corpse, his eyes flooded with unmanly tears. 'I'm your son; not this old mediocrity.' He twisted and slammed a punch at Polyperchon, who dodged it.

'Restrain him,' Hyperia ordered, her voice shrill but commanding as she backed away from her stepson now lashing out in all directions.

The same rough hands grabbed Kassandros' arms and shoulders; this time he could not break free. 'Hyperia, did you know he would do this?'

'Kassandros, your father has just died; show some respect for his wishes and act with decorum; do not bring disgrace upon yourself with histrionics that would shame even one of my sex.'

'Did you know?'

'No, Kassandros, but I suspected it and had your father consulted me upon the matter then I would have agreed with his course of action. You are not of the right temperament to hold too much power.'

'And that faded nobody is?' Kassandros spat at Polyperchon.

'Take him away,' Polyperchon ordered, putting the great ring on his forefinger, 'and lock him in a room until he has calmed down enough to behave in a dignified manner becoming of a grieving son.'

'Dignified manner? Fuck dignity! Grieving son? Robbed son! That's what I am, robbed. I have been robbed of my inheritance and you expect me to be dignified about it?'

But Kassandros ceased to struggle and allowed himself to be escorted from the death chamber, through a crowd of mourners, none of whom could meet his eyes. *That's it, look away, you sheep. There'll be a time, in the very near future, when you will all be begging me for favours and then we shall see who can look me full in the eye.* The thought soothed him to the point that the methodical part of his mind began to restore itself, banishing the hysterical side that had always plagued him when thwarted, since early childhood. *No, this is a situation that cannot just be reversed because I want it so; I have to go quietly and subtly to have my own way. Murder is out of the question; this has to be done legally so that there can be no reversing it. I'm going to need the one commodity I'm short of: friends.*

And so, as the great families of Macedon gathered for the funeral of their erstwhile regent, Kassandros studied each with a renewed interest for the one thing that he had in his favour was the obscurity of Polyperchon's clan; although a noble line, they came originally from Tymphaia, just across the border in Epirus, until Philip had incorporated it into Macedon; despite the fact his father, Simmias, had married a Macedonian kinswoman of high birth and settled in Pella, Polyperchon could scarcely lay claim to true Macedonian blood. Where Polyperchon did have the advantage though – and it pained Kassandros to admit it to himself – was in his war record: he had served with distinction all through Alexander's journey of conquest, commanding the Tymphaean units of the phalanx as a reward for his bravery at the battle of Issos. *But what counts for more with the great families: blood or distinction?* He contemplated the issue as the prayers were recited and the pyre lit.

Hymns accompanied the crackle of the flames and Kassandros felt nothing as the smoke from his father's burning body rose to the sky: no grief, no loss, no remorse, no guilt; nothing. He was empty as far as his father was concerned, the final betrayal had purged him of feeling for the man whom he had never been able to please; whose expectations he had never lived up to and so had never felt the warmth of his unqualified praise; the man who had never liked him and had found it almost impossible, most of the time, to hide the fact. But now he was free of that; no longer would he have to struggle to gain the respect of the one man who had steadfastly refused to bestow it. No, that was all gone now; all gone and forgotten, wiped away by the greatest show of no-confidence and mistrust that could ever be displayed by a father to a son: to pass him over and give his inheritance to another, one who is not even a member of the extended family.

It was a liberating moment, Kassandros realised, for never again would he have any concern for anyone other than himself; now he only had one person to live for, now that he was free of his father.

But he would need help. With Nicanor, his full brother, away in Kappadokia as his father's choice of satrap to replace Eumenes, Kassandros' mind turned to his half-brothers; Hyperia's sons. Nonetheless, they were still of his blood and without doubt anxious to gain renown and would see him as the person who could provide it, not the mediocrity,

212

Polyperchon, who would, in the natural course of event, favour his own son, Alexandros. Iollas had been the oldest, then came the twins, Pleistarchos and Philip, both seventeen and coming into their own; the two youngest, Alexarchos, four, and Triparadeisus, still in his wet-nurse's arms, were prospects for the future. And then, of course, there were his sisters and his brothers-in-law; this is where he would find the most support, for Antipatros had distributed them perfectly: Phila, his full sister in Asia with Demetrios; Nicaea in the north of Europe with Lysimachus and then Eurydike in Egypt with Ptolemy. One on each continent; this is where he would start but, such was his shock at the turn of events, he did not yet know how he would proceed after.

'What if they seize us and keep us as hostages?' Pleistarchos asked as Kassandros, Philip and he stalked a wild boar in the hills across the River Axius, to the east of Pella, the following day.

'You're family,' Kassandros reminded him; do you think that Phila or Eurydike would countenance their brothers being used like that, especially when they've come on a diplomatic mission? No, Ptolemy and Antigonos will listen to you. I need money, men and ships; in return they will have a kinsman ruling in Macedon and not a usurper with his own agenda. We three, along with Lysimachus to whom I shall talk personally after I have summoned our kinsmen and bondsmen from the estates to my banner, will rule all the lands around the sea; we will give each other support but without prying into one another's affairs. Tell them that and then bring me their answers as soon as you can. There will be a ship waiting for you when we reach Amphipolis; it will take you to Tarsus, Pleistarchos, and then deliver Philip to Tyros; it will then bring you both back to me. I'll be in Thrace with Lysimachus.' Kassandros wiped the sweat from his brow and gripped his sturdy boar-spear, determined to finally succeed in killing the beast that had so far eluded him.

'You mean, we're not going back to Pella.'

'No; if I were Polyperchon, I'd kill all three of us.'

The twins looked at one another; silent agreement passed between them. 'We'll do it,' they said in unison.

Kassandros had left Pella with his twin brothers as soon as was decent after the funeral feast; he had received wry looks as he had announced his intention of going hunting for boar so that he could finally earn the right to recline at dinner. It was not that he particularly wanted to take his boar, he was indifferent to how he ate his supper, it was because it was a perfectly plausible excuse for leaving Pella, travelling through the country and staying with families with whom he had ties of hospitality, people who would be sympathetic to his position; people who would calculate that they had more to gain from Kassandros being regent than Polyperchon; for he did not intend to come back to Macedon until he could claim his rightful place.

On they crept, slowly up the hill, the hunting slaves fanned out to either side in a 'V' ahead of them to funnel any game down to the three brothers at the apex. Behind came more slaves leading the horses.

'Where should we tell Antigonos and Ptolemy to send whatever aid they might offer?' Philip asked, his voice now a whisper as the tension of the hunt mounted.

'I will come to Asia once I have spoken with Lysimachus, with our clansmen,' Kassandros replied, trying to ignore the growing unease deep in his belly. *I mustn't let my fear show; whatever happens, I mustn't turn and run.*

It was a shout that heralded the charge and then a scream. With great porcine roars, inflamed by intrusion into its territory, the boar thundered from its lair, slashing the thigh of the slave who had disturbed it, leaving him pumping blood helplessly in its wake. Down the hill it came, its wrath driving the short legs that supported so much muscle and bulk, easily the weight of two men; tiny red eyes flashed from within a thick coating of bristles and the wicked tusks, razor-sharp and already blood-splattered, protruded from a slathering muzzle as it accelerated down the hill, towards Kassandros and his brothers.

Kassandros' heart leaped and he felt urine dribble down his leg but managed to control the flow so that it would not be noticed. *This was a mistake.* But run he could not, especially as his brothers were now moving forward towards the oncoming beast. Kassandros steeled his will and forced himself to follow them as the slaves dashed to circle around the boar, preventing it from escape without killing one of them.

It was Philip that thrust first as, with terrifying speed, the enraged creature swerved towards him; the spearhead flashed down the beast's side, opening a gash but not penetrating the ribcage. Philip jumped to his left a moment before the tusks would have emasculated him, leaving Kassandros directly in the boar's path. He held his spear rigid before him, pointing at the monster's breast; but the beast was canny and with a flick of its head it knocked the spear aside and closed on Kassandros. It was with a streak of pain, intense and stabbing, that Kassandros was launched skyward, screaming his agony, as below him the boar roared a bestial wail, loud and reverberating, drowning out that of Kassandros' completely; down he crashed, somersaulting as he did, clutching his shattered shin that was ripped from knee to ankle, to see Pleistarchos holding onto his spear for all he was worth, being driven backwards by the impaled beast. It was the image of sitting on the couch as his younger brother reclined next to him that came to Kassandros as he passed out.

Pain was not a burden he found easy to bear and it soon hauled Kassandros from the comfortable depths of unconsciousness into the harsh realm of reality. He groaned, his face screwing up with agony, and thumped his fist down onto soft bedding.

'Lie still,' a voice said. 'Your leg was badly hurt but I've set it and stitched it up; you will be fine given time.'

Opening his eyes, he saw a grey-flecked-bearded face looking down at him. 'Who are you?'

'I am Nicanor's physician.'

'My brother Nicanor? But he's in Kappadokia.'

'No, I serve Nicanor of Sindus.'

Pain dulled his mind and he could not focus upon the name.

'I knew your mother,' a middle-aged man with long dark-brown hair and an auburn beard said from a chair on the far side of the room; the evening sun flooded in through an open window draped with fine linen, saffron in hue, that billowed in a soft breeze.

'My mother's dead.'

'I know, and it saddened me greatly when she died.'

Kassandros was immediately suspicious. 'What was she to you?'

Nicanor raised his palm in conciliation. 'Nothing in the way you are imagining it. We were cousins and grew up together, until, of course, our respective sexes started to emerge and we were parted for decency's sake. No, Kassandros, I was very fond of her. I would see her now and again, after she had married your father, when I came to Pella. Her death did grieve me, I can assure you.'

Kassandros winced again through the pain in his leg. 'It grieved me more, I can assure you; and I'm sure that the child that was strangled in her womb wasn't at all happy about it.'

Nicanor got to his feet and crossed the room, dismissing the physician with a wave. 'You have a right to be bitter; in fact you have many reasons to be bitter, not least the way your father has treated you.'

Kassandros looked at Nicanor, puzzled. *Is that sympathy?* 'It is customary that the eldest son should inherit from his father.'

'Indeed. But here's an interesting fact: before I went east with Alexander I spoke with your father just after he had been appointed regent. I asked him what the position entailed as we had not had a regent in Macedon for over a hundred years, so I was interested. He told me that he held all the powers of the king, with one exception.'

'Which was?'

'Which was that he could not pass the title on; only the king could do that.'

'But I was his son!'

Nicanor raised both his hands to quieten Kassandros. 'You're not listening to me, Kassandros: he could not pass the title on, only the king can do that.'

Kassandros frowned; a spasm of pain passed across his face and he suppressed a groan. Slowly the implication of what Nicanor had said percolated through his mind. 'In that case, he didn't have the power to pass on the regency to Polyperchon.'

'Nor could he have passed it on to you; only the kings can do that and, seeing as neither king is fit to rule, they cannot appoint their own regent and without a regent these kings cannot rule. It's a paradox.'

Suddenly the pain ravaging Kassandros' leg was forgotten. *Of course. Why did I not see that before, it's so perfectly obvious: my father did not have the power to pass his power on.* 'Polyperchon's position is therefore not legal.'

'Exactly; he has no right to the regency and nor would you have had, had your father not have passed you over.'

'So I would not be rebelling against him if I were to raise an army.'

'How can you rebel against someone who is not a ruler? Technically, at the moment, Macedon is without a government; so if it were to be spear-won you could argue that you had committed no crime and your seizing of power was legitimate.'

'Why are you giving me this advice? You owe me nothing.'

'And if I help you then you'll owe me something; something that I shall never get from Polyperchon: I know the man, he is a strong subordinate but will be a weak and vacillating leader; in you I see ruthlessness and strength. As I have no ambitions to rule Macedon, I would much prefer it if you were to do so, rather than him. I take it that you are not happy with the situation and plan to do something about it.'

'Yes.'

'May I ask what?'

'I'm sending my brothers to speak to Ptolemy, who's still in Syria and Antigonos who, at the moment, is campaigning against Alketas and Attalus in Pisidia; I'm going to talk to Lysimachus.'

'Your three brothers-in-law; yes, they could help, or if not actively help then they could certainly be induced not to hinder. What other measures are you taking?'

'I'm summoning all the men who owe loyalty to my family to form the basis of an army and that's as far as I've got. I need to know whether they will give me men, ships and money.'

'And if they give you an army and the fleet to transport it, where will you take it?'

Kassandros felt a surge of anger; he did not like to be questioned, especially when the questions exposed a lack of forethought. He had not had time to think things through as it had all happened so quickly; all he had done so far was to escape Pella.

Nicanor was sensitive enough to realise this. 'Pella is out of the question; any Macedonian who defiles the capital with war would be reviled; no, the war has to be won long before you get to Macedon. Fight it down south in Greece; let them bear the suffering of two armies on campaign. You need Piraeus. You need to control the garrison at Munychia there.'

'Menyllus is the commander at the moment; my father appointed him after Athens surrendered.'

'Can you trust him?'

'I've no reason to; I barely know the man.'

'Then send me; if I leave immediately in a fast ship there's a good chance that I can get there before the news of your father's death reaches Athens. I'll bring the news to the garrison and a written order from you to replace Menyllus as commander.'

'And then you can hold Piraeus for me until I arrive with my army.'

'Precisely. Polyperchon will be forced to act; he would lose all face if he let you occupy Greece and did nothing. He would have to come south; defeat him there and then march north in triumph and seize Macedon without a blow being struck within her borders.'

'And what about the kings?'

Nicanor smiled and made a vague gesture with one hand. 'I would just take one step at a time, if I were you; after all, they're not going anywhere.'

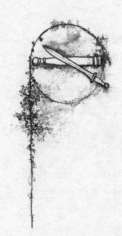

ADEA.
THE WARRIOR.

NOW, PERHAPS, WAS her chance – her last chance, in all likelihood – now that Antipatros was finally dead; how she had wept, tears of joy, at the news of his demise. The man who had denied her the right – her right as a queen – to speak for her husband and to rule in his name could no longer thwart her; he was gone and he had not named his son as his successor.

That Kassandros would rule after Antipatros had plagued Adea ever since she had returned to Europe; it had been clear that the old man would not last the year and it had been obvious that his eldest son should succeed him and she knew that Kassandros bore her no love. Indeed, there were few, if any, among the nobility of Macedon that bore her any affection which was why she had always made her appeals to the common soldiery; their reverence for Alexander and his blood extended to her husband, Philip, as his half-brother and to her as the cousin of the great man.

She looked at her husband, standing in his chamber, high in the palace overlooking Pella; he had a fixed grin on his face as his body-slave fastened his sword and put the final touches to his ceremonial uniform: the uniform of a king of Macedon.

She rubbed a blemish from the muscled, bronze breastplate, inlaid with silver prancing horses with rubies for eyes and diamonds on their hooves, and then adjusted the purple cloak that was draped over his shoulders and hung to the tops of his red-leather calf-boots.

Wiping a trail of drool from the corner of his mouth, she stood back to look at the whole effect. 'Very good, Philip; you look splendid. A veritable king.'

Philip giggled, holding one hand to his mouth – the other clasped his helmet with a red horsehair plume and two tall white feathers on either side. 'Can I ride a horse, Adea? Can I? Can I?'

'Today you can, Philip.'

'Oh, thank you, thank you.' To emphasise his gratitude he sent a small stream of urine down his leg.

Used to such displays of excitement, Adea took no notice as the body-slave wiped his charge dry; he may have been a less than perfect king with the mind of an eight-year-old, but he was perfectly biddable and ridiculously grateful for any treat she allowed him, and "playing kings" was one of his favourites.

She checked herself in the polished bronze mirror: her breastplate, her helmet and her greaves all shone and her sword hung in the correct manner. *An Amazon queen; Mother would be so proud of me.* Satisfied that all was ready, she picked up the scroll that she had prepared for the occasion and, taking her husband's limp hand, led him from the room.

The army of Macedon was by now a very mixed affair made up of beardless recruits, grizzled veterans old enough to be their great grandfathers and relatively untried garrison troops of indifferent quality more used to bullying the unfortunate local populations upon whom they had been forced. But despite its questionability in terms of combat, it could parade with rigid discipline and it was in precise blocks of men, both mounted and on foot, that it was drawn up on the parade ground beyond Pella's North Gate.

Adea sat on her mare, next to her husband on his stallion, as Polyperchon took the salute in the name of the kings; his son, Alexandros, next to him, was as nondescript as his father except that what remaining hair there was on his head was brown rather than grey. *Uninspiring and dull, the both of them; this has to be my chance.*

Glancing to her left she caught the cold stare of her rival, Roxanna, eyes seething with hatred from behind her veil as she sat on a cushion-laden carriage with her four-year-old son next to her. Adea turned away, a feeling of triumph in her breast as she had scored a moral victory over the eastern wild-cat by appearing next to her husband mounted; she was the martial queen, prepared to lead men whereas Roxanna was nothing but a pampered easterner wallowing in luxury, the antithesis of a Macedonian. It had been a point well made and she knew that it would not go unnoticed as she swelled with pride upon the army hailing her husband as king – she ignored the fact that the bitch's whelp was also included in the ovation. Philip beamed and nodded his head furiously, punching his fist into the air until Adea took his elbow and gently brought his arm down. 'Stay still, Philip, act with some decorum or the Ferryman will come and get you.'

'The Ferryman?' Philip froze, his eyes darting left and right, searching for his greatest fear; just the mention of his name was enough to bring the man-child back under control when being unruly.

Adea allowed herself a quick smile at the ease with which she could now control her husband who relied upon her for almost everything and who was, in his own way, passionately devoted to her. Keeping him safe and respected was her priority, for although it was well known that he had the mind of a child he was of Alexander's blood, his half-brother, and that was of great importance to the rank and file of the army and they honoured him as their king and looked upon him as a talisman.

'Soldiers of Macedon,' Polyperchon shouted, as the cheering for the kings died away, his voice a monotone. 'Two days ago we gave funeral rites to Antipatros whose service to our country is beyond all reckoning.' He raised the Great Ring of Macedon into the air. 'I come before you, before this assembly of the army, to say that in his wisdom on his deathbed he passed the ring of Macedon onto me. I ask you, formally, to accept me as regent of Macedon and of the two kings, Alexander and Philip, who appear here before you. What say you, soldiers of Macedon?' The final line went from a monotone to a squeak which rang clear around the parade ground and faded into silence.

Polyperchon, his ring still raised, looked around and, visibly stunned that he had failed to receive a great acclamation, lowered his arm; a hum of muttered conversation began to rise from the assembled troops.

Now is my chance, now I appear before them as a warrior queen. Adea grabbed her husband's horse's reins and walked her mount forward to come to a halt next to Polyperchon whose rage at the move was undisguised. 'Soldiers of Macedon,' she shouted in her clear voice, neither shrill nor deep, and with varying tone so it sounded like sweet music after Polyperchon's dirge. 'My husband, the king, wishes it to be known that he supports Polyperchon.'

Polyperchon looked at her in surprise.

'But it will cost you,' Adea whispered from the corner of her mouth. 'Soldiers of Macedon,' she continued, 'my husband, the king, asks that you too lend your support to Polyperchon knowing that King Philip will guide him in his deliberations. Polyperchon will consult with my husband on all matters both military and civilian and I, Queen Eurydike, shall report the discussions back to your officers. Polyperchon and my husband will have equal status. Support him, soldiers of Macedon, support Polyperchon as your regent and Philip as your king.'

The roar was instant and booming and Adea knew that she had finally achieved her ambition of being at the centre of power as was her right as a granddaughter of Philip, the second of that name. Not for her, this time, the humiliation of failure as when she was outmanoeuvred by Antipatros, first in The Three Paradises and then on the shores of the Hellespont where he had left her with a mutinous army in her hands but without the resources to look after it. No, this time her place was secure; this time she could not be outmanoeuvred for Polyperchon now owed his position to her, she had come to the aid of the uncharismatic nonentity by dazzling the army with her flair.

'What have you done?' Alexandros, Polyperchon's son, hissed at her.

'Come to the rescue of an old man who had underwhelmed the army with a speech lacking in any charisma whatsoever.'

'If you think that I'll be consulting Philip on anything,' Polyperchon said, 'then you are sadly deluded.'

'I don't think anything of the sort, old man; I think that you will be consulting me, acting for the king.' She smiled at him without mirth and then led Philip's horse forward towards the cheering front rankers. 'Wave at them, Philip, don't smile; we're playing kings, remember. Kings don't smile, do they?'

'No, Adea, they don't; kings are gave.'

'Grave, Philip; kings are grave.'

'Yes, Adea,' he agreed, doing his best to wave with gravity as Polyperchon drew level with them to share the accolade.

The nonentity has just agreed to my terms by joining us; I'm there. She looked over to where Roxanna sat helplessly immobile in her carriage. *And she must be furious as I've managed to relegate her son to the second tier; Polyperchon will talk for him at our meetings.*

Thus, for the first time since marrying Philip in Babylon, and taking the name Queen Eurydike, Adea felt a degree of security. No longer did it matter quite so desperately that she had still not conceived; indeed, she had now despaired of ever doing so and had reduced their couplings to just once a month leaving Philip to his own devices the rest of the time. No, now she would have power in her own right, speaking for her husband in a council, protected by the love of the army from Polyperchon trying to remove her.

At last she was going to be listened to.

'We should send Diogenes to Cilicia to meet with Antigenes and Teutamus guarding the imperial treasury in Cyinda,' Adea said to Polyperchon, across the council table set in the centre of the throne-room. She studiously ignored Alexandros sitting – uninvited – next to his father. 'As Antipatros' treasurer he'll have the respect of the two men and the letter signed by you and my husband will release all the money we need into his care; it can be transported back on the same ship that takes him over. The whole thing could be accomplished in ten to twelve days.'

Polyperchon shook his head, clearly not convinced and trying not to look at Philip presiding over the meeting from the raised throne at the end of the table whilst playing with his toy elephant. 'Alketas and Attalus are in neighbouring Pisidia; what if they get wind of the shipment?'

Why does he always come up with unlikely problems; every meeting it's the same: we can't do this because this or that might happen. 'The Rhodians destroyed their navy last year, they're inland and Antigonos is either on his way to face them or is already there; they're far too preoccupied to be looking out for a treasure ship.'

'But they might,' Alexandros said. 'And is it worth the risk of enriching them just to get money that we could squeeze out of Greece?'

'Who asked you your opinion?' Adea barked. 'You represent nobody; you've no place at this council.'

'He's my son and I asked him to be here,' Polyperchon said, thumping his fist on the table. 'And he's right: they might hear of the shipment and end up stronger than they already are.'

Adea shot a venomous glance at Alexandros, smirking at her, and then spoke specifically to his father. 'And a storm *might* blow up and the ship *might* sink. Lots of things *might* happen but nothing will happen if we don't put this in motion; we are desperately short of money here in Macedon and there are hundreds of talents in silver and gold in Cilicia so let's get five hundred over here as quickly as possible. If the situation in Athens is as bad as you say it is then we will need cash to buy support. Who is this Nicanor of Sindus who has taken control of the garrison in Piraeus, anyway?'

'He's no friend of mine, quite the opposite.' Polyperchon looked at his son and nodded.

'According to the people I had follow him,' Alexandros said, 'Kassandros was injured on that hunt he went on and Nicanor's doctor fixed him up; Nicanor left for Athens the same day and got there before the news of Antipatros' death that we'd sent south, arrived and took over the garrison with a letter from Kassandros writing in his father's name. That was almost half a moon ago now.'

'And Kassandros, where is he now?'

Polyperchon looked across the table at her, his eyes full of worry. 'Once his leg was healed enough to travel in a litter he went to Thrace; he's there with Lysimachus.'

A shrill disturbance at the door cut short Adea's response; all turned to see Roxanna force her way past the guards with her son, his nursemaid and two slave-girls following.

'Why was I not informed of this meeting?' Roxanna demanded.

Adea stood and faced her rival. 'Because you're not part of the council.'

'Keep your cunt-kissing mouth shut, bitch, I was asking the regent.' She squared up to Polyperchon, her eyes blazing over the top of her veil. 'There have been four meetings and I have not been informed of any of them. I am the mother of the king.'

'One of the kings,' Polyperchon reminded her.

Roxanna pointed to Philip, now kneeling on the throne and hunched down, over his elephant, as if trying to make himself as inconspicuous as possible. 'You call that a king? It should have been strangled at birth.' She turned to her son, the young Alexander. 'Here is a king; my husband's blood flows in his veins. He should be sitting on that throne instead of that beast. And I should be at this table to speak for him.'

'Polyperchon speaks for him,' Adea shouted. 'He's the regent.'

'And what are you, girl-lover? Are you a regent? No! And yet you sit at this table.'

'I represent my husband.'

'By what right?' Roxanna's voice was now a full-pitched screech.

226

'By the acclamation of the army, you eastern whore!'

It was a lightning action; a flash of blade and a spray of blood from Adea's upper arm. Roxanna raised her hand for another strike with the dagger that had been concealed up her sleeve, but her opponent was too quick.

Warrior-trained and skilled in the art of the blade, Adea grabbed Roxanna's wrist as the blow came down, pushing her back onto the ground and straddling her, with her fist maintaining a vice-like grip. 'Let's see what hideousness you conceal under there.' Ripping the veil from Roxanna's face, she raised her eyes in surprise. 'So you're quite pretty after all; could even be my type except for the nasty scar on your face.' She began to force the blade towards it.

Roxanna screamed, the child howled and clutched his nurse; a stream of urine flowed down from the throne.

'No, Adea!' Polyperchon shouted, hauling her off the writhing easterner as his son secured the blade.

Adea let herself be restrained, both arms pinned behind her, enjoying the look of terror on Roxanna's face just before she flung her veil back over it and got to her knees. 'You think that protects you?' With a jerk, she leaned back on Polyperchon and lashed out with a foot. Back snapped Roxanna's head and she crashed to the floor; blood soaking through the veil from a crushed nose. 'Take her away before I kill the bitch.'

The slave-girls glanced at one another, reluctant to touch their mistress whilst in such an undignified situation and burst into tears.

'Guards!' Alexandros shouted. 'Take the queen to her chambers.'

With little ceremony, for Roxanna had little respect, she was dragged from the room. Her howling son, clinging to his nurse, followed, with the slave-girls weeping for themselves for they feared the punishment for witnessing such humiliation, trailing behind.

'So,' Adea said, ripping off the hem of her tunic, 'where were we before that wicked interruption?'

Polyperchon looked at her with unconcealed surprise. 'You want to carry on the meeting after that?'

She pressed the rag onto the wound on her arm; despite all the blood, it was not deep. 'Of course; the business of government must go on despite that eastern wild-cat.' She sat back down at the table. 'So, Kassandros has left Macedon and is now in Thrace with Lysimachus, his brother-in-law; is that right?'

Polyperchon had to shake his head to realign his thoughts after the brief but violent interlude. 'Yes, that's correct.' He sat back down.

'He's in open rebellion, then?'

'No, not yet, but I'm sure he's thinking about it; he sent his brothers to Ptolemy and Antigonos. He is looking for support.'

'Another brother-in-law and the father of the third one; he's appealing to family ties and perhaps will be successful with at least one of them. All the more reason for us to get some money over here.'

Polyperchon sighed, beaten by her sheer persistence. 'Alright, we'll risk it.'

Adea smiled, still holding the rag to her wound. 'Good. I'm glad we're in agreement, Polyperchon. And don't worry about Alketas and Attalus, Antigonos will be keeping them fully occupied.'

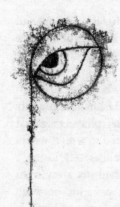

ANTIGONOS.
THE ONE-EYED.

'THEY'RE HOLDING A pass to the east of Termessos, by a little town called Cretopolis,' Demetrios reported, wiping the dust and sweat from his face with a cloth. 'It's a very good position – at least it would be if they were formed up.'

'Alketas still has his army in camp,' Antigonos said, more out of hope than surprise.

'Yes, Father, he doesn't know that we're here yet.'

Antigonos chuckled, rubbing his hands together with more vigour than normally the case. 'We've done it. How far away is this pass?'

'Just over a league, a little bit south of west. There's a negotiable slope on the northern side; we can attack from there with the advantage of the higher ground.'

'Good lad, Demetrios, I'll make a general of you yet.' Antigonos looked at the sun. 'We could be there in an hour which would leave a couple of hours of daylight; just enough time. Best go now rather than wait for dawn and run the risk of their scouts coming across us in the night. I'll lead with the phalanx and you can use the cavalry in conjunction with the elephants to repulse any counter attack as we advance down to them; that'll give them a nasty surprise.'

Demetrios looked at his father, aghast. 'Using elephants on

fellow Macedonians? It's one thing using them against fortifications, but against lads in the field?'

'I know it's never been done before but this is war, Son, and the quicker we get it over with the better. If Eumenes can be brought to terms then this could be the last battle of the struggle.'

But even as he said it he knew that it would be an awful disappointment were it to be so. He loved war and he had thoroughly enjoyed himself during this particular one: phalanx against phalanx, the sheer joy of it. But he also needed to win; it would be pointless prolonging the conflict by deliberately losing a battle and to this end he had forced-marched his army from Kappadokia to Pisidia in just eight days, covering between twelve and fifteen leagues a day. It had been a favourite tactic of Alexander's and now he, Antigonos, had used it successfully, for here he was an hour's march away from his enemy who thought him to be far away in the east.

Gods, this will be good.

'No horns,' he ordered as he gave the command for the army to move off. 'Not until we get there.'

'It's like poking an ants' nest,' Antigonos observed with a laugh, over the trumpeting of his elephants. 'And they were just settling down to the evening meal, by the smell of it.' He looked down the hill into Alketas' camp, astride the main pass leading from the uplands of Pisidia down to the rugged coast of Pamphylia; it was full of tiny figures running around, terrified by the din of the elephants that had suddenly appeared above them. The surprise was perfect and the shouts of the officers rose on the breeze as they desperately tried to get their men formed up in their units. But it was too late; Antigonos' army had the higher ground and it was already formed up. With a simple gesture of his hand, Antigonos signalled the advance and the great phalanx moved forward at a steady pace, down towards the enemy, screened by archers and slingers and flanked by peltasts.

Alketas had many faults but he could never be accused of being a coward: to buy his phalanx time to form up he led his cavalry, three thousand strong, and skirmishing foot, straight at the oncoming mass of infantry in an attempt to frustrate the advance. Up the horses surged, their chests swelling with the effort of the incline as their riders bellowed their war-cries, urging their mounts to greater efforts. The hiss of the first volley rose in the air and the sky darkened with arrows but still Alketas led his men on.

But this was what Antigonos had been waiting for: once Alketas was closer to him than he was to his own phalanx he gave Demetrios the pre-arranged signal; his herd of twenty elephants trumpeted again and lumbered on down the hill, light infantry screening them and cavalry to either flank – the horses having by now been accustomed to the alien smell of the great beasts. Gathering speed with the incline, the animate war-machines closed quickly upon the enemy infantry, still in considerable disarray. Faced with being cut off from his phalanx and then surrounded, Alketas turned his cavalry about and swarmed back down the hill. It was within moments of disaster that he managed to regroup; but it was disaster postponed, and not for long at that, for Antigonos' charge came home into a disorganised phalanx whose unprotected flanks had felt the wrath of an elephant engagement, leaving many mashed, mangled and impaled. They had no choice: they sat down in surrender, like a wave going from the left flank, mauled by the elephants, all the way across the ten thousand man formation to the untouched, but soon to be overwhelmed, right.

'Attalus, Docimus and Polemon,' Antigonos said, addressing each of his prisoners brought, in chains, before him in his tent. 'I wish it were in better circumstances that we are meeting but unfortunately you are to be considered rebels under sentence of death.'

'We're not rebels,' Attalus insisted. 'We're loyal to my brother-in-law, Perdikkas, who was foully murdered by Antigenes,

Seleukos and Peithon; they're the rebels, not us, for killing the man to whom Alexander gave his ring.'

'Well, Antipatros currently wears that ring, although not for much longer I should guess. But because the political situation may well change imminently, I'm minded to spare your lives for the moment and wait to see if there cannot be some sort of rapprochement; until then I shall keep you confined in Celaenae. Now, I suppose it's useless asking you where Alketas is?'

Attalus smiled. 'Not at all. He's in Termessos and they'll never give him up; the young men of the town worship him as a hero.'

Antigonos grunted. 'We'll see about that.' He nodded to the guards. 'Take them away.'

Termessos stood tall on a hill, overlooking a long and wide fertile valley fed by many streams flowing down its sides into a river at the base. Tall towers sprang from the city, some for defence on the walls and others, within the town, just because their owners liked the superiority that the height of their dwelling awarded them. It was a rich town by all appearances and had not suffered, either during the original conquest nor now in the recent civil war as it had remained fervently loyal to the Perdikkans and Alketas in particular. It was before this town, in the fields ripe with a rich harvest, that Antigonos, with an army now of sixty thousand infantry and ten thousand cavalry – having augmented it with Alketas' captured men – stood and smiled at the delegation from the town which had come out to meet him under a branch of truce, just before the setting of the sun.

'So there you have the situation, gentlemen: I'll wait here until Alketas is delivered up to me.' He looked around at the abundance of the harvest. 'I'm in no hurry; there seems to be plenty for my men to eat for months.' He shrugged, his one eye twinkling with mischief. 'Although, the longer you keep me waiting the less you will have to eat this winter; still, it's better than me taking the town by storm, isn't it?'

'It is, Lord,' the greybeard who led the delegation said, wringing his hands, 'and we thank you for that small mercy; but the sad truth of the matter is that our sons will not heed us, they will not give up Alketas and there is nothing that we can do to change their minds.'

'What kind of sons do you have who refuse to obey their fathers?'

'Disrespectful ones, Lord.'

Antigonos mulled this over for a few moments. 'Well, all I can say is that it's going to be a difficult winter for you in there but I think we'll be fine out here so don't you worry about us, will you? I don't think that there is anything else I can say until you teach your sons the meaning of paternal respect and so I shall retire to my dinner; I suggest you do the same and send your sons to bed without theirs.'

Antigonos pulled a leg from whole, roasted goose and looked at his young guest, newly arrived from Tarsus, reclining next to Demetrios across the table, amazed by his news. 'Well, it comes as no surprise, Pleistarchos, he was a broken man after Iollas died; but Polyperchon, that is intriguing. An excellent second in command with a great eye for detail, distribution or orders and supplies and handy with the accounting but by no means a leader – his voice is enough to send you to sleep.' He nudged his old friend, Philotas, reclining next to him. 'Just imagine him trying to give a rousing speech to the army before a battle.'

Philotas choked on his wine. 'You'd have to sound the reveille as soon as he'd finished otherwise the lads would miss the order to advance over the sound of their snores.'

Antigonos laughed as he tore at his goose leg. 'So your brother is a disgruntled man, I take it?'

'It was his inheritance, not Polyperchon's.'

'It wasn't, my lad, it was no one's. Antipatros didn't have the right to pass on the regency without a full meeting of all the satraps, which is very unlikely to happen now. But therein could lie Kassandros' opportunity.'

'So you'll help him?'

'I didn't say that, lad. Firstly: what does he plan to do?'

Antigonos frowned, looking at Pleistarchos once he had finished explaining Kassandros' intentions. 'You're reclining; have you killed your boar?'

A look of pride came over Pleistarchos' face, not as pinched as his elder brother's but similarly pale and with wisps of a ginger beard. 'I did half a moon back.'

'And what about Kassandros?' Demetrios asked – he had killed his boar at the age of fourteen.

Pleistarchos' embarrassed silence was an eloquent response.

'Few men have gone through life always seated on the couch and of those none has done anything remotely memorable, let alone seize Athens and force Polyperchon to fight in Greece. I wonder if your brother might be the exception to that. Go back to him tomorrow morning and tell him I'll think on the matter.'

'But you haven't said no.'

'No, I haven't.'

'And if you decide to help him will you give him money, men and ships?'

'That depends on the situation at the time, were I to decide in Kassandros' favour.'

Any more thoughts on the subject were interrupted by the arrival of the grey-beard who had led Termessos' delegation.

'So,' Antigonos said, having heard the man out, 'you think that if we were to withdraw in the morning then your unruly sons will follow us, leaving the older generation to seize Alketas and deliver him to me.'

'We hope so; they will want to see what damage has been done to the crops and we'll encourage them to do so, most of us going with them. We'll leave some of the younger fathers behind and hope we get the chance to get him.'

Antigonos could not help but be amused. 'You going to have a generational war on your hands if this works; your sons will never trust you again.'

The grey-beard shrugged. 'It was ever thus.'

I've done a better job with mine. 'Very well, I'll withdraw in the morning but on one condition.'

'Name it.'

'That you bring me Alketas, dead.'

The eyes had been pecked out and the air around the corpse reeked of decay as it hung from a gibbet between Antigonos' camp and the walls of Termessos.

'How long will you leave him hanging there, Father?' Demetrios asked as he and Antigonos rode back, under heavy escort, from trying the more vociferous supporters of the dead rebel. 'It's been three days now.'

Antigonos looked up at the body; the elders of the town had been as good as their word: Alketas had been taken and murdered as the younger men had poured from the city to inspect their farms and ensure that the invaders were really on their way; more than a few tried to pick off stragglers. 'I think it's served as a sufficient warning to the youth of the town not to take matters into their own hands.' He turned to the officer commanding his cavalry escort. 'Cut it down and leave it by the side of the road.'

'Father! He was a Macedonian nobleman.'

Antigonos turned his eye onto his son. 'He was a Macedonian nobleman and, as such, he should have known not to kill Cynnane; that's his punishment for murdering Alexander's sister. If the young men who worship him so in the town want to give him his funeral rites then they are more than welcome to. As for me, I'll have nothing to do with him.'

It was an excited Pleistarchos who awaited Antigonos in his tent, along with Philotas.

'I thought you had gone back to your brother three days ago.'

'I did, Antigonos.' The youth's eyes glowed.

'I warn you, old friend,' Philotas said, his voice grave, 'what he has to say could tempt you into a rash course of action. And I speak as one who knows you well.'

Antigonos looked with interest at Pleistarchos. 'Well?'

'I got back to Tarsus yesterday; my ship was waiting for me with my brother on board.'

'I'm very pleased to hear it, but I'm sure you haven't come all this way to tell me that.'

'No, Antigonos. Just before we left, there was another ship arriving from Macedon. I recognised its passenger: Diogenes, my father's treasurer. My brother and I followed him and his escort until we were sure where he was heading and then sailed to find you as fast as possible.'

'And?'

'And he took the road to Cyinda.'

Antigonos looked at Philotas, who gave a knowing smile. 'It looks like Polyperchon is in need of funds.'

'If you take them then you'll be starting a new war just three days after you won the old one.'

Antigonos grinned. 'Let's not get ahead of ourselves.' He looked at Pleistarchos; he was puffed up with pride. 'Can you get a hundred men on your ship?'

'It won't be comfortable, but it's only a day's journey.'

Antigonos slapped the young man on the shoulder. 'Let's get going then.'

It was twilight when the mounted column finally rattled into the river port at Tarsus; in its midst were four sturdy carts loaded with crates; slaves scuttled around, lighting torches so that the lucrative business of trade could carry on into the night.

'It looks like Polyperchon is planning to buy a lot of support,' Philotas commented as the column pulled up to the ship moored next to them.

Antipatros turned away and fiddled with some ropes, in what he hoped was a naval-like fashion, affecting not to notice the goings on so close by. 'We'll let them load it on board so they can't run off with it.'

Philotas came over to help the nautical fiddling with ropes. 'And they save us the trouble.'

Antigonos glanced over to a warehouse across the quay, its

double doors ajar; in the light from the torches blazing to either side of it, Antigonos could just see Demetrios, Pleistarchos and his brother, Philip, waiting, with the men, for his signal.

As the final crate was loaded aboard and Diogenes, standing on the deck, checked it off on his list, the signal came: Antigonos, the hood of his cloak concealing his features, walked down the gangplank of his ship, with Philotas, crossed the jetty and boarded the treasure ship.

'Who are you?' Diogenes snapped. 'Get off my ship!'

'I am the rightful owner of all that money,' Antigonos replied, pulling back his hood.

'Antigonos?'

'That's right, Diogenes. Antipatros made me the supreme commander in Asia and that is Asian money.'

'Antipatros is dead; Polyperchon commands now.'

'I know both those things and neither bothers me in the slightest; now, you can either get off this ship and try to make your own way back to Macedon or you can stay aboard and start serving a new employer.'

'Guards!' But as Diogenes shouted for help he saw that the ship was now surrounded by a hundred men, all with swords drawn; his guards were nowhere to be seen.

'A bit late for that, I think. Which is it to be?'

Diogenes swallowed and his shoulders slumped. 'My family are in Pella; I'll make my own way back.' He handed Antigonos his list and disembarked.

Antigonos whistled as his eye went down the columns. 'Five hundred talents; that really has started a war, Philotas. Still, I was getting bored after three whole days of peace.'

'What are you going to do? Invade Macedon?'

'My arse I will. Why would I do that when I've got somebody who will be quite happy to do it for me?' He looked around and saw who he needed. 'Pleistarchos, Philip, come here.' He watched them come over to him, trying to tell them apart. 'Go back to your brother and tell him that I've got money, ships and men. If he wants me to lend him some of each, so that he can go to

Athens and then take Macedon, he should come and see me before I change my mind.'

'Yes, sir,' they said in tandem. 'Thank you.'

'Oh, and tell him that it was your quick thinking that made it happen; I know he's not the nicest of men but it won't do him any harm to show a bit of gratitude. Now go.'

The twins turned and headed back to their ship as Demetrios began to embark his men onto the treasure ship. 'Back to Pisidia, Father?'

'Yes.'

'And then what? Deal with Eumenes?'

Antigonos smiled, shaking his head. 'In a way; but with a letter rather than a sword. We've got an opportunity here: with war coming to Europe we can use the time to take Asia. Who better to help us plan the campaign than our sly little Greek; after all, the people who don't like us, like him, so we'll get some interesting new friends. I'm going to write to him; Hieronymus, his compatriot, can take the letter so as he will realise that it is a genuine offer.'

'What exactly are you thinking of offering him?'

'To become my second-in-command and join with me in uniting Asia for the kings; he likes that sort of thing, don't you know.'

Demetrios considered the prospect. 'He'll probably take it. What about Polyperchon?'

'Polyperchon will be too busy with Kassandros to stop me; and Kassandros just wants Macedon. I'll leave Ptolemy alone and deal with Seleukos at a later date if he doesn't submit.' He scratched his thick beard in thought. 'No, on reflection there's a second letter I should be writing, and that is to the mother of all mischief encouraging her to make life difficult for Polyperchon.'

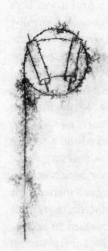

POLYPERCHON.
THE GREY.

T HE NEWS WAS never good; the
outlook rarely, if ever, hopeful.
Polyperchon looked at the pile of
official papers heaped on his desk and
wished it could be like the old days when
Antipatros or Krateros were in charge and all he had to do was
immerse himself in the detail; detail he loved: the minutiae of
organisation, the thrill of a balanced budget, the checking and
double-checking that orders had been passed on, were understood and being effected. And then the joy of a battle in the
front rank of the phalanx; that was soldiering: order, discipline
and violence. That was the life that Polyperchon had chosen,
not this new role that had been thrust upon him without
warning, without consent; not this having to issue orders rather
than take them and then convey them; not this life of poli-
ticking, knowing that to lose would mean not just your career
but your life as well. He glanced down on the Great Ring of
Macedon, worn with such reluctance on his right hand. *And yet
I'm stuck with it; even if I gave this willingly to Kassandros, he
would kill me and my son. I must spend the rest of my life trying to
be what I never was; and all because of one stupid mistake.*

And it had been a stupid mistake: he had distinguished
himself in Alexander's army, first at Issos, after which he had
been given a command of a syntagma of two hundred and fifty-
six of his countrymen and had slowly, during the conquest,

239

worked his way up until he had become a part of Alexander's outer circle, just within reach of his radiance. And it was here that he had made the mistake by laughing at a Persian performing the *proskynesis*, the full prostration that had been the due of the Great King and upon which Alexander had come to insist upon from his Persian subjects. He had laughed at the man who had almost touched his chin to the floor, saying that he should bang it harder; Alexander had flown into a rage, dragged him from his couch and then shamed him before his comrades: he had been forced to perform the homage he had just mocked and although no one had laughed out loud, Polyperchon was well aware that there would be forever sniggering behind his back. And so, when Krateros – himself no lover of Alexander's increasingly Persian ways – had been despatched back to Macedon to replace Antipatros, Polyperchon had been only too pleased to accompany him as his second-in-command. Had he known what it would lead to, Polyperchon had no doubt that he would have stayed out in the east and ignored the sniggering. For although towards the end Alexander had insisted upon the Macedonians performing the humiliating act so as not to differentiate between them and the conquered nations, he had been the first to do so and for that he would always be a laughing stock.

But for that mistake he now could be perhaps Ptolemy's adjutant or Peucestas' quartermaster or even Eumenes' accountant; he wouldn't care, just as long as there was someone to tell him what to do. And that was what he was missing at that moment for he knew not how to react to the news he had just been given. 'So that little bitch Adea was wrong, Antigonos hasn't remained loyal.'

Alexandros, leaning next to the window looking north to the hills, shook his head. 'No, Father.'

Polyperchon turned to the man standing before his desk. 'He stole the whole lot, Diogenes?'

Diogenes lowered his eyes, humiliated by the memory. 'Down to the last denarius.'

Polyperchon put his head in his hands, a posture that he

found himself in remarkably often these days. 'He's declared war on me in effect and I will look stupid and weak if I do not try and fight him. What should I do?'

Alexandros came over to the desk, dismissing Diogenes with a flick of a finger, and sat down. 'Father, this is no time for indecision; it's south you must go, forget about Antigonos. Yes, he's taken the money and, no, we will never be able to draw on the Cyinda treasury again, but it's pointless dwelling on that. The question is: what will Antigonos do with his new wealth? Now, I think the answer to that is obvious.'

Polyperchon looked up at his son, a spark of hope. 'You do?'

'Yes. Antigonos is too busy in Asia to want to come and fight over here so he'll stay there and send a proxy.'

Polyperchon thought for a moment. 'Kassandros?'

'Of course. Diogenes told us that Pleistarchos and Philip were there when the cash was seized; in fact he thinks it was them who betrayed the shipment in the hope of currying favour with Antigonos. Kassandros is clearly the person to do Antigonos' dirty work for him in Europe: he wasn't on the conquest so has no interests in Asia – or many friends, for that matter – so Europe is the obvious place for him to operate and he will need a base.'

'Athens?'

'Yes, Father, Athens. Antigonos will give Kassandros the troops and he will sail to Athens; we must take back Piraeus before he does so and deny him that base.' Alexandros thumped his fist down on the desk. 'We must deny him Greece entirely.'

'How can we do that?'

'All the regimes in the cities are oligarchies set up by Kassandros' father.'

'Yes, but surely that's a good thing. Democracies are reckless; power is best kept in the hands of the wealthy as they are likely to be far more careful with policy in order to protect their wealth and increase it.'

'I agree and those regimes were, as I said, installed by Antipatros; so to whom will they show loyalty if there is a war, us or Kassandros?'

Polyperchon did not need to vocalise the answer.

'So if *we* change the regime,' Alexandros continued, 'that loyalty will come to us. The Athenian oligarchy isn't going to do anything about Nicanor of Sindus in Piraeus; Phocion himself refused to lead their embassy to Antipatros and the rest of the oligarchy, who might have been against it, heard what happened to Demades and his son. So we must get rid of them and install a regime that will be so against the garrison they might even do something about it themselves.'

Polyperchon gestured with open hands for his son to supply the answer, for he could not.

'You proclaim the freedom of the Greeks; all exiles are free to return home. The democrats will come back and the oligarchies will be torn down in a welter of blood; suddenly we shall have all the allies we need down south – especially if we also have an army in close attendance to discourage too much thought of independence.'

'Declare the freedom of the Greeks?'

'Yes; just imagine how popular that would be. With democrats in power in Athens and the Royal Army behind me, I would then be able to threaten Nicanor from a far superior position than we are in now and negotiate his withdrawal from Munychia before Kassandros arrives with his army. He'll have to land it somewhere else but wherever that is he'll be seen as the hostile force and we will be the saviours. That's how we beat him.' Again Alexandros thumped his fist down on the desk making the piles of correspondence jump.

Polyperchon hastily tidied them back to neatness. 'Declare the freedom of the Greeks?'

'Yes, Father. But just saying it again and again is no good; you have to write the document and then distribute it throughout Greece.'

And that was something that Polyperchon could relate to: it was almost an order and it would involve much work to see it to fruition. 'I'll do it.'

'Good. And we'll worry about the consequences of creating so many democracies once Kassandros is beaten. I'll speak to our officers and make sure that the army is ready to march south in two days, with the fleet supporting it. I want to be in Attica when the news spreads so as to receive the thankful delegations and make lots of new friends. When things have settled, you can come south and be lauded as the saviour of Greece where, once again, every citizen in every city has a vote, no matter what their financial status – and may the gods help them.'

Polyperchon gazed, with a good deal of satisfaction, on the fleet, a hundred strong, lying at anchor along the coast at the mouth of the inlet leading up to Pella, three leagues away inland. Too large to be accommodated in Pella's port, it had assembled at sea whilst the army had been mustered on the plain around the city. And now all was set for another Macedonian probe into Greece; already the army had moved off, visible, to the south along the coastal road, leading first to the port of Pydna and then on into Thessaly. With multiple blasts of horns that echoed off cliffs across the bay, the fleet weighed anchor and, taking advantage of a stiff breeze in the north-east, set sail after only a few pulls of the oars from the rowers.

Polyperchon found himself waving at the majestic sight as the wind drove it southward; remembering himself, he brought down his hand, clamped it firmly to his reins and looked around his escort to see if anyone was sniggering at such a childish gesture; no one met his eye.

It was as the fleet dwindled into the distance and Polyperchon turned his mount to head back to Pella that the warning shout came and he looked to the east. Sails, scores of them, could just be seen on the horizon; at least sixty vessels, their hulls just becoming visible.

'What do you think?' Polyperchon asked the officer commanding his escort, shading his eyes with his hand.

'I think they're headed this way; if they were going south they would cut across the bay.'

'Can you make out what manner of ships they are?'

The officer squinted for a few moments. 'I can't be sure, sir, but I don't think they are merchantmen.'

'Warships?'

'I think we should prepare for that, yes, sir.'

Antigonos. Polyperchon turned his eyes to the south where his fleet was now further away from the newcomers. *Even if I could get a message to them they would have to row back against the wind; how did he know the exact moment to attack? With most of my ships away there is no chance of preventing him reaching Pella.* He turned back to the officer. 'We ride to Pella; send a messenger galloping ahead to have the harbour master prepare the harbour defences. We cannot allow that fleet to land.'

'With respect, sir, if that were an invasion fleet it wouldn't try to disembark its army in a hostile port, it would choose a convenient cove nearby or something similar. And if it were a hostile fleet come to destroy our fleet then surely it would be sailing after it and not heading to Pella's port?'

Polyperchon scratched his head. The man's logic made perfect sense and not to follow it would be seen as the action of a panicking old woman, and yet could he afford not to take action on the off-chance that this was a threat coming towards them? 'You're right, of course. I feel it's best to be prepared for any eventuality. With the army and fleet gone and just a small garrison in the port and city, Pella's open. We must hurry.' He kicked his horse forward, closing his eyes and groaning inwardly as he realised that the officer had questioned his judgement and, rather than rebuking him, he had justified himself to him. *That was not leadership.*

The chain was across the harbour entrance when Polyperchon and his escort clattered through its gates; the walls were manned by archers with red-hot braziers interspersed between them to ignite their fire arrows. Artillery pieces were crewed, loaded and trained on the harbour mouth and units of marines stood by at the gates to repel any attempt to land troops outside the walls, should the fleet prove to be hostile. And, should it break through the chain, the last three triremes – kept back as messenger ships – stood, fully manned, ready to be a last line of defence.

'They're definitely coming here, they're just passing that hill a league away,' the harbour master said, pointing into the distance. 'I stationed a man up there; you can see him signalling.'

Polyperchon shaded his eyes; flashes came from a hilltop to the south. 'There's nothing to do but wait then.'

As the lead ship came into sight, Polyperchon toyed with the idea of giving a rousing speech to the defenders and was running over the words he should say in his mind when a voice in the lookout tower shouted, 'Poseidon! Poseidon!'

Again, Polyperchon strained his eyes to see into the distance. Sure enough there, in the prow of the leading ship, stood Poseidon, naked but for some seaweed, and brandishing his trident. Kleitos the White had come to Pella.

'Antigonos moved against Lydia with such speed,' Kleitos reported as he stepped onto the quay, 'that he caught what few troops I had as my satrapy garrison completely unawares; most of them surrendered and then joined his ranks. He was at the walls of Sardis before I even knew he had invaded; he sent me a message giving me the choice of serving under him or serving underground. Fancying neither option very much, I could see that the only thing to do was to save the fleet at Ephesus.' He paused to remove a piece of seaweed that clung, moist, to his cheek, and then pointed to his command with his trident. 'Which, as you can see, I did. The last I heard, he was heading north to Hellespontine Phrygia to give Arrhidaeus the same ultimatum.'

'He's replacing all of Antipatros' nominees with his own,' Polyperchon said, 'one by one.'

'Yes, so I despatched a fast ship to give Arrhidaeus warning, but I doubt he will be able to resist Antigonos: his army is now topping seventy thousand.'

Polyperchon clapped Kleitos on a seaweed-festooned shoulder. 'You did well. What news of Asander in Caria?'

'I expect he'll go over to Antigonos. Meanwhile, Kassandros has crossed into Asia, with two of his brothers and about five hundred of his clansmen, and is on his way to join Antigonos.'

Polyperchon groaned. 'I was hoping his leg would keep him in Thrace for longer. What about Nicanor in Kappadokia? No doubt he's going to pledge himself to Antigonos as well, being Kassandros' brother?'

'Haven't you seen him?'

'Seen him where?'

'Seen him here. He faced a rebellion in his satrapy; he wasn't at all popular, and has been forced out. The locals prefer Eumenes, even though he's still under siege in Nora, and Nicanor didn't have enough forces loyal to him to resist. Anyway, Nicanor passed through Sardis two days before I left; I let him have a ship bound for Macedon. He should have arrived by now.'

'I think I'd better talk to his stepmother.'

'No, I will not,' Hyperia said, her jaw firm in defiance, as she stood before the council table in the palace throne room. King Philip, cradling his elephant, presided with a confused look and a running nose.

Polyperchon brandished his ring. 'I command you in the name of Macedon to tell me where he is.'

Hyperia waved the ring away. 'You can command in the name of your own arse as far as I'm concerned; if I were to give you my stepson you would try and use him as a hostage against Kassandros.'

Polyperchon neither affirmed nor denied the allegation.

'He has nothing to do with Kassandros' rebellion,' Hyperia continued, 'and if I can have a written undertaking from you that he will not be apprehended or harmed in any way then I will get him to swear that he will not move against you.'

'You are in no position to bargain, bitch,' Adea snapped. 'Your stepson is a traitor.'

Hyperia turned stony eyes onto the teenage queen. 'My stepson is not a traitor; to be such a thing you have to take up arms against the rightful leadership of the state. That he has not done.'

'Nicanor is the brother of Kassandros—'

'But has not yet joined him,' Polyperchon pointed out.

'Don't interrupt me, old man.' She glared at Polyperchon and then turned her fire back to Hyperia. 'I am the Queen of Macedon and I speak for the rightful king. You will hand over your stepson or I will see you executed.'

Hyperia stared at her in disbelief. 'You have no right even to issue that threat, and especially not to me.'

'I can do what I like in the name of King Philip. You will hand over your stepson or face the consequences.'

Hyperia shook her head in disbelief. 'Polyperchon, please tell the young lady that she hasn't the power.'

Polyperchon hesitated. *If I back Hyperia against Adea then I am, in effect, supporting Kassandros' rebellion against myself; a ludicrous situation. And yet to support Adea is to endorse her with far more power than she really has. In fact, it would make her more powerful than me; again, a ludicrous situation.* 'I will give you that a written undertaking that he will not be apprehended or harmed in any way.'

'What!' Adea screeched, making her husband jump in his throne.

Hyperia ignored her. 'And I will get him to swear that he will not move against you.'

Polyperchon nodded. 'Thank you, Hyperia. You may go.'

Adea jumped to her feet. 'No, she may not! She is harbouring a traitor.'

'No, Adea, she is protecting her stepson and I am happy that he will behave himself if this high-born lady of Macedon vouches for him.'

Adea looked down at him as if he were the most repellent of insects. 'You are a weak old man who has no business ruling Macedon. You, Polyperchon, are a problem.' She turned and marched to the door. Philip looked at her, then at Polyperchon and then scurried after his wife.

'You need to control that little bitch,' Hyperia said in a matter-of-fact tone before following her out. '*She* is a problem.'

Polyperchon sat back in his chair and sighed. It was true, ever since Adea had won her seat on the council, backed by the army, she had been growing more power-mad by the day. *But how to curb her ambition?* And then Antipatros' last words came back to him: 'Do not ever let Macedon be ruled by a woman.' And that was exactly what he was letting happen. *How to neutralise her?* And then he saw what he must do. *If I can't control her then I must get the help of a woman who can.*

Olympias.
The Mother.

'And so with this ox, boar and ram, given in thanks for the boy-child's life, Father Zeus, I acknowledge him as my own.' Aeacides, the King of Epirus, threw the three hearts of the sacrifices, lying opened on the temple floor, onto the altar fire. 'And I name him Pyrrhus and before the gods and my people declare him to be my heir and heir to the kingdom of Epirus.'

I can only hope that he has a little more backbone and spirit of adventure than you, my chubby cousin. Olympias looked with distaste at her kinsman as he presented his ten-day-old son to the assembled clan leaders of his mountainous kingdom. She stood, with their wives, apart in the women's area. 'The brat is healthy, I take it?' she asked Thessalonike, next to her.

'It would have been given to a slave to be left on a hilltop if it weren't.'

Olympias contemplated the screaming bundle raised in Aeacides' hands, high over his head. 'Well, I'll give the little brute a few years to see if anything can be made of him and then decide.'

'Decide what?'

'Decide whether he has any right to live, of course; Epirus can't afford to have another king like his father or Macedon will swallow it up – or, rather, it would do if it had a ruler in possession of a decent set of balls with some weight to them rather than Polyperchon's old man's eggs.' She spat at the thought of the new regent of Macedon; she was still bemused by the recent news of Polyperchon's elevation and Kassandros' flight from Pella. It had, however, been no surprise when reports of Kassandros joining Antigonos in Asia, along with two of his brothers, had come that morning as she had prepared herself for the *dekate*, the naming ceremony now drawing to a conclusion. But what had surprised her was a letter from Antigonos himself offering an alliance against Polyperchon; an alliance that went right against her nature. As much as she despised Antipatros and his entire family as well as anyone who had ever expressed a positive opinion of any of them, she thoroughly approved of his passing over of Kassandros. *The vile little rat will have been publically humiliated. The rage within him will be all-consuming; it will eat away at him on the inside.* She smiled at the sweet thought of Kassandros' consumption by wrath and hoped that it would be slow and bitter. And yet, if she accepted Antigonos' offer she would effectively be Kassandros' ally.

As Aeacides processed down the temple, showing his son to the high-born families who would one day be his subjects, Olympias considered the options that had occurred to her thus far. Her route to power was through her grandson, King Alexander, currently residing in Pella and now under the guardianship of a man who gave mediocracy a bad name, so it was a question of how she could unite herself and the child and then dispose of the drooling idiot who had, through some weird caprice of the gods, been made joint king.

The men followed their king out of the temple with the women behind them; the citizens of Pella, crammed into the agora, cheered the new addition to the royal family with an eagerness spurred by the thought of the largesse that would be distributed by the proud father. As she reached the top of the steps, Olympias grabbed Thessalonike's arm and pulled her aside. 'Come, we've better things to do than stand in the presence of that filthy mob. We've got decisions to make.'

'I don't believe we know enough of the facts to be able to make a decision,' Thessalonike said, putting Antigonos' letter back down on the table, as she and Olympias sat in the shade of an ancient olive tree in the palace gardens. The celebrations continued in the city below, ignored by both women. 'You need to know whether anyone will back Kassandros in Greece before you persuade Aeacides to invade Macedon.'

'What difference would it make? The very threat of his arrival in Greece will force Polyperchon's hand; he'll have to go south or risk losing control of the whole of Greece and probably Thessaly as well; now that Antigonos has laid claim to the treasury in Cyinda he can't afford to lose the revenue from the Greek states. He has to protect the south; indeed, one of my spies has reported that the order to muster the army has gone out; the army might even have already headed south. Macedon will be left wide open. Now's my chance to take back what is mine and to make up for being ignored by The Three Paradises settlement; never even a mention! I will have their attention if I take Macedon!'

'Yes, Mother.' Thessalonike reached over and rested a soothing hand on Olympias' thigh. 'But try not to think of The Three Paradises; you know it clouds your thoughts.'

Olympias took a deep breath and calmed herself; being totally ignored by the most influential conference of the age had been a bitter blow to her vanity. 'But, nonetheless, this is my opportunity.'

'Perhaps, but if you seize an undefended Macedon with the Epirot army and Polyperchon repels Kassandros, you will have to fight him and the Royal army of Macedon. That will make you the foreign invader; you can avoid that eventuality by just waiting upon results.'

Olympias made no comment to the observation.

'And then consider if Kassandros defeats Polyperchon and comes north to claim the regency, what then? Would you fight him too? That would mean whatever happens after you seize Macedon without a fight you would have one against the winner in the south. Should you really go to war with Kassandros?'

Olympias had no doubts. 'He would still be my enemy after what his family have done to me.'

'But would he, Mother? Would he really? At the moment, Polyperchon, as Antipatros' successor, is your immediate enemy and you always taught me that your enemy's enemy is your friend, no matter how vile they may be. And, granted, none could be much viler than Kassandros. But should he defeat and kill Polyperchon, would it not be better to come to some sort of accommodation with him so that you are not seen to be in power supported by an invading army? The Epirot troops can go home to be replaced by Kassandros' army.'

'This is all assuming that Antigonos does actually give Kassandros an army, that is.'

Thessalonike smiled and sipped her iced wine. 'Mother, there are so many armies around these days; Antigonos is bound to have one to spare.'

Olympias considered her adoptive daughter's advice. *She's right; she's a shrewd one, that's for sure. I need to wait until the outcome is clearer. But somehow, I will be the centre of attention soon.* She picked up Antigonos' letter and reread it to see if there was some hidden meaning that she had missed.

Having now irrevocably split with Polyperchon due to my confiscation of a shipment of five hundred talents bound for Macedon, an ally to his west would be a comfort to me indeed. Although I do not promote the idea of an invasion of Macedon by an Epirot army, I cannot tell what you might do should the so-called Royal Army be called south due to my proxy's arrival at a place of strategic importance. Rest assured that I shall support you whatever your actions, provided they do me no harm, and do not seek to influence events in Asia which I now consider to be under my personal control and not a part of the Kingdom of Macedon. I remain your friend, Antigonos.

No, the meaning was clear enough: he wanted her to invade but could not say so directly; Kassandros was definitely his proxy and he had served notice that Asia and Macedon were now two separate entities, never to be reunited – at least whilst Antigonos still lived.

So what should she do? *I can't trust the snakes anymore, not since I completely misunderstood the last answer; and if I did then what question should I ask?*

'You're not thinking about the snakes again, Mother, are you?'

Olympias looked at Thessalonike in surprise. 'How did you know?'

'Because you always do when you have a decision to make; but what's the point in consulting them when you can't ask a personal question? Look how wrong they were the last time they spoke.'

'I asked the wrong question.'

'That's my point. Why not consult the oldest oracle where you ask just one question?'

'"What should I do?"' Olympias smiled. 'Yes, the Mother Goddess will help; we'll set out for Dodona tomorrow.'

The grove of oaks was a place of peace and of great spirituality situated on the plain between the foothills of snow-capped Mount Tomaros and the town of Dodona, thronged with pilgrims eager to buy religious tat from unscrupulous vendors only too pleased to take advantage of their superstition or religious fervour. It had been a place of worship and divination for centuries. Just eight leagues south of Passaron, it originally was a place sacred to the Mother Goddess, Gaia; she had later been joined by Dione but, by Homer's time, Zeus had taken her place and Dione had been relegated to an aspect of his consort, Hera. But Olympias did not care about the religious hierarchy of the inhabitants, she cared only for the veracity of the oracle, whoever was the deity behind it; she had chosen to consult the priestesses of Gaia.

Soft were the chimes of the bronze circlets suspended in the boughs of the oaks as they moved in the breeze; sharp was the hammer blow that stunned the ram that Olympias had brought as an offering. The beast knew nothing of its throat being slit and succumbed to its duty as an appeasement to the Mother with little struggle and even less understanding.

It was now a time of prayer and hymns and the priestesses, all seven of them, veiled and swathed in voluminous gowns of whitest wool, swayed as they worshipped, delivering their praise and thanks to the earth beneath their feet, the being of the mother herself from which all life springs, whilst clinking small silver cymbals strapped to their thumbs and middle fingers.

Olympias and Thessalonike joined with the priestesses, having been apprised of the sacred texts and given a day to learn them. On they sang and chanted as the sun rose over Mount Tomaros bringing the grove out of the shadow and in doing so freshening the breeze so that the chiming in the trees grew, blending with the rustle of leaves now tinged with autumnal colours.

And as the sun reached its zenith, the worship came to a tinkling climax rounded off with a gasp of religious awe from all present.

'Great Mother,' the high priestess intoned, addressing the ground. 'Show yourself generous to our sister, Olympias, who has come to seek guidance. Use your sight to delve into what has been ordained. Speak through me so that her question may be answered to her satisfaction.' For a while she said nothing, listening to the sound of the chimes in the trees and the wind through their branches. Presently she knelt down on one knee, rang her cymbals and touched the earth with them, deadening the sound. 'She is come,' she announced in a voice that oozed reverence. 'Ask and you shall receive wisdom.'

'What should I do?' Olympias said, moved by the mysticism of the occasion.

No one moved as the priestesses all concentrated their minds on the sound of the trees, interpreting the rustling of the leaves, the creaking of the branches and the clinking of the chimes as the wind rose and then faded and then rose again.

For how long they stood, motionless, Olympias knew not, filled as she was with rapture at the closeness of the Mother. She placed her hand on her womb, now infertile but still a powerful reminder of her femininity and called to mind the two children who had sprung from it: the first now dead and the other sitting in Sardis waiting to be claimed by one who would dare reach for the ultimate prize; but she knew that no man would ever be worthy of her now. She mourned her children's fate and she mourned her inability to change it, as did she mourn the bitterness that now ruled her own life and she prayed that the oracle's answer would sweeten her suffering.

As one, the seven priestesses rang their cymbals and cried: 'She has spoken!'

Olympias felt a thrill of anticipation; her pulse quickened.

The high priestess lifted her veil; her eyes were rolling. 'Take care, Olympias. Do nothing yet for you are to be offered your desire. Seek the advice of your one true friend, for his actions will affect your decisions.'

The eyes rolled once more and then, as they began to focus, the priestess replaced her veil and her colleagues began a low chant, turning their backs to Olympias, the oracle now complete.

'What do you think that means?' Thessalonike asked as they walked out of the grove.

Olympias contemplated the question on the road back to Passaron, dozing in the comfort of deep cushions and furs in her covered travelling wagon: what was her desire, for she had many? Power, revenge, ecstasy, her son alive, the extinction of Antipatros' house; all of them raced around her mind, each stressing its own urgency. And then who was her one true male friend, for she thought she had none?

Nor could Thessalonike throw light on the oracle for she knew many of her adoptive mother's desires but could not say which burned deepest. And so as the wagon trundled through the south gates of Passeron, Olympias was unsure as to whether she should seek an audience with the king and request that he ready his army march west in preparation for an invasion of Macedon, for surely preparing for something was not actually doing it in the sense of taking action? Or should she take the oracle literally, going against all instincts, and bide her time, for inaction at a moment such as this, when Macedon was there for the taking, was an anathema to her?

Thus she entered her apartments as unsure of her course of action as when she had left them but with the knowledge that doing absolutely nothing was sanctioned by the Mother herself.

And it was as she sat contemplating the frustration of inaction that the messenger from Polyperchon arrived; she all but tore at the scroll such was her curiosity to see which of her desires the Mother deemed to have precedence.

She took the letter to the window so as to better read it.

From Polyperchon, Regent of Macedon, to Olympias, Queen, greetings. I write at a time that sees great dangers for Macedon, the kingdom we both love. It is threatened from the south and the east; I would that it not be so from the west. To this end, Queen Olympias, I propose an alliance. I, as you know, am regent to two kings, Alexander and Philip, but I would suggest that now would be the time for you, as Alexander's grandmother, to take him in hand and prepare him for his role in this world. I would deem it, therefore, a great favour if you would return to Macedon and share the regency with me.

Olympias sat and unconsciously scrumpled the letter in her hand. *The regency! Power once again at last.* And then it hit her, her true desire: *To meet my son's son and to see how much of the father is retained in the child. Yes, Great Mother, you are right: of all things, that is my greatest desire.*

She clapped her hands, a slave appeared. 'Send for Thessalonike.'

'And yet you hesitate,' Thessalonike said, having read the letter. 'Why? It is all you want: power and your grandchild?'

Olympias nodded and smiled. 'Yes, but I'm sure it must be a trap; who would give something like that away and ask nothing in return?'

'He secures his western border; that is a great deal for Polyperchon.'

'But he tempts me to Pella where my person will be far more exposed, endangered.'

'Then you must remember the oracle: you must seek the advice of your one true friend.'

It was then Olympias realised who had, ever since her son's death, always supported her family's cause, even though it had led him to be an outlawed exile.

She sat at her desk and began to write.

My truest friend, Eumenes…

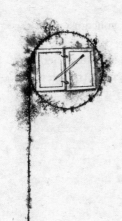

EUMENES.
THE SLY.

EUMENES LAY ON his back looking up at the night sky, willing a cloud of decent proportion to move faster and cover the three-quarter moon. Around him he could hear the breathing of the hundred men he had chosen for the raid, ninety Macedonians and ten of his Kappadokians, many with ropes and grappling hooks; they were concealed in the rock-strewn slope halfway between the sally port of the fortress at Nora and the siege lines that had kept him and his remaining followers prisoners since the spring. Wearing no armour and with weapons and boots muffled with rags, they waited on the cloud's slow progress, the thrill of impending action quickening their hearts.

Finally the moon was shrouded and night became complete. Eumenes turned to Xennias, next to him and pointed down the hill with his finger. Xennias nodded and, at a crouch, threaded his way through the rocks, down the hill, taking the ninety Macedonians with him. Eumenes counted to two hundred in his head, his palm sweating on the leather-bound hilt of his sword, and prayed that the cloud blocking the moonlight would not suddenly find the need for some urgency in its wanderings across the sky.

The allotted time reached, Eumenes got to his feet with care not to dislodge any loose rocks, and beckoned his Kappadokians to follow. Stooped low, he headed in the opposite direction to Xennias and his command for they were but a diversion, the real mission that night was Eumenes', and for it he needed few, if any, men; the ten he was taking, armed with bows and swords, were there only should something unexpected occur and they were obliged to fight their way back up to the fortress.

Down the slope they edged, careful with their footing, in the deep darkness of the cloud-covered night, down towards the trench backed by a wooden palisade, the height of two men, which circumvallated the steep hill upon which Nora perched. Almost a league in circumference and interspersed with fighting towers, the siege line was a huge area to man and Leonidas, Antigonos' commander, did not have sufficient men to do so both day and night. So, if the ringed defence were to be breached, late into the hours of darkness was the best time to do it.

A few times, over their confinement, Eumenes had probed, or even led a full-out attack on the besiegers, only to be repulsed each time; latterly he had continued leading these forays more to keep his men occupied. Both sides realised that the attacks were more for show and a relief to the tedium and so entered into them with good spirit, with very few fatalities ensuing and a free exchange of prisoners afterwards. But this mission was not to attack in order to break out, but, rather, to break someone in. One man, that afternoon, had signalled, reflecting the sun off a polished bronze disc, that he had a letter for Eumenes; that same man had brought letters before and therefore knew what to do and what to expect once he received the acknowledgement.

Now it was just a question of timing.

As he neared the trench, filled with sharpened stakes, Eumenes crouched and listened. A fox barked in the distance and received an answering call; motionless he remained, his men poised and tense behind him. The faint sound of voices floated on the breeze from the west, two perhaps three men talking in hushed tones and seemingly coming closer, most probably guards walking along the fighting platform that ran around the back of the palisade. He signalled to his men to duck down; looking up he could faintly make out the top of the wall as a completely dark line against an almost completely dark background. Sure enough, within a dozen heartbeats, the vague shapes of three heads and shoulders could be made out above the line of the palisade. *Shit! That's not what we needed and it's too dark to try for a head shot.* He looked back up at the sky: the cloud appeared to be holding its position over the moon but for how much longer he could not tell; but even if the moon were to come out the chances of hitting three heads simultaneously with killing accuracy was very slim, even for his Kappadokians who were reckoned the best shots in the fortress – and there had been plenty of time to ascertain the truth of that. And besides, the moon would illumine them just as much as the men on the wall and who knew what other eyes might be watching. *Keep walking and you might get to live.*

But it was the sound of the diversionary attack that put an end to the men's perambulation. Ostentatiously loud, with much shouting and cracking of sword hilts on wood as they scaled the walls using grappling hooks, Xennias' command pierced the night with their din.

The three men on the wall stopped and stared in the direction of the noise. 'Do you think it's just testing our defences or is it another diversionary attack,' one asked his comrades.

'Diversionary attack?'

'Yes, how else do you think Eumenes gets letters? The only thing that Leonidas can't figure out is how the messenger knows where to meet whoever it is who takes the letter up to the fortress.'

I'm afraid you have just sealed your fate, my friends. Signalling to one of his men to follow him and two more to go twenty paces to the far side of the guards, Eumenes crept forward, the cries and halloos from the diversion masking any noise he made as he slid down into the trench. Unslinging his rope and grappling hook, he waited until he considered his other two men would be in position. With a nod to his companion, he whirled the hook around his head and hurled it over the palisade; it clunked on the other side, startling the guards; he pulled the rope taut; it held; he hauled himself up, hand over fist, walking the palisade, his comrade on a rope next to him as the guards ran towards them. Over he leaped, launching himself low at the three men running along the walkway, bowling his body into them, sending them tumbling to the ground. Down a blade hissed, crunching into flesh and bone with the dull thud of a butcher's axe, causing a scream to pierce Eumenes' ears as he jerked his body upright, landing on his two feet and swinging around whilst simultaneously pulling his sword from its muffled scabbard. At them he went, the last two standing, with a silent snarl, as his companion finished off his screaming victim.

Now he wanted to kill, for now he enjoyed it. No longer was he the secretary from Kardia; that Eumenes had disappeared a long time ago when he had fought Neoptolemus single-handed and stripped the corpse of its armour. Now he was a leader of men, a winning general, a fighting man who had had little to do but train at arms for the last few months. He cut the first guard down, slitting his throat with the ease of one sacrificing a lamb whilst ducking under the swipe of the second man. Around he swung, full circle, bringing his blade slicing round into muscled thigh, cutting to the bone, wedging solid so that the hilt was wrenched from his grip as the guard went down with a howl to the gods. Eumenes' two other comrades rushed to join them, weapons bared and in moments all was quiet; the three guards lay motionless just as the moon slid from behind the cloud, its reflection glistening in a growing pool of blood.

'Leave them where they are but lay them out with respect,' Eumenes whispered to his comrades.

As they obeyed his order, Eumenes looked around on the far side of the palisade. He smiled as he saw what he was looking for: a shadowed figure flitted through the various bits of detritus left by months of siege-craft. On he came, racing up the steps to the walkway.

'Well done, Helius,' Eumenes said, taking the proffered scroll case and handing the man a weighty purse.

'I thought they would never go, sir,' Helius said, nodding down at the corpses.

'They didn't; they're still here.'

'Yeah, well, you know what I mean, sir.'

'I do. Next time we'll meet between the first and second towers on the southern side of the fortifications. They've just moved out of the camp there because it's diseased.' Eumenes enjoyed the look of concern on Helius' face. 'Don't worry yourself, you won't be there long enough. In and out quickly and no one gets hurt, just like tonight; apart from those three.' He slapped his messenger on the shoulder. 'Safe trip back.' Turning to go as the noise of the diversionary action began to subside, Eumenes grabbed his rope and slid down, wondering who it was who had written to him this time.

... *and so, therefore I would know your mind on this matter.* Eumenes put down the letter next to that of Antigonos and shook his head in disbelief. Here he was, locked up in a hilltop fortress in Kappadokia with a little under six hundred men and their horses remaining and yet he was being courted by both Antigonos and Olympias. He smiled to himself. *The world really is a different place with Antipatros' death.* The news of the old regent's passing had come the day before with Hieronymus bearing Antigonos' letter; he had been prepared for the political landscape to change after that momentous event, but to become so different as to be almost unrecognisable was pleasing in the extreme. *Kassandros being passed over for Polyperchon! I didn't see that coming; nor did Kassandros and the old nonentity for that matter. It wouldn't surprise me to get an offer from Polyperchon or perhaps even have Kassandros turning up and asking me for help, at this rate.*

He looked again at the offer from Antigonos; he skipped all the formalities and went straight to the relevant passage. *Go to Leonidas and swear loyalty to me and you shall have your freedom and satrapy of Kappadokia back, provided you serve on my staff.*

He mulled over its exact implications before turning back to Olympias' letter. Again he jumped to the relevant passage. *If I were to take up Polyperchon's offer would you be prepared to become the child's protector with responsibility for my own safety as well?*

He smiled to himself. *So everyone is now acting as if I were never condemned to death by the army assembly; my killing of Krateros has been conveniently forgotten. Well, well, Eumenes, you sly little Greek, how are we to take advantage of both offers as it would be a shame to offend one of the two by refusal.*

He then read through the oath that Antigonos wanted him to swear and shook his head, tutting. *Me swearing loyalty to you and to you alone, Antigonos, when I know that you have to rid yourself of the kings; you must think I'm stupid and that won't do.* He took a pen and rewrote the oath in a manner more to his liking.

Satisfied with his efforts, he rose and, placing both letters in a strongbox and locking it, walked out of his room, brandishing the new version of the oath, and on into the noise and chaos of the castle courtyard. Fifty horses were suspended with slings under their chests from a frame built across the entire width of the area; they stood just on their hind legs and were being goaded to thrash their forelegs and buck until the sweat foamed from them. He watched for a while, pleased with himself for having come up with this way of keeping the mounts fit. Once they were exhausted, they were taken down and a further fifty brought out to be exercised. 'How are they today?' he asked Parmida, who was overseeing the exercise.

'No injuries so far, sir.' Parmida went back to supervising the hoisting of the next batch. Many hands pulled on the ropes which, through means of a pulley system lifted the front quarters of the snorting, whinnying beasts who, even after so many months of the same routine, still objected to each new session.

But the regime had worked and the horses had remained, if not battle fit, then fit enough to endure a march should they ever get out of Nora. Indeed, until the arrival of the two letters, first from Antigonos and then, that very morning, that of Olympias, Eumenes had begun to despair of ever getting out. It had been a long, tedious time, but he had kept the men occupied and, in general, he was also happy with their fitness; the raids and the daily exercise of running around the courtyard, wrestling, weapons training and gymnastics had, along with their frugal diet, kept them lean and well-toned and as fit as the horses. Congratulating himself for what he saw as a triumph of leadership, he sought and found the man he was looking for.

'Well, what do you think, Hieronymus?' Eumenes asked after his compatriot had read his work.

'It favours the kings and Olympias much more than the original did.'

'The original only mentioned Antigonos, as you well know. With this I swear loyalty to Antigonos as he seeks to protect the Argead House in the persons of Alexander, Philip and Olympias; I think that is perfectly reasonable.' A cacophony of shouts and a scream made him look back to where a man lay with blood gushing from a head wound; the beast that inflicted it screeched and pummelled the air with its hooves whilst bouncing up and down on its hind legs, completely out of control. Seeing that Parmida was there to contain the situation, he turned back to Hieronymus. 'I still swear loyalty to Antigonos first; it's just that I'm not swearing to support him if he moves against the royal house and I don't think anyone could be asked to do that.'

Hieronymus scratched the back of his head and reread the oath. 'I suppose you could argue that.'

'Take it to Leonidas and ask him what he thinks; say that we think that it's a fairer oath as it doesn't force me into a position that I would have to become a traitor.' He gave his best look of innocence. 'No one would want me to do that, would they?'

Hieronymus chuckled. 'Never in life, dear Eumenes; we all know you to be the most loyal man there is, although why you choose to give your loyalty to a Macedonian child and a Macedonian fool is beyond me; but perhaps I remain too much of a Kardian to really understand. Still, it makes for interesting times and I enjoy observing them; definitely worthy of a history.'

'Perhaps you should begin writing it?'

Hieronymus rolled up the oath. 'Yes, I've been considering it; I would take my starting point as Alexander's death and then carry on until mine. I can foresee some momentous years ahead.' He tapped the scroll. 'I'll bring you Leonidas' answer by nightfall.'

'He debated the matter with his officers,' Hieronymus said upon his return at dusk, 'and they all agreed that it was fair and even, just that you should also name the kings and Olympias in your oath; after all, who would not be loyal to them?'

'Antigonos for one, judging by the original wording.' Eumenes gestured for his friend to sit opposite him at his study desk and poured him a cup of wine. 'So Leonidas is fool enough to accept the wording of my oath? Unbelievable; Antigonos will be furious. What happens next?'

'Leonidas has the authority to take your oath so in theory you could walk out tomorrow and resume your role as Satrap of Kappadokia; you won't even have to remove Antipatros' son, Nicanor, as he fled to Macedon last month.'

'That is very convenient.'

'More interesting than that though: Leonidas heard today that Kassandros has crossed into Asia and is with Antigonos, who's besieging Arrhidaeus in Cius on the Propontis; he's asking for his help.'

So, he's gone to Antigonos; that means he intends to fight for Macedon and he will be no friend of the kings. So if I take Antigonos' oath but then go to Macedon at Olympias' request, I will have Antigonos and Kassandros as enemies; whereas, if I stay here assembling an army, waiting to see what happens under the pretence of staying loyal to Antigonos then a clearer course may present itself. Eumenes contemplated his options for a few more moments. 'So, if I accept Antigonos' offer, I would technically have to refuse Olympias.'

'Technically, yes,' Hieronymus responded after some thought. 'But that doesn't mean an outright refusal.'

Eumenes nodded and sipped his cup, holding it in both hands. 'You're thinking along the same lines as I am. If Leonidas has been so stupid as to accept the wording of my oath then I could quite happily serve as Alexander's and Olympias' protector without breaking my oath to Antigonos and still be able to serve on his staff without seeming to be disloyal to Olympias. I would, as the saying goes, have a foot in both camps.' He leaned over and filled Hieronymus' cup. 'Would you take a letter to Olympias for me?'

'Gladly. I'd be fascinated to meet her.'

'I'm going to advise her to do nothing for the time being; neither decline nor accept Polyperchon's offer until I better know what Antigonos is planning to do with Kassandros.'

KASSANDROS.
THE JEALOUS.

H E WOULD ALWAYS have a limp. A slight limp, granted, but a limp nonetheless; and a limp would always be a sign of weakness. That he got it from a boar hunt was not a mitigating circumstance as it had not been he who had made the kill but his younger brother. Kassandros sighed to himself; it was just another thing that life had sent to try him. It was all mounting up against him but now he intended to fight back; now was to be his time, limp or no limp.

He looked at the great fleet, out in the Propontis, backlit by the sun sinking in the west, blockading the port of Cius where Antigonos had Arrhidaeus cornered, having chased him from Cyzicus and prevented him from sending a force to relieve Eumenes; he was the last of Antigonos' enemies in Anatolia now that Kleitos had fled to Macedon. Eumenes was still trapped but negotiating in Kappadokia, Alketas dead and Attalus, Docimus and Polemon safely locked up in a fortress near Celaenae. One more to go and then Antigonos would be free to turn his attention to the south and maybe, just maybe, he would lend him the great fleet – or at least a part of it – for his expedition to Athens, his starting point for the defeat of Polyperchon and the acquisition of Macedon, his birth-right.

But he still had to wait and during that waiting period there would be more humiliations and he knew that there would be another this evening. He sighed again, turned away from the imposing sight and limped towards Antigonos' tent at the heart of his camp on the Asian shore. Away to the north, trading vessels could be seen sailing to and fro through the mouth of the Bosphoros dominated by the town of Byzantium over on the European side.

The guests were already assembling when he was ushered in; laughter was raucous and wine flowing for Antigonos was entertaining Lysimachus who had just crossed, unexpected, that evening from Thrace.

'Money, that's all you ever ask for,' Antigonos boomed with a grin, slapping Lysimachus on the back and slopping his wine over the cup's rim.

'Money!' Demetrios scoffed. 'We all need money.'

Lysimachus glared at the youth. 'Be a quiet puppy or be a whipped puppy; your choice.'

Demetrios opened his mouth to reply but was silenced by his father clamping a hand over it.

Kassandros did not hide his pleasure at Demetrios' embarrassment; the youth had never failed to make a point of his upright posture at dinner and had also taken to imitating his limp. As a guest of his father there was little that Kassandros could do about it other than endure. *But once I have no need of them, well, then we shall see, you cocky dandy.*

'Money,' Antigonos boomed again, steering Lysimachus away from Demetrios, 'I've barely enough for my own needs.'

Lysimachus attempted a smile; it had never been considered a warm smile and Kassandros could well see how false it was. 'You need money, Antigonos, as you say, for your own needs; I, on the other hand, need it for all our sakes and safety.'

'Are you still building fortresses?'

'I'm fighting the Getae and other hideous tribes to the north, expanding my satrapy, as well as building our defence against the threat from even further north; a real threat; a threat which is heading this way and I need money to carry on. Antipatros promised me a lot, and he was good to his word for a portion of it, but since his death I have received nothing.' He saw Kassandros taking a cup of wine from a slave, and pointed at him. 'Did he not bring my request when he came to you from me?'

Antigonos looked to see who he was talking about. 'Who, him? Kassandros? Well, he did mention something about money but he was more anxious to get an army and a fleet out of me so he didn't labour the point too hard.'

'Only thinks about himself, that one,' Lysimachus said with a sneer.

'Don't we all?' Kassandros retorted.

The look Lysimachus returned was poisonous; their relationship had not improved during Kassandros' sojourn in Thrace. Lysimachus had flatly refused any military help, despite Nicaea's pleas, on the grounds that he completely agreed with Antipatros' choice of successor and just because he was Kassandros' brother-in-law did not mean he had to like him. 'Speaking personally, I think about everyone; why else would I be spending what very limited resources I have building a vast network of fortifications.' Lysimachus turned back to Antigonos. 'Money is what I need and money is what you have.'

'It's not that simple; Antigenes and his Silver Shields guard the treasury at Cyinda and he won't let me make a withdrawal without the permission of Polyperchon who, as far as Antigenes and his second-in-command, Teutamus, are concerned, is the legitimate regent as he holds the Ring of Macedon.'

'Well, then you should kill him and the Silver Shields.'

'My lads wouldn't stand for that; a lot of them have fathers and grandfathers in the Silver Shields.'

'Fuck what your lads think; do what's best for you. But forget Antigenes; I've heard about what happened at Tarsus and I want some of those five hundred talents.'

Antigonos face took on a hurt countenance. 'Is this the only reason you came to see me, old friend?'

'Five hundred talents!'

'We could at least get drunk before you start making demands on me in my own tent.'

'I'll get drunk once you've promised me money,' Lysimachus growled, his voice low.

Antigonos looked at him in earnest. 'And how do we know this *threat* that you are on about is real? What proof do you have?'

Lysimachus made another attempt at a smile, this time it was more successful, although no less chilling. 'That is the other reason why I've come.' He turned to a Thracian officer accompanying him. 'Bring them in.'

It was with a gasp and an unrestrained look of open-eyed awe that Kassandros stared up at the two giants, in their early twenties, shuffling into the tent; they were led by Thracians, holding chains fastened to iron collars, and were weighed down with the heaviest of manacles and leg-irons. At least half a head taller than anyone present – or anyone who Kassandros had ever seen for that matter, Seleukos included – the captives looked taller still with their flame-red hair stiffened to stand upright in spikes; strange swirling patterns, in greens and blues, covered their pale skin, stretched taut over beautifully sculpted physiques that would inspire jealous admiration at the Olympic or any other games. Pale-blue eyes stared straight ahead, disdaining to look around, as they were paraded before an incredulous audience.

'This, gentlemen,' Lysimachus said, evidently pleased at the reaction to his exhibition, 'is what we have to fear: Keltoi. These are two of hundreds of thousands just like them, some even bigger. They have been migrating from the north-east, pushed, no doubt, by other tribes from way beyond the imagination. So far, we have been lucky, they by-passed us and went further west killing and pillaging as they went and then taking whatever land they wanted to settle upon and enslaving the peoples whose ancestral home it was. But soon they will run out of land in the west and then their eyes will be turned back towards us.' He walked up to the nearest captive, grabbed him by the testicles and squeezed.

The man's jaw clenched, his body tautened and his eyes flickered, watering slightly, but he emitted no sound nor displayed any sign of pain.

'You see?' Lysimachus let go of the ravaged scrotum. 'They are either oblivious to pain or just too proud to show it; either way it makes them the most formidable foe.'

'Where did you find them?' Antigonos asked, visibly impressed.

'They were prisoners of the Getae; some of my own Thracians captured them in a raid across the Danubus.' He looked up at their motionless faces, shaking his head in wonder. 'Despite having heard all about them, these are the first that I've seen and they have made me even more determined to keep them away from our lands. Now, Antigonos, before I ask you for money again I shall give you a little demonstration of their prowess.' He turned to the Thracian guards. 'Has the fighting ring been constructed?'

'It is near done, sir.'

It was full darkness by the time the ring was ready: its fencing high and strong so as not to be scaled or broken through; flaming torches burned around it as the two Keltoi were pushed into the middle by their Thracian guards, who beat a hasty retreat leaving a trembling slave to remove their manacles; he was strangled by one as his reward and none of the spectators tried to intervene. Two long slashing swords were thrown into the ring. Lysimachus gestured to one of their Thracian guards to come close; he whispered something in his ear. The Thracian shouted down to the two men in their own language.

The winner gets to live, I suppose. Kassandros was looking forward to seeing this battle of giants.

They looked at each other, nodded, then each picked up a sword and retired to opposite sides of the ring, fifteen paces apart.

For a moment all was silence but then, with a mutual consenting nod, the two men howled, their backs arched, arms down and faces turned to the sky. Their voices mingled in a deathly din that rose and fell.

Kassandros' blood froze. *What formidable allies they would make.* A thrill surged through him at the thought

And then they charged, accelerating at one another at lightning pace, whirling their weapons around their heads before leaping high and slashing them down at their opponent's neck; with a trail of sparks the blades met, resounding in metallic clarity, and bending at the impact. Thrusting their chests out, the Keltoi crashed into each other like two rutting beasts engaged in a mating battle for the pick of the females. Back they rebounded, their footing sure, to slash again with bowed blades at necks, thighs, arms and hips, in a whirr of frenzied motion, parrying, dodging, leaping, ducking as the swords hissed through the air in constant, random cuts, down, across and up, all the while howling their war-cries. And then the first blood splattered onto sweat-sheened flesh but whose it was Kassandros could not tell nor did the combatants seem to care; on their gore-streaked blades scythed. A wet, heavy chop and an incredulous look of the face of one as he watched his arm, sword still gripped, fly through the torchlight; it was the last thing he saw. His head fell from his shoulders and hit the ground at the same time as his knees, blood pulsing from his wounds as his heart pounded on for a few fading beats. The victor looked down at the vacant, staring eyes of his opponent and threw down his sword in disgust.

'That, gentlemen,' Lysimachus said, 'is true fury. And if you think that was impressive then you should know that I had the guard tell them that the winner would be impaled, not freed as you must have supposed. Neither would countenance the shame of offering himself up for an easy death and escape the stake. That's how they think. Now imagine a migration of two hundred thousand of those coming over the Danubus, through the Succi pass in the Haemus mountains and then down into Thrace and from there either into Macedon or across the Hellespont and into Anatolia. Imagine that and then try to refuse my request for money, Antigonos.'

Antigonos looked at the blood-dripping warrior, standing perfectly still as his chest heaved in air. 'You have made your point, Lysimachus.'

'Tell him that this time if he wins, he lives,' Demetrios shouted, jumping into the ring, drawing his blade. 'And get him a new sword.'

'Get out of there, you young fool!' Antigonos shouted. 'What have you got to prove?'

'That they are not invincible. Now, tell him, Lysimachus.'

Lysimachus nodded at the Thracian guard, who then shouted down at the Kelt; the man looked at Demetrios and smiled, thin and grim, he brought his knee up and, placing the flat of his blade upon it, straightened it and then kicked away the Greek sword that had been thrown in to replace his. Working his shoulders, he gave a few experimental slashes, left and right.

This must be my lucky day. Kassandros leaned forward to get a better view. *How I love the arrogance of youth.*

Demetrios crouched, his sword to one side in his right hand his left, palm down, extended out for balance; his weight constantly shifting from one foot to the other.

The Kelt ceased his slashing and withdrew to the ring's edge, directly opposite Demetrios, pulled back his shoulders, arched his back and howled again to the sky. Demetrios raced forward, flashing across the ring, and plunged his blade up into the unsuspecting Kelt's throat as his cry reached its crescendo; it died in his blood-filled gorge. The man's head came forward and he looked with shock down at his killer. Towering over Demetrios, the Kelt wobbled and then collapsed to his knees.

Demetrios pulled his sword free; the man expired, slumping onto the ground. 'And if they do come, Lysimachus, we will just have to work out how to beat them. But I agree: it would be better if they didn't; you should have your money.'

The cocky dandy will be impossible after that; even Lysimachus looks as though he's impressed. Kassandros turned to leave.

'Where are you going?' Antigonos called after him. 'We haven't eaten yet and you are my guest.'

With a sigh Kassandros headed for the tent and took his place, seated on the couch amongst a throng of reclining men.

'What of the goings on in the south and east?' Lysimachus asked once the discussion of the Keltoi's prowess and fearlessness and Demetrios' cunning in overcoming it had been exhausted.

'Seleukos is sitting comfortably in Babylon,' Antigonos replied, breaking off a hunk of bread and wiping his wooden trencher with it. 'He seems to be quietly gathering an army, although where he intends to use it I don't know.'

'With Antigenes and his Silver Shields back in Cilicia, he's probably got his eye on Susiana.'

'Possibly. But how would Peithon in Media and Peucestas in Persis take that? It might be enough for them to find common cause.'

'Maybe so.'

'And what would Ptolemy think?'

'Oh, Ptolemy wouldn't care what happens out east; he seems to be moving back to Egypt, having left garrisons in all the major cities: Damascus, Tripoli, Tyros, Beryrut; I'll not bother with them for the time being. I'll give him time to grow comfortable and then I'll deal with him. Who knows, Seleukos may even do some of the work for me by trying to move west; but I doubt I'll be that fortunate.'

Lysimachus frowned as he inspected a piece of hard cheese. 'What gives you the right to deal with him?'

'Antipatros made me general of all Asia.'

'He's dead. Had you not better get Polyperchon to confirm the appointment?'

Antigonos waved away the suggestion. 'Polyperchon won't be around for much longer.'

'You seem remarkably sure of that; what makes you so?'

'Ah, well, Arrhidaeus is now completely bottled up in Cius so it's just a question of waiting it out; in the meantime I might as well do something positive, especially now as Polyperchon has declared the freedom of all the Greek cities; they'll be executing the oligarchs and restoring democratic regimes which will be queuing up to support him.' He picked up his cup and extended it towards Kassandros. 'Today's your lucky day, Kassandros. I've troops and ships to spare at the moment. Take them to Athens and then beat whatever army Polyperchon sends against you and get rid of those democracies before they take root again.' He drank a large draught, burped and then downed the rest of his wine. 'You owe me, Kassandros.'

That's as maybe but it doesn't mean I necessarily have to pay. Kassandros smiled at Antigonos, raised his cup and drank to him. 'You won't regret it.'

'I had better not. You just make sure that the only person who does is Polyperchon.'

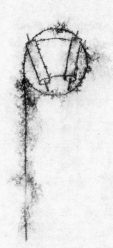

POLYPERCHON.
THE GREY.

P OLYPERCHON GAVE A heavy sigh as
he reread his son's letter.

Upon my arrival in Athens I found that Nicanor of Sindus has hired mercenaries to add to the garrison at Munychia and with this enlarged force has taken control of the entire harbour of Piraeus, including the boom across its mouth. He has barred all our shipping from entering as well as the Athenian grain fleet. His position is secure but not completely so if we were to use overwhelming force against him quickly. Despite receiving a message from Olympias demanding, in the name of her grandson, King Alexander, to disband the garrison, he remains in place and I can only assume that he is expecting Kassandros' arrival imminently. And that might come sooner than we think for the rumour is that Antigonos and Eumenes have come to some sort of agreement and the siege of Nora has been lifted so there are more troops to spare now.

He paused to reflect upon Olympias' demand: *She may be slow in taking up my offer but at least her letter to Nicanor proves that if she isn't exactly on my side then at least she is totally against Kassandros. At least that teenaged thorn in my flesh doesn't suspect my overtures to Olympias.* He glanced at Adea, sitting, beyond

Kleitos, on the other end of the council table, in front of her husband squatting on his throne. *As to Antigonos and Eumenes, I've heard that rumour too so most likely it's true; that leaves Antigonos with only Arrhidaeus to beat in Anatolia and then where will he look: south or west?*

His sigh was even heavier as he returned his attention to the letter.

> *I have taken control of the city itself – as well as the remains of the long walls that used to connect it to Piraeus. Despite the pleas of Phocion and his fellow oligarchs, I have brought Hagnonides, the leader of the democratic faction, back from exile and every day more democrats return so that the assembly will soon be dominated by them. This, however, is not the case in some of the Greek cities where your decree is being fiercely resisted, Megalopolis being a case in point.*
>
> *I have not the resources to deal with Nicanor and to keep control of Athens as well as enforcing the decree on recalcitrant oligarchies; I would therefore ask, Father, that you come south with reinforcements. I have sent Kleitos with this letter so as you can put any questions you might have to him.*

Polyperchon sighed again and then looked down the table to Kleitos seated at its middle. 'Would reinforcements make a difference?'

'Yes, they would,' Kleitos replied, placing down the huge clam shell he had been admiring. 'Piraeus could be taken with sufficient troops storming it and Megalopolis would succumb to a siege but more men are needed to do all that; men and, perhaps, elephants.'

'And with those two things accomplished then Kassandros would have no access to Athens, or potential allies, if he should come, and the last few oligarchies would fall giving me control of all Greece.'

'Precisely.'

'But you would leave Macedon exposed to Antigonos,' Adea pointed out.

Kleitos hid his irritation. 'Assuming Nicanor is holding Piraeus for Kassandros' arrival, which I think is a safe assumption, then he is obviously coming by sea which means he has to get a fleet off Antigonos. Now, our one-eyed friend won't be foolish and give him the entire fleet so he will have to divide his forces.' Kleitos paused and turned to Polyperchon in order to see if his train of thought was being followed.

It was. 'Two weaker half-fleets.'

'Precisely.'

'Each twice as easy to beat.'

Kleitos shrugged. 'Let's hope so. I would suggest that you go south with reinforcements and take Piraeus. Meanwhile, I take my fleet to the Propontis. On the way, I should meet Kassandros and be able to deal with him, and then defeat Antigonos so that he cannot cross into Europe.'

'And then relieve Arrhidaeus in Cius so that we have an ally in Asia.' Polyperchon smiled for what he felt was the first time since he had been cursed with the ring. 'It could be perfect.' He then paused and slapped his forehead. 'Gods! It is perfect. If I write one letter we will get another ally in Asia.'

'Who to?' Adea asked, suspicion in her tone.

'Eumenes.'

'Eumenes? But he's just sworn an oath to Antigonos, if the rumour is true.'

So even she's heard it; it must certainly be true then. 'And I've heard a version of that rumour too: apparently he also added the kings and Olympias into that oath which is why he won't refuse my offer, thereby giving Antigonos such a big problem in Asia, he won't have time to cross to Europe, even if it was on his agenda.'

'What will you offer him?'

It's better to tell her than have her think I'm hiding something. Polyperchon lifted the ring and looked at it with pleasure. 'As regent, I will offer him Antigonos' title of general-in-command in Asia and make him guardian of the kings whom I shall promise to bring to him at some vague date in the future and authorise him to draw five hundred talents from Cyinda and have Antigenes and his Silver Shields under his command.'

Kleitos grinned at the subtlety of the plan. 'That is a big offer. That will make Antigonos the rebel and mean that he and Eumenes will be bound to fight again, just as they had made friends; what a shame.'

'Indeed, it could keep them busy for years. Go over to Ephesus before you go back to Athens and drop the messenger off; the sooner Eumenes is coaxed onto our side the better.'

'I'll be a couple of days and then I'll pick up my fleet, leaving a few ships behind to keep an eye on Nicanor of Sindus in Piraeus, and head for the Propontis.'

'With luck your arrival should coincide with the news of Eumenes' war with Antigonos being back on, with the one difference that this time Eumenes is also fighting on behalf of me, the regent, and both of the kings; he will be completely legitimate and, therefore, in the right. That should give our one-eyed friend pause for thought as he watches his ships go down.'

'Then there's not a moment to be lost,' Kleitos said, getting to his feet with the aid of his trident and picking up his clam shell.

'There is not. I'll march tomorrow, light and fast.'

Polyperchon raised his fist into the air, a single horn sounded and was repeated all the way down the column of three thousand cavalry, ten thousand infantry and twenty-two elephants; it had been shorn of its trail of camp-followers as this was to be a forced march, the baggage could follow in its own time.

The vanguard of two hundred light cavalry, Thessalians in the wide-brimmed leather sun hats, cantered off as the column moved forward and soon got to a speed that would carry it ten leagues in one day; exhausting for any infantry who had not been a part of Alexander's army where speed was one of his major weapons.

Polyperchon glanced sideways at King Philip, riding between him and Adea, grinning and drooling as he looked around admiring his army, as he had put it when he had taken the salute that morning. *And I suppose it his, technically; although what he would do with it if he were in command only the gods know and they're probably laughing about it still.*

Adea rode in stony-faced silence having lost the argument for staying behind as Roxanna was doing with her son.

'The kings' army has to have at least one king with it,' he had told her when she had complained that Roxanna would use the time unsupervised to cultivate dangerous friends.

'The kings' army ought to have both kings with it,' she had retorted.

'It should,' he had agreed, 'but the other king is five years old and has to travel in a wagon, as does his mother, but for other reasons, and we are going to be marching so fast that even if we started out the day with two kings, after less than half a league we would only have one.' *Provided he hasn't fallen off his horse and got himself stuck in a ditch,* he had added to himself. The logic had been undefeatable and Adea had been forced to accept, with reluctance, the arrangement.

Roxanna, unsurprisingly, had been only too pleased to remain behind; that, however, had been a part of Polyperchon's plan: he hoped that when Olympias got wind of the fact that her grandson was in Pella with solely his mother then she might be tempted to take up his offer. *And then, if it all goes to plan, I'll be secure in the south, east and west, with just the wilder hill tribes to the north to worry about as it ever thus was. With luck, that teenage harpy will be the first of Olympias' victims.*

Thus it was in an unusually optimistic mood that Polyperchon set off on the road to Athens and so he remained for the first four days of the march until the column came to Pharygae, on the coast not far from Lamia in Aetolia, where the Athenian Oligarchic delegation met him, led by Phocion, demanding that he hear their side of the argument, and completely ruining his equilibrium.

'And Hagnonides, the leader of the democratic faction, has also just arrived,' the officer of the watch told him as he bathed away the dust of a day's march in preparation for giving an audience to Phocion.

'Has he now? Is there no end to Greeks wanting to put forward their arguments instead of just doing what they are told? Well, I suppose that is convenient; I will listen to them together.' He dried his head and neck and then threw the towel at a waiting slave. 'And they had better be quick. Send for the king, he can chair the proceedings; I shall make this into a court hearing.'

Philip grinned and puffed his chest up as everyone present stood whilst he took his place on the throne, set up on a dais at the head of the open-air court; once settled, a bodyguard to either side, he waved at his wife with his elephant as she took her seat next to Polyperchon, and pointed to himself to make sure that she had seen him. 'I'm playing king!'

Adea gave him a stern glare that caused him to shrink back into his throne, his shoulders hunched and his head bowed, whimpering at her censure.

Polyperchon looked at the two delegations waiting to approach and then beckoned them.

'Lord regent,' Phocion said as he approached. Now in his eighty-fourth year, his beard was pure white, as was the wispy hair on his head. He walked with a stoop and a stick but his voice was still strong. 'I would crave the indulgence of having one far more eloquent speak for me; one but for whom we would have arrived sooner had he not have fallen ill upon the way; but such was my desire that he should present our petition that we tarried while he underwent a full recovery.'

The gods save me from long-winded Greeks. Polyperchon grunted. 'Who?'

'It would be remiss of me not to first praise his qualities both as an orator and—'

'Just tell me his name!' *Gods, these Greeks and their love of their own voices.*

'Deinarchos of Corinth.' Phocion made way for the orator who stood before Polyperchon, looking grave and wordy, with a scroll in his hand.

Polyperchon was astounded and rounded on Phocion. 'You,

Antipatros' great friend, bring Deinarchos, another of Antipatros' great friends, in front of me to plead your case? You, who have been colluding with Nicanor of Sindus. You, who no doubt long for Kassandros' arrival in Athens as he will support your cause, bring this man, this traitor, to plead your case with me?'

'I am no traitor to Macedon,' Deinarchos insisted. 'I have always been a great supporter of Macedon; I prosecuted Demades and secured his conviction.'

'You have always been a great supporter of Antipatros, not Macedon; if you were then you would have realised that Macedon is not Kassandros, Antipatros' son, nor is it supportive of the Athenian oligarchy.' He turned to the officer commanding the guard. 'Take him away and find out what he knows of Kassandros and Nicanor of Sindus' plans and then execute him.'

'You cannot do this!' Deinarchos shouted as he was grabbed by strong soldiery.

'I can and I am.'

'But I came here in good faith, you must see that.'

'I only see a supporter of my enemy come to plead for another old friend of Antipatros who only wants me to reverse my decree on the freedom of the Greeks so that he and his cronies can stay in power and support Kassandros against me; I won't have it! Take him!' The guards dragged the struggling Deinarchos away as Polyperchon reflected upon the justice of summarily executing a man who had made a living out of prosecuting the innocent, far more than the guilty, for large portions of Macedon's treasury.

Uproar gripped the court as both delegations expressed their views on the decision, one for and one against. Hagnonides, a rat-like face and a skinny, loose-fleshed frame, leading the democratic faction, bellowed with laughter, pointing at the unfortunate man. 'That's for all the innocent men you sent to death or exile!'

Polyperchon sat with his eyes closed, willing himself to keep his temper, simmering inside as the noise grew. *I cannot bear these people.* 'Will you be quiet!' he exploded with a vehemence that silenced everyone. 'Silence, I say. Silence!' He took a couple of deep breaths and then looked at Phocion. 'You want me to repeal my freedom of the Greeks' proclamation so that the seventeen thousand or so citizens whom Antipatros exiled to Thrace do not return and therefore the nine thousand citizens whose assets amount to more than two thousand drachmae can remain in power. Is that not so?'

'Lord Regent, it is not a simple question of yes and no; we must first look at all—'

'No, we mustn't, Phocion. Just answer the question: yes or no?'

'But that would be to ignore the essence of the matter; not to get to the very heart of—'

'Yes or no!'

'But to answer so—'

'Yes or no!'

'In substance the answer would be a tentative yes, but—'

'But nothing. I have my answer. Hagnonides, what is your reason for being here?'

'To thank you, Polyperchon, for restoring our rights as citizens of Athens and to help us bring these oligarchs,' he spat the word, 'to justice. We have always been loyal to Macedon and we always will be and we will punish these men in the assembly; in the true democratic assembly of Athens. Send them back to the city in animal cages and we will see it done.'

A roar of laughter interrupted Polyperchon's reply and all turned to the king who was laughing uncontrollably on his throne, knees up and hands clutching his sides in the most un-regal manner.

'Philip!' Adea shouted, getting up from her seat. 'Philip, behave yourself.'

You stupid girl; you don't say that in public to the King of Macedon, no matter how much of an idiot he is.

Philip looked at his wife, tears flowing down his face, trying to get a hold of his mirth.

'Philip, stop it.' Adea leaned over and whispered into his ear.

Philip's laugh came to an abrupt end; he looked around suspiciously. 'The Ferryman? Where?'

Adea whispered again.

Philip nodded slow understanding. 'Yes, I'm king; but it was funny: the man came to speak for that man,' he pointed at Phocion, 'and instead was taken away to be made dead.'

'Yes, Philip, but that was a while ago. You have to concentrate on what is happening at the moment.' She stroked his cheek; he looked up at her and drooled.

It was an embarrassed silence that hung over the court as all pretended that this was the most normal way for the king of Macedon and his consort to behave.

It was Phocion who broke that silence as Adea sat back down.

'May I speak in my defence, Lord Regent?'

'No, I've had enough of long-winded Greeks.' Polyperchon got to his feet and turned away.

'Lord Regent!' a member of Phocion's delegation shouted, rushing forward and grabbing Polyperchon's shoulder. 'Think of all Phocion has done for Macedon; of all we have done for Macedon in keeping our fellow Greeks in peace; leading by example in paying our dues and providing men not only as infantry but also as rowers. We have ever been loyal.'

Polyperchon pulled himself away from the grip. 'Stop lying to me in the presence of the king!'

This was too much for Philip; he leaped from his throne, grabbed one of his bodyguards' spears and charged at the delegate.

'Hegemon!' Phocion shouted, pointing at the incoming threat.

Hegemon turned and jumped to one side, narrowly avoiding the spear-point.

Polyperchon jumped on the king, wrapping his arms about him, halting him as Hegemon scampered away. 'What are you doing?'

Philip looked at Polyperchon, outrage in his dim eyes. 'He told fibs! You said so. You mustn't tell fibs, my wife told me. I never tell fibs, not anymore.'

'Yes, well, that doesn't mean you have to kill someone if they do.'

'I'm playing king; I can do anything I want.'

Taking the spear from Philip's hands, Polyperchon turned to Adea. 'Take him back to his tent and try to impress upon him the need to behave with decorum on this trip.'

'And what about us?' Phocion asked.

'I shall have you all shipped back to Athens and your assembly can deal with you before I arrive. This is not an issue for Macedon; we do not interfere in the internal politics of Greek states.' With that blatant reworking of the truth, Polyperchon left the court in uproar. *Lucky I took the spear away from the idiot; even he would have realised that was a 'fib'.*

With the delegations both sent back by sea, one in chains the other not, Polyperchon continued his march south and it was with relief that he met up with Alexandros encamped on the farmland around the city to make a total of twenty-five thousand men living off Athens' bounty.

'They have already sent a delegation asking me to leave, Father,' Alexandros said as they walked through the camp in order to be seen by the men as they cooked their evening meal, greeting them and sharing a joke with old comrades. 'They claim that there will be a backlash against the new regime if our foraging causes a shortage of food in the city. They're especially worried because they put Phocion to death; they made him and five others drink hemlock after such long service to Athens.'

'Well, that's their own fault for going to extremes. Exile would have been quite sufficient, just as he did to them; he spared them death when he had the chance yet they could not see their way to doing the same.'

'And they botched it by not giving the executioner enough public money to buy sufficient leaves so there was the undignified spectacle of Phocion, half dead, giving money out of his own purse to the executioner to go and buy more; this obviously has got around and there are mumblings in certain quarters against the viciousness of Hagnonides and his faction.

'That's Greeks for you.' Polyperchon looked across to Athens, the grand, brightly painted buildings on the Acropolis glowing in even richer hues in the evening sun, towering over the city that was ancient by any reckoning. 'Then we had better get this done as quickly as possible; once we've got Nicanor of Sindus out of Piraeus, I can take the main bulk of the army over to Megalopolis and the Athenians can stop moaning.' He acknowledged the greeting of a group of veterans he recognised from the storming of a stronghold in Bactria, recalling their names and asking how they did, before turning towards his tent. 'We had better come up with a plan of attack.'

'I have one already, Father. I'll take you through it as we walk.'

'I think that would work admirably, Alexandros,' Polyperchon said as they neared his tent. Did Kleitos leave enough ships to block the harbour mouth to prevent any escape by sea?'

'Yes, Father, twelve should be enough.'

'Good. Will everything be ready by tomorrow night?'

'I'll make sure it is.'

'Has Olympias written again to Nicanor of Sindus?'

'Not to my knowledge, no. I must admit I was surprised that she did so in the first place.'

Polyperchon returned the guards' salute as he entered his tent. 'I believe Olympias did it to demonstrate that she is on my side even though she hasn't taken up the offer I made her after you went south.'

'Which was?'

'Yes, which was?' a female voice echoed.

Polyperchon started, and then turned to see Adea sitting at the council table with the king perched on his throne.

'I sit here, waiting for you to come back so that we can take counsel together on how to proceed and I hear you have made Olympias an offer of some sort without even mentioning it to me. How is that?'

'It was nothing,' Polyperchon said, hoping his embarrassment would not show. 'I offered her a meeting with her grandson on the border between Macedon and Epirus if she would keep her nephew from taking advantage of me taking the army south and leaving no more than five thousand troops in Macedon.'

Adea eyed him with deep suspicion. 'And that was all?'

'Yes.'

She contemplated him for a few moments before coming to an internal decision and then smiling. 'Well, gentlemen, would you like to brief the king on the situation?'

Having briefed the fidgeting king, Polyperchon looked at Alexandros, as Adea led her husband by the hand from the tent, the meeting over. 'Well?'

'Well, what?'

'Do you think she believed me?'

'She might have; it sounded plausible. But what did you really offer Olympias?'

Alexandros whistled once his father had divulged the truth. 'That is a death warrant for the girl.'

'I know. We shall have to keep a sharp watch on her in case she does suspect something.'

But shouting from outside prevented further discussion of the matter as the officer commanding the guard came rushing in. 'Come quickly, sir!'

Polyperchon and Alexandros rushed out and looked in the direction the man was pointing.

Polyperchon's spirits sank. 'Gods above and below, Kleitos missed them and we're too late.' There, on the horizon, lit by the last of the westering sun were sails, scores of them. Kassandros had come to Athens and there was nothing to be done about it. Polyperchon turned, he had seen enough. 'We'll send to parley with him in the morning; perhaps we can avoid an all-out war.'

But the morning held even less hope for Polyperchon as Alexandros hurried into his tent. 'It's Adea!'

'What about her?' Polyperchon said, chewing on a hunk of bread dipped in olive oil.

'She's gone. And the king is missing too.'

287

'Where to?' Polyperchon asked, jumping to his feet.

Alexandros shrugged but Polyperchon had a sinking feeling that he knew as he left his tent to see for himself; and that feeling was confirmed by the sight that presented itself to him as he looked towards Piraeus: the fleet was leaving.

'Is Kassandros going, Father?'

Polyperchon shook his head. 'No, Son. Kassandros is staying with the army that the fleet brought. The fleet is heading for the Propontis. Adea was in on all our plans; she's taken the king over to Kassandros and has told him about Kleitos. Kassandros has sent his fleet to crush him between it and Antigonos.'

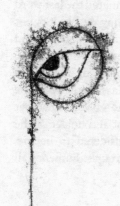

ANTIGONOS.
THE ONE-EYED.

'WHEN I HEARD of it, Leonidas, I was speechless.' Antigonos' one eye glared up at his subordinate, newly arrived in his camp at Chalcedon on the Bosporus, standing to attention before him. 'Speechless in that I was bellowing so incoherently in rage that I was incapable of speech. Does that give you some sort of an idea of just how angry I was, still am, at what you did?'

Leonidas met his commanding officer's glare with defiance. 'You gave me the authority to negotiate with him and that was a part of the negotiations. Besides, it seemed reasonable to me and all my officers that he should swear loyalty to the kings as well. After all, aren't we all loyal to them and to Olympias as the mother of Alexander?'

'My arse!' Antigonos slammed his fist onto the desk. 'My great, pox-ridden arse! You are loyal to me and me alone!'

Leonidas flinched at the outburst. 'And you are loyal to the kings – surely?'

Antigonos collected himself. *I cannot deny that publicly and keep a steady command.* 'The kings are in Europe; they have left Asia. I am the commander-in-chief of Asia; therefore the ultimate loyalty in Asia must be to me and Eumenes is in Asia. But you,' Antigonos raised a shaking finger at Leonidas, 'you have given him a way out of his oath because he can claim that his loyalty to the kings has a higher calling than his oath to me and he would be justified!' He half stood as he shouted the last word and then slumped back down again, breathing deeply. 'So, not only is the sly little Greek back as Satrap of Kappadokia and raising a fresh army, but he can now also use that army to attack anyone whom the kings, or that witch Olympias, deem to be an enemy. And, seeing as I've just supplied Kassandros with the ships and troops to threaten Polyperchon who – if you remember – is, rightly or wrongly, officially the regent and holder of the ring of Macedon, that could well be considered to be me. Because of your stupidity I will now have to fight Eumenes all over again.'

'Unless he sticks to his oath to you.'

Antigonos' mouth dropped open and he stared, incredulous, at Leonidas for many a moment. 'If he was going to do that he wouldn't have changed the oath,' he finally managed to say in a choked voice. 'Now go, before I have your balls ripped off and shoved up your arse for you to shit out in the morning.'

Leonidas saluted, wincing at the image, and stepped smartly out of the tent.

Antigonos drained a full cup of wine, refilled it and then turned to Demetrios and Philotas, sitting in the shadows. 'If he hadn't have provided such good service recently, I would do that.'

'I would still do it,' Philotas said.

Demetrios looked concerned at his father. 'What are you going to do?'

'What else can I do but send a strong force into Kappadokia, capture the little Greek again and give him a choice between swearing a new oath to me alone or going through the same treatment that Leonidas has so narrowly missed. I'll get Menander to do it; I need to show some faith in him or he'll be sloping off back to Europe or south to Ptolemy or Seleukos to sell his services there. Five thousand men should be enough, half and half cavalry and skirmishing infantry, mercenary peltasts and Thracians as well as archers and slingers.' He looked over to his son. 'See to it,

Demetrios. They're to leave tomorrow morning and travel light; I want them to arrive in Kappadokia before news of their coming gets there. Speed, that is the essence. Get going and have Menander report to me.'

'Yes, Father,' Demetrios said, standing and making to leave.

'And make sure none of the lads have ever served with Eumenes,' Antigonos called after his son. 'He has an odd way of inspiring loyalty.'

'And you don't, old friend?' Philotas asked.

'Oh, the lads follow me all right, but I'm Macedonian and I've been a soldier ever since I killed my first boar, so they understand me and I understand them. But Eumenes is a Greek and he used to be a secretary and those two things combined, as far as the lads are concerned, is as good as saying that he takes it up the arse on a professional basis. And yet, there is no denying it, he does command the loyalty of Macedonians serving under him. It's something I find hard to understand but must always take into account.'

'You wanted to see me, sir,' Menander said as the guard held the tent flap open.

'Yes, come and sit down; I need you to do something for me.'

'I'll do my best,' Menander said, having been briefed on the mission.

'I'm sure you will. And when you get him don't let him try and twist you with honeyed words. He can be very persuasive.'

'I know our sly little Greek only too well.'

'Father!' Demetrios shouted, bursting in.

'Well?'

'Father, we're under attack at Cius.'

'Our siege lines there?'

'No, from the sea. They defeated the blockading squadron, sunk or captured every one of our vessels except for the ships holding the harbour as the boom held. When the messenger left, they were attacking the sea walls.'

'The sea walls? How can they do that?'

'I don't know.'

Antigonos swore under his breath. 'Well, well; it would appear that Polyperchon has some military sense after all. My guess is that it's old Poseidon himself, trident, seaweed and all, come to relieve Arrhidaeus, taking advantage of me lending Kassandros more than half of my ships.' And then a thought hit him. 'If he's here then he must have passed Kassandros and either they missed each other somehow or…'

Demetrios picked up on his father's train of thought. 'Or he completely defeated him and we have no navy left worth talking about.'

'We had better get over there.'

And it was a depressing, if impressive, sight that met them as they rowed, in a lembi – small and quick – around the point into the bay at whose end Cius was sited. Antigonos rubbed his eye, disbelieving the evidence before it. 'How have they done that?'

'More to the point,' Philotas said, 'why have they done that? They are meant to be relieving Arrhidaeus, not attacking him.'

All three of them were equally as stunned for, in amongst the enemy fleet, against the sea wall stood a siege tower where it was impossible for such a great construction to be.

'Siege towers don't float,' Demetrios said, rather stating the obvious.

'But ships do,' Philotas said, again stating the obvious, 'and two with a platform lashed between them can support that tower.'

Antigonos then understood what was happening. 'It's not a siege tower – well, it is but it's not being used as such, quite the reverse. Because we hold the harbour, he's taking the garrison off the walls, down through the tower and then transferring them to the other ships and there's nothing we can do about it except watch and marvel at Kleitos' ingenuity. Perhaps I made a mistake threatening him.'

'We'd better not stay here, Father,' Demetrios said, pointing at two ships turning towards them and splitting off from the main body of the fleet. 'I think they're coming to investigate us.'

'Well, there's nothing that we can do without ships other than watch from a distance.' Antigonos turned to the triarchos. 'Get us away from here.'

The twenty rowers on either side of the vessel grunted to their task and the ship turned. Antigonos looked back at the city in a more pragmatic frame of mind. *In a strange way this has done me a big favour: if he takes Arrhidaeus and his four thousand men back to Europe then he's off my hands; if he drops him somewhere along the Asian coast he'll be at my mercy.* A smile crept across his face. *Either way, I'll be safe to start moving back south very soon.*

'Father, look,' Demetrios shouted, pointing west.

There, rounding the island city of Cyzicus appeared five or six ships under oars; four more followed and then another half dozen came after, trailed by even more until at least a hundred were making their way directly into the bay of Cius.

'Kassandros, I take back everything bad I've ever said about you.' Antigonos rubbed his hands together as he looked back to Cius. 'Kleitos is breaking off to face them.' *Gods, a sea battle; this will be good.*

And it was with speed that Kleitos turned his fleet away from Cius, but with speed also came the curse of haste: through some miscommunication between the two triachoi of the ships supporting the platform each went a different way, tearing at the ropes lashing them to their burden so that the tower began to rock, transmitting its momentum down to the vessels at its base so that they too began to share its motion, amplifying it. Tiny figures at the tower's summit could be seen hanging on, terrified, as the motion of the great construction grew wilder until it crashed, booming, into the city wall, dislodging many of the men before ricocheting off and teetering over the sea, pushing the sterns of the two ships bearing it down so that water streamed aboard, causing a mass exit of panicking rowers through their oar ports. Back the great tower went, a slow, deadly pendulum, to smash a second time into the wall, shattering much of its top level and killing many left within. And once more it swung away, out towards the sea, pressing down upon its bearers, pushing with intolerable pressure so that again they were forced beneath the waves, tilting it even further until, with unhurried majesty, it tumbled into a sea already thrashing with hundreds of struggling sailors. Up exploded a burst of displaced water to either side of the tower, white-foamed and glittering in the sun; up the tower bounced, slow and deliberate, as if trying one last time to raise itself from its watery grave, sending huge waves rolling out to rock the ships nearby with angry intent as, for a final time, it slumped back down and began, along with its erstwhile bearers, to founder.

'Sometimes you can be too clever,' Antigonos said with evident satisfaction. 'But that hasn't slowed Kleitos down.'

As they had been watching the mesmerising death of the tower, Kleitos, seaweed flowing from his head and shoulders, trident pointing the way ahead, had extracted most of his fleet from below the sea wall and, with decks crammed with Arrhidaeus' rescued men, had begun to form line of battle as the newly arrived fleet neared.

With less than a league separating the combatants, both now slowed so that they could tighten their formation, neither side wanting to be broken through and then turned.

Antigonos felt helpless as he watched the two fleets square up to each other from a distance. Although always a land general and an infantry one at that, he felt it wrong to be a mere observer at a battle that would decide who had control of the crossing between Europe and Asia; he did not, however, have any illusions about himself as a naval commander and knew that his presence was not being missed by whomever it was commanding his returning fleet.

To the shouted nauticalese of the officers and the shrill calls of pipes, the oarsmen spread their wooden wings and Kleitos' fleet surged forward – the tower, the two sunken ships and hundreds of drowned men forgotten. Antigonos strained to see what was happening with his fleet but Kleitos had his formation so tight that there were few gaps large enough to see the situation beyond.

Antigonos signalled that they should follow at a distance – their ship, a small, fast open-decked lembi being unsuitable for fleet actions.

Now Kleitos was up to cruising speed, the sweeps rising and dipping with studied regularity, the calls of the stroke-masters' pipes blending with the shrieks of the gulls circling and swooping down upon the fleet, plunging into its wake in search of discarded treats. Onwards, away from Antigonos, the great line of warships raced, the beat of its oars increasing to attack speed as it converged with the foe. Then, from the walls of Cius, artillery opened up; flaming bolts rose into the sky to fall amongst the ships.

'Ha! We've taken advantage of the town being emptied and seized it,' Antigonos said with satisfaction. As he did so, the boom across the harbour mouth dropped and the half dozen ships, the last remains of the blockading squadron under the command of the Cretan, Nearchos, slipped out and began to chase Kleitos' fleet. 'That's right, Nearchos, pick off any stragglers,' Antigonos said, rubbing his hands again and turning once more to the triarchos. 'We'll join them and see if there is anything we can do. Open the weapons box.'

The artillery continued until the fleet was at the extreme of their range; with two of the ships burning, flames fed by a freshening northerly breeze, they had done as much as could be expected of them.

Catching up with the ships spilling from the harbour, the lembi slipped in at the rear of their formation as it headed for the burning ships.

The shrill of the pipes grew in tempo as both fleets reached ramming speed and Antigonos, a bunch of javelins now in his left hand, prayed to Poseidon to grant him victory, hoping that Kleitos' constant aping of the god would work against him; but then, he reflected, this earthly Poseidon had won many sea battles, one serving with Antigonos himself on Cyprus little more than two years ago, and another here in these same waters; he did not seem to be lacking in his guardian god's favour. I *needed his talent in Cyprus and now I have to fight against it; I was foolish to alienate him.*

And then the first impacts cracked over the water: shattering blows of metal rams exploding through the bellies of ships; staccato splintering of snapping oars raked, blending with the screams of their wielders as the shafts punched back into the chests, imploding them; high over all came the grinding shriek of metal tearing wood as ships backed oars to extricate themselves from their violent coupling.

Down fell masts, crushing many on Kleitos' full decks, Arrhidaeus' packed men suffering cruelly – partaking in a sea battle had not been what they had expected as they had embarked – as grappling hooks flew through the air to snare a victim and pull it close in deadly embrace. And now Arrhidaeus' men turned their close-packed numbers to their advantage; heavily armed, they swarmed into the enemy ships, leaping across the narrow gaps and overwhelming the more sparsely manned enemy; hurling them overboard, pierced and bloodied, into a sea already churning with the dying.

'They've got the better of us,' Philotas observed as the centre of Kleitos' line appeared to move forward.

Antigonos could see it was the truth of the matter and signalled to the triarchos to turn back. 'Back to Chalcedon, there's nothing that we can do here.'

The six ships that had slipped out of the harbour also turned, having despatched the burning stragglers, being of insufficient force to take on the main body, even from the rear.

The rowers bent their backs to their task as Antigonos gazed out over the stern to the battle still unfolding for the worse. Kleitos had now forced his way through the centre; Antigonos' fleet was riven in two, ready for piecemeal dispatch. The wails of the dying drifted over the waves, disembodied and losing their connection with the nautical chaos whence they had risen. Away they rowed as Antigonos contemplated his next move. As he did so, little pockets of ships filtered from either wing of the main battle, his ships, survivors, to make their way east, towards

Chalcedon whence they had set out for Athens just eight days previously. *I cannot afford to accept defeat; to do so here would mean that I wouldn't have superiority in these waters again for a long time. Somehow I need to defeat a victorious fleet with the remnants of a defeated one.* Still he looked back at the disaster, willing more of his vessels to appear; a few did but not nearly enough for his purposes.

And then the way forward presented itself. 'Philotas, when we get back I want you to go across to Byzantium and hire whatever ships, fishing boats, any vessels that can transport men; I don't care about the price, just do it.'

'Of course. What do you plan to do?'

Antigonos slapped his son on the shoulder. 'Demetrios, remember that force you were gathering for Menander that is due to leave at dawn?'

'Yes, Father.'

'Well, they'll have to leave later. Kleitos' fleet is going to have to spend the night somewhere; get all the archers, slingers and peltasts down to the harbour by midnight and cram them in every available ship; in fact just get everyone who is suited to an operation like this. We're going to give Kleitos a nasty surprise, just as he's toasting a victory.'

And it was, unsurprisingly, on the Thracian side of the water that Kleitos chose to moor or beach his victorious fleet that night; but that did not concern Antigonos, he was not worried about the niceties of asking permission of Lysimachus for venturing onto his territory as he planned to be back in Asia before the Satrap of Thrace even heard about it.

He chuckled to himself as the flotilla, made up of over two hundred ships and boats of all sizes, rowed north, guided by the fires on the beach and the distant drunken shouting and singing. Just how many men Demetrios had managed to cram onto the vessels was unknown as they had been assembled with haste and embarked with even more alacrity. Antigonos' ship and the half dozen who had been in the harbour, along with a dozen triremes and twenty large merchantmen that Philotas had hired in Byzantium – for a price that would have made the eyes of even the most rapacious pirate water – formed the lead squadron. Then came the ships that had been extricated from the disaster, fifty-four of them commanded by Kassandros' man, Nicanor of Sindus; they were followed by over a hundred smaller vessels, some only able to carry five or six men, which brought up the rear with Demetrios in charge of the left flank and Nearchos of the right. But, whatever their size, they were heaving with soldiery, light-armed and quick-moving. *More than five thousand of them and just the kind I need for a thorough massacre.* The thought brought out yet another chuckle; Antigonos was determined to enjoy himself that night to make up for the pain of the day.

As he drew nearer to the celebrating victors, Antigonos could see in the flicker of the firelight that the majority of the ships had been beached with only thirty or so, the larger ones, of the one hundred and twenty rocking at anchor a little way off the shore with skeleton crews left aboard to keep watch.

The plan had already been discussed amidst the flurry of organisation before they had sailed and there was not an officer, neither naval nor infantry, who did not know what was expected of him: nothing short of murder. And thus, still far enough away from the shore to remain invisible to eyes used to the brightness of many driftwood fires, the three squadrons split: Antigonos headed a thousand paces to the west of the fleet, Demetrios with his smaller craft to the eastern side of it, Nicanor of Sindus with the remains of his warships headed straight towards the shore and the ships moored just off it.

Two hundred paces out from the strand, Antigonos signalled for the rowers to cease their grunting labour and let the ships glide in silence over a calm sea beneath a sky brilliant with the wealth of the universe. Through the lapping of small waves kissing the shore, the great keels just nudged the sand, bringing the ships to a gentle, grinding stop. It was not a time for caution – that they had got this far without the alarm being raised was a thing of wonder – Antigonos nodded to Philotas next to him and leaped from the rail down into the shallows; he did not need to beckon his men to follow, each sporting a black headband as a mark of recognition. Helmetless and wearing the same as the mercenary peltasts following him, a tunic and sandals and armed only with a spear and a sword, with his shield on his left arm, he ran, in silence, along the beach towards the fires. Over to his left, the bow- and sling-armed light infantry fanned out, looping inland a couple of hundred paces, moving at a much-faster pace, almost a sprint, so as to be in position as the main body of troops hit from either side.

Antigonos could hear Philotas' breath rasping in his chest and smiled to himself. *I'll enjoy ripping into the old bugger about his fitness over a cup or ten of wine after this. Gods, this is fun.*

The singing and raucous laughter was growing as drunken-ness claimed more and more victims but, even so, the inevitable shouts of alarm soon roared over the celebrations; Antigonos accelerated. At fifty paces out, the first projectiles hissed in from the archers and slingers out in the dark, scores of them, thumping into flesh or kicking up small clouds of sand around recumbent forms. In raced Antigonos, yelling at full pitch now that surprise had been achieved, and it was with joy that he skewered a young lad who had jumped to his feet in fright and then failed to move in shock; he doubled over the spear trans-fixing him as Antigonos kicked his groin and yanked his weapon back, freeing it to leave the lad howling on his knees. On he ploughed, lashing out at throats and bellies with his spear and cracking faces with his shield.

Diving forward, with his fists together, he threw his arms out to either side, shield knocking the senses from one man, his fist the teeth from another, and exploded through a group of four marines, already unsteady on their feet, and then forced himself on into a unit of Arrhidaeus' men mustering into some sort of order. 'Don't let them form up,' he yelled at the troops following him as he buried his spear irretrievably into the ribcage of what seemed to be their officer. Out his sword flashed, scything up under the chin of the next man leaving his jaw hanging by a bloody thread as his tongue slopped to the ground. And then he saw them: Nicanor's warships were amongst the moored ships, trapping them, preventing the escape of all but a few; men swarmed over their sides to overwhelm the holding crews within. With a nonchalant stroke he pierced the eye of a screaming sailor barrelling towards him, sword waving over his head, and then paused to let the men in his wake surge past whilst he worked to regain his breath. Behind him lay the dead; ahead fought the living, but such was the completeness of the surprise and such was the influence that Dionysus had already had on the defenders that the quick soon joined the dead.

Flaming brands from the fires were hurled into the beached ships, contrary to his orders, and in his fury he took off the arm of one of his own men as he went to fire an enemy vessel. 'Leave the ships alone! Do you hear? Leave the ships alone! They are mine!' But such was tumult that very few heard. The flames continued to rise and by those flames he could make out the vessels that had escaped out to sea: most of them were taken but one, the largest, had resisted and, despite many men attempting to board it, grabbing at the oars, it was edging back, away from Nicanor's squadron and out into the night. 'Kleitos!' Looking around his eyes focused on a small boat, with six oarsmen, just coming into land; he ran towards it, wading through the bloodied water. 'Turn around!' he ordered. The helmsman, shouting at his oarsmen, did as he was told with the speed and precision of one that has spent their whole life in boats.

Antigonos struggled aboard. 'Try to get me within hailing reach of that ship.' The helmsman gave a broken-toothed grin, called the stroke and the boat pulled away, leaving the ongoing carnage on the beach behind.

'Kleitos!' Antigonos shouted through cupped hands as they neared the fleeing ship. 'Kleitos, come back and swear to me; fight for me, Kleitos.'

A dim figure could be seen coming to the rail and peering out as the ship slowed. 'Antigonos? Is that you?'

'Kleitos, I was wrong. I should have come to you in peace.'

'It's a little late now, don't you think?'

'Not at all. I'll give you your satrapy back; just come and serve me.'

The laugh that came over the water was hollow; Antigonos could just make out Kleitos pointing his trident at him.

'You cannot give nor take away satrapies, Antigonos; only the regent can do that in the kings' names. Go to Polyperchon and swear to him and the kings and then the fighting will stop and you'll have no need of me. It's you now, Antigonos, you who is continuing the war. You refuse to acknowledge the rightful regent, you gave Kassandros his ships; it's all about you.'

'I am the commander-in-chief of Asia!'

'No, Antigonos, that's where you're wrong. You're not anymore. Polyperchon has written to Eumenes and offered him the position; I'd be very surprised if he refuses it, wouldn't you?'

The information hit Antigonos like a slingshot. 'That's not true.'

'Why would I lie, Antigonos? You are the rebel now; you are the outsider. That being so, why would I want to come and serve you? Goodbye, Antigonos, enjoy your life as an outlaw!' With one final wave of his trident, Kleitos disappeared into the gloom on the deck.

It was in sombre mood that Antigonos waded back to the beach. The fighting was over and the dead lay as thick on the ground as did the smoke in the air; here and there a ship still burnt but work-parties laboured to extinguish them as others went about gathering the weapons and possessions of the defeated.

'Was that Kleitos?' Demetrios asked, coming up to his father with Nicanor of Sindus in tow.

'Yes. He told me that Eumenes has been offered my position in Asia.'

'That's what Adea told us,' Nicanor confirmed. 'I didn't have time to tell you in the rush to get this all ready. She has left Polyperchon, taking King Philip over to Kassandros; she was a mine of information.'

'So it is true then?'

'Yes, but I wouldn't worry too much about it; Polyperchon's days are numbered. We took Adea back to Macedon on our way here. She has claimed the regency of her husband; she will be the one making the decisions in Pella.'

'It's not Pella I'm interested in; it's Asia. Take whatever time you need to make repairs to what's left of the fleet and then back to Athens; give my thanks to Kassandros and tell him that I will aid him in any way that I can in his struggle against Polyperchon. In return I expect him to do the same for me as I take the army south to deal with Eumenes.'

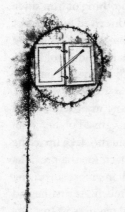

EUMENES.
THE SLY.

'...L OST HIS LITTLE flask of oil!' Eumenes and Hieronymus both doubled up in laughter at the fifth time this punch-line had been repeated as a part of the literary duel between Euripides and Aeschylus in Aristophanes' comedy, *The Frogs*; they had been amusing one another by reading the play aloud in a secluded walled garden at the heart of the palace of Mazaca, the capital of Kappadokia.

'The army is ready to march, sir,' Xennias informed Eumenes from the garden's entrance.

'Thank you. I'll come and address them.' Eumenes wiped his eyes and got to his feet, smiling at Hieronymus, sharing the stone bench underneath an apricot tree.

Hieronymus returned his compatriot's smile with equal warmth. 'Not in the style of Euripides, otherwise at the end of each line the men will shout out...'

'Lost his little flask of oil!' they shouted in unison.

Eumenes suppressed his laughter and put on an exaggeratedly serious face. 'I think a few inspiring words from the new commander-in-chief of Asia should hearten them for a march across the Taurus Mountains down into Cilicia, don't you?'

'I still wish I could have seen Antigonos' face when he was told; have you heard how he took it?'

'He lost his little flask of oil!'

This set them both off again. Once mirth had been controlled, Eumenes managed an answer: 'I've heard nothing of him since he ran Arrhidaeus to ground in Cius and thwarted his attempt at relieving me in Nora, before I swore the oath. I would be more interested in seeing his face when Leonidas told him exactly what oath I'd sworn. Still, that's all by the by: he's the outlaw and I have right and the kings on my side as well as, I should add, the treasury. Pack your things, my friend, we're going to the bank.'

It was light of foot that Eumenes ascended the steps up to the rostrum set before his parading army. In fact, for the previous three days, since he had received Polyperchon's most surprising letter, he had done everything with a light touch. At first he had not believed the letter was genuine, even though its bearer was known to Eumenes to have been with Polyperchon since he had returned west with Krateros; however, the more he thought about it, the more Polyperchon's offer had made sense: it gave the embattled regent an ally in Asia and at the same time outlawed Antigonos; it was a master stroke and something he would have done had he been in Polyperchon's position. He also would have *accidentally* neglected to lift the death sentence hanging over him – a neat little trick – just in case Polyperchon had a change of mind and needed to be rid of the new power in Asia. *All in all very pleasing,* he reflected as he surveyed his army, drawn up on blocks. *Not much of an army; in fact, six thousand men should be called a detachment not an army. Still, the mercenaries will come flocking to me when I prise open the doors of Cyinda. The question is: how do I deal with Antigenes, a prime example of the un-complex Macedonian military mind, if ever there was one?*

The question dwelt foremost in his thoughts for the first few days of the march south, climbing into the Taurus range and then picking up the River Carmalas as it wound its way down into Cilicia.

It was as they descended into the foothills of the southern side of the range that the urgency of finding a solution became paramount: Parmida – left behind with his five hundred

Kappadokian cavalry as a rear guard in Kappadokia – caught up with the column, coming straight to Eumenes to report. 'According to my scouts, Menander was a couple of days away from Kappadokia with a force of five thousand when we left; he'll be there by now.'

Eumenes digested this piece of news, riding at ease on his mare. 'That means that Antigonos has heard of Polyperchon's offer and has, rightly, assumed that I would accept it and therefore sent a force to arrest me or, perhaps, even kill me. If I were him it would certainly be the latter.' He turned to Hieronymus, riding – with far less ease – next to him. 'I'd say that Antigonos has made the first aggressive move.'

'You don't count accepting Polyperchon's offer and then heading to Cilicia as aggressive?'

'How could it be? I'm just obeying the wishes of Polyperchon, the regent of the rightful kings of Macedon, and in doing so I am in no way attacking Antigonos.'

'Neither are you breaking your oath as it was made also to the kings.' Hieronymus chortled; it was rough in his throat. 'Did I mention that you have a reputation for being sly?'

'And little, and a Greek; I wonder which one is the most offensive to the gallant Macedonian military mind?'

'But you're a Greek,' Antigenes said as Eumenes presented Polyperchon's warrant to him at the gates of Cynda, a fortress not unlike Nora, clinging to a bare rock above the Carmalas valley no great distance from Tarsus.

Ah, I thought that would be the main objection. 'Which is why the regent has seen fit to appoint me to the position: as a Greek I cannot challenge for the throne and therefore can be trusted with the powers and the money he has given me, unlike Antigonos who has abused his position for his own gain.'

Antigenes looked again at the warrant and scratched the back of his head. 'So not only do I have to let you withdraw five hundred talents in silver or gold but it says here that I have to place myself and my Silver Shields under your command.'

'Well, seeing as I've been appointed Commander-in-Chief of Asia, by the regent of the two kings of Macedon and you and your lads are in Asia then I would have thought that to be a perfectly logical thing to do.'

Antigenes gave the warrant to the officer standing next to him, a middle-aged veteran with a scar from where his left ear was no more, to where much of his nose should have been. 'What do you make of it, Teutamus?'

Teutamus took the warrant and read it, saying the words out loud, slow and deliberate; he shrugged when he had finally finished and frowned down at Eumenes. 'He's a bit little to be Commander-in-Chief of Asia, isn't he?'

Ah, there we have the second objection; how I value the Macedonian military mind. 'That may well be true but what I might lack in height I make up for in slyness; now, gentlemen, I have come a long way. You have seen my documentation, please show me to my quarters; my men will camp down in the valley. We will inspect the treasury together after I have refreshed myself.'

Xennias looked apologetic as he walked into Eumenes' room. 'They said they are not going to come to you, you have to come to them.'

'Oh, so we're going to play that little game again, are we? How very grown up we are.' Eumenes put down the treasury inventory – which had made for riveting reading this past half hour – got to his feet and walked to the window, looking out over his army making camp down in the valley. 'Well, if I give in and go to them then I'll be the one seen as being weak. What to do? What to do?' He clasped his hands behind his back and took in the view as he contemplated. 'Tell them,' he said eventually, 'that I have decided not to call a meeting before visiting the treasury and instead I will go straight there and we shall discuss matters as we make our tour.' He turned to Xennias. 'That should appease Macedonian pride, I would think.'

Xennias smiled. 'They're old warhorses those two; they would only bow their heads to the king.'

'I am the representative of the kings.'

'You misunderstand me, sir: I said the king, singular; Alexander himself, not the babe and the fool – as they see it – who have taken his place.'

Eumenes nodded his understanding and walked to the door. 'Then we shall have to create the right conditions for them, shan't we?'

But his annoyance with the two men commanding the Silver Shields was temporarily forgotten at the sight of so much wealth glinting in the light of the torches that each of the three held; it seemed as if the hoards of the entire world had been gathered together in one place such was its magnitude: strong-room after strong-room along a corridor, at least a hundred paces long, were filled with crates of coinage, silver and gold bullion, bowls of precious stones – including a ruby so large that Eumenes could not close his fist around it – solid gold and silver statues, plate, furniture and Alexander's ceremonial weapons and armour as well as other trifles in ivory, coloured glass and bronze. 'The wealth of the entire empire,' Eumenes whispered, awestruck by what he was witnessing.

'And beyond,' Antigenes said, in a matter-of-fact tone.

'You wouldn't even notice the five hundred talents that I'm authorised to withdraw.'

'Not at all.'

'Not that I'm going to withdraw it.'

Antigenes frowned. 'But you have a signed warrant saying that you may.'

'I know; but what would I do with all that money? No, I'll take enough to hire a decent amount of mercenaries to bolster my army – our army, I should say, seeing as you and your lads are now a part of it.'

'But you could be a very wealthy man.'

I know, and believe me, my fine friend, it's hurting to do this but I need to show you that I am not in this war just for myself. 'If I need any more, I'll come back for it; until then box up a hundred talents in silver coinage and let us start to make it known that we are recruiting on very generous terms as we move south to take back what Ptolemy's stolen of Syria for the kings.'

'And who says that is what we're going to do?' Antigenes asked, his voice belligerent.

'Alexander does, he told me in a dream.' Eumenes' reply caused both Antigenes and Teutamus to stare at him with something approaching religious awe. 'Yes, my friends, I have had a couple of dreams where Alexander has guided me in recent nights and he has suggested this: we should revert to doing what Perdikkas did in the first few days after Alexander's death, before things went too far; we should set up his throne in his tent and take our deliberations in its shadow so that everything that we decide will have his blessing and he will be our overall commander; he will, once again, be with us.'

'But we haven't got a throne,' Teutamus pointed out.

Well done; full marks for paying attention and getting to the nub of the problem. I can see why you have risen so high in the Silver Shields' ranks. Eumenes put the tips of his fingers to his forehead. 'Thank the gods you are with us, Teutamus, I had completely neglected that point. What would you suggest?' He looked around at all the crates of gold and silver bullion piled up all around. 'I'm sure there must be a way of complying with Alexander's wishes.'

Teutamus followed Eumenes' gaze and scratched his head.

'We could make one,' Antigenes said, his face brightening with inspiration.

Eumenes looked disbelieving. 'Make one?'

'Yes, make one, Eumenes.' Antigenes went to a crate and lifted the lid; he pulled out a bar of gold. 'We'll have one cast from solid gold.'

'Solid gold,' Eumenes exclaimed. 'Surely that would be very heavy to carry around with us; we are going on campaign after all.'

'Then we'll have a gilded one made and on it will lie his ceremonial sword and breastplate.'

'Brilliant!' Eumenes said, with a look of wonder on his face at the sheer cunningness of the plan. 'And I will add one refinement. I have his diadem.'

'What, the one that went missing whilst he was lying in state?'

'The very same.'

'But…'

'But I stole it? No, I didn't; I borrowed it as it was unattended at the time and I thought that one day it could become useful; like today, for example. Have the throne made overnight, nothing too fancy, and we will meet before it tomorrow morning when I shall return to Alexander his diadem.'

'May you guide and inspire us,' Eumenes said with as much reverence as he could muster for the farce, placing the diadem on the throne that stood at the end of the table set in the centre of what was now, officially, Alexander's Tent. But farce or no, the ploy had worked to a remarkable degree: the men, both Eumenes' and Antigenes' Silver Shields, had gathered in clumps around the tent talking in whispers so as not to disturb Alexander's spirit which they firmly believed resided within. This had been re-affirmed when they saw his ceremonial cuirass and sword – a magnificent weapon, the pace of a tall man long, with a leaf-like blade a hand-span at its widest – being taken with all due ceremony from the treasury to the tent; now they truly believed that Eumenes might the issue the orders but those orders came directly from Alexander himself, albeit, his ghost.

And Eumenes was determined to take full advantage of their gullibility.

With the diadem lying on the throne's seat, the sword resting against it and the cuirass hanging over its back, the gilded throne did have a degree of mystery about it, Eumenes conceded as he took his place at the table to Alexander's right. And if that was to help him in his purpose then all was well and good. Antigenes and Xennias sat opposite him whilst Teutamus and Parmida were seated on his sides, splitting the factions up as 'Alexander had wanted'.

'So, gentlemen,' Eumenes said, looking not at his companions but, rather, at the ghost's throne, 'from today we start to win back for Alexander's son and brother, his two rightful heirs, the territory that has been taken from them.'

'And you're proposing,' Antigenes said, 'that we take the army south against Ptolemy's garrisons in Syria and Phoenicia?'

Eumenes raised a placating hand. 'I'm proposing nothing, Antigenes. I am merely suggesting, in Alexander's name, that we do that as it would be what he wants.'

Antigenes frowned but nodded his agreement. 'And where should we strike first?'

'We, that is, Alexander, needs the ports so that this army and that of Polyperchon in Greece can eventually link up. So we are going to need a larger navy. How many ships do we have at present in Tarsus?'

Teutamus put his hand up with surprising child-like eagerness.

Eumenes gave the benevolent look of a grammaticus pleased with an improving pupil. 'Yes, Teutamus?'

'I was there a few days ago and there were about a dozen triremes and a few biremes being used to keep down the pirates who are springing up again along the coast now that there are so many mercenaries looking for employment.'

'Then we will solve two problems by expanding the navy: we will be employing more mercenaries and taking away from them the temptation to go for a pirate and also we will have a stronger force to deal with those pirates that refuse to come and serve in our navy.' He looked at the throne and cocked his head as if he were trying to hear something more clearly and then nodded. 'We should be prepared to march south the day after tomorrow; Teutamus, you will stay in Tarsus recruiting mercenaries for the army and the navy whilst we head south into Phoenicia and take his ship-building ports and all his half-built ships off Ptolemy's hands.'

PTOLEMY.
THE BASTARD.

'IT IS A magnificent sight,' Ptolemy agreed, placing his arm around Thais as they walked along the main quay of the great harbour, the Sidon harbour, of Tyros lined with ships all smelling of freshly hewn timber and swarming with men provisioning them. 'One hundred and thirty-three of them so far and nothing smaller than a trireme; and there are still plenty more under construction. My ship-builders have been busy this season, up and down this coast using some of the finest wood available, cedar for the hulls, masts and decks, oak for the keels and fir for the oars, all very rare in Egypt and although there are reasonable amounts of those materials in Cyprus, I think it much better to utilise someone else's, don't you agree, my dearest?'

Thais took his hand from her shoulder and kissed it as a unit of marines doubled past them, heading for a mighty quinque-reme. 'And now you have built a second navy what are you going to do with it?'

'It's a third navy, actually. Well, fourth if you count the smaller one based at Apollonia in Cyrenaica.' He paused to let a victual-ling party, loaded with kegs, cross his path, their overseer bowing his respects as Ptolemy's dozen bodyguards tensed, the hands resting on the sword-hilts. 'One back at Alexandria, one over in Cyprus and then this one will stay here in Tyros, controlling this

311

coast so that even if I let the interior towns and the lesser ports go, it won't matter as I will still have the largest navy in the vicinity with the ability to supply it, safe in a harbour city that took Alexander, himself, two years to defeat.'

'I didn't ask where it was, I can see that perfectly well for myself; I asked: what are you going to do with it?'

'Ah, that is a good question and one I really didn't know the answer to until very recently; I just had it built because I could and I thought I should.'

'So what was this epiphany?'

'Well, I had a letter from Kassandros, who's recently arrived in Athens in a fleet borrowed from Antigonos; he was requesting that I support his claim to the regency. Personally I can't think of anyone – or thing, for that matter – more unsuited to the title than that poisonous toad, but he does have his uses: one of them is his ability to hate almost as intensely as Olympias; and as he hated Alexander to the core of his being, Kassandros would not worry, like every other Macedonian would, that Olympias was his mother and will, therefore, have no compunction in killing her. He's the only one who can and someone has to soon.'

'Why?' Thais asked as they moved aside for fifteen groups of rowers, eight in each, making up a trireme's complement, with their oars on their shoulders, to snake past.

'Apart from the fact that she is a ruthless, cruel and vindictive serpent?'

'Yes, apart from the obvious reasons.'

'Because Polyperchon has offered her power; Kassandros told me that, according to Adea, who has deserted Polyperchon for Kassandros, taking her pet idiot with her, Polyperchon has invited Olympias to oversee the upbringing of the young Alexander so that he matures into a Macedonian king rather than some luxury-loving, twisted easterner. A noble sentiment, I think you'll agree; but he couldn't have chosen a worse person for the job: Olympias will turn Macedon into a blood-bath of vengeance.'

'Why should you care what she does?'

'Because her ambition will be limitless: she will lay claim to the whole empire in the name of her grandson. And the trouble is that she's the only person who could stand a chance of uniting all the various armies under one banner: Alexander's banner; Alexander in the form of his son and mother. There is no place for me in that scenario. Nor is there for Antigonos, Kassandros, Seleukos or anyone else you care to name. No, she has to be stopped before she goes too far or everything that was gained at The Three Paradises will be under threat.'

'I thought The Three Paradises agreement was in tatters.'

Ptolemy contemplated the remark as he watched another newly built trireme glide through the harbour mouth to join the fleet. *One hundred and thirty-four.* 'Not at all: I still have Egypt; Seleukos is now in Babylon; Peucestas remains in Persis, as does Lysimachus in Thrace and Eumenes is still an outlaw. The gods alone know what Peithon is up to in Media, but, nevertheless, there he is and Antigonos carries on as the commander-in-chief of the army of Asia – although he does seem to be taking the law into his own hands by removing satraps he doesn't like and replacing them with allies, but that's a matter for the future. For now the only thing that has changed markedly is the status of Macedon; the rest of us still remain in our personal paradises and I for one am prepared to help that most unpleasant man if it helps me to remain thus.'

'So when Antigonos asks Kassandros for his fleet back you will offer to lend him some of this one.'

'I will certainly offer; whether I actually do is another matter. But it's definitely in the back of my mind, now it is ready. So, I have a multipurpose fleet. Not a bad year's work, I should say.'

'Not bad at all.' She looked up into his eyes. 'But, tell me, are you really planning on letting the interior go, Damascus, Hierosolyma, Jericho?'

'I'm not planning to; but if anyone comes south to try and take them from me – Antigonos being a case in point – then I see no reason for fighting a war over them – a war, incidentally, that at the moment, I would probably lose in the long run – seeing as they have now served their purpose.'

313

'Which was?'

'Which was to fill Tyros with ships – new ships.' He gestured down to the buzzing port all around. 'And there they all are. No, my dear, now the job is almost done I shall return to Egypt with the army and leave garrisons in the town with orders to retreat into Tyros before an advancing enemy; and they would then be the troops that I would put in these ships should I decide to help Kassandros.' He looked around the horizon and shook his head. 'No, there's no need to have a war for this place – at least, not yet there isn't.'

'My lord,' Lycortas, Ptolemy's chamberlain said, walking towards him as fast as was possible in his long robes.

'What is it, Lycortas?'

'We've finally managed to entice the Exile-Hunter here; Archias is just arriving on that ship.' The steward pointed to the new arrival now docking; in its prow was the unmistakable form of the Exile-Hunter surrounded by his seven formidable Thracians, all still sporting their fox-fur caps despite the southern heat.

'Have him brought to the audience chamber. Alone, mind you; I don't want his little friends to hear what I have to say.'

'Very good, my lord.'

'And send a message to my triarchos to have my ship and escorts ready to sail for Egypt as soon as I've seen Archias.'

'Very good, my lord.'

'That is a piece of luck; I've been wanting to talk to him for a while,' Ptolemy mused as he watched Lycortas waddle off towards the docking trireme. 'He's the key to ensuring that Kassandros really does kill Olympias. Now I have him, we really can go home.' He turned and headed back to the city.

'I for one will be glad to get back to Egypt and see the children,' Thais said, after a companionable silence, as they walked through the harbour gates into the narrow, thronged, streets of Tyros, 'and I'm sure Eurydike will be pleased to have you back and you can meet your baby son finally.'

Ptolemy smiled at the thought of his first legitimate son, his namesake, born in early spring, as his bodyguard cleared a way for him and Thais through what was predominantly a welcoming crowd. He had always made it a policy to treat the towns he had taken with respect, being of the opinion that goodwill brought a lot more for him than heavy taxation. 'Yes, I look forward to meeting my son and heir. I suppose I shall have to get his mother pregnant again; still, better me than someone else.'

'And why just her?'

Ptolemy looked askance at Thais. 'I thought you didn't want any more children.'

Thais shrieked with amusement. 'Me! Oh no, Ptolemy dearest; I'll not go through that again. Three is quite enough; we'll continue to use the safer methods.' She gave a knowing wink and slapped his backside; the bodyguards feigned not to notice. 'No, I'm talking about dynastic politics, my dearest, not shagging your concubine.'

Ptolemy was as intrigued as he was aroused. 'Go on; but make it quick as I think we both have need of a bath when we get back to the palace; and not the soothing sort either.' He returned the slap, stinging his palm as much as her buttocks.

Thais gave a little skip. 'Whoo, thank you; that's got me started. Now, where was I?'

'Dynastic politics?'

'Ah, yes, dynastic politics. But, on second thoughts, it can wait until we can concentrate more effectively, having bathed.'

Thais snuggled into the crook of Ptolemy's arm as they lay on a couch in a shaded corner of the palace's pleasure gardens, her hair still wet and her shift clinging to the contours of her body. 'Now, assuming that you are going to leave whatever you carve out of the empire to your legitimate son, that would mean that the young Ptolemy, whom Eurydike has recently brought into the world, would be your heir.'

Still naked, Ptolemy dragged himself out of the warm haze of sexual satisfaction that had enveloped him ever since a shuddering climax and kissed Thais on the forehead. 'Provided the little brute survives, correct.'

'My question is, given that Antipatros is, or was, his grandfather, and Kassandros is his uncle, is he not too tightly connected with that family? If Kassandros takes Macedon, and it is a fair assumption that he will, especially if you help him, then, obviously, he will have as his power-base the best recruiting ground for Macedonian soldiers. He will become a major power and, no doubt, kill the babe and the fool and make himself king.'

'But he will stay in Europe; he hasn't got the talent to expand from there.'

'You say that, but, consider this: what if he outlives you – which, if both of you die a natural death, is very likely seeing as he's ten years younger than you – and he sees his nephew taking the throne of Egypt? Might he not be tempted to make a dynastic claim?'

'Unlikely, and, besides, he wouldn't have the wherewithal to back it up.'

Thais took his penis and squeezed in an absent-minded way. 'I quite agree. But now look at it from the other way around: you outlive Kassandros because he's killed in battle, murdered, ship-wrecked—'

'Or is eaten from the inside out by worms because he's so unpleasant.'

'Or that, indeed. Anyway, he dies and he leaves young sons, too young to rule without a regent; what claim could be made on the throne of Macedon then?'

Ptolemy's face cleared in slow understanding. 'A nephew would have a serious claim.'

'He would. And especially if that nephew were the son of Ptolemy, who is purported to be Alexander's bastard half-brother. And, whatever happens, young Ptolemy is always going to be a few years older than Kassandros' son; assuming, that is, that there is someone in this world brave enough to open her legs for him.'

Ptolemy turned her towards him and kissed her full on the mouth. 'Thais, you are a genius.'

'I know,' she replied after returning the kiss and feeling his

316

penis swell. 'But would it be possible for one man to rule both Egypt and Macedon?'

'Not unless all the land in between was a part of that empire.'

'So you would need another son, but a son who is not related to Kassandros' family so that he and Ptolemy would not quarrel about Macedon for he would have no dynastic claim to it. But this son must be royal nonetheless – a fact that rules out our sons.'

'Whose son, then?'

'Yours and Berenice's.'

'Berenice?'

'Yes, she's perfect. She's the daughter of Antigone, a Macedonian princess, and is only Kassandros' cousin.'

'But she's also Eurydike's cousin; I can't imagine she'll take too kindly to the idea.'

Thais kissed his chest and began to nibble her way down his torso. 'Eurydike comes from a high-born family; she understands dynastic politics.'

Ptolemy closed his eyes as Thais reached her goal. 'But Berenice already has children of her own.'

'The twin girls will be perfect for marrying off to petty princelings and the boy could be a useful subject ruler of one of your dominions one day; they are an asset rather than a hindrance.'

'And Berenice?'

'Has an eye for you, I know. But stop asking me questions; I'm busy and it's not polite to speak with your mouth full.'

Ptolemy smiled and stretched out with his hands behind his head, looking up into the sun-dappled leaves of an almond tree and listening to the cries of the ubiquitous gulls as they circled the city and harbour.

'Lord,' Lycortas said a respectful time after Thais had returned to the crook of his arm.

So well-timed, in fact, that Ptolemy knew he must have seen them and withdrawn to await the conclusion of the matter. 'What is it?'

'The Exile-Hunter is awaiting you in the audience chamber.'

'I'll be along soon.'

'Indeed, lord. But before you see him, our old friend Babrak has come to see you; he says that he has news that may well interest you concerning Eumenes.'

'Oh, Eumenes, Eumenes, Eumenes,' Ptolemy said, his amusement obvious, 'you are not only a clever and sly little Greek but also a very lucky one.' He turned back to the outrageously eastern-looking man sitting on the terrace of the palace pleasure gardens looking out over Tyros. 'So, Babrak, the little Greek is going to become a naval power, is he?'

The Paktha merchant displayed his red-stained teeth and placed his right hand over his chest, his dark eyes apologetic. 'This I cannot vouch for personally, master. I heard it three days ago from a cousin of mine on his way to Babylon with a caravan loaded with Kappadokian salt. I, as you know, was coming from Babylon. I have no reason to disbelieve him but when buying a boy in the slave market it is always best to check for yourself that he is a virgin rather than take the vendor's word for it.'

'Quite,' Ptolemy said, wondering how one went about checking the virginity of a boy and deciding to leave that sort of thing to experts. Composing his mind, he sat down on a high-backed wicker chair opposite his guest. 'So your cousin says that Antigonos is, to all intents and purposes, an outlaw and that Eumenes is now Polyperchon's commander-in-chief in Asia with Antigenes serving under him.'

Babrak inclined his head and spread his hands: 'I could not have summarised that better myself, master.'

'And they are coming this way.'

'Indeed, master.'

Ptolemy chuckled. 'Oh, Eumenes, Eumenes, Eumenes; you really never give up, do you? Your tenacity will be the death of you.' He stood again, retied the belt of his robe and looked out over the city and beyond up the coast to the north. *It will be a shame to give up Beyrutus, Tripoli, and Damascus, but Eumenes*

318

won't keep them long. And, besides, I won't let him have Tyros.
'When did your cousin think Eumenes will be arriving in Syria, Babrak?'

'He said that he had already left Tarsus and was now somewhere on the coast where Alexander fought Darius.'

'Issos? He's moving fast.' *Moving that fast, he will, no doubt, capture many of my ships still under construction; I shall just have to make sure that I get them back off him. Perhaps I should send some well-financed agitators into his camp to see if I can separate his men's loyalty from him.* He contemplated the issue for a few moments and then picked up a purse from the table next to him, turned back to Babrak and lobbed it to him. 'And what news from the east? How is our good friend Seleukos behaving himself?'

'I had a very interesting conversation with Seleukos, just last month, master, and he was most generous to me in terms of remuneration, victuals and choice of bed companions; the boys of southern Mesopotamia are much prized for their inventiveness, degeneracy and flexibility, did you know?'

'I didn't, Babrak. How fascinating, I shall certainly make a mental note of that.'

A misty look passed over the merchant's eyes that faded as he weighed the purse in his hand. 'But Seleukos seemed to be very settled in Babylon; the city was not overcrowded with soldiery as one so often sees when the local populace have no love of their leaders. I believe he wanted me to tell you how secure he is feeling as he subtly let me glimpse a full parade of his army without seeming to invite me.'

'And?'

'Sixteen and a half thousand strong phalanx, two thousand seven hundred Macedonian and Thessalian cavalry, four thousand mixed eastern cavalry, mainly horse-archers, five thousand three hundred mercenary Greek and Thracian peltasts, thirty-two elephants and over seven thousand light troops, mixed, archers, slingers and javelinmen.'

'You gleaned all that with just a glimpse?'

'Master, when glimpsing such riches of information, my eyes feast like a man having his first fresh boy after a three-month-long journey with the same bed companions: thoroughly and with urgency but not so much haste as to make a mistake.'

The man's obsessed. 'Yes, well, very good, Babrak. That's a decent-enough-sized army for defence but not for attack; how very gratifying. Walk with me.' He turned and began walking along the colonnaded path that bisected the pleasure gardens, perched high in the city where the breeze was fresh. 'Where are you headed?' Ptolemy asked as he paused to admire a bloom, one of many in a bed surrounding a gentle flowing fountain in the shape of a huge fish.

'To your Egypt, master. Alexandria, to be precise. Since you deported so many Jews there recently after you took Hierosolyma it has become a growing place of trade.'

'That was one of the objectives of the exercise; the other was to...well, never mind. Once you've done your business there, will you be heading back east?'

'Yes, master.'

'Then come and see me before you go; I shall be there before you as I'll be leaving later today after I've had what I hope is another fruitful conversation.'

'Once we had killed the men you sent to capture us,' Archias said with a broad and friendly smile on his face, 'I decided that it would be for the best if we should disappear for a while. Eumenes was too well protected, but even if I did manage to get through and kill the little bastard there was no guarantee that I would get my fee as it was obvious that Antipatros had but a short time to live once he had seen Iollas dead. "Hardship can age a man overnight".'

'Indeed,' Ptolemy said, resisting the urge to mentally search for the origin of the quote. 'And what made you decide to come to me after all?'

Archias had no doubts. 'What motivates any man? Money; pure and simple.' He paused to sniff the wine he had been offered by a visibly irked Lycortas. '"When a man is exhausted, wine will build his strength", and I have had a tough journey to get here.' He took a sip and savoured it, his face brightening. 'I can see why your steward was so irritated having to serve this to me, a former tragic actor turned assassin. Far too good for the likes of me, he was thinking; I could tell.' He took another sip and nodded in appreciation. 'Very fine. Not the best I have had and, no doubt, not the best that you could have served; but good enough to flatter me and to show that you mean business.'

Ptolemy inclined his head, unable not to like the man. 'Perhaps when the business is concluded you would join me in Alexandria and we could try a vintage superior to this.'

'That could be the beginnings of a very fruitful relationship.' Archias smiled again, took another sip, placed the cup on a round marble table and, folding his hands in his lap, sat back as if waiting to listen attentively to a proposal.

Ptolemy contemplated the Exile-Hunter for a few moments, surprised by how much he seemed to suit his former trade and how little one would suspect him of his current profession. *He is very sure of himself; that can only be a good thing when dealing with Olympias.* 'Have you read *The Last Days and Testament of Alexander*?'

'I used to be an actor. Of course, I read anything and everything about me.'

'Then obviously you know what part you are meant to have played in Alexander's death.'

'Meant to have played? Ptolemy, I played no part in Alexander's death, I simply procured a certain poison for Kassandros and in return received a great deal of money. What he did with the poison after the exchange had been made was nothing to do with me.'

'So you don't deny getting the poison for Kassandros?'

'Of course not; I don't shy away from things I've done.'

'So would you be prepared, for a substantial fee, naturally—'

'Naturally.'

Ptolemy inclined his head. 'Naturally. Would you be prepared to go to Olympias and tell her that what is written in *The Last*

Days and Testament of Alexander is the truth: Kassandros did get the poison from you.'

'But I had no idea at the time what he wanted it for.'

'Indeed.'

'Until I connected three facts: Kassandros arriving in Babylon bringing a poison that I had procured for him; that his half-brother, Iollas, was Alexander's cup-bearer and mixed his drinks for him; and then Alexander's death a few days later. There can be no doubt that it was Kassandros who was responsible for her son's death.'

'Exactly.'

'And for how long after I've told that to the most vengeful woman in the world do you expect me to live?'

'That danger will be reflected in the fee.'

'Which will be?'

'Ten talents in gold for you and a talent in silver each for your little friends.'

'They are not so little,' Archias said in a failed attempt to keep the astonishment from his face.

'I take it from your expression that the fee meets with your approval?'

'It is most generous.'

'Half payable now; when we have concluded here, Lycortas will see to it. You will receive the other half when you return to me in Alexandria.'

'Fair enough. But, tell me; why are you going to all this effort just to confirm something to Olympias that she must already suspect.'

'Archias, I don't normally share my motives with people but seeing as you are taking a great risk then, just this once, I will. Yes, she already suspects – in fact she is sure that she knows who it was – but she is not certain. I know the nature of the beast I'm goading and when she has absolute proof of who committed the crime there will be no atrocity that she won't commit as she takes her vengeance and each act will be directed against...?'

Archias smiled. 'Kassandros.'

'And his family.'

'He will have to kill her.'

'Or die himself along with all his kin, and I mean all of them.'

'But if you want her dead why not just pay me to kill her?'

'I know you to be a man of discretion but somehow the fact that I had paid for the murder of Alexander's mother would come out and I might start finding it hard to hire men or keep allies, all sorts of things.' Ptolemy stood to show that the audience was at an end. 'I would much rather have my less-creditable deeds done by someone else; in this case you and Kassandros.'

KASSANDROS.
THE JEALOUS.

'AND YOU CAN tell the assembly that I will not release the farm-land back to you until you disenfranchise the poor – that is everyone with less than two thousand drachmas to their name – restore the oligarchy, take my choice as the leader of that group and agree to feed the garrison that I will leave in the fortress of Munychia in Piraeus.' Kassandros looked at the bearded faces of the Athenian delegation, one by one, as they stood before him in his camp outside Athens' walls – the very place where Alexandros and Polyperchon had stayed – and then shrugged in a take it or leave it manner.

A delegate stepped forward. 'But Demetrios of Phalerum is—'

'Is my choice!'

'But he is a philosopher not a politician.'

'He is loyal to me and to my family; that is all I care about. You have no one to blame other than yourselves for killing Phocion and his friends.'

'But Demetrios of Phalerum isn't even yet forty.'

'Neither am I and yet I control Athens at the moment.'

'But he isn't even Athenian; how can he vote in the assembly if he's a foreigner?'

'Do you think I care; if it is so important to you then I suggest that you give him citizenship. But he is not there to vote, he will be there to tell *you* how to vote.'

'A dictator!'

'A guide; now get out of my sight, none of this is negotiable. Come back when you have voted to accept my terms and then I shall move my army on and you will get your land back; until then, I stay and my men eat your food.' Kassandros waved his hand in dismissal as he stood and turned away from the delegation and walked back into his tent trying to disguise his limp. *Argue, argue, argue, that is all Greeks ever do; they will never do as they are told without they give you a thousand reasons why they should do something else or nothing at all. I should have simply executed one of the delegation just to see whether the rest would carry on arguing.* He smiled at the notion. *Perhaps I'll do that next time.* He pulled his helmet off and threw it down on the bed before pouring himself a cup of wine; he took a large swig and felt its calming effects almost immediately.

Slumping down onto a chair with a sigh, he drained the rest of the cup. It had been a rapid few days; days in which he had had to react with haste to take advantage of what seemed to him to be a monumental error on the part of Alexandros: his father, Polyperchon, had only recently moved his army off to Megalopolis when, for some reason that Kassandros did not yet fully understand, Alexandros withdrew. Fearing a trap but unwilling to let the opportunity pass, Kassandros led his army – now reinforced by mercenaries but still not large enough for purpose – out of Piraeus and took up Alexandros' old position; nothing happened, no attack came and he had become the new master of Athens. He shook his head, unable to believe his luck. Now all he needed was more men. *Where is Nicanor?*

Kassandros had been expecting Nicanor of Sindus for the past few days, assuming that he had not been defeated by Kleitos the White's fleet. However, he thought that possibility unlikely if the plan to trap it between Antigonos' fleet in the Propontis and Nicanor's as he came through the Hellespont worked – and there was no reason to think it had not. And yet, despite having left more than half a moon ago, there had been no message from the man. Kassandros thumped his thigh with his fist and immediately regretted it as it was his weak leg. *If Antigonos has kept him back I'll never forgive him.* And that had been his main concern for he needed that fleet to support his army as it moved north and perhaps even to bypass the Gates of Thermopylae should Polyperchon hold it against them. He cursed himself for sending Nicanor off in the first place but Adea's information concerning Kleitos' movements and the opportunity to destroy Polyperchon's navy had proved too irresistible to turn down. However, the exercise did have one unfortunate consequence should it have been successful: it also helped Antigonos; it left him in command of the Asian shore with nothing to stop him crossing his army into Europe, provided he came to some sort of arrangement with Lysimachus.

Kassandros fumed as he realised that what had been an entirely self-serving operation in ridding himself of enemy shipping in Greek and Macedonian waters, might also have had the effect of stripping him of his own fleet – the fleet that he had promised to give back but had no intention of doing so – should Antigonos refuse to let it leave the Propontis.

It therefore came as a relief to him when his younger twin brothers ran into his tent, their faces alight with relief and pleasure. 'He's in sight,' Philip said.

'Who?' Kassandros growled – he had worked himself up into a rage thinking of Nicanor's absence.

'Nicanor of Sindus and the fleet.'

Kassandros jumped to his feet. 'Gods below! At last; I'll go down to Piraeus and greet him personally.'

But it was not with relief that Kassandros watched the arrival of the returning fleet as it glided through the great harbour mouth, it was with fury. Fury not because of the losses the fleet had sustained – a little over two-thirds of the original one hundred and five ships had made it back – but because of the manner of their return. *He makes to be my equal with that display; how dare he claim glory for himself before my eyes.* Again Kassandros thumped his leg and again he regretted it, but the provocation was too much to bear for Nicanor of Sindus was returning to Piraeus in the manner of a victorious general – which, to some extent, he was – with his ships bedecked with the trophies of war at sea: the beaks of enemy ships. And the garrison cheered as Nicanor arrived and his marines and sailors cheered back, all waving hats or pieces of cloth in the air and shouting their praises to the goddess Nike, the personification of victory, and promising lavish sacrifices in her honour that evening.

With an effort of gargantuan proportions, Kassandros prevented himself from shaking with rage, anxious that those around him should not guess his mood and the cause of it. *I need to deal with this quickly; there must be no warning.* So, therefore, it was with a smile, the best he could manage, that he waited on the quay as Nicanor's vessel docked to the cheers of all watching.

'My friend,' Kassandros said, limping towards the victorious general and opening his arms in welcome. 'Am I to take it that the venture was a success?'

Nicanor threw his head back and roared with laughter. 'A success, Kassandros? It was more than just a success: it was annihilation, complete and utter. Just one ship escaped; Polyperchon no longer has a navy. We are masters of these waters, Kassandros; we can go wherever we please.' With that, Nicanor fell into Kassandros' embrace and their palms slapped one another's backs as they made declarations of friendship and mutual support.

'Mutual support!' Kassandros spat, glaring at Pleistarchos and Philip as if they had been the origin of such an outrage. 'Mutual support, as if we are equals! *He* supports *me* with unquestioning loyalty and not the other way around. It is not mutual!' He paused to draw breath; he had been on the subject for a while and had worked himself up into another pleasing state of fury. 'And did you hear him? "We are masters of these waters, Kassandros; we can go wherever we please."' His voice mocked Nicanor's. 'We! *We* are masters! There is only one master in Greece and Macedon and that is me!' He kicked a folding stool at the twins; they each leaned in opposite directions so that it passed between them. 'Get me my secretary, Pleistarchos, and you, Philip, get me half a dozen men whom we can really trust and take them to my suite in Piraeus. I'll show Nicanor the true meaning of mutual support; I'll bring him up so high that the fall will be even more dramatic.'

The twins scuttled from the tent, leaving Kassandros fuming with righteous indignation. *Mutual support; how dare he? Still, it will serve as a good lesson to others as to what to expect if you try to treat me as an equal.*

The arrival of his secretary did nothing to calm Kassandros' rage; he kicked the man up the backside to hurry him over to the desk.

'Is it done?' Kassandros barked as the secretary sprinkled fine sand over the copy of the letter he had just finished writing out in a fair hand.

'Yes, sir,' the secretary whispered, his voice shaky after a tempestuous session of rapid dictation.

Kassandros snatched the letter and ran through it before thrusting it back at his secretary. 'Put the names of all the heads of the leading families in Pella and the surrounding cantons as well as my stepmother, Hyperia, and my brother, Nicanor.' He paused for a thought, remembering Alexander's senior body-guard now in retirement on his estates to the west after his defeat on Cyprus by Antigonos. 'But not Aristonous, that would be stretching credulity too far. Once that is done, do a similar letter as if it were from the leading families of Pydna, understand?'

'Yes, sir,' was the quivering reply.

'Good. Once it's done have them delivered to me, as if they have just arrived in Piraeus, when I'm walking with Nicanor of Sindus this evening.'

And so it was in a state of overt bonhomie that Kassandros strolled along the harbour with his arm around Nicanor's shoulders as the sun burned the western sky. 'Seventy-two ships are seventy-two ships more than Polyperchon has, my friend; yes it was a shame to lose so many but it will be enough for *us* to take the war to Polyperchon and Alexandros in the Peloponnesus.

Polyperchon is bogged down besieging Megalopolis; we'll take the army by sea around to the Bay of Argolis and land it there. I'll move inland and retake Tegea from Polyperchon and then attack him at Megalopolis if he hasn't already been repulsed whilst you keep me supplied from Athens.'

'Together we will sweep Greece free of Polyperchon and his son,' Nicanor said, shaking his fist as they walked.

'Kassandros! Kassandros, sir!' a voice shouted from behind them.

They turned to see the secretary running towards them, waving two scrolls.

'Two letters have just arrived for you, sir! From Macedon.'

Kassandros took the letters from the wheezing secretary, dismissed him with a wave of the hand and unrolled the first. His eyes widened as he mouthed the words and then he read out loud: '…and we ask, no, beg, that you should come immediately to Macedon and take the crown.' He looked at Nicanor, his eyes full of incredulity and showed him the list of names at the end of the letter. 'The crown? Me?'

'But what about King Philip?' Nicanor asked.

'He's dead; poisoned by Roxanna soon after they arrived at Pella. The leading families don't want the Asian babe as their king along with his murderous mother; they want strength and stability and together we could provide them with that.' He slapped Nicanor on the shoulder and gave him his widest grin. 'Go and give the orders for three ships to be prepared for the journey to Macedon; we'll sail tomorrow at dawn, and have the rest of the fleet readied for the expedition to the Peloponnesus which we'll embark upon before the end of the month. Once you've done that join me in my suite here and we'll discuss our futures in Macedon.'

'I won't be long, Kassandros, my good friend,' Nicanor said, grasping the proffered forearm. 'Now is our time.'

Kassandros sat in a darkened room, the shutters pulled, as he listened to Philip escorting Nicanor across the courtyard of his

Piraeus suite. He smiled, cold and resolute, as he realised just how much he was enjoying himself.

Philip opened the door, letting in a bright shaft of light in which many motes of dust wafted as Nicanor breezed in.

'All done?' Kassandros asked, leaning back in his chair.

'All done,' Nicanor confirmed as Philip stepped into the room, closing the door behind him and plunging the room into semi-darkness. Nicanor stopped still at the sound of the lock clicking. 'What's this?'

'What, my friend?' Kassandros asked, his voice innocent.

'Why are we in darkness and why have you locked the door?'

'Oh, that. Well, it's quite simple. We're in darkness so that you wouldn't see these fine gentlemen as you walked into the room.' He waved a hand and six soldiers stepped forward from the shadows. 'And I've had the door locked so as you wouldn't be able to get out. I think that explains it all perfectly simply. Take him.'

Rough hands grabbed Nicanor, easily suppressing his struggles.

'What are you doing, Kassandros?'

'I'm arresting you and now I'm putting you on trial. Did you say: "*We* are masters of these waters, Kassandros; *we* can go wherever *we* please"?'

'You can't do this!'

'I can and I am; answer the question. Did you say that?'

'It was a figure of speech.'

'And parading the beaks of the enemy ships and milking the glory out of my fleet's victory was also a figure of speech, was it?'

'It was a famous victory.'

'Was it? I spoke to a few of the triarchoi and it seems to me that you were roundly defeated at first and it was Antigonos who should claim any glory for the victory. Were you ever going to tell me the truth of the matter or were you just going to carry on with the fiction that you, you! had won a great victory. And what were you going to do with that glory, that kudos? Do you think that I could leave you in command of the most strategic port in Greece? A place that, with enough men inside, is almost impossible to take? Am I that stupid? Is that what you think?'

'No, Kassandros.'

'No, *sir*. I am your superior and yet you use familiar terms with me because, for some reason, you seem to have got it into your head that you are my equal. Now, answer the question. Did you say: "We are masters of these waters, Kassandros; we can go wherever we please."'

'Yes, but I—'

'Guilty; execute him.'

'No...' Nicanor's head was pulled back, Philip's hand clamping on his mouth stifling his protests as the officer commanding the soldiers drew his sword.

Despite his violent resistance, Nicanor was held rigid as the blade approached him, his eyes following it in fear.

It was clean; one punched thrust, and blood spurted from the gut wound. Twisting his wrist, the officer pulled out his weapon and Nicanor was released; he fell to his knees groaning with agony.

Kassandros got to his feet. 'Open the door, Philip.' He looked down at Nicanor as the shaft of light fell on him. 'Does that hurt? I hope so. Well, you've got plenty of time to enjoy it: this is a slow execution, you see; one belly wound and then I lock the door and leave you to die. If you're lucky, you may be dead by the time I sail for Macedon tomorrow.' He looked at the officer. 'Take his sword and dagger; we wouldn't want him cheating on me, would we?' He turned to go and then paused, looking back. 'And, oh, by the way, those letters were fakes; King Philip is still alive and no one has asked me to take the crown, yet. However, I am going to Macedon tomorrow. Not to become king, but to claim the regency. Goodbye, die badly.' He walked from the room with his men following behind him, leaving Philip to close the door, dulling Nicanor's growing cries of pain at every laboured breath and smiled as he heard the click of the lock.

And he smiled again as he saw the size of the crowd waiting for him on the quay of Pella's port: it was more than he had dared hope, even though he had sent a swift boat ahead of him to fore-warn Adea of his coming. *She certainly does have her uses which is more than can be said of her husband.* He scanned the crowd for his brother, Nicanor and stepmother, Hyperia, and allowed himself another smile when he saw them as that meant they would have also received his messages and put in train the gathering of his family's forces.

However, the smile with which he descended the gangplank was far less sincere, but what it lacked in sincerity it made up for in broadness. 'Your Majesty,' he crooned at King Philip, 'it is an honour to come at your summons.'

Philip hopped up and down with excitement, drooling prolifically from both sides of his mouth. 'I did summon you, didn't I?'

'You did,' Kassandros lied, 'and I came immediately. What is Your Majesty's pleasure?'

Philip stopped hopping, squeezed his eyes shut as if trying to remember and then looked down at his toes. 'To play with my elephant,' he said in a low voice.

Adea stepped forward to retrieve the situation, the carefully scripted, simple dialogue that Kassandros had sent ahead having proved too much for her husband. 'The king wishes his loyal subject, Kassandros, to assume, with me, the regency of him and his royal brother, Alexander, the fourth of that name. King Philip hereby decrees that Polyperchon should lay down the office and return the Great Ring of Macedon to him.' Her voice was clear and carried over the crowd, who cheered with great enthusiasm the wisdom of their king.

Kassandros held his hands in the air, waving them for silence. 'It will be an honour for me to serve my king and my country in the manner he has decreed.'

This brought a rapturous reception from the crowd in whose midst his brother Nicanor was leading the applause and gesturing for more volume, as Hyperia encouraged the ladies, to one side, to lend their voices to the ovation.

'We will proceed to the palace,' Adea called, 'where the king will formalise the decree.'

'I didn't think you liked me enough to be *so* enthusiastic in your support, dearest Stepmother,' Kassandros said as he fell back a couple of places in the parade, to be next to Hyperia and Nicanor.

Hyperia looked at him, her expression earnest. 'My feelings for you have nothing to do with it, Kassandros, it's all to do with the safety of our family. Since Adea has allied herself with you, she has ceased to be our enemy; I would like it to remain that way as she is a nasty, vicious girl. But, however vicious she might be, it's nothing compared with Olympias and you being made regent to her grandson, Alexander, will stir that harpy to heights of jealousy hitherto unscaled and bring her east with an army. You mark my words, Kassandros, we need Adea as Olympias is coming to claim her grandson and Roxanna will be only too glad to accept her protection.'

'You think so?'

'We know so,' Nicanor said. 'Letters have passed between her and Olympias; they have been using Aristonous as a go-between as his estates are close to the border with Epirus. Some of our men have been watching the route but we've yet to intercept one.'

'Well, we'll just have to put a stop to that, won't we? But first I need to raise an army up here; how are you doing with that?'

'I've started assembling all of our followers from the estates who didn't follow you to Asia and called upon kinsmen to do the same; we should have a core of almost seven hundred men, four hundred cavalry, two hundred and fifty infantry, completely loyal to our family at the heart of the army.'

Kassandros ruffled the hair on the back of Nicanor's head. 'Well done, brother. Now, I had better do the rest.'

Kassandros looked at the document and then signed it. 'That should bring you an army of about ten thousand if all the discharged veterans pay heed to the call and come to the muster; that should be enough to hold off Olympias if she comes west with the Epirot army.' He passed it over to Adea to sign in the name of her husband.

Adea signed her name and that of Philip and passed the scroll to a waiting clerk. 'Have five hundred copies of that made and sent to every town in Macedon.'

The clerk bowed and reversed out of the council chamber.

'I shall write to Polyperchon in the name of the king,' Adea said, 'demanding that he lay down command of his army and transfer it to you.'

'He won't,' Kassandros said, 'we all know that.'

'Then he will be a traitor.'

'And we know what to do with them.' Kassandros got to his feet. 'I'm going back south to defeat him and his son and then I'll be able to come north and together we will deal with Olympias.'

'What if she invades before you arrive?'

'Then you use that warrior training that you're so proud of and lead the army against her.' *Two female generals facing up to each other; what is the world coming to?* But Kassandros could see by Adea's expression that that was exactly what she dreamed of. 'Just do what you have to do to make sure that Olympias does not get power over her grandson.' He turned and limped from the room with purpose, anxious to be going back south. *Once Polyperchon is defeated and the Greek cities have their oligarchies restored, I'll be back, my little warrior queen, and then we'll deal with Olympias together; and after that? Well, who knows? But there is no room in my plans for either your idiot king nor the half-caste whelped by Roxanna.*

ROXANNA.
THE WILD-CAT.

I T WAS NOT safe; Roxanna felt it more than ever now that the man-woman had allied herself with the coward who did not have the right to recline at table, and Polyperchon was embroiled in the south trying to give freedom to people not much better than slaves who did not deserve it. Her only friend was Olympias and that might be no more than an assumption as, although she had written to her in flattering terms three years previously, her recent couple of letters were far more formal, so who knew where the aging dowager queen stood now. But she was her only hope as Adea's grip on power in Macedon was becoming firmer by the day.

But how was she to escape? Olympias had urged her to do so but had made no suggestions as to the practicalities.

Roxanna sat, in semi-darkness, on a deep cushion and hugged her knees, burying her face in her dress, rocking to and fro as she willed herself to come up with a solution to her predicament: she needed transport, she needed protection for herself and her son as well as the slave-girls she would take with her to keep her in comfort – a considerable amount of protection as the journey was long and across hazardous terrain and her party would not be small – and she needed opportunity, for the three body-guards who constantly watched over her son were there as much to prevent him from leaving Pella as they were to ensure his safety. They were unlikely to agree to fleeing in secret to Epirus and yet that was what Roxanna knew she must do; either that or resign herself to death.

She cursed her inability to get her potions through the security that surrounded the man-woman and her equally disgusting man-child since the one success in administering a poison to Philip all those years ago in Babylon. How many years was it? Five, it must be for that was the age of her son. And what had she done in those years? Nothing but be dragged around Asia following an army and then brought to Europe to be a captive queen kept in what passed for luxury in this backward country. She looked around her chamber on the first floor of the northern side of the palace: it was full of rich decoration in the form of silken drapes, finely woven carpets, deeply upholstered couches piled with cushions, polished wooden tables covered with jewel-encrusted bowls or golden statuettes, all dimly lit by a few guttering lamps, all worthless to her in terms of security; she fought back a sob. *A queen does not cry; a queen stands tall and overcomes her difficulties.* But no sooner had the thought passed through her mind than the futility of the situation hit her. *Stand tall? Stand tall and do what?* And now the sob exploded from her for there was no way of suppressing the impotence she felt and the sense of hopelessness that had been growing in her ever since she had been brought to Pella. There were still another eleven years to go before her son could take up his birth-right in his own name; what were the chances of him surviving until then with the man-woman and the coward in control of Macedon? For the first time in a long while her mind passed back to her youth in the ragged lands of Bactria and the simpler life that she had led. Yes, she had all comforts imaginable but she also had freedom: she roamed the hills and valleys – with a strong escort, naturally – she hunted with her father and brothers, for the girls of her tribe were encouraged to do more than spin and weave; indeed, she would even help her brothers to break the colts each season. But now that was gone, exchanged for what she had thought would be the most privileged position for a woman in the world: the wife of the great Alexander. Instead, she was little more than a prisoner.

The sob repeated itself again and again until it transformed into a wail of despair and Roxanna collapsed onto the soft furnishings, tearing at the delicate fabrics as she wallowed in her self-pity.

It was, therefore, a surprise to Roxanna when she felt strong, masculine hands grip her shoulders and haul her up. Automatically she covered her unveiled face with a ravaged cushion and turned to face the intruder. 'Aristonous? What are you doing in my private apartment? How dare you!'

Aristonous shook her. 'Be quiet and listen. What happens to you is of little concern to me but Alexander's child is in great danger and I've come to help him. You can either stay here or come with me but, if you come, I won't tolerate any histrionics. I'll just abandon you; do you understand?'

'You don't talk to a queen like that.'

'Do you understand? Yes or no?'

'I am a—'

The slap cut her off and she looked in shock at Aristonous, rubbing her cheek, the cushion now discarded. It took much strength to utter her next word: 'Yes.'

'Then come with me.'

'I must pack.'

'If you want to, go and do so; I'm leaving now. You either come now or you don't; it's all one to me.' He turned to go and walked through the door leaving Roxanna fuming, unsure of what to do.

And then she realised that this was the opportunity she had wished for, if not in the form that she had actually wanted. She stamped her foot and clenched her fists by her sides and, for the first time ever did something against her will without being forced into it, she followed Aristonous out of the door.

A couple of her slave-girls crouched, terrified, in the corridor, watched over by a brute of a man, heavily armed. 'Come,' Roxanna ordered the girls.

'They stay,' the brute growled.

'I'm a queen! They do what I say and so do you.'

'And I've got a heavy sword so they're best off obeying me; as are you.' The brute creased his pock-marked face into a leer and grabbed Roxanna's arm, propelling her after Aristonous, along the corridor towards her son's suite.

More men joined them from intersecting corridors lit with torches and adjacent rooms oozing light, until a dozen stood outside the double doors of Alexander's apartment.

Aristonous looked back at her. 'Knock on the door and demand entrance.'

So that's the reason they got me: to get access to Alexander's rooms. She paused, about to object at being used thus, and then thought better of it; she walked up to the doors and thumped them. 'It's the queen; open the doors, I wish to see my son.'

It took but a few moments before the lock clicked. Aristonous heaved his shoulder to the door; it burst open and his men swarmed in behind him, pushing Roxanna aside onto her knees.

'There is no need for bloodshed,' Aristonous said to the young king's three bodyguards, standing, swords drawn, blocking the way. 'You know who I am and you know that my loyalties have always been with the Argead house, as are yours – or, at least, they should be.'

'What do you want, Aristonous?' the middle of the three asked.

'To take the king to safety, Coenus, to Olympias. If he stays here Kassandros and Adea will kill him as soon as they feel secure enough in their rule to be able to murder the flesh and blood of Alexander himself.'

Coenus looked at his two companions and then at Roxanna as she picked herself up off the floor. 'What does his mother say?'

Roxanna fought the urge to snap at the man. 'I know that you are here as much to be our gaolers as to ensure our safety, but if we stay then you will be killed defending us against Kassandros' men and we will all be dead. We must leave.'

Again Coenus looked at his companions and they shared the slightest acknowledgement of agreement. He turned back to Aristonous. 'We've been debating the matter since we heard this morning of Kassandros' coming; we felt that it didn't bode well for the king. It cannot be against our oaths to escort him, with his mother, to his grandmother: we can do that with a clear conscience.'

Aristonous held out his arm, the grip was returned. 'It would have been a great shame to have been obliged to kill you, Coenus.'

Coenus grinned and signalled to an inner door. Roxanna ran forward and opened it; a few heartbeats later she emerged with the spindly form of the five-year-old king of Macedon in her arms, his hands clasped around her neck, and his nurse in hot pursuit.

'She stays,' Aristonous said, pointing to the nurse. 'It's bad enough having a child and a woman with us, I'll not compound it with a crone.'

He turned to go. Roxanna looked at the nurse and knew that she had no choice in the matter; she was being swept along by events over which she had no influence. 'Stay; I will send for you.' With that she turned and ran after her rescuers.

The horses were waiting, looked after by three other men, in a copse four hundred paces north of the city walls. They had descended from her suite via back stairs and labyrinthine passages to exit the complex through a cellar window whose bars had been hacked away in preparation for the escape. It had therefore been some time in the planning and not just a spontaneous action precipitated by Kassandros' arrival and his formal alliance with Adea.

She had struggled as they ran across the open ground, dark as the moon was yet to rise, which sloped up towards the foothills of the mountains overlooking the city, Alexander growing heavier in her embrace by the moment.

Without a word, the men mounted up as Roxanna put Alexander down and looked around, confused.

'Hurry up, woman,' Aristonous hissed.

'But where's my carriage?'

'Don't be stupid, get on that mare.'

'But a queen doesn't ride.'

'A queen does as she's fucking well told; now get on that horse.'

'But Alexander can't ride.'

'Alexander will be dead if he doesn't; now either you take him in front of you or you give him to me.'

Roxanna looked down at the boy, his confused and frightened eyes wide in the night. She took a deep breath and lifted him up in front of the saddle. Then, remembering her girlhood, hunting and breaking colts in far off Bactria, she swung herself up to sit astride, put an arm around Alexander and caught hold of the reins, giving them a rapid double flick to either side of the beast's neck as she kicked it forward after Aristonous. Alive with excitement and the memories of adventures in her youth, Roxanna felt a thrill at her sudden change of fortune. She rubbed her cheek that still smarted from Aristonous' slap and smiled to herself in the darkness; it had been a long while since a man had dominated her so.

On they rode through the night, keeping to the foothills as they made their way ever south and west, increasing their speed at the rising of the moon so that by the time the sky glowed pale on their backs they were ten leagues from Pella, ten leagues closer to the safety of Epirus and the protection of the mother-in-law she had never seen.

The whole of the next day they pressed on, Alexander asleep much of the time in her arms, stopping only to water the horses and feed them from their nosebags as their riders gnawed on bread, apples and onions and took advantage of bushes to relieve nature's call; then on they would set off again. For two days they continued thus, avoiding towns and villages, pausing only for a few hours' sleep on the second night and so they were more than one hundred leagues from Pella, just shy of the border, when the faintest sound of pursuit reached their ears; the sound that all had dreaded but none had spoken of for fear of tempting the gods beyond endurance.

'Ride!' Aristonous cried after a glance over his shoulder. 'Ride!' He kicked his horse forward, accelerating away.

Roxanna looked behind her: there, far in the distance, a league or so away, but clearly following them was a unit of prodromoi, light, lance-armed cavalry, perfect for the pursuit of other horsemen; but what made them a threat at this distance was that each man had a spare mount, they would not be tiring soon.

She urged her mare into a canter but felt her son struggle in his seat, squealing with agitation as the party's nervousness communicated itself to him. 'Keep still! Alexander, curse you, stop struggling!' On she pushed her horse, all the time fighting with one hand to keep her increasingly distressed child secured.

Up they climbed as fast as their mounts could go, up towards the heights of Mount Tymphaea in the Pindus Mountain range and the pass that would take them over into Epirus. And still the boy wriggled and complained, wanting just to be put down and not understanding why he could not have his own way as was normally the case with his nurse. It was the bite on the wrist that made Roxanna loosen her grip and screech; down Alexander tumbled, down onto the rock-strewn parched ground, crashing onto his shoulder-blades to roll two complete somersaults under the momentum of the horse's speed before lying on his back, still.

Roxanna screamed. *If he's dead then so am I.* She leaped from her mare before it had pulled up and ran back to her prostrate son. 'Alexander!' She knelt by the still, small body and cupped his head in her hands; his hair was warm and sticky.

Blood! No, don't let him be dead; I want to live.

She pulled an eyelid open and felt a surge of relief as the pupil dilated.

'Is he alright?' Aristonous shouted, riding his horse back towards them.

'I think so; I think he's just unconscious. He's hit his head, it's bleeding.'

'We have to move him; they are less than half a league behind us. Give him to me.'

With a mixture of reluctance and relief, Roxanna picked up the limp body and handed it up to Aristonous, who, without any ceremony perhaps due to a king, laid him, belly down, across his stallion's neck. 'Now mount up; we must get going.'

Roxanna did as she was told with alacrity, glancing behind to see the pursuers' dust cloud markedly closer after the delay. On she pushed her mare, a sturdy and wide-chested beast with a big heart; it seemed to be enjoying the challenge much more now there was no struggling child around its neck. But the incline grew steeper and they were forced to traverse whilst their pursuers, at least twenty in total, came on in a direct course so that it was not long before the distance between them was no more than five hundred paces in a straight line, although they had the advantage of height. And then Roxanna's heart faltered as she looked down at the prodromoi; still in a canter, they jumped from their tired mounts onto the relatively fresh ones and, with a new turn of speed, accelerated up the hill which Roxanna and her companions, on tired horses, had been obliged to traverse left and right.

On Aristonous pushed, on to the first summit, strewn with ragged rocks, providing places to hide for perhaps a couple of men but not a small party such as they; and still the pursuit gained on their fresher beasts.

'It's no good, Aristonous,' Coenus shouted from the rear of the group, 'they cannot help but catch us unless they are delayed long enough for you to be on the downward slope. We know what we must do to keep our oaths. How far is it to the pass?'

Aristonous pointed up to the crest of the hill about five hundred paces distant; behind it rose another ridge and then, behind that, the mountains soared. 'Just over there it begins; it's narrow at first and then opens out as it cuts through the range.'

Coenus nodded, understanding what Aristonous had implied. 'Then that's there we shall hold true to our oaths.'

Roxanna was reminded of the brave men of her father's household, sworn to the death in the service of her house, lesser lives sacrificed for those of greater worth, as she pushed her mare to the limit of her endurance, ever up, her footing sure despite the loosened scree, in a desperate race for the pass.

The shouts from behind were clearer now, echoing around the hills through clear mountain air; cries assured of success at the end of a long chase.

At last the gradient lessened and the tired horses produced one final surge as the summit was gained; down the slope beyond it they galloped, praying to whatever god seemed the most appropriate in the circumstances that their mounts should not stumble. Ahead, through a maze of scattered boulders, the next ridge climbed aloft but it was not one solid wall of rock, it was two, not quite contiguous but overlapping, and a path led between them into the valley that divided Mount Tymphaea and Mount Lyncus. Up to that path they raced, knowing that a chance of safety lay along it as it entered the pass.

'Go ahead, Aristonous,' Coenus shouted as the first of the party slipped between the gap amid the two ridges. 'We will hold them for as long as possible.'

Roxanna's mare pounded up the path, in the midst of the group before the bottleneck of the entrance slowed them and they were forced to enter just three or four at a time; and then she was through and into a valley that opened up to the west, flanked by steep sides and overlooked by the heights of the Pindus Mountains.

'We will see each other again soon, one way or the other,' Coenus shouted as the last rider was through. With that he and his two comrades turned their horses in the entrance and faced downhill, waiting for the pursuers to close.

It was to the sound of combat that Roxanna and her rescuers fled west: the cries of battle, both triumphant and agonised, the clash of iron and the equine shrieks of the beasts. On they went as the noise faded until it was brought to their ears by just the faintest of echoes whispering on the wind; finally they could relax and let their horses slow to relieve their aching chests.

It was with relief rather than fear, that Roxanna saw an approaching troop of light cavalry, for they came out of the west, from the land of Olympias, from Epirus, into which realm they had just crossed.

'Halt! Come no further,' the officer commanding the Epirot cavalry cried. 'Identify yourselves.'

Aristonous walked his horse forward. 'I am Aristonous, former bodyguard to Alexander himself. We have brought his son and namesake to seek the protection of his grandmother, Queen Olympias, and her kinsman, Aeacides, the King of Epirus.' He lifted the still-unconscious body of the young king. 'He badly needs a physician.'

The commander rode over and looked at Alexander, lifting his chin. 'Then you had better come with me, Olympias is with the king at Decemta.'

Never had words come as such a relief to Roxanna; she looked over her shoulder to see the arrival of their pursuers back down the pass, their number visibly depleted and their threat nullified in the face of a superior force. *Now I'm safe; now I have Olympias to protect me thanks to that man.* She looked at Aristonous and smiled; he nodded back, his expression neutral, but was that desire she saw in his eyes? A thrill ran through her belly.

'Come forward,' Olympias commanded, her voice betraying no familial affection. 'Let me see the child.'

Fighting to keep her temper at being thus addressed, Roxanna advanced, her hands on Alexander's shoulders and her eyes fixed on those of Olympias as she sat, upright and rigid, on an elevated chair looking down at her and her son; Thessalonike stood behind her resting one hand on the chair's back. *She treats me as her inferior. And what is that woman doing, standing behind her? I thought she was no more than a lady in waiting.*

Olympias beckoned to Alexander. 'Come up here, child.'

Still groggy from his fall, the boy froze. Roxanna steered him to the dais' steps.

'Just the child.' Olympias' voice was imperious.

Roxanna hesitated. *How dare she speak to me like that?* But her position as a supplicant had been made abundantly clear to Roxanna since her arrival at the palace earlier that morning: forced to wait for an interview with Olympias for over six hours, Roxanna had been shown into an apartment that was clearly for low-grade diplomatic missions of little import rather than a suite commensurate with her rank as a queen. She had suffered the insult in mute fury, determined to do nothing that would harm her chances of creating a good impression with the woman in whose hands her safety, and that of her child, lay. She would have appealed to Aristonous but, to her disappointment, he and his men had disappeared immediately after they had announced their arrival and placed her in the hands of Thessalonike, of whom she had never heard and with whom she had developed an immediate mutual antipathy.

The look of wicked amusement in Thessalonike's eyes as Roxanna hesitated caused her much cause for concern and she regretted the way she had spoken down to her earlier. *She must be far more in Olympias' confidence than I had imagined.* She pushed Alexander forward to mount the steps on his own, his head low.

Olympias reached out and cupped the boy's chin, raising his gaze to meet her own; she surveyed him for a few moments and then nodded, her lips pursed, as if she had just confirmed what she already suspected. 'You have the look of your father, child, but it is stained by your mother's colour.' She looked down her nose at Roxanna, as if she were a slave barely worthy of notice, and then back to Alexander. 'Tell me your name, child.'

'A…A…Alexander.' The voice was almost inaudible.

Olympias slapped him across the cheek. 'That is not how the true Alexander says his name. Tell me it again, child, this time as if you mean it.'

Alexander recoiled and turned to his mother, who reached up the steps to collect him.

'Leave him! The child must speak for himself and stand on his own feet and not cling to the skirts of his mother. Say your name, child.'

Alexander looked at Roxanna, who encouraged him with a nod; he turned back to Olympias, pulled himself up as tall as his slight stature would allow and puffed out his chest. 'Alexander.' The voice was clear and loud.

'That's better; we shall make a king out of you, despite the barbarian colour of the vessel that bore you.'

This was now too much for Roxanna. 'If you wish to insult me, insult me not to my son but to my face.'

Olympias got to her feet without looking at Roxanna, easing Alexander towards her. 'I'll insult you anyway I like, barbarian, seeing as you have deliberately kept my grandson from me for these many years, despite my pleas to see him. I eventually had to send Aristonous to get him seeing as you were doing nothing to bring him to me and ensure his safety.'

'I wasn't free to come; I was no better than a prisoner.'

Olympias sneered. 'No queen lets herself become a prisoner; any status you thought you had back in Macedon, you have left there. Here you are nothing but what I say you are.' She turned to go, putting her arm around Alexander's shoulders. 'But now that you are here, just remember that you are the supplicant and try not to antagonise me too much; after all, it is now me protecting you from Kassandros and Adea, not Polyperchon.' Without looking back, Olympias glided from the room, taking Alexander with her.

'It's been such a pleasure meeting my nephew,' Thessalonike said as she too turned to leave.

Roxanna was shocked. 'Nephew?'

'Yes, I'm Alexander's half-sister, something that you were evidently unaware of when you treated me with such contempt when we met earlier; perhaps you should have done a little more research before you came running here expecting to be treated like a queen.' She gave a deliberately false smile before following Olympias, leaving Roxanna, stunned, on her own, wishing herself anywhere but there in the clutches of such women.

After a few moments of controlling the urge to slump to the floor and weep, she walked from the audience chamber resolved to appeal to the last person who might help her; she would write to Polyperchon.

POLYPERCHON.
THE GREY.

POLYPERCHON STARED AT the two heads lying on the ground with a trident next to them, and then read the letter that had accompanied them. He sighed with deep regret and looked back down at the gruesome objects, now a playground for maggots. *Kleitos, what have you done? You've lost my fleet. How can I move north along the coast without it?* He turned to Alexandros, looking grim beside him. 'Burn them and have the ashes treated with respect.'

'Yes, Father.' Alexandros pointed at the letter. 'What does it say?'

Polyperchon weighed the scroll in the palm of his hand; it felt heavy, foreboding disaster. 'It's from Lysimachus. After Kleitos defeated Nicanor of Sindus, Antigonos caught him unprepared and, between him and what was left of Nicanor's fleet, completely destroyed Kleitos. Only he managed to escape with Arrhidaeus here,' he nodded to the other head, 'but a Lysimachid patrol took them in Thrace when they landed to pick up water. Lysimachus just announced his support for Antigonos and Kassandros by sending me their heads.' He ripped up the letter and threw the pieces to the breeze. 'To lose the fleet just days after losing so many of my elephants...' He looked over to the walls of Megalopolis, still intact, with bodies littering the ground before them; bodies of men and beasts, huge beasts. The town had refused all offers of terms, unwilling to allow the wild, democratic faction back to rule with the abandon that it had showed before Antipatros had imposed oligarchies on the Greek cities after the Lamian War. 'No,' they had said, rejecting Polyperchon's decree granting freedom to the Greeks, 'it's nothing more than a ruse to gain your support.' And so they had declared for Kassandros and defied Polyperchon to get through or over the strongest walls in the Peloponnesus. Thus, after a few days' constant bombardment with the heaviest artillery in his possession, he had sent his elephant herd in to batter the weakened masonry until it fell. But almost every town or city had a veteran of Alexander's wars in the east and Megalopolis was no exception; knowing what to expect, the veteran had advised the city's elders to commission the forging of hundreds of four-pointed caltrops, so designed so that however they fell there would always be a wicked spike, a hand's-breadth long, pointing straight up.

Unaware of the danger that awaited them, Polyperchon had sent his elephants forward, supported by artillery, archers and slingers to keep the walls clear. But no one needed to be on the walls for the damage was already done. On the great beasts had come; on into a field sown with pain as each step impaled their feet on yet more sprouting iron, sending them trumpeting onto their hind legs. Down did their full weight press on the caltrops already imbedded in them, forcing them to buck and land on shredding forelegs taking the agony to new heights, until, unable to bear it any more, they rolled onto their sides and backs, crushing their mahouts, and lashing out at the light infantry support as they tried to remove the wicked barbs from their feet. In agony they thrashed on the ground, trumpeting their pain to the skies, covering themselves all over in the spiked menace, bleeding from every wound so that they seemed covered in a red skin sprouting ghastly bristles. And there they had lain, their blood flowing freely and their understanding unable to comprehend a way out of their predicament. The first had died on the second day and, even now, four days later, one of the great carcases would occasionally twitch betraying the faintest sign of life.

It was as if the gods had taken all favour from him, Polyperchon reflected, as he considered his position. He turned to Alexandros. 'What news of Kassandros?'

'His army was still disembarking when our scouts returned this morning; it seems pretty certain that he is aiming for Tegea.'

'If he takes that then we've lost the entire Peloponnesus.'

'We've already lost Attica. The Athenian assembly voted the death sentence for Hagnonides and many of his democratic faction; they were executed three days ago shortly after Kassandros arrived back from Macedon.'

Polyperchon rubbed his bald pate and sighed, long and deep. *I need to be decisive or I might just as well go and meet Kassandros and offer him my sword with which to kill me. I have no choices left now; it has to be north.* He drew himself up and looked at his son with what he hoped was a confident expression. 'Take your part of the army and reinforce the garrison in Tegea. Kassandros will be loath to bring his army north until his rear is secure; the city's well stocked so you should be able to hold out until I return.'

'Where are you going?'

'North. I'll travel fast ahead of my army. If Kassandros has been to Macedon that must mean he now has control of it through Adea. I'm going to Epirus; Olympias cannot refuse me now; not with her grandson in such obvious danger. No, she'll bring the Epirot army to my aid; together we can secure Macedon, kill Adea, take the fool back into our protection and then come south to relieve you at Tegea and crush Kassandros between us early next year.'

Alexandros considered his father's plan for a few moments. 'And if she doesn't come?'

'She will.'

'I will,' Olympias said, turning from Polyperchon to Aeacides, seated on his throne in the palace throne-room, looking out over the wooded mountains that surrounded Passeron, 'provided my flabby kinsman will provide me with an army.'

The King of Epirus chuckled mirthlessly, his premature double chin wobbling in an unsightly manner, his eyes bleary with alcohol. 'You have such a way with words, Olympias, it is almost impossible to refuse you – almost.' He quaffed half a cup of wine.

Polyperchon had known that this would be a difficult interview but had not been prepared for the amount of animosity that was evident between Olympias and Aeacides. He needed to make his point vigorously; he stepped forward in what he hoped was an energetic and decisive manner. 'If we do not take an army into Macedon now, when we have Kassandros preoccupied in the Peloponnesus with his siege of Tegea, then Macedon will be lost to the true Argead house for ever. Kassandros is taking advantage of Adea's naivety at the moment. He's using her and Philip to hold Macedon for him until he is free to bring his entire army north and, when he does, he will kill Philip and give Adea the choice between death or becoming his wife, thus legitimizing himself by marrying into the Argead house and opening the door for him to declare himself king.' He slammed a fist into a palm. Olympias and Aeacides both stared at him, momentarily surprised by his vehemence as he stepped back, clearly uncomfortable with his melodrama.

Aeacides recovered first and was dismissive. 'And why would I care about what happens in Macedon? Why would I care about the Argead house?' he asked, quaffing the other half.

'Because if you don't,' Olympias said in the tone of a parent talking to a recalcitrant child, 'then your grandson won't get to sit on the throne of Macedon.'

Aeacides looked confused, holding out his cup for a refill. 'My grandson?'

'Yes, your grandson. Are you so steeped in wine as to have forgotten the conversation we had five years ago when the eastern bitch was about to whelp? The son born of your eldest daughter, Deidamia, and fathered by my grandson, Alexander, son of Alexander. That promise still stands if you help me.'

'Of course I haven't forgotten,' Aeacides lied.

Polyperchon tried to disguise his surprise as he looked at Olympias with a new respect. *That is a brilliant plan; both children may only be five years old but they would represent stability in the future. Only the hardest-bitten supporters of Kassandros and Antigonos would find that unacceptable.*

Aeacides was also making that mental calculation, pulling on the lobe of an ear and swilling his wine around. Eventually his expression indicated he had come to a decision. 'That would be a powerful union indeed, a glory to my house.'

'A glory to both houses,' Olympias corrected.

'Indeed, to both houses.' He looked fleetingly anxious. 'And the mother, Roxanna?'

'Is irrelevant now that I have Alexander in my power; she will do as she's told if she wishes to live. She'll be comfortable enough, although, naturally, she will not be allowed access to anything with which she can brew her potions, so she won't be able to pursue her little hobby.'

'Wouldn't it be better if...' He left the question standing, and concentrated on his cup.

'I've thought about that too, but if I kill her it might adversely affect the child, turn him against me, which wouldn't do for what I have in mind.'

Ruling through him; I don't doubt. Where will that leave me? Dead, unless I voluntarily submit to her. He took hold of the Great Ring of Macedon, twisted it from his finger and offered it to Olympias. 'It would seem that now Alexander is reunited with his grandmother and Adea and Philip have turned traitor with Kassandros, my duty is done; take it. It is yours now and I shall serve you.'

Olympias' eyes lit up with power-lust. She took the ring, slipped it onto her forefinger and then raised her hand in the air to admire it. 'Very pretty; very pretty indeed. You've done well,

Polyperchon, not many people could give up such power. I thought that I would have to kill you for it.'

Polyperchon was relieved that he had guessed correctly. 'To tell the truth, I never wanted it; I have always preferred to follow rather than lead.'

'Now you have your chance again to do so.' She lowered her hand and turned to Aeacides. 'So that army we were talking about; when can I have it by?'

The king shook his head, smiling to himself. 'You don't ever give up, do you, Olympias?'

'Not when I'm pursuing what is rightfully mine, no. The army? When?'

Aeacides raised his hands in surrender. 'Alright, we'll invade Macedon.'

'We?'

'Yes, I shall come with you and lead the attack in person.'

'And be seen as a foreign invader at the head of a foreign army? Are you even more stupid than I thought? Surely not? No, you're just drunk. *I* shall lead the army and I shall be the mother of the great Alexander returning to Macedon with his son to reclaim his inheritance. No Macedonian will stand before such a claim, especially as the army behind me will not be foreign but, rather, the army of Alexander's betrothed who will one day give birth to a true son of the Argead house. As her father, Aeacides, you may be present, but I think you will agree that you cannot lead, even if you could stand up.'

Aeacides' smile was cold, his teeth stained. 'You think of everything, Olympias.'

'I have to as no one else seems able to.'

'Very well, you lead the army if you wish, but who will actually command it in a way that it doesn't fall to pieces?'

'Implying that I know nothing of military command.'

'I'm not implying it, I'm stating it.'

'And for once I would agree with you, which is why I had Aristonous bring the boy from Macedon; he will be my general. Now, when will the army be ready?'

Aeacides gestured his helplessness in the face of such determination. 'Seven days at the earliest.'

'Good,' Olympias said in approval. 'We'll be through the pass before there's any danger of snow; we should be in Pella before the onset of winter.' She glanced again at the ring and then looked at Polyperchon. 'When will your army arrive here in the north?'

'Ten days or so.'

'Excellent. How long can Tegea hold out?'

'Until next spring at least.'

'Does Kassandros know that?'

'I would have thought so,' he replied with a shrug. 'There is always so much toing and froing between the men as so many know each other from before.'

Olympias considered this for a few moments and then came to a decision. 'Kassandros will break off his siege once he hears that we've invaded; I'm sure of it. He will see Macedon as the greater prize and calculate that he can deal with Tegea in his own time. You come with me and then once we have Macedon secure, I'll send you south, Polyperchon, to speak to the Aitolians; we need them as our allies, whatever the cost. Get them to hold the Gates of Thermopylae for us against Kassandros.'

'What if they refuse?'

'They won't, not if you offer them complete independence in the name of the king should they do as they are asked.'

Polyperchon almost sighed with relief to be once again receiving orders from one with complete confidence in what they were about; and then a thought occurred to him. 'He has a fleet; he could just sail around them.'

Olympias smiled at him with cold eyes. 'Because *you* managed to lose *your* fleet? Yes, I've thought of that. But you did accomplish one sensible thing whilst you wore the ring: you made Eumenes the general commanding Asia with the right to draw on the treasury at Cynda. I wrote to him when you first made the offer of my returning to Macedon; he advised me to wait until a more suitable time. That time has now come: I have the child

354

who gives me legitimacy and Eumenes will have ships by now; I'll order him to bring them, his army and plenty of gold and silver across the Aegean. Kassandros will be crushed between me and Eumenes.'

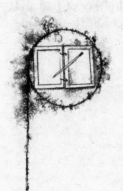

EUMENES.
THE SLY.

I T WAS, EUMENES had to acknowledge, a bold plan that Olympias put
forward. He admired it because it
would achieve three things: it would get
rid of Kassandros; unite his, Olympias'
and Polyperchon's forces in Europe thus securing Macedon
and Greece; and leave Antigonos and Ptolemy facing one
another in Asia. *Very satisfactory; let them duel with each other
for a while and then we'll secure Lysimachus' loyalty – or at least
his non-belligerence – and bring our combined armies across the
Hellespont and deal with Antigonos with Ptolemy's help because he
would be a fool to refuse us. Perfect.* He handed Olympias' letter
to Hieronymus, reclining next to him at the low table covered
with the fruits of the sea. 'I think I should do as she asks; what
say you, old friend? And when you've finished, you can keep it
for your history.'

Leaving Hieronymus to peruse the letter, Eumenes took his
cup, crossed to the window and, leaning on the windowsill,
looked down at the busy Syrian port of Rhosus, on the
southern shore of the large bay where Alexander had won his
stunning victory at Issos. It was a pleasing sight: the harbour,
with the theatre standing tall on a slope behind it, was now
bursting with the ships he had commandeered in Tarsus and
along the coast in his push south into Phoenicia as Ptolemy's
garrisons withdrew before him. Having reached Tyros and

realising that he had not the strength – yet – to take it, he had left garrisons in all the major towns and withdrawn to Rhosus where he was amassing his fleet and recruiting hundreds of local Phoenician oarsmen and sailors. He had chosen Rhosus as it was the closest port to Europe that he could safely use for he had intended to send coinage to the cash-starved Polyperchon in Greece in return for Macedonian troops; but now Olympias had offered a bigger prize. He took a long draught of wine in her honour.

With a growing sense of well-being, he sucked in a deep breath of salt-tanged air and drew himself up to his diminutive full height as he appreciated the sight of such sea-power; almost fifty fighting ships, and as many again of transport, all under the command of his Rhodian naval commander, Sosigenes. He then cast his gaze south to the army camp, just beyond the city walls, covering almost the same area as Rhosus itself and full of newly arrived mercenaries; he did a mental calculation as to how many of them he would be able to embark. *Most of them, I should think; I'll stiffen the garrisons with those we have to leave behind. I'll speak to Sosigenes and get him to do the arithmetic.*

When news of Eumenes' new-found wealth and desire to recruit mercenaries had spread throughout Greek cities of Europe and Asia, thousands had flocked to his call; his army had swelled. *It's not far off being a respectable size,* he mused as he felt pride in his achievements since withdrawing funds from Cyinda. He had maintained the illusion of Alexander remaining in overall command from beyond the grave by holding a council every morning in the royal tent with the empty throne presiding; Antigenes along with Teutamus had both found it acceptable to receive orders from Eumenes so long as they were framed as Alexander's will. His other commanders, Sosigenes, Xennias and Parmida had no need of such a ruse.

Thus Eumenes' strength had grown by the day and with it his confidence, for he now had legitimacy: he commanded in Asia in the name of the kings and Antigonos was the outlaw. Granted, the sentence of death still hung over his head but that was now no more than a technicality to be rescinded as soon as a full army assembly could be convened once he got to Europe. *Defeat Kassander, unite with Olympias and Polyperchon and then take up once again the cause of the kings back in Asia. Or king, more likely. I don't imagine that Olympias will let the fool live for a moment longer than she can decently allow once we've captured him.* Eumenes shrugged at the thought. *No bad thing so long as the Argead house carries on in the form of the young Alexander; if only half the rumours are true then Adea is just as bad as the eastern wild-cat. Still, now that Olympias has finally got her clutches on the boy-king and Adea has sided with Kassandros, regicide is inevitable; better the fool than the child. And there always remains Kleopatra...*

'What news of Antigonos?' Hieronymus asked from behind him, rolling up Olympias' letter.

Eumenes turned, screwing up his face. 'That's my one concern: it seems that his fleet, under Nearchos' command, is still in the north repairing damage and wiping out any last little pockets of resistance to him; but he himself headed south with the bulk of his army as soon as he heard I had gone back on our agreement and taken up Polyperchon's offer. He could be spotted by our scouts any day.'

'You'll have to be quick then.'

'I will be; I'll speak to Sosigenes immediately.'

'The fleet is almost completely crewed and the coinage is due to arrive from Cyinda tomorrow; as soon as it is stowed, lord, we can start embarking the troops,' Sosigenes, bald but full-bearded with slits for eyes from years of squinting into weather of all kinds, replied with encouraging confidence as they toured the harbour. 'The whole process should then take no longer than the rest of the day and most of the following one.'

Eumenes stepped over a large coil of rope. 'So we could sail for Europe in three days' time.'

'Depending on the currents in the bay.'

'What do you mean?'

'They change all the time, lord. To get a fleet this size safely out to sea it would be best if the current is flowing from north to south around the bay, then it will sweep us out, clear of the land. Sometimes it reverses, which is fine for a single ship or a small squadron but not for a fleet this numerous; so many ships getting forced to the apex of the bay would be dangerous.'

'Then we had better hope that Poseidon is with us.'

Sosigenes pointed to the cliffs to the north of the port. 'I climb them every morning to see for myself just what the god is up to and he seems to have been behaving himself for the last few days.' His face took on a mischievous aspect revealing five, almost useless, teeth. 'But then again it might be nothing to do with Poseidon and solely because the weather has remained settled for so long.'

Ah, a rational man, I'm beginning to like you, my Rhodian friend. Eumenes grinned and clapped the man on the shoulder. 'Nevertheless, I'll have some sacrifices made to the god for his continued cooperation.'

'If you think it will help, lord.'

'Probably not, but it will make the troops feel easier about putting to sea if they know that I've despatched a few white bulls. Especially the Silver Shields.'

'Don't waste your money on good bulls just for the Silver Shields; they are rich enough to afford their own if they really are so frightened of Poseidon.'

'You may well have a point, Sosigenes. I'm going to give them orders to get ready and let them have time to get used to the idea.' Eumenes turned to go, amused to have found a sailor who did not seem to be one bit superstitious.

But it was the Silver Shields who were the cause of Eumenes' next problem as he met with their commander in the royal tent before the empty throne; and it was nothing to do with their superstitions.

'Ptolemy, you say, Antigenes?'

The grizzled veteran commander of the most elite unit in the whole army nodded and shifted uncomfortably on his folding stool. 'And not just Ptolemy's letters but Antigonos' messengers as well; he's sent his long-time friend, Philotas, and thirty old soaks who know many of the lads; they're offering large amounts of money for them to mutiny, kill you and then come over to Antigonos. They're going to address the lads later.'

'What's Ptolemy offering?'

'His messengers were just to me and Teutamus; he wants *us* to kill you.'

Eumenes was shocked. 'And you're admitting this to me?'

'You would have found out sooner or later and then you could well have had me executed for not telling you.'

'And so why did you remain loyal; I'm sure the bounty offered was considerable?'

Antigenes looked rueful. 'It was, believe me, it was. But what is money compared to life? Teutamus was all for it, but I reasoned him around. You see, Eumenes, you are a Greek.'

'You don't say! I'm astounded that you've noticed since I've tried all these years to hide it. You'll be telling me you've perceived that I'm small in stature next.'

'What I mean, Eumenes, is that you need friends far more than Ptolemy or Antigonos. If we murdered you and then went over to either of them, what's to stop them killing us for being demonstrably unreliable allies? You, on the other hand, need me and Teutamus alive.'

Eumenes could not contain his mirth. 'That is the first time I've had the advantage of being Greek explained properly to me by a Macedonian: Greeks need Macedonian friends, however questionable their loyalty, whereas Macedonians can be a little choosier.'

Antigenes did not share the joke. 'It's a genuine consideration, Eumenes, I haven't come this far just to have my head cut off by someone who paid me to kill a Greek and then decides that I'm expendable; I've got far too much wealth in the baggage-train for that. No, I'll stick with you.'

'And what about your lads?'

Antigenes' sun-battered face took on a concerned countenance. 'That's the main reason I've come to you, Eumenes. They're about to hold a meeting. If they decide to kill you and go over to Antigonos or Ptolemy, their lives will be spared; no one can ever be responsible for killing the Silver Shields, but—'

'Antigonos or Ptolemy won't be so squeamish when it comes to you, is that it?'

'Well, yes, I suppose so.'

Eumenes was enjoying himself. 'And you need me to come and address the lads in order to save your life?'

'And yours.'

Ah, the Macedonian military mind at its best; brazenly making out he gives a whore's discharge for a Greek's safety whilst all the time it's solely about the consequences for him of my lack of safety. 'I'm touched by your concern. Shall we go?'

Antigenes went to the entrance and looked up at the westering sun. 'They'll be meeting at dusk; Philotas will be addressing them on their parade ground.'

'And this is signed by Antigonos.' Philotas held the letter in the air and turned slowly so that all the three thousand men surrounding him could see in the flicker of many flaming torches. 'And he demands that you should do your duty towards him.'

Duty to an outlaw; now there's a new concept, Eumenes considered with a raise of an eyebrow as he stood in the shadows at the rear of the meeting. *And I suppose their duty to Antigonos is to murder the legally appointed Commander-in-Chief of Asia.*

'You must seize Eumenes immediately and put him to death.'

Now there's a surprise.

'If not, Antigonos will consider you to be traitors and bring his army against you.'

This statement brought howls of protest from the assembly.

Philotas stood his ground, holding a hand up, palm out, hoping for silence; after a while he could just be heard. 'One man must speak for you and tell me what is so unreasonable about Antigonos' demand.'

An old timer, strong and fit, well into his seventies, shoved his way forward. He stood before Philotas and wagged his finger in his face. 'We have been ordered by the regent, in the name of the two kings of Macedon, to follow Eumenes and to treat Antigonos as a rebel. By what authority does Antigonos overrule that order?'

This brought more than a few growls of agreement. *Good lads; they may be old and bigoted Macedonians of very little brain, but they know how to obey an order – when it suits them.*

'Antigonos was made the overall commander in Asia by Antipatros who, in turn, was appointed regent by Alexander himself.' Philotas paused to let that name sink in; its magic worked and there was absolute silence. 'The regency cannot be passed on from one regent to the next; it can only be given by the king. Polyperchon is, therefore, not the regent and therefore his order is not legal; thus Antigonos remains the overall commander in Asia and the little Greek is still outlawed.'

I was wondering when my height was going to become an important factor in this debate. Mind you, he has made a very good point that I shall be obliged to counter. Eumenes began easing his way through the crowd.

'If Polyperchon is not the regent, then who is?' the veteran demanded.

Philotas shrugged in a melodramatic fashion. 'That is not Antigonos' problem; he cannot sort out the legal conundrum of how a regent can be appointed when neither king is competent to do so, he can only—'

'Take advantage of the uncertainty for his own ends,' Eumenes said, his voice loud and carrying as he pushed his way into the light at the centre of the gathering. 'Because that's what he's doing, isn't it, Philotas?'

'Eumenes!'

'Yes, well spotted; the sly little Greek in person. I can only assume that Antigonos values your friendship for your powers of observation because it certainly isn't for your ability to form a coherent argument. It is Antigonos' problem, in fact it's everyone's problem: who is legally the regent? And until that legal conundrum – as you so elegantly put it – is sorted out, then what do we have?' Eumenes looked around but none seemed to have an answer. 'Then I shall tell you. We have the next best thing to a regent appointed by Alexander: we have a regent appointed by Alexander's regent.' He spread his arms with a flourish, pushing his head forward and widening his eyes. 'What more can we hope for at the moment? Face it: without Polyperchon we would be leaderless for he is the one who looks after the interests of the Argead royal house, not Antigonos or Ptolemy or even Kassandros for that matter, but Polyperchon. He has the kings' interests at heart and I support him for that.' *The fact that Adea has taken her pet idiot over to Kassandros can be overlooked for the time being.* 'That being the case you can either do what Antigonos has urged you to do and kill me – and here I am – or accept that I am the legitimate representative of the kings in Asia.' He held his arms wide and turned full circle. 'Here I am, lads. Come on, kill me if that's your decision but know this if you do: you would have committed treason and your lives will be forfeit; not perhaps tomorrow or the next month but once Antigonos is defeated. And defeated he will be, for when the sons of Macedon see that he has no love or honour for the Argead royal house, the rightful rulers of Macedon, they will turn on him and he shall fall and the ancient law of Macedon will prevail.'

The roar was sudden and deafening; Eumenes punched both arms into the air to milk it. *Well, it might have been a bit melodramatic but that's never a bad thing and it seems to have done the trick – for now. There's nothing like appealing to a Macedonian's sense of patriotism; gods, how they love a king.*

And then the shouting changed into something more malevolent as thirty or so men were hauled out of the crowd and thrust into the middle. 'Kill them!' the chant became.

Eumenes signalled for silence and looked at Philotas; the veteran showed no fear. As the shouting died down, Eumenes approached Antigonos' envoy and addressed the crowd. 'Do you also think that this man should die?'

The shouts were in the affirmative.

Eumenes shook his head, slow and deliberate. 'And I say no. I say that this man was just doing as he was ordered by his misguided general, as were all these men. No, let's not kill old comrades for obeying orders; if we start doing that then where will it lead us? Send them back so they can tell their comrades that we wish no harm towards them; we wish only for the soldiers of Macedon to unite behind the Argead royal house.'

With another flourish, Eumenes unleashed more roars of approval and the erstwhile condemned men were lifted up and drawn into brotherly embraces.

Eumenes got close to Philotas. 'Tell your chum that he is welcome to surrender to me anytime without fear for his life.' He clapped him on the shoulder and made his way through a jubilant crowd. By the time he reached Antigenes and Teutamus, he was bruised from congratulatory slaps. 'You owe me, gentlemen. Just remember that next time we're in a tight spot.'

The two commanders nodded and mumbled their thanks.

Eumenes sighed. *Well, I suppose that is the most thanks a Greek can expect from two such illustrious Macedonian veterans.* 'Tell me when the detachment bringing the strongboxes from Cyinda arrives tomorrow; I want that coinage and bullion loaded onto the ships as soon as it is here.'

'That makes me feel much better,' Eumenes observed to Sosigenes the following afternoon as the last of the thirty boxes crammed with treasure was safely battened down in the hold of a new-smelling trireme. He turned to Xennias standing next to him. 'So, we start embarking the lads now.'

Xennias snapped a salute. 'They are standing by ready in the camp, sir.'

'Wait, I should check the currents first,' Sosigenes said,

looking up at the cliffs, 'there's no point in having them board if we can't sail.'

'We need to hurry.'

'I know, sir, I will only delay if absolutely necessary.'

'I'll come with you to be a constant reminder of that fact.'

'As you can see, sir,' Sosigenes said, almost an hour later, pointing down to a brown stain in the otherwise turquoise water, 'the effluent from the river is coming south, our way, showing that the current is favourable and will sweep us out to sea.'

Eumenes frowned and shaded his eyes as his gaze rested on the west in the glare of the afternoon sun reflecting on a smooth sea. 'And what about for them?' he asked, his voice tightening. 'Will the current be as favourable to that fleet?'

Sosigenes followed his look and drew breath. 'Whose fleet is that?'

'I'm not sure but I can take a guess and it's not a nice answer. It would seem that Nearchos has made his repairs to Antigonos' fleet. How far away are they?'

Sosigenes studied the three or four dozen silhouettes backlit by the sinking sun. 'No more than two leagues; less than an hour.'

Eumenes turned and ran.

But speed was of no avail to him for, as the approaching fleet came closer, the marks of victory adorning individual ships became clear: the beaks of the defeated enemy were proudly displayed in their bows and the ends of their yards were festooned with captured banners, ripped and torn. And fast they came for they had the wind in their favour and were far enough off the coast to be unaffected by the current.

And then the first of Eumenes' ships cleared the harbour mouth, followed by two more in quick succession and after came a steady stream of them. As Eumenes, with Sosigenes puffing behind him, ran along the quay he saw bodies floating in the water and slumped on the ground: the bodies of the officers unwilling to be a part of the mutiny.

'Philotas and his men came as soon as the other fleet appeared,' Xennias said as they approached. 'They pointed out to our Phoenician sailors that the fleets were evenly matched, but Antigonos' was fresh from victory and full of confidence, as was plain to see. So they decided that they were better off joining with them than trying to fight their way out. You know Phoenicians: ever untrustworthy and very quick to back a winner.'

'And steal a fortune,' Eumenes said, unable to keep the bitterness from his voice as he watched the two fleets meld together, cheers drifting across the water. *That's what you get when you spare someone's life. Well, next time, Philotas, I won't be so stupid.*

'What do we do?' Xennias asked, shaking his head in disbelief.

But Eumenes' attention was distracted by the sight of Teutamus jogging towards him, his mutilated face registering urgency.

The news can't be any worse than what's just happened.

'The scouts have just come in, Eumenes,' Teutamus said, catching his breath. 'Antigonos is crossing the Taurus Mountains with a force of over fifty thousand. What do we do?'

Eumenes smiled. 'That's the second time I've been asked that in the space of a hundred heartbeats, and both times by Macedonians. I must be looking less Greek all of a sudden.'

Teutamus ignored the remark and looked, astounded, at the empty harbour, only now registering the lack of ships. 'Where are they?'

Eumenes resisted the urge to do a comic double-take and pointed, instead, to the combined fleet now lying off Rhosus. 'There.'

Teutamus swallowed. 'What do we do?'

'I suppose if I get asked that question by a Macedonian a third time it is deserving of an answer.' He looked west, towards Europe. 'Well, with Antigonos to our north and without a fleet to take us across the sea then we must forget the idea of combining our forces in Europe.' Eumenes turned away from the west. 'We head inland to the eastern satrapies and try to raise an army big enough to deal with Antigonos who will surely follow us.'

And thus Eumenes headed east, leaving Olympias to face Kassandros and Adea alone.

ADEA.
THE WARRIOR.

DOWN SHE WENT, ducking under the blade that swept not a hand's breadth over the horsehair plume of her helm, putting her weight onto her right foot and leaning out to stab low into the warrior's thigh only to strike the leather-bound wood of a hastily lowered shield. Back Adea jumped, raising her shield to cover her throat from a lightning thrust as her opponent stamped his right foot forward, kicking up dust into her face now far closer to the ground than his own. Resisting the urge to rub her eyes, stinging from a mixture of sweat and grit, Adea stabbed down at the foot, striking it just below the greave with the tip of her blunted sword with enough force to make her opponent grunt in pain and withdraw a couple of paces. Now was her chance; she pounced, still keeping low, side on, leading with her shield to crack into that of her opponent, forcing him back onto his injured foot to steady himself. With another pained grunt, the man hopped onto his left leg as Adea brought her blade up between his legs, freezing the motion as it made contact with soft flesh. 'My kill!'

Cries of astonishment erupted from the gathered men witnessing the defeat of their commander, Kassandros' brother, Nicanor, by a woman barely out of her teens.

'You fight like a man,' Nicanor said with grudging respect, looking down at the blade that would have struck a mortal blow had the contest been for real in the heat of battle.

Adea whipped off her helmet, handed it to her bodyguard, Barzid, and shook out her hair. 'You're wrong there, Nicanor: I fight like my mother who taught me and she was patently not a man.' She wiped the back of her hand over her eyes, clearing the sweat-clogged dust.

'She taught you well,' Nicanor said, bending down to rub his foot; the bruising could already be seen between the straps of his sandal. 'I've not been beaten in a long while and certainly never so publicly as this.' He gestured around the seven hundred-strong crowd of his family's personal followers; cavalry of exceptional quality and hard-marching infantry, the balance of those who did not follow Kassandros to Asia, now come to Pella to be the nucleus of the army. 'And certainly never by a woman; what will they think of me?' He raised his arms, demanding silence. 'You have seen how the queen, Queen Eurydike, can fight, have you not?'

The response was positive, if still a little bewildered, for none of these men knew much of Adea as they had always served in Macedon with Antipatros.

'I will command you in the field but she is the queen, she will command the whole army in the name of her husband, King Philip. Soldiers loyal to my house, do you accept Queen Eurydike as the overall commander of the army of Macedon?'

This time the response was a rousing cheer accompanied by the raising of weapons and helmets into the air.

Adea nodded in satisfaction. 'They think you are right to give me command of the army.'

'Joint command, as I will still be leading my men.'

'Perhaps so, but I will make the decisions in the name of my husband; you will support those decisions, whether you like them or not.'

Nicanor looked at her, his dignity evidently suffering; it had not been an easy rapprochement since finding himself allied with the woman who had wanted him dead just a few months ago. 'The men from my family's estates who always served my father will follow you if I tell them to, and perhaps the new recruits will as well, but what about all the veterans of Alexander's campaigns who have answered the call? Where do their loyalties lie if they march for a king against a king?'

'We shall tell them tomorrow when we review the complete muster. It's still not certain that Aristonous got Roxanna and the boy out of Macedon.'

'Coenus and his fellow bodyguards held the mouth of the pass against us, long enough for them to be picked up by an Epirot border patrol,' the officer commanding the pursuit of the fugitives reported to the council now ruling Macedon that evening. 'By the time we caught up with them they heavily outnumbered us; we lost nine good lads in the fight.'

'Fools!' Adea shouted, thumping the council table with her palm, causing Philip to release a squirt of urine in alarm and to hurl his elephant at the man who had clearly upset his wife. 'How do three men kill nine of you and delay you long enough for the boy to escape?'

The officer dodged the elephant and narrowed his eyes at Adea as one of two of Philip's bodyguards to either side of the throne retrieved the toy. 'They were brave men we faced who had sworn to protect their king. My lads were unwilling, at first, to go at them full-heartedly; it wasn't until we had lost three men that we realised that we really had to do this. We killed them for doing their duty to theirs and our king; how can that be right?'

Nicanor, seated next to Hyperia, leaned forward, resting his elbows on the table. 'That king is a traitor.'

'How can a king be a traitor? We were the traitors for going against his bodyguard.'

Adea pointed to the drooling fool on the throne. 'You went in this king's name! He's the king!'

'And so is Alexander! And he is now with Olympias in Passeron; I know because we followed them there. They arrived seven days ago. Does that mean he is no longer King of Macedon?'

Adea bit back a reply as the man was absolutely right: now that Aristonous had taken the young king to his grandmother there could never be a chance of the dual monarchy functioning – if it ever could be said to have functioned – again. *One of the kings has got to die and I will make sure that it is not my Philip.* 'Just go! And think yourself lucky that you've escaped punishment for failing in your duty.'

The officer sketched a vague salute. 'So we are threatened with punishment for failing in our duty, whilst his brother,' he pointed at Nicanor, 'executes good men for succeeding in theirs. We have all heard what happened to Nicanor of Sindus. Where do the men of Macedon stand now? Answer me that when you have had time to think about it. Who actually do we serve?' He turned, marched to the door, past Philip's other two bodyguards to either side of it, and kicking it open, walked out without closing it.

'I should have the man executed,' Adea spat.

'And have a mutiny on your hands in the morning?' Nicanor said, indicating with his head to Philip's bodyguards.

'No one would mutiny against the rightful king!'

Hyperia put her hand on Adea's arm. 'This is a very finely balanced situation; we cannot afford to alienate anyone. A few months ago you were threatening me with all sorts of things because I wouldn't give up Nicanor here to you, no doubt, for execution. Now we sit at the same table and govern Macedon in Kassandros' absence in the name of the kings, even though one is now in Epirus. It could easily be argued that the reason we are now on the same side is because you played the traitor by bringing Philip over from the regent who holds the ring of Macedon, given to him by my husband on his deathbed, to the man who feels that it should have been him who received that prize.'

'I'm no traitor.'

'No? And yet you've now pitched your fool against Roxanna's babe; someone has to be in the wrong, surely?' Hyperia smiled with a mixture of sympathy and amusement and rose to her feet.

'Sometimes I don't even know whose side I'm on or, more to the point, sometimes I don't even know if there are opposing sides or just too many women wanting to influence things.' It was with a questioning look that she turned and left the chamber.

Nicanor got up to follow her. 'She has a point, Adea. And, unfortunately, it's gone too far to draw back now. The war has come home to Macedon rather than staying in the south and in Asia, and it's because of you.'

'You think that Olympias will invade?'

'She's bound to. She has a king with her now; a king who will give her legitimacy. She will come sooner rather than later. In fact, I wouldn't be surprised if she is already mustering the army of Epirus.'

'Then we had better march out to meet her and prevent her from crossing the border.'

'And we had better be successful because if Olympias wins...' He left the sentence hanging, gave a brief acknowledgement to the king and left.

Adea sat in silence for a few moments, contemplating Hyperia's and Nicanor's words. *Of course they're right, but I can never admit it. Roxanna, Olympias, me...if it hadn't been for the rivalry between that eastern wild-cat and me there would still be a dual monarchy and Polyperchon would have a just cause to resist Kassandros. And now that Olympias, through her desire for power and attention, has grabbed Alexander, the fight is against her with absolute right on neither side. We've been the catalysts who have brought this war that will rip Macedon apart; it will be a duel to the death with only one survivor.* She looked at her husband, who whimpered on his throne, concerned by her serious countenance. 'When we inspect the army tomorrow, Philip, I want you to play king harder than you have ever done before. We want the men to be right behind you.'

And it was with his best efforts, the following morning, that Philip stood still, resisting the temptation to fidget or pick his nose, as Tychon dressed him in the uniform of a King of Macedon; bronze, silver and purple topped with gold and scarlet so that, to the untutored eye, he was the very image of his father and namesake: the conqueror of Greece, Thrace and southern Illyria come back to life to review the army that was destined to sweep all before it.

But the army that this new Philip had paraded before him as he rode, with fanfares blaring and the common populace cheering, from the palace along the Sacred Way was a shadow of the armies that had once graced Macedon. Gone were the numbers, spread now throughout the empire and all fighting for different warlords, so that the army of today resembled more a flying column of yesteryear. But, nevertheless, an army it was; built around a central corps of Kassandros' followers, ever loyal to Antipatros and now his sons. Men who had stayed behind in Macedon rather than share the great adventure that Alexander had led; men whose loyalty was first to the Antipatrid clan, who would follow that leadership whatever king it backed. They cheered as Philip, with Nicanor and Adea to either side, drew up his mount before them and hailed them with a raised hand. And the rest of the army followed their lead, though with less enthusiasm, for these were either young, almost beardless, recruits to whom Alexander was a potent myth or discharged veterans answering their country's call to return to arms and come to its defence. Middle-aged or even old, these men, beards flecked with grey, were passionate in their loyalty to the now-dead king who had led them on a conquest of half the known world, and, despite Philip's resemblance to his and Alexander's shared father, under whom they had all served in their youth, their support for him was expressed with less zest than Adea had hoped.

It was at the first sign of the ovation dying that Adea rode forward and held her hands to the sky. With bronze cuirass and greaves, leather boots and pteruges, and with helm high-plumed with horsehair and feathers, she looked the picture of a high-ranking officer of Macedonian Companion cavalry: elite, experienced and loyal. 'Men of Macedon,' she shouted as the cheering faded, 'your king is before you.' The pause she left for a cheer was sparsely filled. 'It is for him we march to defend our country from foreign invaders, for they are coming from the west and we must counter them. It is no use staying here sheltering behind the walls of Pella and Pydna, no, we must take to the field and repel these trespassers at the border. We must not let the sacred earth of Macedon be soiled by Epirot feet. It falls to us, therefore, to march west and defend our motherland's honour and integrity. Are you with us, soldiers of Macedon? Do you answer your king's call?'

The roar was not overwhelming but it was sufficient.

'Then we march tomorrow at first light; we march for our king and for our country! We march for all of us, for Macedon and for Philip!'

This time the cheering was thunderous; Adea breathed deep in relief. *Now it's you or me, Olympias.*

OLYMPIAS.
THE MOTHER.

OLYMPIAS LOOKED AT the eight men standing before her, outside her tent in the army of Epirus' camp, two days out of Passeron, and wrinkled her nose; she had never liked Thracians and seven of them were garbed as such in their stinking fox-fur hats, as red as their beards, knee-length boots and foul tunics and cloaks. They had refused to give up their rhompaia, slung over their backs, and were therefore heavily guarded and held at a distance from her. But it was the eighth man, unarmed and just five paces away, who intrigued her for she had often heard of Archias the Exile-Hunter but she had never seen him. And yet here he was, looking nothing like she had imagined: a round, smiling face and humorous eyes; he was not a killer, surely? And yet there was a coldness about him; his reputation went before him, bringing fear into all with cause to be looking over their shoulder for the assassin's blade. Indeed, she had often expected Antipatros to send Archias to murder her, but even though they had been mortal enemies and she had tried to have the old regent killed or poisoned on numerous occasions, he had never attempted to assassinate her; perhaps he had been too wary of killing Alexander's mother whereas, despite his mild looks, Olympias could sense that Archias would have no such compunction.

'Whether it was Iollas who administered the poison to Alexander, if, indeed, he was poisoned,' Archias said, coming straight to the point, his voice level and matter-of-fact, 'I cannot say as I was not in Babylon at the time. However, what I can say with certainty is that Kassandros asked me to obtain a certain poison in Tarsus, which I did for a very handsome fee, and he travelled south to Babylon with it hidden in a hollowed-out mule's hoof. All else is pure conjecture. I just present the facts; this is no mere reflection derived from hearsay.' With this quote, he gave an exaggerated bow as if acknowledging the applause of an adoring audience.

Olympias sat motionless, only just able to control her cold hatred. She had always suspected this version of events; in fact, she had continually claimed them to be the truth, but in her heart she never had complete conviction. Even when *The Last Days and Testament of Alexander* had been sent to her by her daughter, Kleopatra, claiming exactly this story, she had still feared that it could be just propaganda however much she wanted it to be true and believed it so. But now, to have one of the protagonists admit his part in the deed to her face was almost too much to bear; she did not know whether to weep with relief or scream with a burning desire for vengeance.

Eventually, Olympias steeled herself and turned to Aristonous, whose men guarded the new arrivals to the camp. 'Well?' she asked, her voice tight. 'You were there; does that make sense to you?'

'I wasn't in Tarsus, so I cannot vouch for Archias claiming that he procured the poison for Kassandros, but Polyperchon was in Cilicia at the time.'

'I remember Kassandros coming through,' Polyperchon said, 'but I didn't see Archias; he might have got the poison, he might not have; but either way, we all know what happened shortly after Kassandros' arrival in Babylon and we all know that Iollas was, inexplicably, Alexander's cup-bearer. I have no reason to doubt this man and yet I have every reason to believe him, for why would he risk the depths of your considerable wrath by lying to you?'

Olympias nodded and looked back to Archias, whose face seemed as placid and unconcerned as one having a pleasant daydream. 'And why have you risked my wrath to come here and tell me this to my face?'

'Ptolemy paid me to; he wanted you to be sure of the truth.'

So Ptolemy's goading me into action, is he? 'Ah, so I'm to be Ptolemy's weapon now, am I? I can see how his devious mind works. Very clever.' Olympias considered Archias with hard eyes for a few moments; he remained unmoved, unconcerned even, under the intense scrutiny. 'And so the story really is true, then? You provided the poison to the man who killed my son.'

'I provided the poison to the man who may have killed your son, I will not deny that. I will also say that the poison works in a remarkably similar way to how Alexander died. But what I will deny is that I knew what Kassandros intended to do with the poison when he paid me to acquire it for him; it is because of that fact that I felt I could take Ptolemy's commission and travel all the way here to confirm the truth to you.'

'And why should I not kill you just because you didn't know what he would do with that poison?'

Archias feigned a look of surprise. 'I would have thought that was reason enough; but should you require further cause to spare our lives rather than lose thirty or more men trying to kill us – and even then you cannot be sure that you would – then consider this: if you win this little war you seem to be embarked upon, then you may well have some prisoners who are a singular embarrassment to you; prisoners who you would love to see dead but not by your own hand. And what Macedonian would be willing to commit such an act against the sacred blood? I leave it at that.' Again he bowed, acknowledging the plaudits of an imaginary crowd.

He's right and he would be eminently suitable; suitable for many of my tasks. 'How much was Ptolemy paying you?'

Archias looked mortally offended. 'To expect me to discuss my dealings with a client is not just, Queen Olympias. I am a man of great discretion.'

Olympias resisted the urge to order the impertinent man's death. 'Very well, Exile-Hunter, you will stay here with the army as we go into Macedon. If I can find a use for you then you will be paid with your lives; if not then they are forfeit.'

Again he bowed as she turned and stormed off. '"Like blasts of wind her will drives her on.'

'So it really is true,' Olympias said, hissing through her teeth such was her agitation, as she stomped back into her tent. 'I believe the man.'

Thessalonike looked up from the book she was reading. 'Yes, I heard what he had to say. What will you do?'

Olympias' eyes burned with hatred. 'Do? I will wipe every trace of Antipatros' family from the earth, down to fifth and sixth cousins no matter how many times they are removed. I will wreak such vengeance on the family that killed Macedon's greatest son; my son!'

And it was with a black heart that Olympias led her army through the pass in the Pindus Mountains to bring it within sight of Macedon; a heart that had grown blacker every day of the six-day march since she had had what she always suspected confirmed. But she did nothing to ease the growing canker within her. Indeed, quite the opposite; she nursed it, cherished it almost, for it was, to her, the fuel upon which she would feed as she inflicted her will on the country that had excluded her from power and rejected her; the country that she had not seen for five years and then only briefly after nine more years of exile; the country that harboured the murderous clan that had, in its jealousy, assassinated her son at the height of his success; the clan that had then gone on to exclude her from the settlement made at The Three Paradises. No, Olympias wished only that her heart would be blacker still once she reached Pella so that her will would drive her on, like blasts of wind, as Archias had so rightly observed in his quote from Sophocles. None of that clan would be left alive.

It was with a great relief that her scouts informed her that the army of Macedon, about ten thousand strong, was but half a day's march away. 'We will face them in the morning, Aristonous.'

'I would prefer to choose my ground and wait for them here.'

Olympias shook her head. 'I am worth any amount of high ground flanked by rivers or woods. No, we march on and meet them as soon as we might; I wish to be in Pella by the full of the moon. My business there is grown urgent.'

The three-quarter moon gave a pale light to the grove as Olympias, swaying to the rhythm of the music, raised her phallus, made of fig tree wood, above her ivy headdress; with a clash of cymbals the congregation broke out in song, a hymn to Dionysus: 'I call upon loud-roaring and revelling Dionysus, primeval, double-natured, thrice-born, Bacchic lord...' Joy swirled through her entire being as she sang the oh-so-familiar hymn; so close was she now to the culmination of all her scheming and plotting that she could almost taste the blood that she would spill, could almost hear the screams and the unheeded cries for mercy and it made her black heart thump deliciously in her throat, such was the anticipation.

'...hearken to my voice, O blessed one, and with your fair-girdled nymphs breathe on me in a spirit of perfection.'

The hymn ended with the roll of drums; the white bull was stunned and then despatched with the double-headed axe that flashed in the hands of a huge man wreathed in ivy and sporting a prodigious erection. Down sliced the blade to carve its way through the bull's neck, severing the spine and sending blood spurting, dark in the torchlight.

'Euoi! Euoi!' the congregation roared in unison; the men pumping a thyrsus, a wand of giant fennel covered in ivy and topped with a pine cone, into the air in time to the chant as the women brandished their phalluses ready for the next phase of the ceremony. As there were no new initiates to induct, the ivy-wreathed wielder of the great axe was ritually stoned to a rising tempo of pipes, drums and cymbals; wine was devoured by the gyrating congregation as a goat was led, terrified, into their midst.

Oblivion approached Olympias as, after a bloody chase, she ripped the flesh from the animal's torn and twitching body, its blood mingling with the wine that stained the fawn skin draped over her naked body; and oblivion was achieved as she was roughly entered, by whom she knew not, and worked with relentless thrusting into a sexual and religious state of ecstasy.

And thus, as a bacchant, bloodied and dripping, she appeared at the head of her army as it formed up in the dawn that rose to greet it: the ivy headdress was still in place but very much the worse for wear, as was her fawn skin, stained with wine and bodily fluids; but she had abandoned her phallus, preferring instead to go into battle with a masculine thyrsus.

If Aristonous felt any surprise at his commander-in-chief's appearance and the lack of sleep writ clear across her face, he hid it well. 'We shall be ready shortly, Queen Olympias,' he announced. 'My cavalry on either flank are in position, as are the skirmishers; I'm just waiting upon the report from Polyperchon that the phalanx is formed, before we can advance.'

Olympias breathed deep, the air refreshing her. 'Very good; where's the boy?'

Aristonous indicated to a troop of cavalry stationed at the front of the assembling phalanx. 'Thessalonike's looking after him.'

'And the barbarian?'

'Roxanna is under guard in her tent; she's been demanding to see you.'

'She can demand as much as she likes. She'll soon get the idea that she is irrelevant now I have the child; useless baggage which, unfortunately, can't be discarded – yet. Tell Thessalonike to watch for my signal.' She turned to gaze over to the army of Macedon, now coming out of its camp, not a third of a league distant, forming up on the summit of the long, gentle slope that it had seized the evening before. 'Their having the high ground will be of no avail to them; not after I show myself and the boy. Has there been much contact between our camps during the night?'

'A fair amount; I gave orders not to discourage it as you were otherwise…well, not present.'

'That's good; so they will already know that they are facing

Alexander's son. That will give them something to think about as the armies approach one another.'

And it was with drums beating all around her that Olympias, now mounted, led her army forward as soon as Polyperchon indicated that the phalanx, seven thousand strong, was set. Up the slope they advanced, at the pace of men keen for battle; skirmishers screening their frontage and light cavalry swirling around their flanks as the heavier Companions trotted, lances at ease, in noble ranks and files, a sight to impress.

But the army of Macedon was equally impressive. It stood its ground on the slope's summit; almost a mirror image of its opponent in both size and make-up, it would be an even contest in normal circumstances. But Olympias was determined that this would be anything but normal as horns sounded the halt, two hundred paces from the enemy.

But for the occasional equine whinny or stamp of hoof and rattle of harness, a silence brooded over the field as the two sides faced each other, skirmishers to the fore, the breeze pulling at helmet plumes, cloaks and banners. For a long while did Olympias allow the tension to build, knowing that Adea would not order the attack first as she would be happy to keep to the high ground. On and on the face-off went, the silence growing more profound as the apprehension grew in the midst of the wilderness that lay between the two kingdoms, practically deserted due to centuries of cross-border raids.

Soon, when she could bear it no longer, Olympias ordered the skirmishers to withdraw; they filed back through the gaps left in the formation, leaving her exposed, a mounted bacchant at the head of an army. And forward she urged her horse, forward onto the open ground between the two forces; until, midway, she halted and raised her thyrsus high above her head.

Again she allowed silence to reign as she let every man in the opposing army look at her; many, as she well knew, for the first time. Ahead she could see Adea and Philip, both also mounted, at the centre of the phalanx. *She appears in a soldier's uniform as if that will give her authority over the men; well, we'll see about that.*

'Men of Macedon!' Her voice was clear despite the sleepless night of excess. 'Many of you know me but for those who do not, I am Olympias, the mother of Alexander and the grandmother of the current king of the same name.' She turned and beckoned Thessalonike forward; she came with Alexander riding astride before her. They stood together, side by side, facing the army of Macedon; again she let the silence grow as she allowed the enemy to see the boy.

'Here stands Alexander's son and here stands Alexander's mother and half-sister; will you, men of Macedon, come against us?'

Let me see you try to make them, Adea.

ADEA.
THE WARRIOR.

ADEA LOOKED TO either side as Olympias' challenge rang out, aware that this was a crucial time in testing the willingness of her men to fight against Alexander's closest kin.

It was hardly anything at first, just a slight murmur floating on the breeze, an undertone, but it was there. And Olympias must have heard, or sensed it too, for again she called out: 'Will you come against us?'

It was an arrow to her heart, the first shout of: 'No!' She turned her horse as the cry was replicated through the ranks of veterans.

'That is your enemy!' she screeched, pointing behind her; and then she pointed to Philip. 'And this is your king.' It was then that she realised the magnitude of her miscalculation.

The first pike was pitched to the ground.

And then came the second and third to unlock a wave of discarded weapons surging left and right along the whole line. 'No! No! No!' went the shout as shields followed pikes hurled to the ground. Adea looked around, panic mounting in her breast as the mutiny grew; nowhere could she see a sympathetic face, until, at the extreme right of the phalanx, she saw a small section of it standing firm, and beyond that, Nicanor's cavalry.

Men started to break ranks, not to offer her or Philip any violence but to walk over towards Olympias, still sitting there waving her thyrsus high in the air and singing the hymn to

Dionysus. Now in danger of being swamped by her erstwhile troops as they changed sides, Adea grabbed Philip's mount's reins and kicked her horse to the right along the line towards the steady Antipatrid command.

But it was then that something deep in the dark channels of Philip's clouded mind detected a threat to both himself and his wife; the urge to protect surged to the fore. He yanked the reins from Adea's grip and, holding his elephant towards Olympias, pushed his horse forward.

'No, Philip!' Adea shouted as the king charged, knocking aside many of the troops now swapping allegiance. 'No! Come back!' But it was too late: in his simplicity it was enough to charge with a toy elephant to achieve the same effect as a herd of the actual beasts and on he went, waving the carved creature and trumpeting its call, bringing first astonishment and then laughter from all witnessing the bizarre battlefield manoeuvre. On he went with his bodyguards chasing him, but they were hampered by men in their path.

Helpless, Adea watched her husband's brave and well-meaning gesture as he was slowly swamped by the tide of troops changing sides, his horse trapped, unable to make progress, his bodyguards pulled from their mounts and despatched. To ride to his aid was to ride into Olympias' clutches and so, as none had yet tried to lay hands on her, her Argead blood still holding her sacrosanct, she waded through the tide of turncoats, with Barzid at her side, towards the relative safety of Nicanor and his men.

But although her blood kept her safe it was not so for Barzid; as blades hacked at him he offered no strokes in return for fear of enraging his attackers, goading them into action against his charge for whom he was now a proxy.

Adea screamed as he went down, ripped and bloodied.

'Keep going!' he shouted as he disappeared into the scrum hauling at him. 'Go!'

And go she did, knowing that his sacrifice would only buy her a few heartbeats before the mob turned upon her, their blood-lust up and the respect forgotten.

She kicked her mount on, pushing through the throng, avoiding meeting any man's eye.

'They have Philip,' Nicanor shouted as she came within hail, 'we must go, we have no legitimacy here anymore.'

And the truth of the statement hit Adea with breath-taking force. *I'm nothing now, without him; nothing at all in my own name other than the granddaughter of Alexander's father but what is that compared to his mother, son and half-sister all standing together?* Tears welled as she looked behind to see Philip, still mounted and waving his elephant, being led away by the men who had only recently sworn themselves to him.

'Come,' Nicanor said, 'there's nothing to be done other than to try to escape back to Macedon and hold out on my estates until Kassandros comes north to relieve us.'

Adea nodded, unable to say anything coherent, her world and ambitions having been shattered in such a short time and by a woman against whom, she should have realised, it had been foolish to pit herself.

But now there were more immediate priorities, such as how to extricate five hundred cavalry and two hundred infantry from the disintegrating army and take them all the way back to Nicanor's estates to the north of Pella. 'I'll give you an escort,' Nicanor said, 'you have to get away from here quickly. We'll both be safer that way.'

Adea looked at him quizzically. 'How so?'

'They'll be less likely to want to spend their lives attacking us if you aren't with us and I'll be able to use my cavalry to slow down any pursuit they might send after you.'

Adea considered her options; it did not take long. 'I'll go.'

Nicanor detailed a dozen of his men to ride with her. 'Ride fast and take a ship south to my brother; you will be safe with him.'

Thanking Nicanor, despite the fact that she realised that her escort were probably more like her guards, she turned to head west with no intention of taking his advice for she knew that without her husband, Kassandros would have no use for her; she was dead if she went south. There was only one direction for her to go now and that was north to the land of her grandmother, north to Illyria. *I'll wait until darkness and then slip away into the night.*

Night had come fast now that the autumnal equinox had passed and the year waned. Adea lay curled up in her cloak in the darkness, no fire having been set for fear of alerting pursuers. With eyes closed she waited, feigning sleep, as the snores of her companions multiplied. One man remained on guard close by her but not so close as to seem it was her he was keeping an eye on and not intruders.

Judging the mid-point between the changing of the guard, she slipped from her cloak and wrapped it around her shoulders, creeping off, crouching low, in the opposite direction to the man.

'Where are you going?' the guard asked in a hissed whisper.

Adea paused and turned to him. 'To have a private moment, if you must know the movements of a queen.'

The guard grunted and got to his feet. 'Not so private as I can't see you.'

Then you are dead. Adea shrugged and moved off. 'Then that wouldn't be private at all.'

The guard said nothing and followed her as she went past the horse line.

He never saw the knife as it punched through the darkness to take his throat, a hand clamping tight on his mouth so that naught but a gurgle escaped him. Down he went, knees buckling, unable to struggle as the life flooded from him.

Adea waited until the final judder became a sequence of weakening twitches; she released her grip. Working fast, she took the dead man's sword and dagger, unhitched her horse and another and then, on foot, led them, west, into the night. It was not until she was well away from the camp that she dared mount and ride under the dim but adequate light of the three-quarter moon.

With no sound of pursuit after an hour, she reckoned it was time to turn north-west and work her way through the hills towards the course of the River Haliaomon that would take north towards Illyria. On she pressed as the moon sank, climbing and twisting through rugged terrain that was barely discernible, but gave her heart as her tracks would be nigh on impossible to trace until after first light. And so it was more than three leagues distance from her guards that the sun bathed its first light upon her as it broke over the mountains to the east and she looked down into the Haliaomon valley.

With a new confidence, Adea changed mounts and increased her pace, the new mare's footing increasingly sure as the light grew and she followed the course of the valley. Stopping solely to water her horses in the river and let them chew on some rough grazing as she eased herself and tugged on a piece of staling bread, she carried on, keeping as northwards as the country would allow, until well after midday when she halted again to rest for a couple of hours during the hotter part of the day. It was with a feeling of hope, slowly blooming within her, that she began to scale the mountain in which the river had its source and then search for the pass that would take her over into the valley of the Eordaicus River that led down into Illyria. Much at home in this wild country, having hunted in the border lands between the land of her birth and the land of her grandmother's blood, the blooming hope within her flowered into full-grown optimism so that the sight of horsemen up ahead at the entrance to the narrow pass leading to her destination was a relief to her rather than a cause for concern. It was not until it was too late that she realised they were not her countrymen but, rather, a unit of prodromoi, the same unit she had sent to pursue Roxanna from Macedon to Epirus, now sworn to Olympias and Alexander. They had guessed her plan and had reached the pass before her.

Adea turned to run but another troop of cavalry emerged from the hills to either side, blocking her escape. Caring not, now that her life was over, she charged directly for them, drawing her sword and shouting the war-cry of the warriors of country of her youth, now so close and yet barred from her. But her horse was tired and the footing rugged so that the charge was more of a gentle canter towards the lowered lance-points of the oncoming cavalry; such were their reach that her mare was dead and falling to the ground before her sword could reap the last blood it ever would. She closed her eyes as she tumbled onto her back, prepared for the multiple piercings that she knew would come, only to feel a blazing pain as her head struck rock.

'Olympias knew that you would never wish to return to Macedon without the protection of your fool,' the officer informed her with a cheerful smile, looking down into her slowly focusing eyes. 'It was obvious that you would head for Illyria and it was obvious that you would have to use this pass. She sent us to wait here as soon as you were seen heading west with Nicanor's escort. We've only been waiting for you for half a day. You did well to get here so quickly.'

Adea struggled to sit, but her arms would not obey her, numb from the bindings. 'Untie me; I am a queen!'

'You used to be my queen; but you are my prisoner. A very valuable one and one I must take to Pella; I can't afford to take any risks with you escaping. My life will be over so quickly if I report back to Olympias without you.'

Olympias looked down at Adea as two soldiers each pushed her shoulders down, forcing her to kneel. Despite her humiliation, Adea would not give her captor the pleasure of outright capitulation and returned her gaze with a steady glare.

'So, there is still some fight left in the man-woman, is there?' Olympias mused, tapping her forefinger on the arm of Macedon's throne.

The movement caught Adea's attention; her eyes widened.

Olympias smiled, cold and triumphant, and looked at the Great Ring of Macedon on her finger. 'Pretty, isn't it? And it suits me well, don't you think?'

Adea did not trust herself to reply.

'The thing about rings,' Olympias continued, 'is that they can only be worn by one person at a time.' She patted the arm of the throne. 'It's the same with thrones: there's not enough room for two.' She paused to consider her captive, still gazing up at her in defiance. 'Which leads us to the question: what to do if there's a second person who insists upon sharing what cannot be shared?' She turned to Thessalonike, standing, as ever, just behind her. 'What would you do with that person, my dear?'

'I would do what has always been done to rivals for the throne of Macedon.'

Olympias nodded at the sagacity of this opinion, her lips pursed. 'Wisdom indeed from one so young.' She looked over to the guards standing to either side of the doors. 'Tell Archias to bring in the usurper.'

Unable to restrain herself, Adea turned as the doors opened, to reveal, first the Exile-Hunter and then Philip, ragged and filthy, his wrists bound before him; one of Archias' Thracians led him by a lead around his neck.

'Adea!' Philip cried, trying to run to her and being brutally hauled back; he choked, tears rolling down his grimed face. 'Adea, they took my elephant. Tell them to give it back to me, Adea; I want my elephant.'

'Silence!' Olympias roared.

Philip looked up at her and whimpered, wetting himself.

Olympias glanced down at the resulting pool in disgust. 'Is this…thing yours, Adea?'

Again, Adea refused to speak.

'The very idea that this monstrosity was worthy to be King of Macedon is a stain upon us all. Nevertheless by some collective madness he was proclaimed king by the army assembly and who am I to go against the wishes of the army?' Olympias' eyes narrowed with wicked glee. 'He shall have his kingdom, Adea, and you shall share it with him. Escort them to it, Archias.'

Through the streets of Pella Archias and his Thracians led Adea and Philip; past the sombre faces of the populace looking on in silence as the woman who had in effect ruled over them in her husband's name was ritually humiliated. Into the agora they were taken where, at its far end, there was a new construction: a small, low building with no windows and one door with a narrow opening in it. Next to the door, Polyperchon waited.

Adea saw the two slaves with a pile of bricks and the tub of mortar waiting next to the entrance and turned to Polyperchon in panic. 'Don't do this; don't. We're friends, surely?'

Polyperchon shook his head. 'You have done nothing for me other than make my life more difficult, Adea. I serve Olympias now; I'm happy to obey orders, I always have been, and this is one I shall enjoy.' He opened the door, cut her bonds and pushed her through into the dark interior. Philip followed her in, unperturbed, not realising where he went.

'No!' Adea screamed as the door slammed shut, banging her fists upon it.

Polyperchon's eyes appeared in the narrow opening. 'You will be fed once a day through this hole; other than that your time is your own.' He turned to go and then came back. 'Oh, I nearly forgot. Philip dropped this.' He pushed the toy elephant through the hole and left.

Philip grabbed his prized possession, chortling with pleasure, and then looked at his wife in confusion as she wailed to the gods both above and below. Whether or not he had heard the noise from outside, Adea did not know, but if he had he did not realise it was the sound of the slaves sealing the entrance with mortar and bricks.

Adea cursed Olympias, cursed her with all that was left of her being; cursed her not for bringing her death but for extending her life.

OLYMPIAS.
THE MOTHER.

NOW, AT LAST, was her time; now she could realise all the dark ambitions that had haunted her through waking nights. Now she would no longer be on the periphery, ignored by the men seated around a table in the far off Three Paradises. Now she would make all take notice of her and regret not having given her their full attention in the past.

Now she would make herself the centre of all things.

Olympias smiled as she stepped from her carriage, the door held open by Archias, and walked the twenty paces to stand before the tomb of Iollas, high on its cliff, overlooking the sea. It stood alone from the tombs of his forebears with one exception: that of Antipatros; for he had chosen to be close to his beloved son in death. She felt warm and that warmth was strengthened by the presence of Hyperia, guarded by two of Archias' Thracians. Captured by the Exile-Hunter as she attempted to flee south with her two youngest children, Hyperia stood silent but, Olympias well knew, churning on the inside, for she had seen the two score of slaves, each holding a heavy hammer, commanded by another of Archias' Thracians.

Olympias savoured the moment, refraining from giving the order immediately for the imminent prospect of vengeance was as delicious as the act itself; she saw no reason to deprive herself of a moment of her pleasure. She had time, after all, as much time as she wanted to wreak her revenge that had been so long in coming, her will driving her on like blasts of the wind.

She turned to Hyperia. 'It's such a shame you didn't beg. Still, I can't have everything, I suppose; although, why, I don't know.'

Hyperia returned her hate-filled gaze with equal measure. 'Everything? You have nothing, Olympias; nothing at all. You are just a husk burnt out by bitterness. Yes, you can destroy the tombs of my husband's family; yes, you can destroy the tomb of my son; yes, you can kill me and most of my family but what will you have when you've done all that? Satisfaction? No; you'll have nothing but fear because touch just one of these tombs and Kassandros will kill you.'

'No one would dare kill the mother of Alexander; the people love me for what I brought into the world. If Kassandros were to come against me his army would desert just as Adea's did. Besides, the Exile-Hunter will soon see to that weasel stepson of yours. Once he's finished here, that is.' She filled her lungs and looked to the sky. 'I am Macedon! Me, and none other. I spit on your tombs.' She pointed at the Thracian in charge of the wrecking party.

With a shouted order, many hammers slammed into Iollas' tomb, shattering its marble walls almost instantaneously; another combined blow broke through the brickwork behind, exposing the casket within, in which lay the bones.

'Enough!' Olympias cried, stepping forward. 'Drag it out.' The Thracian grabbed the casket and pulled it from its resting place, dropping it to the ground. 'Open it.'

It took but a moment to prise the lid off revealing the bones placed within.

Now I have you, treacherous son of a traitor; now you are mine. Olympias reached inside and pulled out the skull, throwing it to the floor. 'Break it!' One hammer blow was enough for her command. She looked over to Hyperia, who stood motionless and emotionless, watching the fruit of her body's desecration. *I'll make you plead yet, bitch.* 'Throw the rest over the cliff!' But it was not with the satisfaction that she had expected that she

392

watched the remains hurtle down onto the rocks below, for Hyperia still refused to vent any emotion. Not even when the bones of her husband suffered the same fate did she cry; not one tear, not one sound as the rest of the family's tombs suffered the same fate.

In desperation she marched up to Hyperia and slapped her, forehand and back. 'You think you are above all this, do you?'

Hyperia did not even acknowledge her.

Another slap; another snub.

'Very well, you've forced me into this; I will have your attention, Hyperia.' She looked over to Archias, waiting by her carriage. 'Bring them here.'

'I know you have my two youngest children, Olympias,' Hyperia said, her voice steady and calm. 'And I know that you will kill them in front of me so that I will die with their deaths in my heart.'

Olympias' smile was of naked cruelty. 'I might have spared them had you had pleaded earlier.'

'No, you wouldn't have; you don't have that in you.'

'Mother,' Alexarchos cried as Archias hauled him from the carriage by his arm.

Hyperia did not turn to look at her five-year-old son, nor did she turn when she heard the frightened wail of the three-year-old Triparadeisus. 'I'll not give you the pleasure. I'll show them the way.' She spat in Olympias' face. Swift as a youth, catching all by surprise, she darted forward, sprinting the thirty paces to the cliff's edge and launching herself high into the air, arms aloft, head back. 'Vengeance, Kassandros,' she cried as she fell. 'Vengeance! Venge—'

Olympias screamed, a claw of hatred squeezing her heart; but it was too late, her moment had been stolen from her and she was powerless to bring it back. She turned and stormed back to her carriage, past the two frightened children staring with unbelieving eyes at the point where their mother had disappeared. 'They can join the bitch,' Olympias snapped at Archias as she stepped into her carriage, slamming the door.

'You did what?' Aristonous exclaimed in shock as they walked, heavily guarded, through the agora towards Adea and Philip's place of confinement.

'I reunited the little beasts with their mother,' Olympias stated again.

'And you expect the people of Macedon to accept you as the regent of your grandson if you behave like that?'

'I expect the people of Macedon to do as the mother of Alexander tells them to.' She looked with distaste at the crowd, forced aside by her bodyguards, staring at her in silence as she passed. 'Whether they like me or not is irrelevant.'

'Beware of arrogance, Olympias,' Aristonous said, his voice sharp.

'Beware of overreaching your station, Aristonous.' Her tone was low and iced. 'Leave the politics to me and concentrate on what I demand of you as a soldier; how long before your men bring me Nicanor and his cavalry?'

Aristonous composed himself before he replied. 'They'll be here soon.'

'How soon is soon?'

'Today or tomorrow.'

'All of them?'

'Of the three hundred or so who survived the retreat to his estates after their infantry surrendered, we've captured almost two-thirds, including Nicanor; the rest will probably flee to Asia, taking their families with them.'

'Then hold their families.'

'I do not make war on Macedon's women and children, Olympias.'

'You make war on whomever I tell you to, Aristonous, or I'll stop Polyperchon from rejoining his army in the south and he can come and do my bidding; he seems far more anxious to serve than you do.'

Aristonous made no comment.

Olympias scowled but took the matter no further. 'Have them put in the compound with their infantry when they arrive and bring Nicanor to me.'

'It will be done.'

'Good; now what is so important that you've dragged me here to the man-woman and her fool's kingdom?'

Aristonous sighed. 'You need to hear this for yourself and then judge whether you have made a mistake.'

'I don't make mistakes.'

'You'll be the best judge of that.'

The crowd grew thick as they neared the bricked-up cell; thicker and more vocal, the tone one of anger. And then Olympias heard a wail rise above the hubbub: 'I am the daughter and granddaughter of Macedonian kings; I am your queen and Philip is your king and look how we are treated by a foreigner from Epirus. I am your queen.'

The crowd grew more restless in its mutterings.

'I am your queen!'

'It's been getting progressively worse since she started this a couple of hours ago,' Aristonous said as they looked on.

The cell was surrounded by hundreds of the local populace, including many soldiers. Such was the press of people that the guards had to fight to push them back from the building.

'I am your queen and yet I am treated worse than a beast in a cage!'

The crowd's discontent was growing.

Olympias was flummoxed. 'How can this be? They're meant to be enjoying her humiliation, not sympathising with the little bitch.'

Aristonous looked at her with exaggerated patience. 'Not everyone feels the same way as you, Olympias; for some, she really is their queen.'

'I'm their queen!'

'No, your king is dead; you cannot be the queen in your own right. You are the regent.'

'Look how she treats us,' Adea wailed again.

'Silence!' Olympias screamed. 'Silence, bitch!'

The crowd turned and stared at Olympias amidst her body-guards. 'Shame,' many of them muttered.

'Olympias? Is that you? Release us!'

'Yes, release them,' a voice in the crowd shouted.

'Release them,' another echoed; and then another and another until the shout became a chant.

Be careful what you wish for. Olympias turned on her heel and walked, with dignity, away.

'The debt is paid?' Archias asked as he took the three items up from the table in front of the throne.

'The debt *will have* been paid once you have done as I've ordered,' Olympias corrected. 'And then come back to me and we will discuss your fee for killing Kassandros. Now go, and do it cleanly; I don't want to be accused of unnecessary cruelty seeing as some of my people seem to harbour a misguided affection for Adea and her fool.'

ADEA.
THE WARRIOR.

ADEA SAT ON the dirt floor, hugging her knees, watching Philip play with his elephant in the meagre light seeping in through the narrow slit left in the bricked-up door. Oblivious to his predicament, his legs and tunic soiled with his own filth, he made charge after charge across the cell, vanquishing all enemies before him. She almost smiled, envying him his isolation from the ghastly reality they shared.

Yet for her, there was a way out; an easy way. She fingered the belt around her waist: it would do. She looked up at the beams supporting the roof: the central one would do very well too. It was a simple matter, but for one thing: she could not leave Philip. She wondered at herself, at how sentimental she had become in that she cared for this man-child and felt the need to protect him; and yet she did. It was a plain fact. He had never asked for any of this; indeed, he would be happy playing with his elephant for the rest of his life if only people would let him and he was fed and warm.

Nor could she take him with her. He would not understand the concept of suicide with honour and would fight for survival should she try to kill him; he would probably kill her as he defended himself, such was his enormous strength, thus solving the problem. But that she could not allow either, for he would be wracked with guilt and his simple life would become a burden to him; a burden he could not escape.

No, she was trapped.

How she had failed and allowed herself to come to this, she could not tell. All had been well with her in Babylon after Cynnane, her mother, had been killed by Alketas. She had ridden high in the army's estimation, fighting for their rights, their back-pay, anything that would curry favour with them. And then she had been outwitted by Antipatros at The Three Paradises; outwitted and then pushed aside. But that did not dishearten her, no, she fought back, once more using the men's grievances as her way into their hearts only to be outwitted again by the same man when Antipatros left her with the army stranded in Asia as he slipped back across to Europe without acceding to her demands. The humiliation of having no solutions to the problems she had created had been deep; the army had deserted her and crawled back to the dying regent, begging forgiveness. But then Antipatros had died and she had been able to dominate the weak Polyperchon until she had found out that he had invited Olympias to help him counter her and share his burden; and Adea knew enough about that harpy to know that she shared nothing. Had it been her going over to Kassandros thus putting her irrevocably on the opposite side to Alexander's demon mother that had been her gravest error? Should she have stayed with the legitimate regent and fought her corner against Olympias? Did it matter anymore? No, she supposed not, for all was lost whatever the cause was.

Once again she raised her mouth and cried with a voice hoarse from much usage: 'I am your queen and see how I am treated.' And once again there was no response, not like there had been earlier. She smiled, grim and mirthless: Olympias had been shamed into clearing the area around her cell so that she would not be able to feed on the sympathy of the people. She would be moved soon, she had no doubt, so that Olympias could carry on tormenting her in private, having realised the depth of her miscalculation when she had seen for herself just how much the people resented such brutal treatment of members of the royal house.

And it was with that thought in mind, as the light faded outside, that she heard the first of the bricks being levered away with ease, the mortar not yet fully dry. *They will take us away in the dark. I suppose we will disappear into a dungeon in the palace to be kept alive for years.* She could have wept had Philip not have been there, but she knew she had to stay strong for him.

The bricks continued to tumble and be scraped aside; the lock clicked; the door opened.

'Good evening,' Archias said, standing in the darkened doorway. He turned back to his men behind him. 'Come; let there be light upon the stage.' And a flaming torch was brought in. Archias looked down at Adea and then Philip, smiling, as if it was a real pleasure to see them both. 'Our business will not take long, my friends.'

Philip whimpered and hid his elephant behind his back.

'Oh, it's not your elephant I want, dear child,' Archias said, flashing his sword from its scabbard in his right hand, 'it's your life.' He stamped his left foot forward and, in a blur, threw his sword into his left hand to carry on the motion, plunging the tip deep into the unsuspecting Philip's throat.

Adea screamed as the weapon was twisted and Philip's eyes bulged and then dimmed.

'There now,' Archias said, withdrawing the blade, 'that didn't hurt, did it?'

Adea stared at Philip as he slumped forward, dead. She scampered over to him and knelt down; picking up his elephant, she stroked his hair. 'You are free to play all you like now, my big man-child.' She felt a surge of relief: she was able now to choose her own end.

'Yes, you are in luck,' Archias said, reading her mind. 'Olympias has taken pity on you.'

Adea scoffed. 'That word isn't a part of her vocabulary.'

Archias considered the statement. 'Very true; I got my lines wrong. My apologies.' He bowed and then acknowledged an unseen audience. 'Nevertheless, she does offer you death which is far preferable to life in these conditions. To that end she sends you three items.' He clicked his fingers and one of his men passed the three items in question. 'A sword, a noose and a phial of hemlock; you choose.' He paused, dramatically holding his chin as if he had forgotten something. 'A chair; what use is a noose without a chair? Bring the lady a chair.'

A chair was duly brought in and set before Adea.

Archias examined the scene and nodded in satisfaction. 'I believe you have all the props you need for the final act; I will bid you farewell.'

'Before you go,' Adea said, unbuckling her belt and feeding the end through the buckle, 'I have a message for Olympias. Thank her for the items that she sent me. But tell her that I have no need of her tender mercies as I will make my own arrangements. Be sure she knows that I died at my own hand and not through any means provided by her.'

'Alas, dear girl; I will not be seeing Olympias. I have seen quite enough of her to realise that she is mad even by the standards of the age. No, it is south for me. "A cautious man is safest".' He turned and, leaving the door open, left with his men.

Adea made no attempt to follow for the guards were still posted outside; she was not going to humiliate herself even more. No, there was only one thing left to do now and that was to salvage whatever dignity she could. She laid out Philip's body; wiped what filth she could from him and closed his startled eyes. Satisfied with her efforts, she picked up Philip's elephant and then set the chair beneath the central beam. Climbing onto the seat she reached up and slung her belt around the wood, fastening it with a secure knot. She took a deep breath and glanced towards the door. The guards were watching her; their commander nodded in approval, his face grave.

It was time; she slipped the loop of the belt around her neck and pulled it tight. Holding her husband's elephant in both hands, she briefly pictured her mother. *Be there when I come, Mother.*

'May you receive the same items one day soon, Olympias!' She kicked the chair away and felt the leather tight around her throat, her eyes bulging, their light fading as her mind composed her death curse. *Olympias.* Kicking, she dropped the elephant. *I curse you with my final breath, Olympias.*

OLYMPIAS.
THE MOTHER.

'SHE DIED WELL! Well!' Olympias screamed into Aristonous' face; even Thessalonike, standing by the window of Olympias' day chamber, flinched at the vehemence. 'How can that little bitch be said by the people to have died well when she died at my hand?'

Aristonous wiped a droplet of spittle from his eye and took a deep breath. 'Archias left the door open so the guards saw her hang herself with her own belt; not one of your *gifts*.'

The harpy defied me at the last. Olympias ran to the open window, pushing Thessalonike aside and howled out of it over Pella: 'Bitch!'

'They said she did it with a calmness and bravery that they would have expected from her and said so to the people who came to see the bodies.'

Olympias turned, she was now puce. 'See the bodies! Who let the people see the bodies?'

'The door was open.'

'I know it was open! Why didn't the guards close it?'

'What for? Adea and Philip were both dead.'

He's smirking. Olympias struggled to control herself and then looked, with wicked intent, at Aristonous. 'You're enjoying this, aren't you?'

Aristonous shrugged. 'I can see nothing to enjoy in what's happened: one of the two kings of Macedon has just been murdered by the regent and his queen has hung herself, dying with dignity; what is there to enjoy?'

Olympias' eyes narrowed even further. 'Just whose side are you on, Aristonous? And think carefully before answering.'

'I don't need to think about that; I'm on Macedon's side.'

'I am Macedon.'

'So you keep saying.'

'Then you are on my side.'

Aristonous remained silent.

How can I trust this man? He has sympathy for the little bitch. Perhaps I should get Archias to deal with him before... Archias? 'Where is Archias? He was meant to come straight back to me.'

'Archias took a ship as soon as he had completed his mission.'

'A ship!'

'Yes, a ship. The one he arrived on waited for him; it was in Ptolemy's pay.'

'But he was going to...' Olympias checked herself. 'Send a vessel after him to bring him back.'

'I don't think he would come even if we could catch up with him.'

Olympias slumped down in a chair. 'Right; we need to remedy the situation. Where are the bodies?'

'I've had them brought here to the palace awaiting their funeral rites.'

'Funeral rites? Ha! I want them thrown into an unmarked pit. There'll be no easy passage across the Styx for that little harpy and her pet idiot. See it done.'

Aristonous drew himself up to his full height. 'I do not desecrate bodies, especially those of the King of Macedon and his queen.' He turned and walked away, looking over his shoulder. 'That would be the act of a savage.'

Olympias clenched her teeth, suppressing the urge to scream after him, ordering him to stop. *He'll just keep going and I will lose face.*

'That went well,' Thessalonike observed.

Olympias looked up at her and snarled, 'When I want your opinion, I'll ask for it.'

Thessalonike smiled, sweet and unconcerned. 'And sometimes I'll give it for free. And it is this: if you want to maintain power here you are going to need men like Aristonous—'

'I don't need anyone; I'm the mother of Alexander.'

'As I was saying: you're going to need men like Aristonous and to keep them you are going to have to modify your behaviour.'

'Modify?'

'Yes, modify. Start acting through reason and not through hatred. There will always be a time for revenge but men like Aristonous hold their honour in highest esteem and won't have it tainted by malicious acts of vengeance.'

'Pah!'

Thessalonike opened her mouth to admonish her adoptive mother's attitude but thought better of it and sat down instead.

The two women sat in silence for a while, each immersed in their own thoughts.

'I can't afford to give Adea and Philip a grave,' Olympias said eventually. 'It would become a focal point for dissent.'

Thessalonike inclined her head in appreciation. 'That is a reasoned course of action which also has the advantage of tasting sweetly of revenge.'

Olympias nodded, pleased with herself. She clapped her hands; her elderly body-slave appeared in the doorway. 'Bring my cloak.'

Olympias looked down at the bodies of Adea and Philip lying next to a narrow hole dug in the corner of a lesser-used courtyard on the north side of the palace; a warm glow ran through her as all thoughts of modifying her behaviour evaporated. She turned to the slaves who had brought them out. 'Strip them! And then throw them in.'

'Mother!' Thessalonike warned.

Olympias waved her warning away. 'I'm enjoying myself. Allow me that at least.'

Naked, the bodies were heaved into the hole, Philip first and then Adea on top of him, facing up, her body completely exposed.

Olympias straddled the hole and, lifting her skirts, urinated; the warm glow intensifying the more she was enjoying herself.

Thessalonike turned away, unwilling to be a party to her stepmother's excess, to see Aristonous emerge into the court-yard leading a prisoner, hands tied behind his back, guarded by two soldiers. 'Mother, have some dignity; we have company.'

Olympias looked up and smiled. 'Nicanor! The day is just getting better and better.' She stood back up, adjusting her dress and waited for the prisoner to cross the courtyard. 'Have him kneel before me.'

'I promised to bring Nicanor to you but, remember, he is a Macedonian noble,' Aristonous cautioned. 'I have given him my word that he will be treated as such.'

'Then you have wasted your breath. Where are his cavalry?'

'They are being put into the compound with the rest of the prisoners, as you ordered.'

'Good. You can go.' She glared at the two guards. 'Force him to his knees.'

The guards looked at Aristonous who shrugged and then walked away; they glanced at each other before pushing Nicanor down with well-muscled arms.

'Does that make you feel good?' Nicanor asked, contempt in his voice.

Olympias looked down at him, triumphant. 'It helps.' She considered her enemy, taking pleasure in his humiliation. 'Your stepmother cheated me yesterday by jumping off a cliff before I could kill your two young half-brothers in front of her. Did you know that?'

Nicanor's eyes remained hard. 'You'll get nothing from me, bitch.'

'Wrong; I'll get a lot of pleasure from sending your head to Kassandros.'

Nicanor snorted in disbelief. 'You can't see what you're doing, can you? My brother has many failings, one of which is that he is very hard to like, even by his own family. But when he comes in triumph to Pella and puts your head on a spike people are going to worship him, love him, call him their saviour for ridding them of the foulest monster to have ever been given life. You're turning Kassandros into a nice man.'

'Kassandros will never rule here.' She thrust the ring into his face. 'I hold the ring and when I hold something nothing will make me let it go.' With a fleet movement she reached up, grabbed a long hairpin from her headdress and, bringing it down, pierced Nicanor's left eye, thrusting it through, into the brain. Nicanor convulsed.

Leaving the pin in place, she spat in his face as he fell back and then spoke, low, to the guards. 'Take his head and send it to his brother; throw the remains in with the other rubbish and then kill the slaves once they have filled in the hole.' With one final look down at the quivering body on the ground she walked away, bliss flooding through her. 'I'm going to have a look at the prisoners now, Thessalonike; do you want to come along and see me really enjoying myself?'

Thessalonike ran after her. 'Mother; you're losing control. This has to stop or Nicanor will be proven right.'

'Never! I am the mother of Alexander; I am Macedon.'

If Olympias had felt the elation of vengeance as she watched Nicanor quiver on the ground then it was to a new height that her spirit soared as she looked down upon over five hundred captives all sitting, heads hanging, hands tied on the dusty ground of the prisoner compound; guards wandered amongst them beating those who showed any sign of resistance. 'What's left of Antipatros' kinsmen and bondsmen are languishing down there in defeat,' she said, moistening her lips with the tip of her tongue. 'How sweet is that sight?'

'You can't,' Thessalonike said in a hushed, disbelieving voice. 'Surely, you can't.'

'Oh, but I can; the real question is: will I?' She gave an impression of someone considering a deeply complex problem.

Thessalonike looked at her in mounting horror, seeing the game she was playing. 'I'll not be a part of this any more, Mother. I'll let you dig your own grave but I won't let you dig mine.'

Olympias' expression was one of contempt as her adopted daughter walked away. 'I thought I'd made you of stronger stuff than that. Suit yourself, weakling, but I won't let you interfere with my enjoyment.' She turned back to the suffering below. 'Kill them, guards! Kill them! Kill them all!'

It was as the first throat was cut and the wail of desperation rose to the sky from five hundred men, doomed to an ignominious death, that Olympias raised her head, arching her back, and spread her arms, shouting her triumph to the gods, revelling in just how much she was enjoying herself.

The settlement made by men at The Three Paradises meant nothing now.

Olympias was Macedon.

Author's note and Acknowledgements

This fiction is, in part, based on the works of Diodorus and Plutarch; however, I have relied heavily on, and am indebted to, modern histories of the time and biographies: *Ghost on the Throne* by James Romm and *Dividing the Spoils* by Robin Waterfield distill the primary sources into very readable and enjoyable narratives and are highly recommended. Jeff Champion's biography of Antigonos the One-Eyed, John Grainger's *Rise of the Seleukid Empire* and *The Wars of Alexander's Successors* by Bob Bennett and Mike Roberts are also excellent explorations of the time and my thanks go to them all.

Again, almost every event that occurs in the novel is attested to by one or more of the few primary sources and once again I had very little reason to make things up as it would be hard to outdo the facts. The most interesting of these to my mind, is the propaganda war between Ptolemy and Antipatros with the publishing of *The Last Days and Testament of Alexander*, putting names to the people alluded to by Onesecritus in his *Voyages with Alexander* and then the repudiation and development of 'alternative facts' by Antipatros in *The Royal Journals* – it seems it was ever thus!

Iollas' death is my fiction; we do not know how he died, only that he was dead by the time Olympias siezed power as she did desecrate his tomb as well as execute Nicanor and his followers. Her murder of Antipatros' wife – fictionally called Hyperia, as we know not her real name – and her two youngest children is my fiction, although I'm sure they would have met with an unpleasant end at Olympias' hands.

Seleukos' method of taking Babylon is my fiction although we do know that fire in the temple complex was involved.

For narrative reasons I have moved Adea and Philip's imprisonment from Pydna to Pella. Whether it was Archias the Exile-Hunter and his Thracians who did the deed, we do not know; however, it is stated that Thracians killed them so it seemed to me to be a reasonable guess.

Interestingly, a tomb close to the site of Termessos has been uncovered that is believed to be that of Alketas; the young men of the town evidently did recover his body to give it a decent burial.

Some readers did not like the way I removed the line breaks in the first book; I'm very sorry if it annoyed you. I did it because I wanted to keep the action going by – in filmic terms – having jump-cuts rather than a slow dissolves. I have now seen the folly of my ways and have reintroduced the much-loved line break in this book.

My thanks also go to Will Atkinson and Sarah Hodgson at Atlantic/Corvus for continuing to publish my books – welcome to Corvus, Sarah; I wish you all the best. I'm also indebted to my agent, Ian Drury, for all his work on my behalf and his great insight into the period. Thank you also to Gaia Banks and Alba Arnau in the foreign rights department at Sheil Land Associates, for selling the series abroad. I would also like to thank Susannah Hamilton, Poppy Mostyn-Owen, Kate Straker, Hanna Kenne and everyone at Atlantic/Corvus for all the work that goes into publishing a book. My thanks also to Nicky Lovick for copy-editing the manuscript so thoroughly.

My love and thanks to my wife, Anja, for putting up, once again, with me being distracted for the six months that it took to write this and for her constant support, not to mention her fantastic map and chapter headings.

And, finally, my thanks to you, dear reader, for continuing to join me on this adventure; I hope we will carry on down history's path together. Alexander's Legacy will continue in *An Empty Throne*.

LIST OF CHARACTERS

(Those in italics are fictional.)

Adea	Daughter of Cynnane and Alexander's cousin Amyntas.
Aeacides	The young king of Epirus.
Alexander	The cause of all the trouble.
Alexander	Alexander's posthumously born son by Roxanna.
Alexandros	Polyperchon's son.
Alexarchus	Infant son of Antipatros and *Hyperia*.
Alketas	Brother of Perdikkas.
Antigenes	Veteran commander of the Silver Shields.
Antigonos	Satrap of Phrygia appointed by Alexander.
Antipatros	Regent of Macedon in Alexander's absence.
Apama	Seleukos' Persian wife.
Apollonides	A cavalry officer in Eumenes' army.
Archias	A one-time dramatic actor turned bounty-hunter.
Aristonous	The oldest of Alexander's bodyguards.
Arrhidaeus	A Macedonian officer in Ptolemy's army.
Asander	Alexander's satrap of Caria.
Atalante	Perdikkas' sister, married to Attalus.
Attalus	A Macedonian officer, brother-in-law to Perdikkas.
Babrak	*A Paktha merchant.*
Barsine	Alexander's Persian mistress and mother of his bastard, Heracles.
Barzid	An Illyrian nobleman.
Berenice	Antipatros' niece and cousin to Eurydice.
Callias	*A mercenary in Ptolemy's pay fighting for Seleukos.*
Coenus	*Commander of the young Alexander's bodyguard.*
Cynnane	Murdered half-sister to Alexander. Mother of Adea.

Deidamia	Daughter of Aeacides, King of Epirus.
Deinarchos	A Corinthian lawyer.
Demades	A pro-Macedon Athenian.
Demeas	Demades' son.
Demetrios	Son of Antigonos.
Diocles	*The leader of the deserters from Eumenes' army.*
Diogenes	Antipatros' and then Polyperchon's treasurer.
Docimus	A Macedonian noble and supporter of Perdikkas.
Dreros	*Commander of the Macedonian garrison in Damascus.*
Eudamus	Alexander's satrap of India.
Eumenes	First Philip's and then Alexander's secretary, a Greek from Kardia.
Eurydike	One of Antipatros' daughters, married to Ptolemy.
Hagnonides	Leader of the Athenian democratic faction.
Hecataeus	Tyrant of Kardia.
Hegemon	A member of the Athenian oligarchy.
Helius	*A mercenary in Eumenes' pay.*
Hephaistion	A deceased Macedonian general; the love of Alexander's life.
Heracles	Alexander's bastard by Barsine.
Hieronymus	A soldier turned historian; a compatriot of Eumenes.
Holcias	*The leader of deserters from Antigonos' army.*
Hyperia	*Antipatros' wife.*
Iollas	Antipatros' son, half-brother to Kassandros.
Karanos	*A Macedonian veteran.*
Kassandros	Antipatros' eldest son, half-brother to Iollas.
Kleitos	A Macedonian admiral with a Poseidon complex.
Kleopatra	Daughter of Philip and Olympias, Alexander's full sister.
Krateros	The great Macedonian general killed in battle with Eumenes.
Leonidas	An officer in Antigonos' army specialising in subterfuge.
Lycortas	*Steward to Ptolemy.*

Lysimachus	One of Alexander's seven bodyguards.
Magas	Antipatros' kinsman and second-in-command.
Menander	Alexander's satrap of Lydia.
Nearchos	A Cretan, Alexander's chief admiral, now in Antigonos' pay.
Nicaea	One of Antipatros' daughters once married to Perdikkas.
Nicanor	The second eldest son of Antipatros; brother to Kassandros.
Nicanor of Sindus	A Macedonian noble and supporter of Kassandros.
Olympias	One of Philip's wives, mother to Alexander and Kleopatra.
Onesecritus	A naval commander and author of *Voyages with Alexander.*
Parmida	*A Kappadokian cavalry officer.*
Peithon	One of Alexander's seven bodyguards. Satrap of Media.
Perdikkas	One of Alexander's seven bodyguards, now deceased.
Peucestas	One of Alexander's seven bodyguards. Satrap of Persis.
Phila	Antipatros' recently widowed daughter.
Philip	Alexander the Great's father and predecessor.
Philip – formally Arrhidaeus	The mentally challenged half-brother to Alexander.
Philip	Son of Antipatros and *Hyperia*, half-brother to Kassandros.
Philotas	Friend of Antigonos.
Philoxenus	Satrap of Cilicia.
Phocion	Athens' veteran general and friend of Antipatros.
Phthia	Wife of Aeacides, King of Epirus.
Pleistarchos	Son of Antipatros and *Hyperia*, half-brother to Kassandros.
Polemaeus	Antigonos' nephew.
Polemon	A Macedonian noble and supporter of Perdikkas.
Polyperchon	Krateros' erstwhile second-in-command.

Ptolemy	One of Alexander's seven bodyguards, perhaps Philip's bastard.
Pyrrhus	Son of Aeacides, King of Epirus.
Roxanna	A Bactrian princess, wife of Alexander and mother to Alexander.
Seleukos	An ambitious Macedonian officer.
Sextus	*Ptolemy's body-slave.*
Sosigenes	A Rhodian naval commander in Eumenes' pay.
Stratonice	Wife of Antigonos and mother to Demetrios.
Temenos	*The Macedonian commander of the southern fortress in Babylon.*
Teutamos	A Macedonian officer, second-in-command to Antigenes.
Thais	Long-time mistress of Ptolemy.
Thessalonike	Daughter of Philip the second in the care of Olympias.
Thetima	*Slave to Kleopatra.*
Triparadeisos	Infant son of Antipatros and *Hyperia.*
Tychon	Companion and doctor to Philip/Arrhidaeus the Fool.
Xennias	A Macedonian cavalry officer.

COMING SOON FROM
ROBERT FABBRI

THE LATEST INSTALMENT OF
ALEXANDER'S LEGACY

AVAILABLE 06.01.2022